Will the Last Person
to Leave the Planet
Please Shut Off
the Sun?

MIKE RESNICK

Will the Last Person to Leave the Planet Please Shut Off the Sun?

ORB

A Tom Doherty Associates Book
New York

WILL THE LAST PERSON TO LEAVE THE PLANET PLEASE SHUT OFF THE SUN?

Copyright © 1992 by Mike Resnick

This book was originally published as a Tor hardcover in August 1992.

This book is printed on acid-free paper.

An Orb Edition
Published by Tom Doherty Associates, Inc.
175 Fifth Avenue
New York, N.Y. 10010

Library of Congress Cataloging-in-Publication Data

Resnick, Michael D.
    Will the last person to leave the planet please turn off the sun?
  / Mike Resnick.
        p.   cm.
        "A Tom Doherty Associates book."
        ISBN 0-312-89010-9
        1. Science fiction, American.   I. Title.
    [PS3568.E698W55   1994]
    813'.54—dc20   94-7147
                                                                CIP

First Orb edition: August 1994

Printed in the United States of America

0 9 8 7 6 5 4 3 2 1

COPYRIGHT ACKNOWLEDGMENTS

CONTENTS

FOREWORD:
The Man Who Hated Short Stories

I've got a confession to make.

I feel like a fool making it—but what the hell, it's not the first time I've felt like a fool, and I'm reasonably certain it won't be the last.

Science fiction is a field which has produced at least thirty demonstrably great short stories, and, at best, two or three near–great novels. And yet, as recently as 1986, I held firmly to the conviction that short fiction was somehow trivial, that if an idea or a character was worth anything at all, then it belonged in a novel.

So I wrote novels. Some pretty good ones, if I say so myself. One was a national bestseller. Others came close. A few were optioned to Hollywood. Most of them sold to half a dozen or more additional countries, and were translated into any number of exotic languages.

The late Terry Carr, whose greatest fame was as a book editor, the creator of the Ace Specials, was the first to take me aside and gently explain that if I ever wanted recognition within the field, I was going to have to write some short stories, since most of my peers were too damned busy writing their own stuff to be bothered reading novels by an author with whose work they were unfamiliar. I thanked him for his advice, and explained to him that this was all well and good in theory, but short stories were pieces of fluff. Novels had *substance.*

He looked at me as if I was crazy. (I wasn't. Wrong, yes, but not crazy. Although in this case, that's merely a quantitative difference.)

I kept writing novels.

Then my friend Barry Malzberg, author of *Galaxies* and *Herovit's World,* probably the two finest science-fiction novels of the 1970s, spent the better part of a year trying to convince me that short stories were predestined to be trivial only if you set out to write trivial short stories.

I listened politely, nodded sagely, and kept writing novels.

Finally my wife, line editor, and uncredited collaborator, Carol, took up the gauntlet. Carol doesn't lose a lot of arguments.

So I gave in. Officially. Just enough to obey the absolute letter of the law. I wrote one short story a year from 1977 through 1986. Sold most of 'em. Even won a couple of awards. Got picked up for a best-of-the-year anthology.

Trivial.

The awards were minor. The pay was minor. Even the year's-best anthology was minor; it appeared once and never again.

Then a strange thing happened. Usually, when I finished a novel, I would loaf for a week or two and then get right to work on the next one. But in the summer of 1987, I finished *Ivory* in mid-June, and the next novel on my schedule was *Paradise,* a science-fictional allegory of Kenya's past and future history. And since I was going to Kenya in September, it seemed counter-productive to start writing the book prior to taking a very expensive trip that had been arranged for the express purpose of researching it.

So I was looking at ten weeks of unproductive dead time, and I decided that I might as well finally give short stories an honest shot.

So I sat down, and before I left for Kenya, I had written and sold nine of them. Not only that, but even *I* had to admit they weren't all trivial. One of them, "Kirinyaga," was nominated for a Nebula, won a Hugo, and did more for my reputation than any novel I'd ever written.

Something else strange happened, too.

I found—to my absolute amazement—that I *enjoyed* writing short stories.

So after I finished *Paradise,* I took two months off and wrote another ten. And sold them all. And included in that batch was another Hugo and Nebula nominee.

And while the pay wasn't quite up to what my novels brought in, I found that if you sell enough short stories to enough major markets, it does a lot more for your bank account than sitting around the house watching the Reds and Bengals blow one lead after another.

My next novel after *Paradise* was *Second Contact,* and this time I didn't even wait to finish it: I wrote and sold seven more stories *while* I was writing it—and two of *them* were nominated for Hugos (and one of them, "The Manamouki," won me my second Hugo). More recently, while I was writing the Oracle Trilogy for Ace over a period of about fourteen months, I wrote and sold another twenty-two.

Some of them, admittedly, were good-natured pieces of fluff. I like humor, science fiction is one of the few remaining markets for it, and I've included some of the better ones here.

But a number of them *weren't* trivial. Some of them have substance I once thought impossible for works of short fiction (or at least for *my* short fiction) and I take an enormous pride in them. The Kirinyaga stories, the Teddy Roosevelt stories, such personal pieces as "Winter Solstice" are as ambitious and meaningful as any novels I have written.

Back in 1986, I seriously wondered if I would have enough short stories to form a respectable collection by the turn of the century. Now here it is, 1991, and my biggest problem in preparing this book is which thirty stories to eliminate. Life just gets curiouser and curiouser.

So what you have in your hands is a collection by an avowed novelist who spent most of his life shunning short stories, and who has won two Hugos for short fiction and received eight Hugo and Nebula nominations in the past thirty months—seven of them for short fiction.

Go figure.

—Mike Resnick
September, 1991

Will The Last Person to Leave the Planet Please Shut Off the Sun?

When I sold this collection to Tor, my longtime (and long-suffering) editor, Beth Meacham, asked me what the title would be. I gave her what I thought were four or five of the catchier titles in the book, and she seemed vaguely dissatisfied, so out of the blue I suggested "Will the Last Person to Leave the Planet Please Shut Off the Sun?"

I love it, said Beth.

There's only one problem, I pointed out; I don't have a story with that title.

So write one, she said.

So I did.

(Postscript: I then sold it to Alan Dean Foster, who asked me to change the title. It appears elsewhere as "Final Solution." For what that's worth.)

Will the Last Person to Leave the Planet Please Shut Off the Sun?

It started with the Jews.

One day they announced that they were immigrating to the world of New Jerusalem. Just like that. Not even so much as a by-your-leave.

"We are tired of being underappreciated and overpersecuted," said their statement. "We gave you the Old Testament and the Ten Commandments, relativity and quantum mechanics, the polio vaccine and interstellar travel, Hollywood and Miami Beach and Sandy Koufax, the Six-Day War of 1967 and the Twenty-three-Minute War of 2041, and frankly, we've had it with you guys. Live long and prosper and don't call us, we'll call you."

And the next day they were gone, every last one of them.

It was June 21, 2063. I still remember my friend Burt passing out *Earth: Love It Or Leave It* t-shirts to all the guys at work, and saying that we were well rid of them and that *now* things were going to get better in a hell of a hurry.

Then, three months later, Odingo Nkomo announced

that the Kikuyu were leaving for Beta Piscium IV, and then Joshua Galawanda took the Zulus to Islandhwana II, and almost before you could turn around, Africa was empty except for a few Arabs in the north and a handful of Indians who quickly booked passage back to Bombay.

Well, this didn't bother anyone very much, because nobody really cared about Africa anyway, and suddenly there were two billion less mouths to feed and some of the game parks started showing signs of life. But then Moses Smith demanded that the U.S. government supply transportation to all American blacks who wanted to leave, and Earl Mingus ("the Pride of Mississippi"), who had just succeeded to the presidency, agreed on the spot, and suddenly we had an all-white nation.

Well, *almost* all-white. Actually, it took another year for Harvey Running Horse to convince all his fellow Amerinds to accompany him to Alphard III, which he had renamed Little Big Horn.

"Now," said Burt, popping open a beer, "if we could just get rid of the Hispanics, and maybe the Catholics . . . "

The Hispanics headed off for Madrid III two months later, and Burt threw a big party to celebrate. "I'm finally proud to be an Amurrican agin!" he announced, and hung a huge flag outside his front door.

Of course, it wasn't just the blacks and Jews and Hispanics who were emigrating, and it wasn't just America and Africa that were getting emptier. The Chinese left the next year, followed by the Turks, the Bulgarians, the Indians, the Australians, and the French Polynesians. It didn't even make headlines when the Cook County Democratic Machine went off to Daleyworld, which figured to be the only planet that was ever turned into a smoke-filled back room.

"Great!" proclaimed Burt. "We finally got room to breathe and stretch our legs."

Things kind of settled down for a couple of years then, and life got pretty easy, and we hardly noticed that the Brits, the Germans, the Russians, the Albanians, the Sunnis and the Shiites had all gone.

"Wonderful!" said Burt on the day the Greeks and the Pakistanis left. "So maybe we still wear gas masks because of the pollution, and the water still ain't safe to drink, and we ain't quite gotten over our little problem with Eight Mile Island"—that was the problem that turned it into thirty-two Quarter Mile Islands—"but, by God, what's a little inconvenience compared to a world run by and for 100 percent pure Amurricans?"

I suppose we should have seen the handwriting on the wall when the NFL moved the Alaska Timberwolves and the Louisiana Gamblers, the last two franchises still on Earth, to the Quinellus Cluster. There were other little hints, too, like using downtown Boston to test out the new J-Bomb, or the day the Great Lakes finally turned solid with sludge.

That was when the *real* emigration started, right in our back yard, so to speak. Nevada, Michigan, and Florida were the first to go; then New Hampshire and Delaware, then Texas, and then it was Katie-bar-the-door. For the longest time I really thought California would stick around, but they finally located a world with a 9,000-mile beach and a native populace that specialized in making sandals and cheap gold jewelry, and suddenly the United States of America began at St. Louis and ended about 60 miles west of Council Bluffs.

"Let 'em go," counselled Burt. "We never needed 'em anyway. And there's just that much more for the rest of us, right?"

Except that things kept happening. The ice cap slipped south all the way to Minneapolis, Mount Kilimanjaro started pouring lava down onto the Serengeti Plains, the Mediterranean boiled away, the National Hockey League went bankrupt, and people kept leaving.

That was almost ten years ago.

There are only eight of us left now. Burt was pressed into duty as World President this week, because Arnie Jenkins hurt his wrist and can't sign any documents, and Sybil Miller, who was supposed to succeed Arnie, has her period and says she doesn't feel like it.

We haven't gotten any mail or supplies in close to a year now. They say that Earth is too polluted and dangerous to land on anymore, so Burt figured it was his Presidential duty to take one of our two remaining ships to Mars Base and pick up the mail, and bring Arnie back his yearly supply of cigarettes.

I stopped by his office this morning to return a socket wrench I had borrowed, and I saw a letter addressed to me sitting on his desk, so I opened it and read it.

I been mulling it over, and I decided that I was all wrong about this after all. I mean, being World President is all well and good, but not when your only duties are taking out the garbage and picking up the mail. A World President needs a army and navy to keep the peace, and lots of people paying taxes, and stuff like that. I hate to leave now that we're finally down to nothing but 100% pure and loyal Americans, but the fact of the matter is that there ain't no point to being President every eighth week without no perks and no fringes, so I'm off to the big wide galaxy to see if anyone out there wants a guy with Presidential experience. I'll be happy to take over the reins of any government what wants me, so long as it's white and Christian and mostly American and has a football team. In fact, I don't even have to be President; I got no serious objections to hiring on as King.

Do me a favor and post this one last official message for me.

And there was a printed sign saying, WILL THE LAST PERSON TO LEAVE THE PLANET PLEASE SHUT OFF THE SUN?

I can't tell you how relieved the rest of us are. Burt was okay for a Baptist, but you know what they say about Baptists.

Now if we can just find a way to get rid of Myrtle Bremmer and that Presbyterian claptrap she's always spouting, we'll finally have an America that *I'm* proud to be a part of.

INTRODUCTION
Kirinyaga

Back in 1987, Orson Scott Card called me up and asked me to contribute a story to his shared-world collection, *Eutopia.* The best career decision I ever made was to tell him I'd be happy to create an East African Utopia within his guidelines. I handed him the story at the World Science Fiction Convention in Brighton, England, while on my way to Kenya.

The second-best career decision I ever made was to ask him for permission to market it to one of the magazines before the anthology came out. Ed Ferman made it the cover story for *The Magazine of Fantasy and Science Fiction,* it was nominated for a Nebula, it won the 1989 Hugo for Best Short Story, it has been resold nine times and has appeared in five countries to date, and it probably did more for my career than any other piece I've written.

(And, five years later, *Eutopia* still hasn't appeared. I sometimes wonder what might have happened had Orson *not* graciously allowed me to submit it to Ed. From such musings come nightmares you wouldn't believe.)

Kirinyaga

In the beginning, Ngai lived alone atop the mountain called Kirinyaga. In the fullness of time He created three sons, who became the fathers of the Masai, the Kamba, and the Kikuyu races, and to each son He offered a spear, a bow, and a digging-stick. The Masai chose the spear, and was told to tend herds on the vast savannah. The Kamba chose the bow, and was sent to the dense forests to hunt for game. But Gikuyu, the first Kikuyu, knew that Ngai loved the earth and the seasons, and chose the digging-stick. To reward him for this Ngai not only taught him the secrets of the seed and the harvest, but gave him Kirinyaga, with its holy fig tree and rich lands.

The sons and daughters of Gikuyu remained on Kirinyaga until the white man came and took their lands away, and even when the white man had been banished they did not return, but chose to remain in the cities, wearing Western clothes and using Western machines and living Western lives. Even I, who am a *mundumugu*—a witch doctor—

was born in the city. I have never seen the lion or the elephant or the rhinoceros, for all of them were extinct before my birth; nor have I seen Kirinyaga as Ngai meant it to be seen, for a bustling, overcrowded city of three million inhabitants covers its slopes, every year approaching closer and closer to Ngai's throne at the summit. Even the Kikuyu have forgotten its true name, and now know it only as Mount Kenya.

To be thrown out of Paradise, as were the Christian Adam and Eve, is a terrible fate, but to live beside a debased Paradise is infinitely worse. I think about them frequently, the descendants of Gikuyu who have forgotten their origin and their traditions and are now merely Kenyans, and I wonder why more of them did not join with us when we created the Eutopian world of Kirinyaga.

True, it is a harsh life, for Ngai never meant life to be easy; but it is also a satisfying life. We live in harmony with our environment, we offer sacrifices when Ngai's tears of compassion fall upon our fields and give sustenance to our crops, we slaughter a goat to thank him for the harvest.

Our pleasures are simple: a gourd of *pombe* to drink, the warmth of a *boma* when the sun has gone down, the wail of a newborn son or daughter, the foot-races and spear-throwing and other contests, the nightly singing and dancing.

Maintenance watches Kirinyaga discreetly, making minor orbital adjustments when necessary, assuring that our tropical climate remains constant. From time to time they have subtly suggested that we might wish to draw upon their medical expertise, or perhaps allow our children to make use of their educational facilities, but they have taken our refusal with good grace, and have never shown any desire to interfere in our affairs.

Until I strangled the baby.

It was less than an hour later that Koinnage, our paramount chief, sought me out.

"That was an unwise thing to do, Koriba," he said grimly.

"It was not a matter of choice," I replied. "You know that."

"Of course you had a choice," he responded. "You could have let the infant live." He paused, trying to control his anger and his fear. "Maintenance has never set foot on Kirinyaga before, but now they will come."

"Let them," I said with a shrug. "No law has been broken."

"We have killed a baby," he replied. "They will come, and they will revoke our charter!"

I shook my head. "No one will revoke our charter."

"Do not be too certain of that, Koriba," he warned me. "You can bury a goat alive, and they will monitor us and shake their heads and speak contemptuously among themselves about our religion. You can leave the aged and the infirm out for the hyenas to eat, and they will look upon us with disgust and call us godless heathens. But I tell you that killing a newborn infant is another matter. They will not sit idly by; they will come."

"If they do, I shall explain why I killed it," I replied calmly.

"They will not accept your answers," said Koinnage. "They will not understand."

"They will have no choice but to accept my answers," I said. "This is Kirinyaga, and they are not permitted to interfere."

"They will find a way," he said with an air of certainty. "We must apologize and tell them that it will not happen again."

"We will not apologize," I said sternly. "Nor can we promise that it will not happen again."

"Then, as paramount chief, *I* will apologize."

I stared at him for a long moment, then shrugged. "Do what you must do," I said.

Suddenly I could see the terror in his eyes.

"What will you do to me?" he asked fearfully.

"I? Nothing at all," I said. "Are you not my chief?" As he relaxed, I added: "But if I were you, I would beware of insects."

"Insects?" he repeated. "Why?"

"Because the next insect that bites you, be it spider or mosquito or fly, will surely kill you," I said. "Your blood will boil within your body, and your bones will melt. You will want to scream out your agony, yet you will be unable to utter a sound." I paused. "It is not a death I would wish on a friend," I added seriously.

"Are we not friends, Koriba?" he said, his ebony face turning an ash gray.

"I thought we were," I said. "But my friends honor our traditions. They do not apologize for them to the white man."

"I will not apologize!" he promised fervently. He spat on both his hands as a gesture of his sincerity.

I opened one of the pouches I kept around my waist and withdrew a small polished stone from the shore of our nearby river. "Wear this around your neck," I said, handing it to him, "and it shall protect you from the bites of insects."

"Thank you, Koriba!" he said with sincere gratitude, and another crisis had been averted.

We spoke about the affairs of the village for a few more minutes, and finally he left me. I sent for Wambu, the infant's mother, and led her through the ritual of purification, so that she might conceive again. I also gave her an ointment to relieve the pain in her breasts, since they were heavy with milk. Then I sat down by the fire before my *boma* and made myself available to my people, settling disputes over the ownership of chickens and goats, and supplying charms against demons, and instructing my people in the ancient ways.

By the time of the evening meal, no one had a thought for the dead baby. I ate alone in my *boma,* as befitted my status, for the *mundumugu* always lives and eats apart from his people. When I had finished I wrapped a blanket around my body to protect me from the cold and walked down the dirt path to where all the other *bomas* were clustered. The cattle and goats and chickens were penned up for the night, and my people, who had slaughtered and eaten a cow, were now singing and dancing and drinking great quantities of *pombe*. As they made way for me, I walked over to the caldron and took a drink of *pombe,* and then, at Kanjara's request, I slit open a goat and read its entrails and saw that his youngest wife would soon conceive, which was cause for more celebration. Finally the children urged me to tell them a story.

"But not a story of Earth," complained one of the taller boys. "We hear those all the time. This must be a story about Kirinyaga."

"All right," I said. "If you will all gather around, I will tell you a story of Kirinyaga." The youngsters all moved closer. "This," I said, "is the story of the Lion and the Hare." I paused until I was sure that I had everyone's attention, especially that of the adults. "A hare was chosen by his people to be sacrificed to a lion, so that the lion would not bring disaster to their village. The hare might have run away, but he knew that sooner or later the lion would catch him, so instead he sought out the lion and walked right up to him, and as the lion opened his mouth to swallow him, the hare said, 'I apologize, Great Lion.'

" 'For what?' asked the lion curiously.

" 'Because I am such a small meal,' answered the hare. 'For that reason, I brought honey for you as well.'

" 'I see no honey,' said the lion.

" 'That is why I apologized,' answered the hare. 'Another lion stole it from me. He is a ferocious creature, and says that he is not afraid of you.'

"The lion rose to his feet. 'Where is this other lion?' he roared.

"The hare pointed to a hole in the earth. 'Down there,' he said, 'but he will not give you back your honey.'

" 'We shall see about that!' growled the lion.

"He jumped into the hole, roaring furiously, and was never seen again, for the hare had chosen a very deep hole indeed. Then the hare went home to his people and told them that the lion would never bother them again."

Most of the children laughed and clapped their hands in delight, but the same young boy voiced his objection.

"That is not a story of Kirinyaga," he said scornfully. "We have no lions here."

"It *is* a story of Kirinyaga," I replied. "What is important about the story is not that it concerned a lion and a hare, but that it shows that the weaker can defeat the stronger if he uses his intelligence."

"What has that to do with Kirinyaga?" asked the boy.

"What if we pretend that the men of Maintenance, who have ships and weapons, are the lion, and the Kikuyu are the hares?" I suggested. "What shall the hares do if the lion demands a sacrifice?"

The boy suddenly grinned. "Now I understand! We shall throw the lion down a hole!"

"But we have no holes here," I pointed out.

"Then what shall we do?"

"The hare did not know that he would find the lion near a hole," I replied. "Had he found him by a deep lake, he would have said that a large fish took the honey."

"We have no deep lakes."

"But we do have intelligence," I said. "And if Maintenance ever interferes with us, we will use our intelligence to destroy the lion of Maintenance, just as the hare used his intelligence to destroy the lion of the fable."

"Let us think how to destroy Maintenance right now!" cried the boy. He picked up a stick and brandished it at an imaginary lion as if it were a spear and he a great hunter.

I shook my head. "The hare does not hunt the lion, and the Kikuyu do not make war. The hare merely protects himself, and the Kikuyu do the same."

"Why would Maintenance interfere with us?" asked another boy, pushing his way to the front of the group. "They are our friends."

"Perhaps they will not," I answered reassuringly. "But you must always remember that the Kikuyu have no true friends except themselves."

"Tell us another story, Koriba!" cried a young girl.

"I am an old man," I said. "The night has turned cold, and I must have my sleep."

"Tomorrow?" she asked. "Will you tell us another tomorrow?"

I smiled. "Ask me tomorrow, after all the fields are planted and the cattle and goats are in their enclosures and the food has been made and the fabrics have been woven."

"But girls do not herd the cattle and goats," she protested. "What if my brothers do not bring all their animals to the enclosure?"

"Then I will tell a story just to the girls," I said.

"It must be a long story," she insisted seriously, "for we work much harder than the boys."

"I will watch you in particular, little one," I replied, "and the story will be as long or as short as your work merits."

The adults all laughed and suddenly she looked very uncomfortable, but then I chuckled and hugged her and patted her head, for it was necessary that the children learned to love their *mundumugu* as well as hold him in awe, and finally she ran off to play and dance with the other girls, while I retired to my *boma*.

Once inside, I activated my computer and discovered that a message was waiting for me from Maintenance, informing me that one of their number would be visiting me the following morning. I made a very brief reply—"Article II, Paragraph 5," which is the ordinance forbidding intervention—and lay down on my sleeping blanket, letting the rhythmic chanting of the singers carry me off to sleep.

I awoke with the sun the next morning and instructed my computer to let me know when the Maintenance ship had landed. Then I inspected my cattle and my goats—I, alone of my people, planted no crops, for the Kikuyu feed their *mundumugu,* just as they tend his herds and weave his blankets and keep his *boma* clean—and stopped by Simani's *boma* to deliver a balm to fight the disease that was afflicting his joints. Then, as the sun began warming the earth, I returned to my own *boma,* skirting the pastures where the young men were tending their animals. When I arrived, I knew the ship had landed, for I found the droppings of a hyena on the ground near my hut, and that is the surest sign of a curse.

I learned what I could from the computer, then walked outside and scanned the horizon while two naked children took turns chasing a small dog and running away from it. When they began frightening my chickens, I gently sent them back to their own *boma,* and then seated myself beside my fire. At last I saw my visitor from Maintenance, coming up the path from Haven. She was obviously uncomfortable in the heat, and she slapped futilely at the flies that circled her head. Her blonde hair was starting to turn grey, and I could tell by the ungainly way she negotiated the steep, rocky path that she was unused to such terrain. She almost lost her balance a number of times, and it was obvious that her proximity to so many animals frightened her, but she never slowed her pace, and within another ten minutes she stood before me.

"Good morning," she said.

"*Jambo,* Memsahib," I replied.

"You are Koriba, are you not?"

I briefly studied the face of my enemy; middle-aged and weary, it did not appear formidable. "I am Koriba," I replied.

"Good," she said. "My name is—"

"I know who you are," I said, for it is best, if conflict cannot be avoided, to take the offensive.

"You do?"

I pulled the bones out of my pouch and cast them on the dirt. "You are Barbara Eaton, born of Earth," I intoned, studying her reactions as I picked up the bones and cast them again. "You are married to Robert Eaton, and you have worked for Maintenance for nine years." A final cast of the bones. "You are forty-one years old, and you are barren."

"How did you know all that?" she asked with an expression of surprise.

"Am I not the *mundumugu?*"

She stared at me for a long minute. "You read my biography on your computer," she concluded at last.

"As long as the facts are correct, what difference does it make whether I read them from the bones or the computer?" I responded, refusing to confirm her statement. "Please sit down, Memsahib Eaton."

She lowered herself awkwardly to the ground, wrinkling her face as she raised a cloud of dust.

"It's very hot," she noted uncomfortably.

"It is very hot in Kenya," I replied.

"You could have created any climate you desired," she pointed out.

"We *did* create the climate we desired," I answered.

"Are there predators out there?" she asked, looking out over the savannah.

"A few," I replied.

"What kind?"

"Hyenas."

"Nothing larger?" she asked.

"There *is* nothing larger anymore," I said.

"I wonder why they didn't attack me?"

"Perhaps because you are an intruder," I suggested.

"Will they leave me alone on my way back to Haven?" she asked nervously, ignoring my comment.

"I will give you a charm to keep them away."

"I'd prefer an escort."

"Very well," I said.

"They're such ugly animals," she said with a shudder. "I saw them once when we were monitoring your world."

"They are very useful animals," I answered, "for they bring many omens, both good and bad."

"Really?"

I nodded. "A hyena left me an evil omen this morning."

"And?" she asked curiously.

"And here you are," I said.

She laughed. "They told me you were a sharp old man."

"They were mistaken," I replied. "I am a feeble old man who sits in front of his *boma* and watches younger men tend his cattle and goats."

"You are a feeble old man who graduated with honors from Cambridge and then acquired two postgraduate degrees from Yale," she replied.

"Who told you that?"

She smiled. "You're not the only one who reads biographies."

I shrugged. "My degrees did not help me become a better *mundumugu*," I said. "The time was wasted."

"You keep using that world. What, exactly, *is* a *mundumugu?*"

"You would call him a witch doctor," I answered. "But in truth the *mundumugu*, while he occasionally casts spells and interprets omens, is more a repository of the collected wisdom and traditions of his race."

"It sounds like an interesting occupation," she said.

"It is not without its compensations."

"And *such* compensations!" she said with false enthusiasm as a goat bleated in the distance and a young man yelled at it in Swahili. "Imagine having the power of life and death over an entire Eutopian world!"

So now it comes, I thought. Aloud I said: "It is not a matter of exercising power, Memsahib Eaton, but of maintaining traditions."

"I rather doubt that," she said bluntly.

"Why should you doubt what I say?" I asked.

"Because if it were traditional to kill newborn infants,

the Kikuyus would have died out after a single generation."

"If the slaying of the infant arouses your disapproval," I said calmly, "I am surprised Maintenance has not previously asked about our custom of leaving the old and the feeble out for the hyenas."

"We know that the elderly and the infirm have consented to your treatment of them, much as we may disapprove of it," she replied. "We also know that a newborn infant could not possibly consent to its own death." She paused, staring at me. "May I ask why this particular baby was killed?"

"That *is* why you have come here, is it not?"

"I have been sent here to evaluate the situation," she replied, brushing an insect from her cheek and shifting her position on the ground. "A newborn child was killed. We would like to know why."

I shrugged. "It was killed because it was born with a terrible *thahu* upon it."

She frowned. "A *thahu?* What is that?"

"A curse."

"Do you mean that it was deformed?" she asked.

"It was not deformed."

"Then what was this curse that you refer to?"

"It was born feet-first," I said.

"That's it?" she asked, surprised. "That's the curse?"

"Yes."

"It was murdered simply because it came out feet-first?"

"It is not murder to put a demon to death," I explained patiently. "Our tradition tells us that a child born in this manner is actually a demon."

"You are an educated man, Koriba," she said. "How can you kill a perfectly healthy infant and blame it on some primitive tradition?"

"You must never underestimate the power of tradition, Memsahib Eaton," I said. "The Kikuyu turned their backs on their traditions once; the result is a mechanized, impoverished, overcrowded country that is no longer populated by

Kikuyu, or Masai, or Luo, or Wakamba, but by a new, artificial tribe known only as Kenyans. We here on Kirinyaga are true Kikuyu, and we will not make that mistake again. If the rains are late, a ram must be sacrificed. If a man's veracity is questioned, he must undergo the ordeal of the *githani* trial. If an infant is born with a *thahu* upon it, it must be put to death."

"Then you intened to continue to kill any children that are born feet-first?" she asked.

"That is correct," I responded.

A drop of sweat rolled down her face as she looked directly at me and said: "I don't know what Maintenance's reaction will be."

"According to our charter, Maintenance is not permitted to interfere with us," I reminded her.

"It's not that simple, Koriba," she said. "According to your charter, any member of your community who wishes to leave your world is allowed free passage to Haven, from which he or she can board a ship to Earth." She paused. "Was the baby you killed given such a choice?"

"I did not kill a baby, but a demon," I replied, turning my head slightly as a hot breeze stirred up the dust around us.

She waited until the breeze died down, then coughed before speaking. "You do understand that not everyone in Maintenance may share that opinion?"

"What Maintenance thinks is of no concern to us," I said.

"When innocent children are murdered, what Maintenance thinks is of supreme importance to you," she responded. "I am sure you do not want to defend your practices in the Eutopian Court."

"Are you here to evaluate the situation, as you said, or to threaten us?" I asked calmly.

"To evaluate the situation," she replied. "But there seems to be only one conclusion that I can draw from the facts that you have presented to me."

"Then you have not been listening to me," I said, briefly closing my eyes as another, stronger breeze swept past us.

"Koriba, I know that Kirinyaga was created so that you could emulate the ways of your forefathers—but surely you must see the difference between the torture of animals as a religious ritual and the murder of a human baby."

I shook my head. "They are one and the same," I replied. "We cannot change our way of life because it makes *you* uncomfortable. We did that once before, and within a mere handful of years your culture had corrupted our society. With every factory we built, with every job we created, with every bit of Western technology we accepted, with every Kikuyu who converted to Christianity, we became something we were not meant to be." I stared directly into her eyes. "I am the *mundumugu,* entrusted with preserving all that makes us Kikuyu, and I will not allow that to happen again."

"There are alternatives," she said.

"Not for the Kikuyu," I replied adamantly.

"There *are,*" she insisted, so intent upon what she had to say that she paid no attention to a black-and-gold centipede that crawled over her boot. "For example, years spent in space can cause certain physiological and hormonal changes in humans. You noted when I arrived that I am forty-one years old and childless. That is true. In fact, many of the women in Maintenance are childless. If you will turn the babies over to us, I am sure we can find families for them. This would effectively remove them from your society without the necessity of killing them. I could speak to my superiors about it; I think that there is an excellent chance that they would approve."

"That is a thoughtful and innovative suggestion, Memsahib Eaton," I said truthfully. "I am sorry that I must reject it."

"But why?" she demanded.

"Because the first time we betray our traditions this world will cease to be Kirinyaga, and will become merely another Kenya, a nation of men awkwardly pretending to be something they are not."

"I could speak to Koinnage and the other chiefs about it," she suggested meaningfully.

"They will not disobey my instructions," I replied confidently.

"You hold that much power?"

"I hold that much respect," I answered. "A chief may enforce the law, but it is the *mundumugu* who interprets it."

"Then let us consider other alternatives."

"No."

"I am trying to avoid a conflict between Maintenance and your people," she said, her voice heavy with frustration. "It seems to me that you could at least make the effort to meet me halfway."

"I do not question your motives, Memsahib Eaton," I replied, "but you are an intruder representing an organization that has no legal right to interfere with our culture. We do not impose our religion or our morality upon Maintenance, and Maintenance may not impose its religion or morality upon us."

"It's not that simple."

"It is precisely that simple," I said.

"That is your last word on the subject?" she asked.

"Yes."

She stood up. "Then I think it is time for me to leave and make my report."

I stood up as well, and a shift in the wind brought the odors of the village: the scent of bananas, the smell of a fresh caldron of *pombe,* even the pungent odor of a bull that had been slaughtered that morning.

"As you wish, Memsahib Eaton," I said. "I will arrange for your escort." I signalled to a small boy who was tending three goats and instructed him to go to the village and send back two young men.

"Thank you," she said. "I know it's an inconvenience,

but I just don't feel safe with hyenas roaming loose out there."

"You are welcome," I said. "Perhaps, while we are waiting for the men who will accompany you, you would like to hear a story about the hyena."

She shuddered involuntarily. "They are such ugly beasts!" she said distastefully. "Their hind legs seem almost deformed." She shook her head. "No, I don't think I'd be interested in hearing a story about a hyena."

"You will be interested in *this* story," I told her.

She stared at me curiously, then shrugged. "All right," she said. "Go ahead."

"It is true that hyenas are deformed, ugly animals," I began, "but once, a long time ago, they were as lovely and graceful as the impala. Then one day a Kikuyu chief gave a hyena a young goat to take as a gift to Ngai, who lived atop the holy mountain Kirinyaga. The hyena took the goat between his powerful jaws and headed toward the distant mountain—but on the way he passed a settlement filled with Europeans and Arabs. It abounded in guns and machines and other wonders he had never seen before, and he stopped to look, fascinated. Finally an Arab noticed him staring intently and asked if he, too, would like to become a civilized man— and as he opened his mouth to say that he would, the goat fell to the ground and ran away. As the goat raced out of sight, the Arab laughed and explained that he was only joking, that of course no hyena could become a man." I paused for a moment, and then continued. "So the hyena proceeded to Kirinyaga, and when he reached the summit, Ngai asked him what had become of the goat. When the hyena told him, Ngai hurled him off the mountaintop for having the audacity to believe he could become a man. He did not die from the fall, but his rear legs were crippled, and Ngai declared that from that day forward, all hyenas would appear thus—and to remind them of the foolishness of trying to become something that they were not, He also gave them a fool's laugh." I paused again, and stared at her. "Memsahib Eaton, you do not hear the Kikuyu laugh like fools, and I will not let them become crippled like the hyena. Do you understand what I am saying?"

She considered my statement for a moment, then looked into my eyes. "I think we understand each other perfectly, Koriba," she said.

The two young men I had sent for arrived just then, and I instructed them to accompany her to Haven. A moment later they set off across the dry savannah, and I returned to my duties.

I began by walking through the fields, blessing the scarecrows. Since a number of the smaller children followed me, I rested beneath the trees more often than was necessary, and always, whenever we paused, they begged me to tell them more stories. I told them the tale of the Elephant and the Buffalo, and how the Masai *elmoran* cut the rainbow with his spear so that it never again came to rest upon the earth, and why the nine Kikuyu tribes are named after Gikuyu's nine daughters, and when the sun became too hot I led them back to the village.

Then, in the afternoon, I gathered the older boys about me and explained once more how they must paint their faces and bodies for their forthcoming circumcision ceremony. Ndemi, the boy who had insisted upon a story about Kirinyaga the night before, sought me out privately to complain that he had been unable to slay a small gazelle with his spear, and asked for a charm to make its flight more accurate. I explained to him that there would come a day when he faced a buffalo or a hyena with no charm, and that he must practice more before he came to me again. He was one to watch, this little Ndemi, for he was impetuous and totally without fear; in the old days, he would have made a great warrior, but on Kirinyaga we had no warriors. If we remained fruitful and fecund, however, we would someday need more chiefs and even another *mundumugu,* and I made up my mind to observe him closely.

In the evening, after I ate my solitary meal, I returned to the village, for Njogu, one of our young men, was to marry Kamiri, a girl from the next village. The bride-price had been decided upon, and the two families were waiting for me to preside at the ceremony.

Njogu, his faced streaked with paint, wore an ostrich-feather headdress, and looked very uneasy as he and his betrothed stood before me. I slit the throat of a fat ram that Kamiri's father had brought for the occasion, and then I turned to Njogu.

"What have you to say?" I asked.

He took a step forward. "I want Kamiri to come and till the fields of my *shamba,"* he said, his voice cracking with nervousness as he spoke the prescribed words, "for I am a man, and I need a woman to tend to my *shamba* and dig deep around the roots of my plantings, that they may grow well and bring prosperity to my house."

He spit on both his hands to show his sincerity, and then, exhaling deeply with relief, he stepped back.

I turned to Kamiri.

"Do you consent to till the *shamba* of Njogu, son of Muchiri?" I asked her.

"Yes," she said softly, bowing her head. "I consent."

I held out my right hand, and the bride's mother placed a gourd of *pombe* in it.

"If this man does not please you," I said to Kamiri, "I will spill the *pombe* upon the ground."

"Do not spill it," she replied.

"Then drink," I said, handing the gourd to her.

She lifted it to her lips and took a swallow, then handed it to Njogu, who did the same.

When the gourd was empty, the parents of Njogu and Kamiri stuffed it with grass, signifying the friendship between the two clans.

Then a cheer rose from the onlookers, the ram was carried off to be roasted, more *pombe* appeared as if by magic, and while the groom took the bride off to his *boma,* the remainder of the people celebrated far into the night. They stopped only when the bleating of the goats told them that some hyenas were nearby, and then the women and children went off to their *bomas* while the men took their spears and went into the fields to frighten the hyenas away.

Koinnage came up to me as I was about to leave.

"Did you speak to the woman from Maintenance?" he asked.

"I did," I replied.

"What did she say?"

"She said that they do not approve of killing babies who are born feet-first."

"And what did *you* say?" he asked nervously.

"I told her that we did not need the approval of Maintenance to practice our religion," I replied.

"Will Maintenance listen?"

"They have no choice," I said. "And *we* have no choice, either," I added. "Let them dictate one thing that we must or must not do, and soon they will dictate all things. Give them their way, and Njogu and Kamiri would have recited wedding vows from the Bible or the Koran. It happened to us in Kenya; we cannot permit it to happen on Kirinyaga."

"But they will not punish us?" he persisted.

"They will not punish us," I replied.

Satisfied, he walked off to his *boma* while I took the narrow, winding path to my own. I stopped by the enclosure where my animals were kept and saw that there were two new goats there, gifts from the bride's and groom's families in gratitude for my services. A few minutes later I was asleep within the walls of my own *boma.*

The computer woke me a few minutes before sunrise. I stood up, splashed my face with water from the gourd I keep by my sleeping blanket, and walked over to the terminal.

There was a message for me from Barbara Eaton, brief and to the point:

> *It is the preliminary finding of Maintenance that infanticide, for any reason, is a direct violation of Kirinyaga's charter. No action will be taken for past offenses.*
>
> *We are also evaluating your practice of euthanasia, and may require further testimony from you at some point in the future.*
>
> *Barbara Eaton*

A runner from Koinnage arrived a moment later, asking me to attend a meeting of the Council of Elders, and I knew that he had received the same message.

I wrapped my blanket around my shoulders and began walking to Koinnage's *shamba,* which consisted of his *boma,* as well as those of his three sons and their wives. When I arrived I found not only the local elders waiting for me, but also two chiefs from neighboring villages.

"Did you receive the message from Maintenance?" demanded Koinnage, as I seated myself opposite him.

"I did."

"I warned you that this would happen!" he said. "What will we do now?"

"We will do what we have always done," I answered calmly.

"We cannot," said one of the neighboring chiefs. "They have forbidden it."

"They have no right to forbid it," I replied.

"There is a woman in my village whose time is near," continued the chief, "and all of the signs and omens point to the birth of twins. We have been taught that the firstborn must be killed, for one mother cannot produce two souls— but now Maintenance has forbidden it. What are we to do?"

"We must kill the firstborn," I said, "for it will be a demon."

"And then Maintenance will make us leave Kirinyaga!" said Koinnage bitterly.

"Perhaps we could let the child live," said the chief. "That might satisfy them, and then they might leave us alone."

I shook my head. "They will not leave you alone. Already they speak about the way we leave the old and the feeble out for the hyenas, as if this were some enormous sin against their God. If you give in on the one, the day will come when you must give in on the other."

"Would that be so terrible?" persisted the chief. "They have medicines that we do not possess; perhaps they could make the old young again."

"You do not understand," I said, rising to my feet. "Our society is not a collection of separate people and customs and traditions. No, it is a complex system, with all the pieces as dependent upon each other as the animals and vegetation of the savannah. If you burn the grass, you will not only kill the impala who feeds upon it, but the predator who feeds upon the impala, and the ticks and flies who live upon the predator, and the vultures and maribou storks who feed upon his remains when he dies. You cannot destroy the part without destroying the whole."

I paused to let them consider what I had said, and then continued speaking: "Kirinyaga is like the savannah. If we do not leave the old and the feeble out for the hyenas, the hyenas will starve. If the hyenas starve, the grass eaters will become so numerous that there is no land left for our cattle and goats to graze. If the old and the feeble do not die when Ngai decrees it, then soon we will not have enough food to go around."

I picked up a stick and balanced it precariously on my forefinger.

"This stick," I said, "is the Kikuyu people, and my finger is Kirinyaga. They are in perfect balance." I stared at the neighboring chief. "But what will happen if I alter the balance, and put my finger *here?"* I asked, gesturing to the end of the stick.

"The stick will fall to the ground."

"And here?" I asked, pointing to a stop an inch away from the center.

"It will fall."

"Thus is it with us," I explained. "Whether we yield on one point or all points, the result will be the same: the Kikuyu will fall as surely as the stick will fall. Have we learned nothing from our past? We *must* adhere to our traditions; they are all that we have!"

"But Maintenance will not allow us to do so!" protested Koinnage.

"They are not warriors, but civilized men," I said, allowing a touch of contempt to creep into my voice. "Their chiefs and their *mundumugus* will not send them to Kirinyaga with guns and spears. They will issue warnings and findings and declarations, and finally, when that fails, they will go to the Eutopian Court and plead their case, and the trial will be postponed many times and reheard many more times." I could see them finally relaxing, and I smiled confidently at them. "Each of you will have died from the burden of your years before Maintenance does anything other than talk. I am your *mundumugu;* I have lived among civilized men, and I tell you that this is the truth."

The neighboring chief stood up and faced me. "I will send for you when the twins are born," he pledged.

"I will come," I promised him.

We spoke further, and then the meeting ended and the old men began wandering off to their *bomas,* while I looked to the future, which I could see more clearly than Koinnage or the elders.

I walked through the village until I found the bold young Ndemi, brandishing his spear and hurling it at a buffalo he had constructed out of dried grasses.

"*Jambo,* Koriba!" he greeted me.

"*Jambo,* my brave young warrior," I replied.

"I have been practicing, as you ordered."

"I thought you wanted to hunt the gazelle," I noted.

"Gazelles are for children," he answered. "I will slay *mbogo,* the buffalo."

"*Mbogo* may feel differently about it," I said.

"So much the better," he said confidently. "I have no wish to kill an animal as it runs away from me."

"And when will you go out to slay the fierce *mbogo?*"

He shrugged. "When I am more accurate." He smiled up at me. "Perhaps tomorrow."

I stared at him thoughtfully for a moment, and then spoke: "Tomorrow is a long time away. We have business tonight."

"What business?" he asked.

"You must find ten friends, none of them yet of circumcision age, and tell them to come to the pond within the forest to the south. They must come after the sun has set, and you must tell them that Koriba the *mundumugu* commands that they tell no one, not even their parents, that they are coming." I paused. "Do you understand, Ndemi?"

"I understand."

"Then go," I said. "Bring my message to them."

He retrieved his spear from the straw buffalo and set off at a trot, young and tall and strong and fearless.

You are the future, I thought, as I watched him run toward the village. *Not Koinnage, not myself, not even the young bridegroom Njogu, for their time will have come and gone before the battle is joined. It is you, Ndemi, upon whom Kirinyaga must depend if it is to survive.*

Once before the Kikuyu have had to fight for their freedom. Under the leadership of Jomo Kenyatta, whose name has been forgotten by most of your parents, we took the terrible oath of Mau Mau, and we maimed and we killed and we committed such atrocities that finally we achieved Uhuru, for against such butchery civilized men have no defense but to depart.

And tonight, young Ndemi, while your parents are asleep, you and your companions will meet me deep in the woods, and you in your turn and they in theirs will learn one last tradition of the Kikuyu, for I will invoke not only the strength of Ngai but also the indomitable spirit of Jomo Kenyatta. I will administer a hideous oath and force you to do unspeakable things to prove your fealty, and I will teach each of you, in turn, how to administer the oath to those who come after you.

There is a season for all things: for birth, for growth, for death. There is unquestionably a season for Utopia, but it will have to wait.

For the season of Uhuru is upon us.

Me and My Shadow

Back in the early 1980s, my friend Barry Malzberg asked me to read Robert Silverberg's *The Second Trip,* which showed what could go wrong with the Demolition process briefly described at the end of Alfred Bester's classic *The Demolished Man.* I read it and told Barry that it was a fine book, but that things wouldn't happen that way. He asked me how they *would* happen, and I wrote this story to show him.

I wasn't exactly a household name back then, and "Me and My Shadow" was turned down by every magazine in the field. I wound up practically giving it away to a semi-professional publication—where Jerry Pournelle, bless him, spotted it and bought it for *Science Fiction Yearbook,* his Best of the Year anthology.

Me and My Shadow

It all began when—

No. Strike that.

I don't know when it all began. Probably I never will.

But it began the second time when a truck backfired and I hit the sidewalk with the speed and grace of an athlete, which surprised the hell out of me since I've been a very *un*athletic businessman ever since the day I was born—or born again, depending on your point of view.

I got up, brushed myself off, and looked around. About a dozen pedestrians (though it felt like a hundred) were staring at me, and I could tell what each of them was thinking: Is this guy just some kind of nut, or has he maybe been Erased? And if he's been Erased, have I ever met him before? Do I *owe* him?

Of course, even if we *had* met before, they couldn't recognize me now. I know. I've spent almost three years trying to find out who I was before I got Erased, but along with what they did to my brain, they gave me a new face and wiped my fingerprints clean. I'm a brand-new man: two years, eleven months, and seventeen days old. I am (fanfare and trumpets, please!) ***William Jordan***. Not a real catchy name, I'll admit, but it's the only one I've got these days.

I had another name once. They told me not to worry about it, that all my memories had been expunged and that I couldn't dredge up a single fact no matter how hard I tried, not even if I took a little Sodium-P from a hypnotist, and after a few weeks I had to agree with them—which didn't mean that I stopped trying.

Erasures *never* stop trying.

Maybe the doctors and technicians at the Institute are right. Maybe I'm better off not knowing. Maybe the knowledge of what I did would drive the New Improved Me to suicide. But let me tell you: whatever I did, whatever *any* of us did (oh, yes, I speak to other Erasures; we spend a lot of time hanging around the newstape morgues and Missing Persons Bureaus and aren't all that hard to spot), it would be easier to live with the details than the uncertainty.

Example:

"Good day to you, Madam. Lovely weather we're having. Please excuse a delicate inquiry, but did I rape your infant daughter four years ago? Sodomize your sons? Slit your husband open from crotch to chin? Oh, no reason in particular; I was just curious."

Do you begin to see the problem?

Of course, they tell us that we're special, that we're not simply run-of-the-mill criminals and fiends; the jails are full of *them.*

Ah, fun and games at the Institute! It's quite an experience.

We cherish your individuality, they say as they painfully extract all my memories. (Funny: the pain lingers long after the memories are gone.)

Society needs men with your drive and ambition, they

smile as they shoot about eighteen zillion volts of electricity through my spasmodically-jerking body.

You had the guts to buck the system, they point out as they shred my face and give me a new one.

With drive like yours there's no telling how far you can go now that we've imprinted a new personality and a new set of ethics onto that magnificent libido, they agree as they try to decide whether to school me as a kennel attendant or perhaps turn me into an encyclopedia salesman. (They compromise and metamorphize me into an accountant.)

You lucky man, you've got a new name and face and memories and five hundred dollars in your pocket and you've still got your drive and ambition, they say as they excruciatingly insert a final memory block.

Now go out and knock 'em dead, they tell me.

Figuratively speaking, they add hastily.

Oh, one last thing, they say as they shove me out the door of the Institute. *We're pretty busy here, William Jordan, so don't come back unless it's an emergency. A BONA FIDE emergency.*

"But where am I to go?" I asked. "What am I to do?"

You'll think of something, they assure me. *After all, you had the brains and guts to buck our social system. Boy, do we wish we were like you! Now beat it; we've got work to do—or do you maybe think you're the only anti-social misanthrope with delusions of grandeur who ever got Erased?*

And the wild part is that they were right: most Erasures make out just fine. Strange as it sounds, we really *do* have more drive than the average man, the guy who just wants to hold off his creditors until he retires and his pension comes through. We'll take more risks, make quicker decisions, fight established trends more vigorously. We're a pretty gritty little group, all right—except that none of us knows why he was Erased.

In fact, I didn't have my first hint until the truck back-fired. (See? I'll bet you thought I had forgotten all about it.

Not a chance, friend. Erasures don't forget things—at least, not once they've left the Institute. What most Erasures do is spend vast portions of their new lives trying to *remember* things. Futilely.)

Well, my memory may have been wiped clean, but my instincts were still in working order, and what they told me was that I was a little more used to being shot at than the average man on the street. Not much to go on, to be sure, but at least it implied that the nature of my sin leaned more toward physical violence than, say, Wall Street tycoonery with an eye toward sophisticated fraud.

So I went to the main branch of the Public Library, rented a quarter of an hour on the Master Computer, and started popping in the questions.

LIST ALL CRIMINALS STANDING SIX FEET TWO INCHES WHO WERE APPREHENDED AND CONVICTED IN NEW YORK CITY BETWEEN 2008 A.D. AND 2010 A.D.

***CLASSIFIED.

That wasn't surprising. It had been classified the last fifty times I had asked. But, undaunted (Erasures are rarely daunted), I continued.

LIST ALL MURDERS COMMITTED BY PISTOL IN NEW YORK CITY BETWEEN 2008 A.D. AND 2010 A.D.

The list appeared on the screen, sixty names per second.

STOP.

The computer stopped, while I tried to come up with a more limiting question.

WITHOUT REVEALING THEIR IDENTITIES, TELL ME HOW MANY CRIMINALS WERE CONVICTED OF MULTIPLE PISTOL MURDERS IN NEW YORK CITY BETWEEN 2008 A.D. AND 2010 A.D.

***CLASSIFIED. Then it burped and added: NICE TRY, THOUGH.

THANK YOU. HAS ANY ERASURE EVER DIS-

COVERED EITHER HIS ORIGINAL IDENTITY OR
THE REASON HE WAS ERASED?

NOT YET.

DOES THAT IMPLY IT IS POSSIBLE?

NEGATIVE.

THEN IT IS IMPOSSIBLE?

NEGATIVE.

THEN WHAT THE HELL DID YOU MEAN?

ONLY THAT NO IMPLICATION WAS IN-
TENDED.

I checked my wristwatch. Five minutes left.

I AM AN ERASURE, I began.

I WOULD NEVER HAVE GUESSED.

Just what I needed—sarcasm from a computer. They're
making them too damned smart these days.

RECENTLY I REACTED INSTINCTIVELY TO A
SOUND VERY SIMILAR TO THAT MADE BY A PIS-
TOL BEING FIRED, ALTHOUGH I HAD NO CON-
SCIOUS REASON TO DO SO. WOULD THAT IMPLY
THAT GUNFIRE PLAYED AN IMPORTANT PART IN
MY LIFE PRIOR TO THE TIME I WAS ERASED?

***CLASSIFIED.

CLASSIFIED, NOT NEGATIVE?

THAT IS CORRECT.

I got up with three minutes left on my time.

My next stop was at Doubleday's, on Fifth Avenue. The
sign in the window boasted half a million microdots per cubic
yard, which meant that they had one hell of a collection of
literature crammed into their single ten-by-fifty-foot aisle.

I went straight to the True Crime section, but gave up
almost immediately when I saw the sheer volume of True
Crime that occurred each and every day in Manhattan.

I called in sick, then hunted up a shooting gallery in the
vidphone directory. I made an appointment, rode the Mid-
town slidewalk up to the front door, rented a pistol, and went
downstairs to the soundproofed target range in the basement.

It took me a couple of minutes to figure out how to insert the ammunition clip, an inauspicious beginning. Then I hefted the gun, first in one hand and then the other, hoping that something I did would feel familiar. No luck. I felt awkward and foolish, and the next couple of minutes didn't make me feel any better. I took dead aim at the target hanging some fifty feet away and missed it completely. I held the pistol with both hands and missed it again. I missed it right-handed and left-handed. I missed it with my right eye closed, I missed it with my left eye closed, I missed it with both eyes open.

Well, if the only thing I had going for me was my instinct, I decided to give that instinct a chance. I threw myself to the floor, rolled over twice, and fired off a quick round—and shot out the overhead light.

So much, I told myself, for instinct. Obviously the man I used to be was more at home ducking bullets than aiming them.

I left the gallery, hunted up a couple of Erased friends, and asked them if they'd ever experienced anything like my little flash of *déjà vu*. One of them thought it was hilarious—they may have made him safe, but I have my doubts about whether they made him sane—and the other confessed to certain vague stirrings whenever she heard a John Philip Sousa march, which wasn't exactly the answer I was looking for.

I stopped off for lunch at a local soya joint, spent another fruitless fifteen minutes in the library with my friend the computer, and went back to my brownstone condo to think things out. The whole time I was riding the slidewalk home I kept shadow-boxing and dancing away from imaginary enemies and reaching for a nonexistent revolver under my left arm, but nothing felt natural or even comfortable. After I got off the slidewalk and walked the final half block to my front door, I decided to see if I could pick the lock, but I gave up after about ten minutes, which was probably just as well since a passing cop was giving me the fish-eye.

I poured myself a stiff drink—Erasures' homes differ in locale and decor and many other respects, but you'll find liquor in all of them, as well as cheap memory courses and the Collected Who's Who in Organized Crime tapes—and tried, for the quadrillionth time, to dredge up some image from my past. The carnage of war, the screams and supplications of rape victims, the moans of old men and children lying sliced and bleeding in Central Park, all were grist for my mental mill—and all felt unfamiliar.

So I couldn't shoot and I couldn't pick locks and I couldn't remember. All that was on the one hand.

On the other hand was just one single solitary fact: I had ducked.

But somewhere deep down in my gut (certainly not in my brain) I knew, I *knew,* that the man I used to be had screamed wordlessly in my ear (or somewhere) to hit the deck before I got my/his/our damned fool head blown off.

This was contrary to everything they had told me at the Institute. I wasn't even supposed to be in communication with my former self. Even emergency conferences while bullets flew through the air were supposed to be impossible.

The more I thought about it, the more I decided that this definitely qualified as a bona fide Institute-visiting emergency. So I put on my jacket and left the condo and started off for the Institute. I didn't have any luck flagging down a cab—like frightened herbivores, New York cabbies all hide at the first hint of nightfall—so I started walking over to the East River slidewalk.

I had gone about two blocks when a grungy little man with watery eyes, a pock-marked face, and a very crooked nose jumped out at me from between two buildings, a wicked-looking knife in his hand.

Well, three years without being robbed in Manhattan is like flying 200 missions over Iraq or Paraguay or whoever we're mad at this month. You figure your number is up and you stoically take what's coming to you.

So I handed him my wallet, but there was only a single small bill in it, plus a bunch of credit cards geared to my voiceprint, and he suddenly threw the wallet on the ground and went berserk, ranting and raving about how I had cheated him.

I started backing away, which seemed to enrage him further, because he screamed something obscene and raced toward me with his knife raised above his head, obviously planning to plunge it into my neck or chest.

I remember thinking that of all the places to die, Second Avenue between 35th and 36th Streets was perhaps the very last one I'd have chosen. I remember wanting to yell for help but being too scared to force a sound out. I remember seeing the knife plunge down at me as if in slow motion.

And then, the next thing I knew, he was lying on his back, both his arms broken and his nose spouting blood like a fountain, and I was kneeling down next to him, just about to press the point of the knife into his throat.

I froze, trying to figure out what had happened, while deep inside me a voice—not angry, not bloodthirsty, but soft and seductive—crooned: *Do it, do it.*

"Don't kill me!" moaned the man, writhing beneath my hands. "Please don't kill me!"

You'll enjoy it, murmured the voice. *You'll see.*

I remained motionless for another moment, then dropped the knife and ran north, paying no attention to the traffic signals and not slowing down until I practically barreled into a bus that was blocking the intersection at 42nd Street.

Fool! whispered the voice. *Didn't I save your life? Trust me.*

Or maybe it wasn't the voice at all. Maybe I was just imagining what it would say if it were there.

At any rate, I decided not to go to the Institute at all. I had a feeling that if I walked in looking breathless and filthy and with the mugger's blood all over me, they'd just Erase me again before I could tell them what had happened.

So I went back home, took a quick Dryshower, hunted up Dr. Brozgold's number in the book, and called him.

"Yes?" he said after the phone had chimed twice. He looked just as I remembered him: tall and cadaverous, with a black mustache and bushy eyebrows, the kind of man who could put on a freshly-pressed suit and somehow manage to look rumpled.

"I'm an Erasure," I said, coming right to the point. "You worked on me."

"I'm afraid we have a faulty connection here," he said, squinting at his monitor. "I'm not receiving a video transmission."

"That's because I put a towel over my camera," I told him.

"I assume that this is an emergency?" he asked dryly, cocking one of those large, thick, disheveled eyebrows.

"It is," I said.

"Well, Mr. X—I hope you don't mind if I call you that—what seems to be the problem?"

"I almost killed a man tonight."

"Really?" he said.

"Doesn't that surprise you?"

"Not yet," he replied, placing his hands before him and juxtaposing his fingers. "I'll need some details first. Were you driving a car or robbing a bank or what?"

"I almost killed this man with my bare hands."

"Well, whoever you are, Mr. X, and whoever you *were*," he said, stroking his ragged mustache thoughtfully, "I think I can assure you that *almost* killing people probably wasn't your specialty."

"You don't understand," I said doggedly. "I used karate or kung fu or something like that, and I don't *know* any karate or kung fu."

"Who *is* this?" he demanded suddenly.

"Never mind," I said. "What I want to know is: What the hell is happening to me?"

"Look, I really can't help you without knowing your case history," he said, trying to keep the concern out of his voice and not quite succeeding.

"I don't have a history," I said. "I'm a brand-new man, remember?"

"Then what have you got against telling me who you are?"

"I'm trying to find out who I am!" I said hotly. "A little voice has been telling me that killing people feels good."

"If you'll present yourself at the Institute first thing in the morning, I'll do what I can," he said nervously.

"I know what you can do," I snapped. "You've already done it to me. I want to know if it's being *un*done."

"Absolutely not!" he said emphatically. "Whoever you are, your memory has been totally eradicated. No Erasure has ever developed even partial recall."

"Then how did I mangle a professional mugger who was attacking me with a knife?"

"The human body is capable of many things when placed under extreme duress," he replied in carefully-measured tones.

"I'm not talking about jumping ten feet in the air or running fifty yards in four seconds when you're being chased by a wild animal! I'm talking about crippling an armed opponent with three precision blows."

"I really can't answer you on the spur of the moment," he said. "If you'll just come down to the Institute and ask for me, I'll—"

"You'll what?" I demanded. "Erase a little smudge that you overlooked the first time?"

"If you won't give me your name and you won't come to the Institute," he said, "just what is it that you want from me?"

"I want to know what's happening."

"So you said," he commented dryly.

"And I want to know who I was."

"You know we can't tell you that," he replied. Then he paused and smiled ingratiatingly into the camera. "Of course, we might make an exception in this case, given the nature of your problem. But we can't do that unless we know who you are now."

"What assurances have I that you won't Erase me again?"

"You have my word," he said with a fatherly smile.

"You probably gave me your word the last time, too," I said.

"This conversation is becoming tedious, Mr. X. I can't help you without knowing who you are. In all likelihood nothing at all out of the ordinary has happened or is happening to you. And if indeed you are developing a new criminal persona, I have no doubt that we'll be meeting before too long anyway. So if you have nothing further to say, I really do have other things to do." He paused, then looked sharply into the camera. "What's *really* disturbing you? If you are actually experiencing some slight degree of recall, why should that distress you? Isn't that what all you Erasures are always hoping for?"

"The voice," I said.

"What about the voice?" he demanded.

"I don't know whether to believe it or not."

"The one that tells you to kill people?"

"It sounds like it *knows,*" I said softly. "It sounds convincing."

"Oh, Lord!" he whispered, and hung up the phone.

"Are you still here?" I asked the voice.

There was no answer, but I really didn't expect any. There was no one around to kill.

Suddenly I began to feel constricted, like the walls were closing in on me and the air was getting too thick to breathe, so I put my jacket back on and went out for a walk, keeping well clear of Second Avenue.

I stayed away from the busier streets and stuck to the

residential areas—as residential as you can get in Manhattan, anyway—and spent a couple of hours just wandering aimlessly while trying to analyze what was happening to me.

Two trucks backfired, but I didn't duck either time. A huge black man with a knife handle clearly visible above his belt walked by and gave me a long hard look, but I didn't disarm him. A police car cruised by, but I felt no urge to run.

In fact, I had just about convinced myself that Dr. Brozgold wasn't humoring me after all but was absolutely right about my having an overactive imagination, when a cheaply-dressed blonde hooker stepped out of a doorway and gave me the eye.

This one, whispered the voice.

I stopped dead in my tracks, terribly confused.

Trust me, it crooned.

The hooker smiled at me and, as if in a trance, I returned the smile and let her lead me upstairs to her sparsely-furnished room.

Patience, cautioned the voice. *Not too fast. Enjoy.*

She locked the door behind us.

What if she screams, I asked myself. We're on the fourth floor. How will I get away?

Relax, said the voice, all smooth and mellow. *First things first. You'll get away, never fear. I'll take care of you.*

The hooker was naked now. She smiled at me again, murmured something unintelligible, then came over and started unbuttoning my shirt.

I smashed a thumb into her left eye, heard bones cracking as I drove a fist into her rib cage, listened to her scream as I brought the edge of my hand down on the back of her neck.

Then there was silence.

It was fabulous! moaned the voice. *Just fabulous!* Suddenly it became solicitous. *Was it good for you, too?*

I waited a moment for my breathing to return to normal, for the flush of excitement to pass, or at least fade a little.

"Yes," I said aloud. "Yes, I enjoyed it."

I told you, said the voice. *They may have changed your memories, but they can't change your soul. You and I have always enjoyed it.*

"Do we just kill women?" I asked, curious.

I don't remember, admitted the voice.

"Then how did you know we had to kill this one?"

I know them when I see them, the voice assured me.

I mulled that over while I went around tidying up the room, rubbing the doorknob with my handkerchief, trying to remember if I had touched anything else.

They took away your fingerprints, said the voice. *Why bother?*

"So they don't know they're looking for an Erasure," I said, giving the room a final examination and then walking out the door.

I went home, put the towel back over the vidphone camera, and called Dr. Brozgold.

"You again?" he said when he saw that he wasn't receiving a picture.

"Yes," I answered. "I've thought about what you said, and I'll come in tomorrow morning."

"At the Institute?" he asked, looking tremendously relieved.

"Right. Nine o'clock sharp," I replied. "If you're not there when I arrive, I'm leaving."

"I'll be there," he promised.

I hung up the vidphone, checked out his address in the directory, and walked out the door.

Smart, said the voice admiringly as I walked the twenty-two blocks to Brozgold's apartment. *I would never have thought of this.*

"That's probably why they caught you," I whispered into the cold night air.

It took me just under an hour to reach Brozgold's place. (They turn the slidewalks off at eight o'clock to save money.)

Somehow I had known that he'd be in one of the century-old four-floor apartment buildings; any guy who dressed like he did and forgot to comb his hair wasn't about to waste money on a high-rise to impress his friends. I found his apartment number, then walked around to the back, clambered up the rickety wooden stairs to the third floor, checked out a number of windows, and knew I had the right place when I came to a kitchen with about fifty books piled on the floor and four days' worth of dirty dishes in the sink. I couldn't jimmy this lock any better than my own, but the door was one of the old wooden types and I finally threw a shoulder against it and broke it.

"Who's there?" demanded Brozgold, walking out of the bedroom in his pajamas and looking even more unkempt than usual.

"Hi," I said with a cheerful smile, shoving him back into the bedroom. "Remember me?"

I closed the door behind us, just to be on the safe side. The room smelled of stale tobacco, or maybe it was just the stale clothing in his closet. His furniture—a dresser, a writing desk, a double bed, a couple of nightstands, and a chair—had cost him a bundle, but they hadn't seen a coat of polish, or even a dust rag, since the day they'd been delivered.

He was staring at me, eyes wide, a dawning look of recognition on his face. "You're . . . ah . . . Jurgins? Johnson? I can't remember the name on the spur of the moment. You're the one who's been calling me?"

"I am," I said, pushing him onto the chair. "And it's William Jordan."

"Jordan. Right." He looked flustered, like he wasn't fully awake yet. "What are you doing here, Jordan? I thought we were meeting at the Institute tomorrow morning."

"I know you did," I answered him. "I wanted to make sure that all your security was down there so we could have a private little chat right here and now."

He stood up. "Now you listen to me, Jordan—"

I pushed him back down, hard.

"That's what I came here for," I said. "And the first thing I want to listen to is the reason I was Erased."

"You were a criminal," he said coldly. "You know that."

"What crime did I commit?"

"You know I can't tell you that!" he yelled, trying to hide his mounting fear beneath a blustering exterior. "Now get the hell out of here and—"

"How many people did I kill with my bare hands?" I asked pleasantly.

"What?"

"I just killed a woman," I said. "I enjoyed it. I mean, I *really* enjoyed it. Right at this moment I'm trying to decide how much I'd like killing a doctor."

"You're crazy!" he snapped.

"As a matter of fact," I replied, "I have a certificate stating that the State of New York considers me to be absolutely sane." I grinned. "Guess who signed it?"

"Go away!"

"As soon as you tell me what I want to know."

"I can't!"

"Are you still with me?" I whispered under my breath.

Right here, said the voice.

"Take over at the proper moment or I'm going to break my hand," I told it.

Ready when you are, it replied.

"Perhaps you need a demonstration of my skill and my sincerity," I said to Brozgold as I walked over to the dresser.

I lifted my hand high above my head and started bringing it down toward the dull wooden surface. I winced just before impact, but it didn't hurt a bit—and an instant later the top of the dresser and the first two drawers were split in half.

"Thanks," I whispered.

Any time.

"That could just as easily have been *you,*" I said, turning back to Brozgold. "In fact, if you don't tell me what I want to know, it *will* be you."

"You'll kill me anyway," he said, shaking with fear but blindly determined to stick to his guns.

"I'll kill you if you *don't* tell me," I said. "If you do, I promise I won't harm you."

"What's the promise of a killer worth?" he said bitterly.

"You're the one who gave me my sense of honor," I pointed out. "Do you go around manufacturing liars?"

"No. But I don't go around manufacturing killers, either."

"I just want to know who I was and what I did," I repeated patiently. "I don't want to do it again. I just need some facts to fight off this damned voice."

Well, I like that, said the voice.

"I can't," repeated Brozgold.

"Sure you can," I said, taking a couple of steps toward him.

"It won't do you any good," he said, on the verge of tears now. "Everything about you, every last detail, has been classified. You won't be able to follow up on anything I know."

"Maybe we won't have to," I said. "How many people did I kill?"

"I can't."

I reached over to the little writing desk and brought my hand down. It split in two.

"How many?" I repeated, glaring at him.

"Seventeen!" he screamed, tears running down his face.

"Seventeen?" I repeated wonderingly.

"That we know about."

Even I was surprised that I had managed to amass so many. "Who were they? Men? Women?" He didn't answer, so I took another step toward him and added menacingly, "Doctors?"

"No!" he said quickly. "Not doctors. Never doctors!"

"Then who?"

"Whoever they paid you to kill!" he finally blurted out.

"I was a hit man?"

He nodded.

"I must really have enjoyed my work to kill seventeen people," I said thoughtfully. "How did they finally catch me?"

"Your girlfriend turned state's evidence. She knew you had been hired to kill Carlo Castinerra—"

"The politician?"

"Yes. So the police staked him out and nailed you. You blundered right into their trap."

I shook my head sadly. "That's what I get for trusting people. And *this,*" I added, bringing the edge of my hand down on his neck and producing a snapping noise, "is what *you* get."

That was unethical, said my little voice. *You promised not to hurt him if he told you what you wanted to know.*

"We trusted someone once, and look where it got us," I replied, going around and wiping various surfaces. "What about that hooker? Had someone put out a contract on her?"

I don't remember, said the voice. *It just felt right.*

"And how did killing Dr. Brozgold feel?" I asked.

Good, said the voice after some consideration. *It felt good. I enjoyed it.*

"So did I," I admitted.

Then are we going back in business?

"No," I said. "If there's one thing I've learned as an accountant, it's that everything has a pattern to it. Fall into the same old pattern and we'll wind up right back at the Institute."

Then what will we do? asked the voice.

"Oh, we'll go right on killing people," I assured it. "I must confess that it's addictive. But I make more than enough money to take care of my needs, and I don't suppose *you* have any use for money."

None, said the voice.

"So now we'll just kill whoever we want in any way that pleases us," I said. "They've made William Jordan a stickler for details, so I think we'll be a lot harder to catch than we were when I was you." I busied myself wiping the dresser as best I could.

"Of course," I added, crossing over to the desk and going to work on it, "I suppose we could start with Carlo Castinerra, just for old time's sake."

I'd like that, said the voice, trying to control its excitement.

"I thought you might," I said dryly. "And it will tidy up the last loose end from our previous life. I hate loose ends. I suppose it's my accountant's mind."

So that's where things stand now.

I've spent the last two days in the office, catching up on my work. At nights I've cased Castinerra's house. I know where all the doors and windows are, how to get to the slidewalk from the kitchen entrance, what time the servants leave, what time the lights go out.

So this Friday, at 5:00 P.M. on the dot, I'm going to leave the office and go out to dinner at a posh French restaurant that guarantees there are no soya products anywhere on the premises. After that I'll slide over to what's left of the theater district and catch the old Sondheim classic they've unearthed after all these years. Then it's off to an elegant nearby bar for a cocktail or two.

And then, with a little help from my shadow, I'll pay a long-overdue call on the estimable Mr. Castinerra.

Only this time, I'll do it right.

Erasures are, by and large, pretty lonely people. I can't tell you how nice it is to finally have a hobby that I can share with a friend.

INTRODUCTION
Mrs. Hood Unloads

I have this strange relationship with Marty Greenberg. I appear in maybe a dozen of his anthologies every year, usually with stories of under 3,000 words. This is because Marty, a dear man with whom I have co-edited a number of anthologies, invariably calls me on a Monday night to tell me he's got a hole to fill and could I please have the story in his hands by Friday morning? I unfailingly say No, you can't do this to me again—and I can almost see him grin when I slam down the phone, because sure enough, within twenty or thirty minutes, I have not only come up with another of my against-the-grain stories, but I have fallen in love with it and am desperate to write it.

Like this one, which appeared in *The Fantastic Robin Hood*. Anyone can write about Robin and Little John and Friar Tuck, but how many of you remember that even the mighty Robin had a mother?

(I'm especially proud of this anthology, because my daughter, Laura Resnick, who is an award-winning romance novelist under the *nom de plume* of Laura Leone, made the first of her many science-fiction appearances here, alongside her old man—and under her real name, too.)

MRS. HOOD UNLOADS

Yes, Mrs. Grobnik, it's a new set of tiles. My son the Most Wanted Felon gave them to me. Probably they used to belong to the rabbi's wife.

He just gave them to me last week. He'd been keeping them for me for three months. Two nights a week he can sneak into the castle and annoy the King, but can he come by for dinner with his mother more than once in three months?

You think you've got *tsouris?* Well, God may ignore you from time to time, but He *hates* me.

I don't mean to complain . . . but what did I ever do to deserve such a *schmendrik* for a son? I think they must have switched babies at the hospital, I really do. Twenty-six hours I spent in labor, and for what? You work and you slave, you try to give your son a sense of values, and then even when he stops by he gulps his food and can never stay for dessert because the army is after him.

So at least you can write and tell me how you're doing, Mr. Big Shot, I tell him. And do you know what he says to that? He says he can't write because he's illiterate. Me, I say he's just using that as an excuse.

You break the wall, Mrs. Noodleman. Can I bring anyone some tea?

Well, of course he robs from the rich, Mrs. Grobnik. I mean, what's the sense of robbing from the poor? But why does he have to rob at all? Why couldn't he have been a doctor? But he says no, he's got this calling, that God told him he has to rob from the rich and give to the poor. When I was fourteen, God told me that I was a fairy princess, but you didn't see me going out and kissing any frogs. Anyway, I tell him that maybe he's misinterpreting, that maybe God is telling him to be a banker or a real estate broker, but he says no, his holy mission is to rob the rich and give to the poor. So I ask him why he can't at least charge the poor a ten percent handling fee, and he gives me that look, the same one I used to smack his *tuchis* for when he was a boy.

Pong! Very good, Mrs. Katz.

No, we're happy to have you here, Mrs. Katz. I just couldn't take any more of that Mrs. Nottingham. She's so hoity-toity and walks around with her nose in the air, and acts like her boy is a lawyer instead of just a policeman. My son the criminal gives away more in a week than her son makes in a year.

You heard *what,* Mrs. Noodleman? You heard him say that he moved to Sherwood Forest because he went off to the Crusades and came back to find out he wasn't the Lord of the Manor? Well, of course he wasn't the Lord of the Manor! Was my late husband, Mr. Hood, God rest his soul, the Lord of the Manor? Are my brothers Nate and Jake the Lords of the Manor? Probably ten thousand boys came home and found they weren't Lords of the Manor—but did *they* go live in the forest and rob their mothers' friends?

He was an apprentice blacksmith, that's what he was. He probably made up all this Lord of the Manor stuff to impress that *shikse* Marian.

And while I'm thinking of it, what's all this *Maid* Marian talk? She doesn't look like a maid to *me*.

Not so fast, Mrs. Noodleman. I have a flower, so I get an extra tile.

Anyway, you work and you slave, and what does it get you? Your son runs off to the forest and starts wearing a *yarmulke* with a feather in it, that's what.

And look who he runs around with—a bunch of merry men! I don't know if I can bear the shame! I just wish I knew what I ever did to make God hate me so much.

Thank you for your kind words, Mrs. Grobnik, but you just can't imagine what it's like. I try to raise him with proper values, and look how it all turns out—he's dating this Marian person, and his closest friend is a priest, Friar someone-or-other.

Oh, it's not? Now his best friend is Little John? Well, I don't want to be the one to gossip, but the stable girl told me what's so little about *him*.

Chow, Mrs. Noodleman. I lost track—whose turn is it now?

So he comes by last Thursday, and he gives me these tiles, and he says he can only stay for five minutes because the Sheriff's men are after him, and he gulps his *gefilte* fish down, and I notice he's looking thin, so I ask him if he's getting his greens, and he gives me that look, and he says Ma, of course I'm getting my greens, I live in a forest. So sue me, I say, better I should just sit here in the dark and never even mention that you're too skinny because you never come by for dinner unless the Sheriff's men are watching your hide-in.

Hide-out, hide-in, what's the difference, Mrs. Katz? At least *your* son comes by for dinner every Sunday. The only time I know I'll see *my* son is when I go to the post office, and there's his picture hanging on the wall.

Oy! You're showing four white dragons, Mrs. Noodleman! You see? I *knew* God hated me!

And he says the next time he comes by—if I haven't died

of old age and neglect by then—he's going to bring his gang
with him. And I say not without a week's notice, and that I'm
not letting this Marian person in the house, no matter what,
and even if I do, she isn't allowed to use the bathroom. And
he just laughs that Mr. Big Shot laugh, ho-ho-ho, like he
thinks he can wrap me around his little finger. Well, I'll Mr.
Big Shot him right across the mouth if he doesn't learn a little
respect for his mother.

Mah-Jongg!

All right, so God doesn't hate me full-time, once in a
while He blinks long enough for me to win a game.

By the way, what do you cook for seventy merry *goys,*
anyway?

INTRODUCTION
Over There

When Axolotl Press, *Isaac Asimov's Science Fiction Magazine,* and Tor Books were all asking me for a novella set in Africa, I came up with the notion of writing an alternate history story featuring Teddy Roosevelt's attempts to bring American know-how and democracy to the Belgian Congo. The resultant story was "Bully!," which sold to all three markets, and was nominated for the 1991 Hugo Award for Best Novella.

I have always found Teddy Roosevelt to be the most accomplished and fascinating American of this century, and the success of "Bully!" encouraged me to write a second series of related stories (the Kirinyaga stories were the first), a set of alternate histories featuring that remarkable man. Gardner Dozois, a good friend, a fine writer, and, most important to this introduction, the editor of *Asimov's,* gave me the go-ahead, and has purchased all the Roosevelt stories that I've written to date.

Each begins with two historical quotes, showing what actually *did* happen, followed by the date that I start skewing history. Of those I've written thus far, I think "Over There" may be the best of them.

Over There

I respectfully ask permission immediately to raise two divisions for immediate service at the front under the bill which has just become law, and hold myself ready to raise four divisions, if you so direct. I respectfully refer for details to my last letters to the Secretary of War.
>—Theodore Roosevelt
>Telegram to President Woodrow Wilson, May 18, 1917

I very much regret that I cannot comply with the request in your telegram of yesterday. The reasons I have stated in a public statement made this morning, and I need not assure you that my conclusions were based upon imperative considerations of public policy and not upon personal or private choice.
>—Woodrow Wilson
>Telegram to Theodore Roosevelt, May 19, 1917

The date was May 22, 1917.

Woodrow Wilson looked up at the burly man standing impatiently before his desk.

"This will necessarily have to be an extremely brief meeting, Mr. Roosevelt," he said wearily. "I have consented to it only out of respect for the fact that you formerly held the office that I am now privileged to occupy."

"I appreciate that, Mr. President," said Theodore Roosevelt, shifting his weight anxiously from one leg to the other.

"Well, then?" said Wilson.

"You know why I'm here," said Roosevelt bluntly. "I want your permission to reassemble my Rough Riders and take them over to Europe."

"As I keep telling you, Mr. Roosevelt—that's out of the question."

"You haven't told *me* anything!" snapped Roosevelt. "And I have no interest in what you tell the press."

"Then I'm telling you now," said Wilson firmly. "I can't just let any man who wants to gather up a regiment go fight in the war. We have procedures, and chains of command, and . . . "

"I'm not just *any* man," said Roosevelt. "And I have every intention of honoring our procedures and chain of command." He glared at the President. "I created many of those procedures myself."

Wilson stared at his visitor for a long moment. "Why are you so anxious to go to war, Mr. Roosevelt? Does violence hold so much fascination for you?"

"I abhor violence and bloodshed," answered Roosevelt. "I believe that war should never be resorted to when it is honorably possible to avoid it. But once war has begun, then the only thing to do is win it as swiftly and decisively as possible. I believe that I can help to accomplish that end."

"Mr. Roosevelt, may I point out that you are fifty-eight years old, and according to my reports you have been in poor health ever since returning from Brazil three years ago?"

"Nonsense!" said Roosevelt defensively. "I feel as fit as a bull moose!"

"A one-eyed bull moose," replied Wilson dryly. Roosevelt seemed about to protest, but Wilson raised a hand to silence him. "Yes, Mr. Roosevelt, I know that you lost the vision in your left eye during a boxing match while you were President." He couldn't quite keep the distaste for such juvenile and adventurous escapades out of his voice.

"I'm not here to discuss my health," answered Roosevelt

gruffly, "but the reactivation of my commission as a colonel in the United States Army."

Wilson shook his head. "You have my answer. You've told me nothing that might change my mind."

"I'm about to."

"Oh?"

"Let's be perfectly honest, Mr. President. The Republican nomination is mine for the asking, and however the war turns out, the Democrats will be sitting ducks. Half the people hate you for entering the war so late, and the other half hate you for entering it at all." Roosevelt paused. "If you will return me to active duty and allow me to organize my Rough Riders, I will give you my personal pledge that I will neither seek nor accept the Republican nomination in 1920."

"It means that much to you?" asked Wilson, arching a thin eyebrow.

"It does, sir."

"I'm impressed by your passion, and I don't doubt your sincerity, Mr. Roosevelt," said Wilson. "But my answer must still be no. I am serving my second term. I have no intention of running again in 1920, I do not need your political support, and I will not be a party to such a deal."

"Then you are a fool, Mr. President," said Roosevelt. "Because I am going anyway, and you have thrown away your only opportunity, slim as it may be, to keep the Republicans out of the White House."

"I will not reactivate your commission, Mr. Roosevelt."

Roosevelt pulled two neatly-folded letters out of his lapel pocket and placed them on the President's desk.

"What are these?" asked Wilson, staring at them as if they might bite him at any moment.

"Letters from the British and the French, offering me commissions in *their* armies." Roosevelt paused. "I am first, foremost, and always an American, Mr. President, and I had entertained no higher hope than leading my men into battle under the Stars and Stripes—but I am going to participate in this war, and you are not going to stop me." And now, for the first time, he displayed the famed Roosevelt grin. "I have some thirty reporters waiting for me on the lawn of the White House. Shall I tell them that I am fighting for the country that I love, or shall I tell them that our European allies are more concerned with winning this damnable war than our own President?"

"This is blackmail, Mr. Roosevelt!" said Wilson, outraged.

"I believe that is the word for it," said Roosevelt, still grinning. "I would like you to direct Captain Frank McCoy to leave his current unit and report to me. I'll handle the rest of the details myself." He paused again. "The press is waiting, Mr. President. What shall I tell them?"

"Tell them anything you want," muttered Wilson furiously. "Only get out of this office."

"Thank you, sir," said Roosevelt, turning on his heel and marching out with an energetic bounce to his stride.

Wilson waited a moment, then spoke aloud. "You can come in now, Joseph."

Joseph Tummulty, his personal secretary, entered the Oval Office.

"Were you listening?" asked Wilson.

"Yes, sir."

"Is there any way out of it?"

"Not without getting a black eye in the press."

"That's what I was afraid of," said Wilson.

"He's got you over a barrel, Mr. President."

"I wonder what he's really after?" mused Wilson thoughtfully. "He's been a governor, an explorer, a war hero, a police commissioner, an author, a big-game hunter, and a President." He paused, mystified. "What more can he want from life?"

"Personally, sir," said Tummulty, making no attempt to hide the contempt in his voice, "I think that damned cowboy is looking to charge up one more San Juan Hill."

* * *

Roosevelt stood before his troops, as motley an assortment of warriors as had been assembled since the last incarnation of the Rough Riders. There were military men and cowboys, professional athletes and adventurers, hunters and ranchers, barroom brawlers and Indians, tennis players and wrestlers, even a trio of Masai *elmoran* he had met on safari in Africa.

"Some of 'em look a little long in the tooth, Colonel," remarked Frank McCoy, his second-in-command.

"Some of *us* are a little long in the tooth too, Frank," said Roosevelt with a smile.

"And some of 'em haven't started shaving yet," continued McCoy wryly.

"Well, there's nothing like a war to grow them up in a hurry."

Roosevelt turned away from McCoy and faced his men, waiting briefly until he had their attention. He paused for a moment to make sure that the journalists who were traveling with the regiment had their pencils and notebooks out, and then spoke.

"Gentlemen," he said, "we are about to embark upon a great adventure. We are privileged to be present at a crucial point in the history of the world. In the terrible whirlwind of war, all the great nations of the world are facing the supreme test of their courage and dedication. All the alluring but futile theories of the pacifists have vanished at the first sound of gunfire."

Roosevelt paused to clear his throat, then continued in his surprisingly high-pitched voice. "This war is the greatest the world has ever seen. The vast size of the armies, the tremendous slaughter, the loftiness of the heroism shown and the hideous horror of the brutalities committed, the valor of the fighting men and the extraordinary ingenuity of those who have designed and built the fighting machines, the burning patriotism of the peoples who defend their homelands and

the far-reaching complexity of the plans of the leaders—all
are on a scale so huge that nothing in past history can be
compared with them.

"The issues at stake are fundamental. The free peoples of
the world have banded together against tyrannous militarism,
and it is not too much to say that the outcome will largely
determine, for those of us who love liberty above all else,
whether or not life remains worth living."

He paused again, and stared up and down the ranks of
his men.

"Against such a vast and complex array of forces, it may
seem to you that we will just be another cog in the military
machine of the allies, that one regiment cannot possibly make
a difference." Roosevelt's chin jutted forward pugnaciously.
"I say to you that this is rubbish! We represent a society
dedicated to the proposition that every free man makes a
difference. And I give you my solemn pledge that the Rough
Riders will make a difference in the fighting to come!"

It was possible that his speech wasn't finished, that he
still had more to say . . . but if he did, it was drowned out
beneath the wild and raucous cheering of his men.

One hour later they boarded the ship to Europe.

Roosevelt summoned a corporal and handed him a
hand-written letter. The man saluted and left, and Roosevelt
returned to his chair in front of his tent. He was about to pick
up a book when McCoy approached him.

"Your daily dispatch to General Pershing?" he asked
dryly.

"Yes," answered Roosevelt. "I can't understand what is
wrong with the man. Here we are, primed and ready to fight,
and he's kept us well behind the front for the better part of
two months!"

"I know, Colonel."

"It just doesn't make any sense! Doesn't he know what
the Rough Riders did at San Juan Hill?"

"That was a long time ago, sir," said McCoy.

"I tell you, Frank, these men are the elite—the cream of the crop! They weren't drafted by lottery. Every one of them volunteered, and every one was approved personally by you or by me. Why are we being wasted here? There's a war to be won!"

"Pershing's got a lot to consider, Colonel," said McCoy. "He's got half a million American troops to disperse, he's got to act in concert with the French and the British, he's got to consider his lines of supply, he's . . . "

"Don't patronize me, Frank!" snapped Roosevelt. "We've assembled a brilliant fighting machine here, and he's ignoring us. There *has* to be a reason. I want to know what it is!"

McCoy shrugged helplessly. "I have no answer, sir."

"Well, I'd better get one soon from Pershing!" muttered Roosevelt. "We didn't come all this way to help in some mopping-up operation after the battle's been won." He stared at the horizon. "There's a glorious crusade being fought in the name of liberty, and I plan to be a part of it."

He continued staring off into the distance long after McCoy had left him.

A private approached Roosevelt as the former President was eating lunch with his officers.

"Dispatch from General Pershing, sir," said the private, handing him an envelope with a snappy salute.

"Thank you," said Roosevelt. He opened the envelope, read the message, and frowned.

"Bad news, Colonel?" asked McCoy.

"He says to be patient," replied Roosevelt. "Patient?" he repeated furiously. "By God, I've been patient long enough! Jake—saddle my horse!"

"What are you going to do, Colonel?" asked one of his lieutenants.

"I'm going to go meet face-to-face with Pershing," said Roosevelt, getting to his feet. "This is intolerable!"

"We don't even know where he is, sir."

"I'll find him," replied Roosevelt confidently.

"You're more likely to get lost or shot," said McCoy, the only man who dared to speak to him so bluntly.

"Runs With Deer! Matupu!" shouted Roosevelt. "Saddle your horses!"

A burly Indian and a tall Masai immediately got to their feet and went to the stable area.

Roosevelt turned back to McCoy. "I'm taking the two best trackers in the regiment. Does that satisfy you, Mr. McCoy?"

"It does not," said McCoy. "I'm coming along, too."

Roosevelt shook his head. "You're in command of the regiment in my absence. You're staying here."

"But—"

"That's an order," said Roosevelt firmly.

"Will you at least take along a squad of sharpshooters, Colonel?" persisted McCoy.

"Frank, we're forty miles behind the front, and I'm just going to talk to Pershing, not shoot him."

"We don't even know where the front *is*," said McCoy.

"It's where we're *not*," said Roosevelt grimly. "And that's what I'm going to change."

He left the mess tent without another word.

The first four French villages they passed were deserted, and consisted of nothing but the burnt skeletons of houses and shops. The fifth had two buildings still standing—a manor house and a church—and they had been turned into Allied hospitals. Soldiers with missing limbs, soldiers with faces swatched in filthy bandages, soldiers with gaping holes in their bodies lay on cots and floors, shivering in the cold damp air, while an undermanned and harassed medical team did their best to keep them alive.

Roosevelt stopped long enough to determine General Pershing's whereabouts, then walked among the wounded to offer words of encouragement while trying to ignore the unmistakable stench of gangrene and the stinging scent of disinfectant. Finally he remounted his horse and joined his two trackers.

They passed a number of corpses on their way to the front. Most had been plundered of their weapons, and one, lying upon its back, displayed a gruesome, toothless smile.

"Shameful!" muttered Roosevelt as he looked down at the grinning body.

"Why?" asked Runs With Deer.

"It's obvious that the man had gold teeth, and they have been removed."

"It is honorable to take trophies of the enemy," asserted the Indian.

"The Germans have never advanced this far south," said Roosevelt. "This man's teeth were taken by his companions." He shook his head. "Shameful!"

Matupu the Masai merely shrugged. "Perhaps this is not an honorable war."

"We are fighting for an honorable principle," stated Roosevelt. "That makes it an honorable war."

"Then it is an honorable war being waged by dishonorable men," said Matupu.

"Do the Masai not take trophies?" asked Runs With Deer.

"We take cows and goats and women," answered Matupu. "We do not plunder the dead." He paused. "We do not take scalps."

"There was a time when *we* did not, either," said Runs With Deer. "We were taught to, by the French."

"And we are in France now," said Matupu with some satisfaction, as if everything now made sense to him.

They dismounted after two more hours and walked their horses for the rest of the day, then spent the night in a bombed-out farmhouse. The next morning they were mounted and riding again, and they came to General Pershing's field headquarters just before noon. There were thousands of soldiers bustling about, couriers bringing in hourly reports from the trenches, weapons and tanks being dispatched, convoys of trucks filled with food and water slowly working their way into supply lines.

Roosevelt was stopped a few yards into the camp by a young lieutenant.

"May I ask your business here, sir?"

"I'm here to see General Pershing," answered Roosevelt.

"Just like that?" said the soldier with a smile.

"Son," said Roosevelt, taking off his hat and leaning over the lieutenant, "take a good look at my face." He paused for a moment. "Now go tell General Pershing that Teddy Roosevelt is here to see him."

The lieutenant's eyes widened. "By God, you *are* Teddy Roosevelt!" he exclaimed. Suddenly he reached his hand out. "May I shake your hand first, Mr. President? I just want to be able to tell my parents I did it."

Roosevelt grinned and took the young man's hand in his own, then waited astride his horse while the lieutenant went off to Pershing's quarters. He gazed around the camp: there were ramshackle buildings and ramshackle soldiers, each of which had seen too much action and too little glory. The men's faces were haggard, their eyes haunted, their bodies stooped with exhaustion. The main paths through the camp had turned to mud, and the constant drizzle brought rust, rot and disease with an equal lack of cosmic concern.

The lieutenant approached Roosevelt, his feet sinking inches into the mud with each step.

"If you'll follow me, Mr. President, he'll see you immediately."

"Thank you," said Roosevelt.

"Watch yourself, Mr. President," said the lieutenant as

Roosevelt dismounted. "I have a feeling he's not happy about meeting with you."

"He'll be a damned sight less happy when I'm through with him," said Roosevelt firmly. He turned to his companions. "See to the needs of the horses."

"Yes, sir," said Runs With Deer. "We'll be waiting for you right here."

"How is the battle going?" Roosevelt asked as he and the lieutenant began walking through the mud toward Pershing's quarters. "My Rough Riders have been practically incommunicado since we arrived."

The lieutenant shrugged. "Who knows? All we hear are rumors. The enemy is retreating, the enemy is advancing, we've killed thousands of them, they've killed thousands of us. Maybe the general will tell you; he certainly hasn't seen fit to tell *us.*"

They reached the entrance to Pershing's quarters.

"I'll wait here for you, sir," said the lieutenant.

"You're sure you don't mind?" asked Roosevelt. "You can find some orderly to escort me back if it will be a problem."

"No, sir," said the young man earnestly. "It'll be an honor, Mr. President."

"Well, thank you, son," said Roosevelt. He shook the lieutenant's hand again, then walked through the doorway and found himself facing General John J. Pershing.

"Good afternoon, Jack," said Roosevelt, extending his hand.

Pershing looked at Roosevelt's outstretched hand for a moment, then took it.

"Have a seat, Mr. President," he said, indicating a chair.

"Thank you," said Roosevelt, pulling up a chair as Pershing seated himself behind a desk that was covered with maps.

"I mean no disrespect, Mr. President," said Pershing,

"but exactly who gave you permission to leave your troops and come here?"

"No one," answered Roosevelt.

"Then why did you do it?" asked Pershing. "I'm told you were accompanied only by a red Indian and a black savage. That's hardly a safe way to travel in a war zone."

"I came here to find out why you have consistently refused my requests to have my Rough Riders moved to the front."

Pershing lit a cigar and offered one to Roosevelt, who refused it.

"There are proper channels for such a request," said the general at last. "You yourself helped create them."

"And I have been using them for almost two months, to no avail."

Pershing sighed. "I *have* been a little busy conducting this damned war."

"I'm sure you have," said Roosevelt. "And I have assembled a regiment of the finest fighting men to be found in America, which I am placing at your disposal."

"For which I thank you, Mr. President."

"I don't want you to thank me!" snapped Roosevelt. "I want you to unleash me!"

"When the time is right, your Rough Riders will be brought into the conflict," said Pershing.

"When the time is right?" repeated Roosevelt. "Your men are dying like flies! Every village I've passed has become a bombed-out ghost town! You needed us two months ago, Jack!"

"Mr. President, I've got half a million men to maneuver. I'll decide when and where I need your regiment."

"When?" persisted Roosevelt.

"You'll be the first to know."

"That's not good enough!"

"It will have to be."

"You listen to me, Jack Pershing!" said Roosevelt heatedly. "I *made* you a general! I think the very least you owe me is an answer. When will my men be brought into the conflict?"

Pershing stared at him from beneath shaggy black eyebrows for a long moment. "What the hell did you have to come here for, anyway?" he said at last.

"I told you: to get an answer."

"I don't mean to my headquarters," said Pershing. "I mean, what is a fifty-eight-year-old man with a blind eye and a game leg doing in the middle of a war?"

"This is the greatest conflict in history, and it's being fought over principles that every free man holds dear. How could I not take part in it?"

"You could have just stayed home and made speeches and raised funds."

"And you could have retired after Mexico and spent the rest of your life playing golf," Roosevelt shot back. "But you didn't, and I didn't, because neither of us is that kind of man. Damn it, Jack—I've assembled a regiment the likes of which haven't been seen in almost twenty years, and if you've any sense at all, you'll make use of us. Our horses and our training give us an enormous advantage on this terrain. We can mobilize and strike at the enemy as easily as this fellow Lawrence seems to be doing in the Arabian desert."

Pershing stared at him for a long moment, then sighed deeply.

"I can't do it, Mr. President," said Pershing.

"Why not?" demanded Roosevelt.

"The truth? Because of you, sir."

"What are you talking about?"

"You've made my position damnably awkward," said Pershing bitterly. "You are an authentic American hero, possibly the first one since Abraham Lincoln. You are as close to being worshipped as a man can be." He paused. "You're a goddamned icon, Mr. Roosevelt."

"What has *that* got to do with anything?"

"I am under direct orders not to allow you to participate

in any action that might result in your death." He glared at Roosevelt across the desk. *"Now* do you understand? If I move you to the front, I'll have to surround you with at least three divisions to make sure nothing happens to you—and I'm in no position to spare that many men."

"Who issued that order, Jack?"

"My Commander-in-Chief."

"Woodrow Wilson?"

"That's right. And I'd no more disobey him than I would disobey you if you still held that office." He paused, then spoke again more gently. "You're an old man, sir. Not old by your standards, but too damned old to be leading charges against the Germans. You should be home writing your memoirs and giving speeches and rallying the people to our cause, Mr. President."

"I'm not ready to retire to Sagamore Hill and have my face carved on Mount Rushmore yet," said Roosevelt. "There are battles to be fought and a war to be won."

"Not by you, Mr. President," answered Pershing. "When the enemy is beaten and on the run, I'll bring your regiment up. The press can go crazy photographing you chasing the few German stragglers back to Berlin. But I cannot and will not disobey a direct order from my Commander-in-Chief. Until I can guarantee your safety, you'll stay where you are."

"I see," said Roosevelt, after a moment's silence. "And what if I relinquish my command? Will you utilize my Rough Riders then?"

Pershing shook his head. "I have no use for a bunch of tennis players and college professors who think they can storm across the trenches on their polo ponies," he said firmly. "The only men you have with battle experience are as old as you are." He paused. "Your regiment might be effective if the Apaches ever leave the reservation, but they are ill-prepared for a modern, mechanized war. I hate to be so blunt, but it's the truth, sir."

"You're making a huge mistake, Jack."

"You're the one who made the mistake, sir, by coming here. It's my job to see that you don't die because of it."

"Damn it, Jack, we could make a difference!"

Pershing paused and stared, not without sympathy, at Roosevelt. "War has changed, Mr. President," he said at last. "No one regiment can make a difference any longer. It's been a long time since Achilles fought Hector outside the walls of Troy."

An orderly entered with a dispatch, and Pershing immediately read and initialed it.

"I don't mean to rush you, sir," he said, getting to his feet, "but I have an urgent meeting to attend."

Roosevelt stood up. "I'm sorry to have bothered you, General."

"I'm still Jack to you, Mr. President," said Pershing. "And it's as your friend Jack that I want to give you one final word of advice."

"Yes?"

"Please, for your own sake and the sake of your men, don't do anything rash."

"Why would I do something rash?" asked Roosevelt innocently.

"Because you wouldn't be Teddy Roosevelt if the thought of ignoring your orders hadn't already crossed your mind," said Pershing.

Roosevelt fought back a grin, shook Pershing's hand, and left without saying another word. The young lieutenant was just outside the door, and escorted him back to where Runs With Deer and Matupu were waiting with the horses.

"Bad news?" asked Runs With Deer, as he studied Roosevelt's face.

"No worse than I had expected."

"Where do we go now?" asked the Indian.

"Back to camp," said Roosevelt firmly. "There's a war

to be won, and no college professor from New Jersey is going to keep me from helping to win it!"

"Well, that's the story," said Roosevelt to his assembled officers, after he had laid out the situation to them in the large tent he had reserved for strategy sessions. "Even if I resign my commission and return to America, there is no way that General Pershing will allow you to see any action."

"I knew Black Jack Pershing when he was just a captain," growled Buck O'Neill, one of the original Rough Riders. "Just who the hell does he think he is?"

"He's the supreme commander of the American forces," answered Roosevelt wryly.

"What are we going to do, sir?" asked McCoy. "Surely you don't plan to just sit back here and then let Pershing move us up when all the fighting's done with?"

"No, I don't," said Roosevelt.

"Let's hear what you got to say, Teddy," said O'Neill.

"The issues at stake in this war haven't changed since I went to see the general," answered Roosevelt. "I plan to harass and harry the enemy to the best of our ability. If need be we will live off the land while utilizing our superior mobility in a number of tactical strikes, and we will do our valiant best to bring this conflict to a successful conclusion."

He paused and looked around at his officers. "I realize that in doing this I am violating my orders, but there are greater principles at stake here. I am flattered that the President thinks I am indispensable to the American public, but our nation is based on the principle that no one man deserves any rights or privileges not offered to all men." He took a deep breath and cleared his throat. "However, since I *am* contravening a direct order, I believe that not only each one of you, but every one of the men as well, should be given the opportunity to withdraw from the Rough Riders. I will force no man to ride against his conscience and his beliefs. I would like to you go out now and put the question to the men; I will wait here for your answer."

To nobody's great surprise, the regiment voted unanimously to ride to glory with Teddy Roosevelt.

3 August, 1917

My Dearest Edith:

As strange as this may seem to you (and it seems surpassingly strange to me), I will soon be a fugitive from justice, opposed not only by the German army but quite possibly by the U.S. military as well.

My Rough Riders have embarked upon a bold adventure, contrary to both the wishes and the direct orders of the President of the United States. When I think back to the day he finally approved my request to reassemble the regiment, I cringe with chagrin at my innocence and naivete; he sent us here only so that I would not have access to the press and he would no longer have to listen to my demands. Far from being permitted to play a leading role in this noblest of battles, my men have been held far behind the front, and Jack Pershing was under orders from Wilson himself not to allow any harm to come to us.

When I learned of this, I put a proposition to my men, and I am extremely proud of their response. To a one, they voted to break camp and ride to the front so as to strike at the heart of the German military machine. By doing so, I am disobeying the orders of my Commander-in-Chief, and because of this somewhat peculiar situation, I doubt that I shall be able to send too many more letters to you until I have helped to end this war. At that time, I shall turn myself over to Pershing, or whoever is in charge, and argue my case before whatever tribunal is deemed proper.

However, before that moment occurs, we shall finally see action, bearing the glorious banner of the Stars and Stripes. My men are a finely-tuned fighting machine, and I daresay that they will give a splendid account of themselves before the conflict is over. We have not made contact with the enemy yet, nor can I guess where we shall finally meet,

*but we are primed and eager for our first taste of battle.
Our spirit is high, and many of the old-timers spend their
hours singing the old battle songs from Cuba. We are all
looking forward to a bully battle, and we plan to teach the
Hun a lesson he won't soon forget.*

*Give my love to the children, and when you write to
Kermit and Quentin, tell them that their father has every
intention of reaching Berlin before they do!*

*All my love,
Theodore*

Roosevelt, who had been busily writing an article on
ornithology, looked up from his desk as McCoy entered his
tent.

"Well?"

"We think we've found what we've been looking for, Mr.
President," said McCoy.

"Excellent!" said Roosevelt, carefully closing his note-
book. "Tell me about it."

McCoy spread a map out on the desk.

"Well, the front lines, as you know, are *here,* about
fifteen miles to the north of us. The Germans are entrenched
here, and we haven't been able to move them for almost three
weeks." McCoy paused. "The word I get from my old outfit
is that the Americans are planning a major push on the German left, right about *here.* "

"When?" demanded Roosevelt.

"At sunrise tomorrow morning."

"Bully!" said Roosevelt. He studied the map for a moment, then looked up. "Where is Jack Pershing?"

"Almost ten miles west and eight miles north of us,"
answered McCoy. "He's dug in, and from what I hear, he
came under pretty heavy mortar fire today. He'll have his
hands full without worrying about where an extra regiment of
American troops came from."

"Better and better," said Roosevelt. "We not only get to

fight, but we may even pull Jack's chestnuts out of the fire."
He turned his attention back to the map. "All right," he said,
"the Americans will advance along this line. What would you
say will be their major obstacle?"

"You mean besides the mud and the Germans and the
mustard gas?" asked McCoy wryly.

"You know what I mean, Frank."

"Well," said McCoy, "there's a small rise here—I'd
hardly call it a hill, certainly not like the one we took in
Cuba—but it's manned by four machine guns, and it gives the
Germans an excellent view of the territory the Americans
have got to cross."

"Then that's our objective," said Roosevelt decisively.
"If we can capture that hill and knock out the machine guns,
we'll have made a positive contribution to the battle that even
that Woodrow Wilson will be forced to acknowledge." The
famed Roosevelt grin spread across his face. "We'll show him
that the dodo may be dead, but the Rough Riders are very
much alive." He paused. "Gather the men, Frank. I want to
speak to them before we leave."

McCoy did as he was told, and Roosevelt emerged from
his tent some ten minutes later to address the assembled
Rough Riders.

"Gentlemen," he said, "tomorrow morning we will meet
the enemy on the battlefield."

A cheer arose from the ranks.

"It has been suggested that modern warfare deals only in
masses and logistics, that there is no room left for heroism,
that the only glory remaining to men of action is upon the
sporting fields. I tell you that this is a lie. *We matter!* Honor
and courage are not outmoded virtues, but are the very ideals
that make us great as individuals and as a nation. Tomorrow
we will prove it in terms that our detractors and our enemies
will both understand." He paused, and then saluted them.
"Saddle up—and may God be with us!"

* * *

They reached the outskirts of the battlefield, moving silently with hooves and harnesses muffled, just before sunrise. Even McCoy, who had seen action in Mexico, was unprepared for the sight that awaited them.

The mud was littered with corpses as far as the eye could see in the dim light of the false dawn. The odor of death and decay permeated the moist, cold morning air. Thousands of bodies lay there in the pouring rain, many of them grotesquely swollen. Here and there they had virtually exploded, either when punctured by bullets or when the walls of the abdominal cavities collapsed. Attempts had been made during the previous month to drag them back off the battlefield, but there was simply no place left to put them. There was almost total silence, as the men in both trenches began preparing for another day of bloodletting.

Roosevelt reined his horse to a halt and surveyed the carnage. Still more corpses were hung up on barbed wire, and more than a handful of bodies attached to the wire still moved feebly. The rain pelted down, turning the plain between the enemy trenches into a brown, gooey slop.

"My God, Frank!" murmured Roosevelt.

"It's pretty awful," agreed McCoy.

"This is not what civilized men do to each other," said Roosevelt, stunned by the sight before his eyes. "This isn't war, Frank—it's butchery!"

"It's what war has become."

"How long have these two lines been facing each other?"

"More than a month, sir."

Roosevelt stared, transfixed, at the sea of mud.

"A month to cross a quarter mile of *this?*"

"That's correct, sir."

"How many lives have been lost trying to cross this strip of land?"

McCoy shrugged. "I don't know. Maybe eighty thousand, maybe a little more."

Roosevelt shook his head. "Why, in God's name? Who cares about it? What purpose does it serve?"

McCoy had no answer, and the two men sat in silence for another moment, surveying the battlefield.

"This is madness!" said Roosevelt at last. "Why doesn't Pershing simply march around it?"

"That's a question for a general to answer, Mr. President," said McCoy. "Me, I'm just a captain."

"We can't continue to lose American boys for *this!*" said Roosevelt furiously. "Where is that machine gun encampment, Frank?"

McCoy pointed to a small rise about three hundred yards distant.

"And the main German lines?"

"Their first row of trenches are in line with the hill."

"Have we tried to take the hill before?"

"I can't imagine that we haven't, sir," said McCoy. "As long as they control it, they'll mow our men down like sitting ducks in a shooting gallery." He paused. "The problem is the mud. The average infantryman can't reach the hill in less than two minutes, probably closer to three—and until you've seen them in action, you can't believe the damage these guns can do in that amount of time."

"So as long as the hill remains in German hands, this is a war of attrition."

McCoy sighed. "It's been a war of attrition for three years, sir."

Roosevelt sat and stared at the hill for another few minutes, then turned back to McCoy.

"What are our chances, Frank?"

McCoy shrugged. "If it was dry, I'd say we had a chance to take them out . . . "

"But it's not."

"No, it's not," echoed McCoy.

"Can we do it?"

"I don't know, sir. Certainly not without heavy casualties."

"How heavy?"

"*Very* heavy."

"I need a number," said Roosevelt.

McCoy looked him in the eye. "Ninety percent—if we're lucky."

Roosevelt stared at the hill again. "They predicted 50 percent casualties at San Juan Hill," he said. "We had to charge up a much steeper slope in the face of enemy machine gun fire. Nobody thought we had a chance—but I did it, Frank, and I did it alone. I charged up that hill and knocked out the machine gun nest myself, and then the rest of my men followed me."

"The circumstances were different then, Mr. President," said McCoy. "The terrain offered cover, and solid footing, and you were facing Cuban peasants who had been conscripted into service, not battle-hardened professional German soldiers."

"I know, I know," said Roosevelt. "But if we knock those machine guns out, how many American lives can we save today?"

"I don't know," admitted McCoy. "Maybe ten thousand, maybe none. It's possible that the Germans are dug in so securely that they can beat back any American charge even without the use of those machine guns."

"But at least it would prolong some American lives," persisted Roosevelt.

"By a couple of minutes."

"It would give them a *chance* to reach the German bunkers."

"I don't know."

"More of a chance than if they had to face machine gun fire from the hill."

"What do you want me to say, Mr. President?" asked McCoy. "That if we throw away our lives charging the hill we'll have done something glorious and affected the outcome of the battle? I just don't know!"

"We came here to help win a war, Frank. Before I send my men into battle, I have to know that it will make a difference."

"I can't give you any guarantees, sir. We came to fight a war, all right. But look around you, Mr. President—*this* isn't the war we came to fight. They've changed the rules on us."

"There are hundreds of thousands of American boys in the trenches who didn't come to fight this kind of war," answered Roosevelt. "In less than an hour, most of them are going to charge across this sea of mud into a barrage of machine gun fire. If we can't shorten the war, then perhaps we can at least lengthen their lives."

"At the cost of our own."

"We are idealists and adventurers, Frank—perhaps the last this world will ever see. We knew what we were coming here to do." He paused. "Those boys are here because of speeches and decisions that politicians have made, myself included. Left to their own devices, they'd go home to be with their families. Left to ours, we'd find another cause to fight for."

"This isn't a cause, Mr. President," said McCoy. "It's a slaughter."

"Then maybe this is where men who want to prevent further slaughter belong," said Roosevelt. He looked up at the sky. "They'll be mobilizing in another half hour, Frank."

"I know, Mr. President."

"If we leave now, if we don't try to take that hill, then Wilson and Pershing were right and I was wrong. The time for heroes is past, and I *am* an anachronism who should be sitting at home in a rocking chair, writing memoirs and exhorting younger men to go to war." He paused, staring at the hill once more. "If we don't do what's required of us this day, we are agreeing with them that we don't matter, that men of courage and ideals can't make a difference. If that's true, there's no sense waiting for a more equitable battle, Frank—we might as well ride south and catch the first boat home."

"That's your decision, Mr. President?" asked McCoy.

"Was there really ever any other option?" replied Roosevelt wryly.

"No, sir," said McCoy. "Not for men like us."

"Thank you for your support, Frank," said Roosevelt, reaching out and laying a heavy hand on McCoy's shoulder. "Prepare the men."

"Yes, sir," said McCoy, saluting and riding back to the main body of the Rough Riders.

"Madness!" muttered Roosevelt, looking out at the bloated corpses. "Utter madness!"

McCoy returned a moment later.

"The men are awaiting your signal, sir," he said.

"Tell them to follow me," said Roosevelt.

"Sir . . . " said McCoy.

"Yes?"

"We would prefer you not lead the charge. The first ranks will face the heaviest bombardment, not only from the hill but also from the cannons behind the bunkers."

"I can't ask my men to do what I myself won't do," said Roosevelt.

"You are too valuable to lose, sir. We plan to attack in three waves. You belong at the back of the third wave, Mr. President."

Roosevelt shook his head. "There's nothing up ahead except bullets, Frank, and I've faced bullets before—in the Dakota Badlands, in Cuba, in Milwaukee. But if I hang back, if I send my men to do a job I was afraid to do, then I'd have to face myself—and as any Democrat will tell you, I'm a lot tougher than any bullet ever made."

"You won't reconsider?" asked McCoy.

"Would you have left your unit and joined the Rough Riders if you thought I might?" asked Roosevelt with a smile.

"No, sir," admitted McCoy. "No, sir, I probably wouldn't have."

Roosevelt shook his hand. "You're a good man, Frank."

"Thank you, Mr. President."

"Are the men ready?"

"Yes, sir."

"Then," said Roosevelt, turning his horse toward the small rise, "let's do what must be done."

He pulled his rifle out, unlatched the safety catch, and dug his heels into his horse's sides.

Suddenly he was surrounded by the first wave of his own men, all screaming their various war cries in the face of the enemy.

For just a moment there was no response. Then the machine guns began their sweeping fire across the muddy plain. Buck O'Neill was the first to fall, his body riddled with bullets. An instant later Runs With Deer screamed in agony as his arm was blown away. Horses had their legs shot from under them, men were blown out of their saddles, limbs flew crazily through the wet morning air, and still the charge continued.

Roosevelt had crossed half the distance when Matupu fell directly in front of him, his head smashed to a pulp. He heard McCoy groan as half a dozen bullets thudded home in his chest, but looked neither right nor left as his horse leaped over the fallen Masai's bloody body.

Bullets and cannonballs flew to the right and left of him, in front and behind, and yet miraculously he was unscathed as he reached the final hundred yards. He dared a quick glance around, and saw that he was the sole survivor from the first wave, then heard the screams of the second wave as the machine guns turned on them.

Now he was seventy yards away, now fifty. He yelled a challenge to the Germans, and as he looked into the blinking eye of a machine gun, for one brief, final, glorious instant it was San Juan Hill all over again.

*   *   *

ber, 1917
from General John J. Pershing to Commander-
ident Woodrow Wilson.

*egret to inform you that Theodore Roosevelt died
uesday of wounds received in battle. He had dis-
d his orders, and led his men in a futile charge against
ntrenched German position. His entire regiment, the
alled "Rough Riders," was lost. His death was almost
tainly instantaneous, although it was two days before his
dy could be retrieved from the battlefield.*

*I shall keep the news of Mr. Roosevelt's death from the
press until receiving instructions from you. It is true that he
was an anachronism, that he belonged more to the 19th
Century than the 20th, and yet it is entirely possible that he
was the last authentic hero our country shall ever produce.
The charge he led was ill-conceived and foolhardy in the
extreme, nor did it diminish the length of the conflict by a
single day, yet I cannot help but believe that if I had 50,000
men with his courage and spirit, I could bring this war to a
swift and satisfactory conclusion by the end of the year.*

*That Theodore Roosevelt died the death of a fool is
beyond question, but I am certain in my heart that with his
dying breath he felt he was dying the death of a hero. I
await your instructions, and will release whatever version
of his death you choose upon hearing from you.*
                                                        —*Gen. John J. Pershing*

22 September, 1917
Dispatch from President Woodrow Wilson to General
John J. Pershing, Commander of American Forces in Europe.

John:
That man continues to harass me from the grave.
*Still, we have had more than enough fools in our his-
tory. Therefore, he died a hero.*

Just between you and me, the time for heroes is past.
I hope with all my heart that he was our last.
                                —*Woodrow Wilson*

And he was.

The Last Dog

This one was written simply because I was getting sick of every dog in science fiction either having *psi* powers or being a cute bassett puppy. My wife, Carol, and I bred some twenty-three collie champions, and I am still a licensed AKC judge, and it seemed to me that someone, somewhere, ought to draw a true portrait of a dog.

Like "Me and My Shadow," this was turned down by every magazine in the field. So I sold it to *Hunting Dogs Magazine,* where it won the American Dog Writers' Association Award for the Best Short Fiction of 1977. I have resold it some fifteen times since, almost always to canine markets, despite the fact that it is indisputably a science-fiction story.

The Last Dog

The Dog—old, mangy, his vertebrae forming little ridges beneath the slack skin that covered his gaunt body—trotted through the deserted streets, nose to the ground. He was missing half an ear and most of his tail, and caked blood covered his neck like a scarf. He may have been gold once, or light brown, but now he looked like an old red brick, even down to the straw and mud that clung to those few portions of his body which still retained any hair at all.

Since he had no true perception of the passage of time, he had no idea when he had last eaten—except that it had been a long time ago. A broken radiator in an automobile graveyard had provided water for the past week, and kept him in the area long after the last of the rusty, translucent liquid was gone.

He was panting now, his breath coming in a never-ending series of short spurts and gasps. His sides ached, his eyes watered, and every now and then he would trip over the rubble of the decayed and ruined buildings that lined the tortuously fragmented street. The toes of his feet were covered by sores and calluses, and both his dew claws had long since been torn off.

He continued trotting, occasionally shivering from the cold breeze that whistled down the streets of the lifeless city. Once he saw a rat, but a premature whine of hunger had sent it scurrying off into the debris before he could catch it, and so he trotted, his stride a little shorter, his chest hurting a little more, searching for sustenance so that he would live another day to hunt again and eat again and live still another day.

Suddenly he froze, his mud-caked nostrils testing the wind, the pitiful stump of a tail held rigidly behind him. He remained motionless for almost a minute, except for a spasmodic quivering in one foreleg, then slunk into the shadows and advanced silently down the street.

He emerged at what had once been an intersection, stared at the thing across the street from him, and blinked. His eyesight, none too good even in the days of his youth and health, was insufficient to the task, and so he inched forward, belly to ground, flecks of saliva falling onto his chest.

The Man heard a faint shuffling sound and looked into the shadows, a segment of an old two-by-four in his hand. He, too, was gaunt and dirty, his hair unkempt, four teeth missing and another one half rotted away. His feet were wrapped in old rags, and the only thing that held his clothes together was the dirt.

"Who's there?" he said in a rasping voice.

The Dog, fangs bared, moved out from between buildings and began advancing, a low growl rumbling in his throat. The Man turned to face him, strengthening his grip on his makeshift warclub. They stopped when they were fifteen feet apart, tense and unmoving. Slowly the Man raised his club to striking position; slowly the Dog gathered his hind legs beneath him.

Then, without warning, a rat raced out of the debris and ran between them. Savage cries escaped the lips of both the

Dog and the Man. The Dog pounced, but the Man's stick was even faster; it flew through the air and landed on the rat's back, pulping it to the ground and killing it instantly.

The Man walked forward to retrieve his weapon and his prey. As he reached down, the Dog emitted a low growl. The Man stared at him for a long moment; then, very slowly, very carefully, he picked up one end of the stick. He sawed with the other end against the smashed body of the rat until it split in half, and shoved one pulpy segment toward the Dog. The Dog remained motionless for a few seconds, then lowered his head, grabbed the blood-spattered piece of flesh and tissue, and raced off across the street with it. He stopped at the edge of the shadows, lay down, and began gnawing at his grisly meal. The Man watched him for a moment, then picked up his half of the rat, squatted down like some million-years-gone progenitor, and did the same.

When his meal was done the Man belched once, walked over to the still-standing wall of a building, sat with his back against it, laid his two-by-four across his thighs, and stared at the Dog. The Dog, licking forepaws that would never again be clean, stared back.

They slept thus, motionless, in the ghost city. When the Man awoke the next morning he arose, and the Dog did likewise. The Man balanced his stick across his shoulder and began walking, and after a moment the Dog followed him. The Man spent most of the day walking through the city, looking into the soft innards of stores and shops, occasionally cursing as dead store after dead store refused to yield up shoes, or coats, or food. At twilight he built a small fire in the rubble and looked around for the Dog, but could not find it.

The Man slept uneasily and awoke some two hours before sunrise. The Dog was sleeping about twenty feet away from him. The Man sat up abruptly, and the Dog, startled, raced off. Ten minutes later he was back, stopping about eighty feet distant, ready to race away again at an instant's warning, but back nonetheless.

The Man looked at the Dog, shrugged, and began walking in a northerly direction. By midday he had reached the outskirts of the city and, finding the ground soft and muddy, he dug a hole with his hands and his stick. He sat down next to it and waited as water slowly seeped into it. Finally he reached his hands down, cupping them together, and drew the precious fluid up to his lips. He did this twice more, then began walking again. Some instinct prompted him to turn back, and he saw the Dog eagerly lapping up what water remained.

He made another kill that night, a medium-sized bird that had flown into the second-floor room of a crumbling hotel and couldn't remember how to fly out before he pulped it. He ate most of it, put the rest into what remained of a pocket, and walked outside. He threw it on the ground and the Dog slunk out of the shadows, still tense but no longer growling. The Man sighed, returned to the hotel, and climbed up to the second floor. There were no rooms with windows intact, but he did find one with half a mattress remaining, and he collapsed upon it.

When he awoke, the Dog was lying in the doorway, sleeping soundly.

They walked, a little closer this time, through the remains of the forest that was north of the city. After they had proceeded about a dozen miles they found a small stream that was not quite dry and drank from it, the Man first and then the Dog. That night the man lit another fire and the Dog lay down on the opposite side of it. The next day the Dog killed a small, undernourished squirrel. He did not share it with the Man, but neither did he growl or bare his teeth as the Man approached. That night the Man killed an opossum, and they remained in the area for two days, until the last of the marsupial's flesh had been consumed.

They walked north for almost two weeks, making an occasional kill, finding an occasional source of water. Then one night it rained, and there was no fire, and the Man sat, arms hugging himself, beneath a large tree. Soon the Dog approached him, sat about four feet away, and then slowly, ever so slowly, inched forward as the rain struck his flanks. The Man reached out absently and stroked the Dog's neck. It was their first physical contact, and the Dog leaped back, snarling. The Man withdrew his hand and sat motionless, and soon the Dog moved forward again.

After a period of time that might have been ten minutes or perhaps two hours, the Man reached out once more, and this time, although the Dog trembled and tensed, he did not pull away. The Man's long fingers slowly moved up the sore-covered neck, scratched behind the torn ears, gently stroked the scarred head. Finally the Man withdrew his hand and rolled over on his side. The Dog looked at him for a moment, then sighed and lay up against his emaciated body.

The Man awoke the next morning to the feeling of something warm and scaly pressed into his hand. It was not the cool, moist nose of the dogs of literature, because this was not a dog of literature. This was the Last Dog, and he was the Last Man, and if they looked less than heroic, at least there was no one around to see and bemoan how the mighty had fallen.

The Man patted the Dog's head, arose, stretched, and began walking. The Dog trotted at his side, and for the first time in many years the nub of his tail moved rapidly from side to side. They hunted and ate and drank and slept, then repeated the procedure again and again.

And then they came to the Other.

The Other looked like neither Man nor Dog, nor like anything else of earth, as indeed it was not. It had come from beyond Centauri, beyond Arcturus, past Antares, from deep at the core of the galaxy, where the stars pressed so close together that nightfall never came. It had come, and had seen, and had conquered.

"You!" hissed the Man, holding his stick at the ready.

"You are the last," said the Other. "For six years I have

scoured and scourged the face of this planet, for six years I have eaten alone and slept alone and lived alone and hunted down the survivors of the war one by one, and you are the last. There is only you to be slain, and then I may go home."

And, so saying, it withdrew a weapon that looked strangely like a pistol, but wasn't.

The Man crouched and prepared to hurl his stick, but even as he did so a brick-red, scarred, bristling engine of destruction hurtled past him, leaping through space for the Other. The Other touched what passed for a belt, made a quick gesture in the air, and the Dog bounced back off of something that was invisible, unsensible, but tangible.

Then, very slowly, almost casually, the Other pointed its weapon at the Man. There was no explosion, no flash of light, no whirring of gears, but suddenly the Man grasped his throat and fell to the ground.

The Dog got up and limped painfully over to the Man. He nuzzled his face, whined once, and pawed at his body, trying to turn it over.

"It is no use," said the Other, although its lips no longer moved. "He was the last, and now he is dead."

The Dog whined again, and pushed the Man's lifeless head with his muzzle.

"Come, Animal," said the Other wordlessly. "Come with me and I shall feed you and tend to your wounds."

I will stay with the Man, said the Dog, also wordlessly.

"But he is dead," said the Other. "Soon you will grow hungry and weak."

I was hungry and weak before, said the Dog.

The Other took a step forward, but stopped as the Dog bared his teeth and growled.

"He was not worth your loyalty," said the Other.

He was my— The Dog's brain searched for a word, but the concept it sought was complex far beyond its meager abilities to formulate. *He was my friend.*

"He was my enemy," said the Other. "He was petty and barbarous and unscrupulous and all that is worst in a sentient being. He was Man."

Yes, said the Dog. *He was Man.* With another whimper, he lay down beside the body of the Man and rested his head on its chest.

"There are no more," said the Other. "And soon you will leave him."

The Dog looked up at the Other and snarled again, and then the Other was gone and the Dog was alone with the Man. He licked him and nuzzled him and stood guard over him for two days and two nights, and then, as the Other had said he would, he left to hunt for food and water.

And he came to a valley of fat, lazy rabbits and cool, clear ponds, and he ate and drank and grew strong, and his wounds began to scab over and heal, and his coat grew long and luxuriant.

And because he was only a Dog, it was not too long before he forgot that there had ever been such a thing as a Man, except on those chilly nights when he lay alone beneath a tree in the valley and dreamt of a bond that had been forged by a gentle touch upon the head or a soft word barely audible above the crackling of a small fire.

And, being a Dog, one day he forgot even that, and assumed that the emptiness within him came only from hunger. And when he grew old and feeble and sick, he did not seek out the Man's barren bones and lie down to die beside them, but rather he dug a hole in the damp earth near the pond and lay there, his eyes half closed, a numbness setting in at his extremities and working its way slowly toward his heart.

And just before the Dog exhaled his last breath, he felt a moment of panic. He tried to jump up, but found that he couldn't. He whimpered once, his eyes clouding over with fear and something else; and then it seemed to him that a bony, gentle hand was caressing his ears, and, with a single wag of his tail, the Last Dog closed his eyes for the last time and prepared to join a God of stubbled beard and torn clothes and feet wrapped in rags.

INTRODUCTION
King of the Blue Planet

The "shared-world" story is relatively new to science fiction. A writer/editor creates a world and some characters, and then asks a number of other writers to contribute stories about them.

When David Drake and Bill Fawcett sent me the "bible" for *The Fleet,* which consisted mostly of descriptions of starfaring battleships and nasty aliens, I agreed to be in it if I could do something funny instead of warlike, without breaking any of their rules. To my surprise, they agreed—and I have been writing "against the grain" for shared-world anthologies ever since.

King of the Blue Planet

Lizard O'Neal leaned back on his straw chair, folded his dirty hands across his grubby shirt, and surveyed his empire.

The empire, such as it was, extended for some 200 feet in all directions from him, as he sat at its very center. To the right were six small huts, each and every one (or so he liked to tell his customers) serviced by a reborn virgin; no one had ever asked exactly what a reborn virgin was, so he hadn't quite gotten around to defining it yet. To the left was the bar, a huge tree trunk imported ("at considerable expense") from the forest some sixty yards away, framed by wanted posters of the most notorious outlaws of the Rim, each of them personally autographed. Behind him was his royal palace, all two rooms of it, kept together by spit and bailing wire and held in place by pile upon pile of unwashed laundry. In front of him was the Royal Spaceport, a burnt and blackened strip of ground barely large enough to hold six two-man ships at a time, and right next to it was the Imperial Fuel Station.

Beyond the perimeter of his empire there were forests

and mountains, rivers and streams and ultimately the enormous ocean that made his world glow like a blue gemstone in the night sky. There were also placid furry aliens who might or might not be intelligent. Word had it that there was even a desert out there, waiting for someone even crazier than him to try crossing it.

O'Neal ran his fingers through his thick, uncombed shock of red hair, stretched, sighed, and finally turned to the carefully-groomed man who looked so out of place in these surroundings.

"You've got your answer," he said, flicking a blue-and-gold insect away from his neck. "What are you waiting for?"

"The answer is unacceptable," replied Reinhardt.

"So is your proposition."

"Mr. O'Neal, the Alliance absolutely must have—"

"Look around you," interrupted O'Neal, "and tell me what you see."

"Absolutely nothing," said Reinhardt contemptuously.

"Right," agreed O'Neal. "No banks, no lawyers, no tax collectors, no police—and no Alliance," he added pointedly.

"That's precisely why the Alliance needs this planet," insisted Reinhardt, wiping a little trickle of sweat from his left cheek.

"Well, this planet doesn't need the Alliance. We're 75,000 light-years from Tau Ceti. We mind our own business, we enjoy ourselves, we get a lot of sun and sex and fresh air, and nobody is bothering us—except for you, of course."

"The fact that you're in a totally unpopulated area of the galaxy is precisely why we must have the use of your world for a few weeks."

"No."

"I could *order* you to acquiesce to my demands."

O'Neal shrugged. "Whatever makes you happy."

"This planet is within the Alliance's sphere of influence," noted Reinhardt.

"This planet declared independence five years ago," replied O'Neal.

"There is no record of that."

"Maybe you don't have a record of it, but we do." He gestured to the huge cash box behind the bar. "It's in there somewhere with the receipts."

"Totally illegal."

"Fine. Take me to court."

"In point of fact, we can take you to court over a number of matters, if we so desire," said Reinhardt calmly. " 'Lizard O'Neal,' " he quoted, " 'wanted for gun-running, smuggling, pandering, swindling, consorting with known—' "

"A series of misunderstandings," replied O'Neal with yet another shrug.

"We can let a court of law decide that."

"As a matter of fact, you can't," replied O'Neal. "We don't have any extradition treaties with the Alliance."

"Then I will speak to the ruler of this world."

"You're looking at him," said O'Neal with a lazy smile. "King Lizard the First."

"You are an alien here. I am speaking about the lawful leader of the native population."

"That's me. We took a vote. I won."

"*Who* took a vote?" demanded Reinhardt.

"The planetary population."

"How many ballots were cast?"

"Just one," answered O'Neal. "But it was an absolutely open election. You can hardly blame me for voter apathy."

"I can see that we'll have to add enslavement of a sentient race to your list of crimes."

"It'll take you 500 years to find out whether or not they're sentient," replied O'Neal. "I thought you needed the world next month."

"We do—and we will have it, one way or another."

"What's so special about this world?" asked O'Neal curiously. "Uranium? Gold? Platinum?"

"This world is valuable to us precisely because it has no value," responded Reinhardt.

"What have you been drinking?"

"Whatever your barman served me," was the distasteful reply.

"Well, you can't be drunk; we water our liquor down too much." O'Neal paused and stared at Reinhardt from beneath half-lowered lids. "So why is a little dirtball out in the middle of nowhere so important that the Alliance is making threats to me, a peaceable businessman who never caused any harm to anyone?"

Reinhardt stared silently at him for a moment.

"Well?" persisted O'Neal.

"I was just trying to envision you as a peaceable businessman," he said. "And believe me, it isn't easy."

"Use your imagination," said O'Neal easily. "And I still want to know: why do you need my planet?"

"It should be obvious to you."

"I'm sure it is," replied O'Neal. "But suppose you tell me why it's obvious to *you.*"

"Have you ever heard of Switzerland?" asked Reinhardt, leaning forward intently.

"Nope."

"It was a little country, back on Earth, that was never conquered."

"Tough sons of bitches, huh?" asked O'Neal without much show of interest.

"Not especially."

"Well, it's probably better to be lucky than tough."

"Switzerland was never conquered because it was far too valuable as a neutral country." Reinhardt paused. "Warring nations had to have a place where their diplomats could meet, where international banking could be done, where . . . "

"Spare me the details," said O'Neal. "What you're trying to say is that you want to set up a meet with the Khalia, and that you want to do it on my world."

"That is correct."

"Well, why didn't you just come out and say so in the first place, instead of making all those threats?"

"Then you'll agree to it?" asked Reinhardt, surprised.

"No—but think of the time we could have saved."

"O'Neal, I have been assigned to procure the services of this world for a secret meeting with the Khalia. I really can't return with my mission unfulfilled."

"And I really can't agree with my pockets unfulfilled," replied O'Neal.

"So it comes down to money?"

"Doesn't it always?"

"Have you no concept of loyalty at all?" demanded Reinhardt. "You have an opportunity to be of inestimable service to your own race!"

"I belong to the race of capitalist beachcombers," said O'Neal, "to whom I am intensely loyal. As for you and the Khalia, you're just a bunch of guys with money for beer."

"All right," said Reinhardt. "What are your terms?"

O'Neal shrugged. "Make me an offer."

"The Alliance can spend up to 200,000 credits for the use of your planet."

"Come on," said O'Neal. "You'll spend more than that just getting here."

"250,000."

"Forget it."

"And a pardon for all previous crimes."

"I'm never going back. What do I need a pardon for?"

"What *do* you want?" demanded Reinhardt in exasperation.

"Got a pen?"

"I have my pocket computer."

"All right," said O'Neal. "First, I want one million credits."

"That's out of the question."

"Second, I want the pardon you offered me."

"I told you, the amount is—"

"Let me finish," said O'Neal. "Then we can negotiate." He leaned back comfortably. "Third, I want it—in writing—that the Alliance can't erect any competitive bars while they're here. Any soldier who wants a drink has to come to the Devil's Asshole."

"The Devil's Asshole?"

"That's where we are."

"We simply can't have that name, O'Neal. You will have to change it."

"I like it."

"Nevertheless."

"Who's making the rules here, anyway?"

"This is to be the site of a diplomatic meeting. We can't have you calling it the Devil's Asshole!"

"I'll think about it," replied O'Neal. "Fourth, if any special buildings have to be erected for the Khalia, the Alliance has to pay for them."

"Is that all?" asked Reinhardt dryly.

"Nope. I can't seem to get vodka out here. I want twenty-four cases of top-quality vodka. And finally, I want official recognition as King Lizard I."

"Surely you're jesting!"

"Not at all."

"Your conditions are totally unacceptable."

"Well, as I said, they're negotiable. I'll take sixteen cases of vodka if I have to."

"You'll take 200,000 credits and nothing else, and be glad we don't blow your planet right out of orbit."

"You'll give me what I asked or I'll mine every inch of this place."

"You can't mine an entire planet," said Reinhardt confidently.

"Maybe not, but I can make the air and water awfully dirty."

"We'll go elsewhere," threatened Reinhardt.

"Fine. I wish you would."

"Damn it, O'Neal—we've only got a month!"

"So you said." O'Neal grinned. "I've done a little math, and according to my figures, if you've only got a month the Khalia are already on their way."

"Only in this general direction."

"And your engineers must be within a day's flight of here if you want the Khalia sleeping anywhere besides grass huts." O'Neal took a long sip from his drink. "I'd say this is a seller's market."

"I'll have to contact my superiors and get back to you."

"I've got all the time in the world," said O'Neal pleasantly.

Reinhardt stalked off, hoping that O'Neal couldn't see the trace of a smile forming at the corners of his mouth.

The Alliance approved O'Neal's terms within three hours.

"Oh dear, oh dear," said the little diplomat. "This won't do at all, Mr. O'Neal. Not at all."

"What won't?" asked O'Neal.

"We can't have our men sleeping in a . . . a *whorehouse*. It would do terrible things for discipline and morale."

"As a matter of fact," contradicted O'Neal, "it would be the best thing in the world for morale. They'd wake up smiling every morning."

"No, it just won't do, Mr. O'Neal. I'm afraid your female employees will have to go."

"Go? Go where?"

The little man stared at him. "That's hardly *my* problem."

"They stay right where they are."

"Then I shall advise the Alliance that you have broken the spirit if not the letter of your agreement, and that payment not be made."

"Fine," said O'Neal. "You do that. And while you're at it, get the hell off my planet."

"I have every right to be here, Mr. O'Neal."

"I'm the king, and I said Scram!"

"Allow me to refer to you Section 19, sub-section 3, paragraph 21 of your signed agreement with the Alliance . . ."

"Why don't you just tell me what you think it says?"

"It gives me permission to survey the construction sites and—"

"Sites?" repeated O'Neal. "You mean there's more than one?"

"I hope you didn't think we would permit our troops to sleep in thatched huts, Mr. O'Neal!" said the little diplomat, quite shocked. "And of course, we shall have to erect a dwelling fully commeasurate with the needs of the Khalia."

"What has that got to do with my girls?"

"Really, Mr. O'Neal, I've no time for levity. And of course the name of your establishment must be changed."

"It already has been."

The little diplomat looked severe. "Satan's Sphincter has to go. If you won't change it, one of our people will be happy to come up with a new name."

"You've knocked down all my trees!" complained O'Neal.

"We can't have the Khalia thinking we have any men hidden out there," said the General, who was supervising the defoliation.

"There's nothing out there! I've been here for three years, and I've never seen anything but a few birds!"

"You know it and I know it, Mr. O'Neal," replied the General, "but the Khalia may not believe it, and I won't have the conference fall apart over a trivial matter of a few trees."

"Do you know how long those trees have been standing there?" demanded O'Neal.

"I haven't the slightest idea."

"Centuries!"

"Then they'll be glad to have a rest, won't they?"

"You're desecrating my planet!" complained O'Neal.

"It's *our* planet for the next few weeks," replied the General. "And by the way, you're going to have to come up with a new name for your establishment."

"I already did."

"I don't know who approved of Lucifer's Rectum, but I assure you it's totally unacceptable."

O'Neal glared at him and began wishing he had put an escape clause into the contract.

"Reinhardt! Where the hell have you been?"

"Around," replied Reinhardt calmly. "I've had numerous details to look after."

"I want to talk to you!"

"Well, here I am. Start talking."

"This isn't working out," said O'Neal.

"Nonsense," said Reinhardt, staring at the cold gray steel structures. "Construction is actually two days ahead of schedule."

"That's not what I mean."

"Then please explain yourself."

"There are too damned many people here, and your buildings are eyesores."

"Most of the people will be gone before long, and you can decorate the builldings any way you like once we've finished here."

"I plan to tear them down."

Reinhardt uttered an amused laugh. "They're made of fortified titanium with a tight molecular bonding."

"What the hell does that mean?"

"It means that they're virtually indestructible. After all, it wouldn't do to have a saboteur try to blow them up during the meeting, would it?"

"You mean they're going to be here forever?"

"You'll get used to them. And I'm sure your—ah—lady-friends will appreciate them come winter."

"We don't *have* any winters here!" yelled O'Neal.

"So you don't. My mistake."

"Then what am I going to do with them?"

Reinhardt grinned at him. "War is hell, O'Neal."

"Ready for your physical?" asked the Major.

"What physical?" replied O'Neal suspiciously.

"The Khalia are due to land here in just six more days."

"What the hell does that have to do with my health?"

"It's not *your* health we're worried about," answered the Major. "But they're mammals, and very likely subject to many of the same diseases that afflict humans. What if you have a cold, or a minor viral infection? For all we know, it could kill the Khalia—and we can't have them all dying on us, can we?"

"I thought that was the whole purpose of going to war with them," muttered O'Neal.

"What a refreshing sense of humor you have!" laughed the Major. "Now be a good fellow and report to Building #4 for your physical, won't you?"

"You go to hell."

"You can report voluntarily or I can call the guard, but you *will* report, Mr. O'Neal. Allow me to refer you to your written agreement with the Alliance, page 7, paragraph . . . "

"Now breathe out."

O'Neal, his face a bright red, exhaled and began gasping for air.

"We're just a bit out of shape, aren't we?" asked the doctor with a smile.

"We didn't realize that holding our breath for ten minutes was a prerequisite for being king," replied O'Neal caustically.

"Come, now, Mr. O'Neal," chuckled the doctor. "You held it for barely thirty seconds."

"What does that have to do with carrying some disease that can wipe out the Khalia?" demanded O'Neal.

"Nothing," replied the doctor. "On the other hand, we don't want a reigning monarch to die during our occupation. It wouldn't look at all good back at headquarters."

"I have no intention of dying."

"Well, we seem to be in total agreement on that point."

"You bet your ass we are."

"Therefore, I'm certain you won't mind going on an immediate 800-calorie-per-day diet."

"What?"

"Just until you've lost twenty-five pounds or so," said the doctor. "And of course, the tobacco and liquor will have to go."

"They're not going anywhere!" snapped O'Neal.

"Really, Mr. O'Neal, a man with your blood pressure should try not to get so excited. I think a brisk three-mile walk every morning and evening is also called for."

"Then *you* take it."

"Please, Mr. O'Neal—your health is my resposibility."

"Not unless the Khalia can get high blood pressure by visiting my planet, it isn't."

"This is most awkward," said the doctor. "You are calamitously out of condition, Mr. O'Neal. I really *must* insist that you follow my instructions."

"Not a chance."

"Then I shall have to use my authority, under Section 34 of—"

"You have no authority! I'm the goddamned king!"

"Under Section 34 of the Occupying Army Specifications," continued the doctor doggedly. " 'If, in the opinion of the presiding medical officer,' " he quoted, " 'there is just and ample cause for . . . ' "

"Never mind," said O'Neal wearily.

"It's for your own good," said the doctor. "Someday you'll thank me."

"Don't hold your breath," muttered O'Neal.

"I won't," said the doctor agreeably. "But with luck, and a considerable amount of self-discipline, you may someday be able to hold yours."

"What now?" demanded O'Neal as Reinhardt approached him.

"It's time for you to leave," replied Reinhardt. "The Khalia are expected within the next ten hours."

"So what? It's *my* planet. I'm curious to see what they look like."

"We can't have you representing the human race dressed like *that!* When was the last time you wore a pair of shoes?"

"What's that got to do with anything? For all you know, the Khalia don't even wear clothes."

"They may not, but *humans* do," answered Reinhardt severely. "You're simply not presentable."

"Then I'll get a pair of shoes."

"And a whole new outfit."

"Right," muttered O'Neal wearily.

"And a shave."

"What? No manicure?" said O'Neal sardonically.

"I was about to suggest that," agreed Reinhardt.

"Somehow I'm not surprised."

The Khalia came and the Khalia went, accusations were hurled back and forth, and nothing very much was resolved, to nobody's great surprise.

"Thank God *that's* over!" muttered O'Neal thankfully as the last of the Khalia ships departed.

"I should think that you, of all people, would be delighted," remarked Reinhardt. "After all, you made a million credits."

"I also lost sixteen pounds, I haven't had a drink or a

woman in three weeks, my feet are covered with blisters, my suit is too tight, and I don't recognize my home."

"Well, one can't have everything."

"I *had* everything a month ago. Evidently one can't *keep* everything as long as you military bastards continue to play your idiot games. Which reminds me," added O'Neal, "when are you clearing out?"

"I'm afraid I don't understand you," said Reinhardt.

"What's to understand?" snapped O'Neal. "When are you taking your men and going away?"

"I have absolutely no idea. It depends on headquarters."

"But the meeting's over, for all the good it did you."

"True," admitted Reinhardt. "But we do have an option to renew our lease."

"What the hell for?" demanded O'Neal. "You're never going to make peace with those bastards."

"Probably not," agreed Reinhardt. "Still, I don't see why it should bother you in the least. You'll get a renewal fee."

"I don't *want* your money! I just want to be left alone!" He stood up. "Look at me. I'm in danger of turning into *you!*"

"Then you shouldn't have leased us the planet in the first place."

"You came to *me,* damn it! I didn't come to you!"

"I can't see what difference that makes."

"Look," said O'Neal desperately, "why don't you just buy the damned world from me?"

"Oh, we couldn't do that," said Reinhardt. "Then it wouldn't be a neutral planet any longer." He paused. "No, we're quite pleased with our present arrangement."

Reinhardt was sitting in the bar of the Angel's Anus, sharing a drink with the General, when the speaker on his wrist beeped twice.

"Yes?" said Reinhardt.

"He's gone, sir."

"He took all his possessions with him?"

"Yes, sir."

"Did you remember to put a tracer on his ship?"

"As you ordered."

"Good. Let me know where he winds up." Reinhardt deactivated the speaker and turned to the General. "A pity that we're going to have to freeze his account. One could almost feel sorry for him, if he hadn't tried to hold us up." He allowed himself the luxury of a smile. "I do love dealing with an amoral man!"

"Where do you suppose he'll come to rest?"

Reinhardt shrugged. "Who knows? Wherever it is, it'll be as far from us and the Khalia as possible." He grinned and leaned back comfortably on his chair. "The perfect place for another Switzerland, once this world has outlived its usefulness. I look forward to negotiating its use with him."

Watching Marcia

This one's not science fiction at all. In fact, it was written on commission for *The Arbor House Treasury of Mystery and Suspense,* and to this day I do not really know what a suspense story is, except that it's sort of a mystery story in which the Bad Guys don't necessarily have to lose.

But it was a breakthrough story for me, and a type that I haven't written in any of my science fiction. After its appearance, editors began soliciting work from me, rather than the other way around, and for that reason I've got a soft spot in my heart for it.

Watching Marcia

Tuesday, June 7

Marcia walks from the living room to the bathroom and I panic for a minute as I lose sight of her, but then she comes back in view and I peer intently through my telescope (a Celestron C90, two hundred and thirty-nine dollars retail and worth every penny of it).

She lets her robe drop to the floor and a little moan escapes my lips. Then she is in the shower and the bathroom fills with steam, and it seems that even through the steam I can see her rubbing soap over her naked breasts, sliding her hands down her body, stroking that delicious area between her legs with just the hint of a smile on her face.

After an eternity she emerges, clean and pink and glowing with health, her skin still slick with water, and for a moment I can imagine myself in the bathroom with her, rubbing the water away from secret areas that only she and I share, licking her dry and then licking her moist again.

The thought fascinates me, and I find, to my surprise, that I have been rubbing my own body in the very same way, and producing, not surprisingly, the very same results.
I think I'm in love.

Wednesday, June 8

My lunch break is almost over and I wait by a tobacco stand in Marcia's office building. The smell of the cigars, even though they're all wrapped in cellophane and stacked in boxes, irritates my nostrils, and I find myself wondering why Royal Jamaicans cost twice as much as Royal Caribbeans when they both look so much alike. Finally she emerges from the elevator, her tight little ass fighting against her tight little skirt, her heels click-click-clicking in an almost sexual rhythm on the dirty tile floor.

She walks right by me without noticing, which is not unexpected—after all, I am the watcher and she is the watched—and I fall into step behind her, mesmerized by the twin globes of her buttocks as they race ahead of me like some sexual incarnation of Affirmed and Alydar locked in an eternal neck-and-neck struggle. I think of a horrible pun about no quarter being asked and emit a falsetto cackle which draws a few strange stares, but Marcia, everything moving in sync, shaking, bobbing, twitching, does not turn around.

She walks into the bookstore (I know her habits and could have been waiting for her there, but then I wouldn't have been able to watch her walk) and goes right to the romance section while I punch in and walk to my station at the cash register. She bends over to look at a title at the bottom of one of the racks, and her skirt climbs up her thighs and it is all I can do not to scream as inch after inch of that smooth white flesh which I know so well is revealed to me. I wonder if she is wearing panties (I woke up late this morning and didn't get a chance to check) and hope that she is; that soft, slippery little mound of ecstasy is for my eyes only. I start thinking of all the things I want to do to it with my lips, my tongue, my teeth, my fingers—and suddenly I realize that I have been staring blankly at the place where Marcia had been but that now she is standing in front of me with a pile of paperbacks and I am so nervous that I have to count her change three times before I get it right.

She smiles at me, an amused kind of smile, and I mumble and apologize and have to dig my fingers into my palms to keep from ripping her blouse open and covering her tits with love-bites right there in front of everyone. She takes her books and her change and walks out, Alydar and Affirmed jostling each other furiously for position. I wipe the sweat from my face and feel very stupid.

Which, by the way, is all wrong. Would a stupid person have had enough sense to demand that Marcia write down her phone number the first time she paid for her books with a Visa card? Without her name and number I'd never have been able to confirm her address in the directory, and without her address I wouldn't have been able to rent the apartment across the street, or set up my Celestron C90 three-and-one-half-inch refractive scope with its off-axis guiding system, or learned about the tiny mole on the inside of her left thigh. So there.

In point of fact, I am possessed of enormous animal cunning (which is a very nice word and reminds me of all kinds of things I'd like to do with Marcia). When I started writing notes and slipping them under her door, I knew better than to do it in my own handwriting or even on my own typewriter. Do you know how much work it was to cut out the letters from newspaper headlines to spell I WANT TO EAT YOU? (I did it all in 48-point Tempo Bold, but I couldn't find a capital *Y* for *YOU*. I hope she doesn't think she's dealing with an illiterate.)

And I drove all the way to Greenwich, Connecticut, to mail her the vibrator and the K-Y Jelly. I mean, not just to the Bronx or even Scarsdale, but to *Connecticut* for God's sake!

So I guess that shows you who's stupid and who's not.

Thursday, June 9

Marcia and I wake up together, or maybe I should say that we wake up at the same time. I place my eye to the Celestron and zero in and can almost see her clit pulsating. Then I look at her breasts and utter a howl of anguish because her nipples are not erect and she should know—damn it, she *must* know!—that she looks like only half a woman when they're like that. I want to suck and bite them erect, but I just stare and stare and get madder and madder at her.

She yawns, and hangs up her robe, and starts to get dressed. She puts her bra on first and then her panties, and I am beside myself with rage. *Everyone* knows that you're supposed to do it the other way around. It's just out-and-out *wrong,* and if I were there I'd take that goddamned vibrator and shove it so far up her ass that it would break her teeth.

I'm so upset that I don't even follow her to work like I always do. Ordinarily I like to watch her raise her hand and jiggle her breasts when she signals the bus, and try to get a peek up her skirt as she takes an aisle seat, but she has ruined everything today.

If she doesn't start showing a little consideration, I'll do something bad to her.

Yes I will.

Friday, June 10

I'm so mad I could almost kill her!

She didn't wear a bra today, and just walked up to the bus stop, bouncing and flopping for everyone to see. I mean, you could see *everything!* The bus was a couple of minutes late, and some tall, gray-haired guy carrying a briefcase stopped to talk to her while we were waiting, and her nipples almost stuck right through her sweater. They didn't have any goddamned trouble standing up for *him!*

And the bus driver, who never notices anything, not even dogs crossing the street in front of him, gave her a great big smile when she shook her boobs in his face. If she'd have paused in front of him one more second I'd have cut his cock off and fed it to those dogs that he's always trying to hit.

Those tits and that cunt and that ass are *mine* to look at—nobody else's! No woman I love can flaunt herself like some five-buck-a-shot hooker, that's all I've got to say.

It had just better never happen again.

Or else.

Saturday, June 11

She goes to the beach today, and I sit a few hundred yards away on a park bench, binoculars in hand, and watch her.

She finds a nice secluded spot and removes her wrap-around, and she is wearing a skimpy little royal-blue bikini, and it seems like the second she takes a deep breath her tits will pop right out of it. I tremble a little as I study her through the binoculars (Power Optics 30 x 80, one hundred and sixty-nine dollars without the tripod, lens cap free), and I decide that I don't want anyone else to see her like this. Bikinis may be all very well for unattached girls, but Marcia is mine, and you can even see that mole right next to her pussy, for Christ's sake! I make a mental note to tell her to dress more modestly in the future, wipe away a little stream of spittle that has somehow rolled down to my chin, and go back to looking at her.

A young blond man, all tanned and hairy and with his

cock almost bursting out of his tight swimming trunks, stops
by to talk to her. To *my* Marcia!

I reach into my purse and fondle the .22-caliber Beretta,
letting my fingers slide over it and seek out all its crevices,
much as they would like to do with Marcia, and decide to
count to twenty. But on fourteen he shrugs and walks away,
and Marcia turns onto her belly, golden buttocks reflecting
the sun, begging, *begging* to be violated, and never knows that
she saved his life by only six seconds.

Sunday, June 12

I get up at seven-thirty, turn off my alarm (a General
Electric clock-radio, AM/FM, twenty-two-ninety-five at the
local discount house, but it doesn't have a Snooze-Alarm,
which was a terrible mistake but one with which I must live),
and train my Celestron on her, but Marcia is becoming slov-
enly and she just lays there, eyes shut, the succulent mounds
of her breasts rising and falling regularly, sound asleep.

Nine comes, then ten, and she's still asleep, and I don't
dare take my eyes off her for fear that when I'm not looking
she'll wake up and I'll miss the daily unveiling of her trea-
sures, and suddenly I am overcome by a sense of having been
misused. Has she no consideration for me? Doesn't she know
how long I have been sitting motionless, my eye glued to the
telescope? It's unfair, no two ways about it, and I make up my
mind to alleviate the situation, so without taking my eyes
from her body I reach blindly behind me and finally manage
to locate the telephone.

I call her, and a moment later she sits up in the bed, the
covers falling to her thighs, and I see that her nipples are
erect, but it doesn't please me because I know she has been
dreaming of *him*, of shoving her tits into his blond face and
sticking his blond cock in her mouth and having his corrupt
blond hands exploring every inch of her, and when she picks

up the phone a moment later I am so mad that I don't trust myself to speak and all I can do is breathe heavily into the receiver.

I wait until my head stops throbbing and the screeching noise in my ears goes away, and then I dial her number again.

"Hello?" she says.

I stare at her and forget the receiver is in my hand, and she hangs up again. But now she is up for the day, and after I watch her go into the shower and come out and dry herself off and powder her body, I call a third time. This time I am in perfect control of myself. This time I will lay down the law to her.

"Hello?" she says again.

"Hello, Marcia," I say softly.

"Who is this?" she says.

"Marcia, I don't like the way things have been going between us," I say. "You've got to stop."

"Is this some kind of joke?" she asks, but I am looking at her through the scope and I know she doesn't think it's funny.

"If we're going to remain lovers," I say, "if you're going to open your ripe juicy body to me, then we've got to come to an understanding."

"Marlene, is this you?" she snaps. "I don't think much of your sense of humor, Marlene!"

"Who's Marlene?" I demand. "Are you seeing someone named Marlene?"

"Who *is* this?" she yells.

"You keep away from Marlene," I warn her. "I don't want to hear about her again." Then I realize that I am getting away from the point and that I am yelling too, so I take a deep breath and lower my voice and say, very casually and conversationally, "If you say one word to the blond guy, just one word, I'll kill him."

She hangs up the phone and starts pacing around her apartment.

She looks worried.

I smile. I have made my point. Things will improve between us now.

Monday, June 13

Marcia wears a bra today, and very unrevealing pants. She scrutinizes everyone at the bus stop, scanning each face ever so carefully, but I am too smart for her and I stay in my room, watching her from the window. I don't wait for her at the cigar stand either. When she walks into the bookstore I nod to her and smile pleasantly and she looks right through me. She browses for a few minutes but doesn't buy anything, and I can tell she is still thinking about our little chat.

Good. Even though it was our very first conversation and we haven't even been properly introduced, I am glad to see that she is a serious girl and considers what I have said very carefully.

I think this is the beginning of a very long and beautiful and trusting relationship.

Tuesday, June 14

I leave work early and race home to watch Marcia's face when she opens the package. I wait an hour for her, but finally she arrives, and puts the package down next to her mail on the kitchen table and looks at it like it might be a bomb. Finally she opens it and pulls out the black bra with the little holes cut out so that her nipples can peek through, and the black lace panties with the crotch removed, and then she sees the message: I ACHE FOR YOUR HOT LITTLE BODY. (I have given up on Tempo Bold and switched to 96-point Erber, which is much more impressive and really gets my message across.)

She begins to cry, and a warm glow suffuses me as I realize that I have brought tears of happiness to the woman I love.

Wednesday, June 15

Today begins like all other days, with the unveiling, and proceeds like all the others, but somewhere along the way something goes wrong, because when I get on the bus to go home Marcia is not on it. Panic-stricken, I get off at the next block and begin back-tracking. I bump into people without noticing, and twist my ankle painfully on a curb, but I continue and finally I find her.

She is sitting at a bar, and as I look in the window I see that she has a drink in her hand, but because of my inexperience in such matters I cannot tell from the shape of the glass what kind of drink it is. The place is not doing much business at this hour. There is a couple seated at a table, and three businessmen are positioned at various spots along the bar, but that is enough.

I go into a drugstore across the street and look up the bar's number in the directory and dial it and ask for Marcia. The bartender sounds surprised, but he calls her name and then I see him bring the phone over to her.

"Marcia," I say harshly, "this can't go on."

"Who is this?" she says, her voice shaking.

"You can't keep exhibiting yourself like this," I continue, "flaunting your ass in front of those three men like some kind of trollop. I won't stand for it."

"Why can't you leave me alone?" she shrieks.

"Get out of there at once or I'm going to be very cross with you," I warn her and hang up the phone.

I watch her scream something into the receiver before she realizes the line is dead. Everyone turns and stares at her and suddenly she throws a handful of money on the bar and walks out and summons a cab.

I must remember to tell her not to overtip bartenders in the future.

Thursday, June 16

Marcia doesn't get out of bed to take her shower this morning. I know she's not having her period and I start to worry that she might be feeling under the weather, but then she jumps like she's had an electric shock and stares at the phone, and I can tell by her attitude that it must be ringing and she is probably afraid that I am still mad at her.

Once she gets to know me better she'll discover that I'm really a very warm and caring person who almost never carries a grudge. I decide to call her and tell her that she is forgiven, but when the phone rings she buries her head under a pillow and there is nothing more to watch except for a few trembling lumps under the blanket. I decide to go to work without her.

All day long I wonder who would have been calling her at eight in the morning, and it puts me in a very foul mood by the time I return home. I watch Marcia for a few hours before going to bed and I feel better.

Friday, June 17

The unveiling is glorious today, as always, and I become so engrossed that I almost miss the bus. Still, there is a certain sameness to it, it lacks a certain spark, and I find myself wishing that she would do something a little different, so I call her at her office just after lunchtime.

"Hello?" she says in a brisk, businesslike voice. "May I help you?"

"You certainly may," I answer. "I sent you a present three days ago and you haven't even tried it on yet." I think I hear something at the other end of the line, perhaps a gasp or a sob, but she doesn't say anything, so I continue: "I think you should wear it to bed tonight, Marcia. After all, I spent a lot of time selecting it, and it seems very ungracious of you not to wear it at least once."

She hangs up the phone, or perhaps we are cut off. I spend the rest of the afternoon putting new mystery and science-fiction titles in the racks and setting aside the old ones for the distributor to take away. Someone comes in right at closing and I miss my regular bus, but somehow it doesn't bother me at all because I have already seen Marcia in the dress she is wearing today and I am looking forward with almost frenzied eagerness to seeing her wear my present tonight.

I walk up the stairs to my apartment and unlock the door. I haven't eaten all day and suddenly I realize that I am ravenously hungry, but I decide to take a quick look at Marcia first. I race to the Celestron, hoping against hope that she has decided against waiting until bedtime to put on the bra and panties. I press my eye to the sight, and I stare, and suddenly I emit a howl of rage.

She has pulled all her shades down!

Horrified, I turn the scope from her bedroom to the other rooms. In each of them the flimsy curtains have been pulled together and the shades have been drawn. I dial her on the phone to demand an explanation, and the operator tells me she has just changed to an unlisted number.

This is intolerable! All ties are broken, all vows unmade, and I race down the stairs and across the street. I know that the ungrateful, spiteful, back-stabbing bitch will never answer the doorbell, so I climb up the creaky wooden stairs to her back door. It is locked, but I break the window and reach my hand through and let myself in.

She is running from the bedroom when I get there but I

grab her by the arm (it doesn't feel anywhere near as soft as I had thought it would) and hurl her onto the bed.

"Who are you?" she blubbers, tears streaming down her face and mingling with her mascara. "I know you from somewhere! What do you want with me?"

"You can't treat me like this!" I scream. "Not after all we've meant to each other!"

"My God!" she says, her eyes suddenly going wide with horror. "You're that strange woman from the bookstore!"

I pull the knife from my purse.

"Slut!" I scream, and plunge it into her belly.

She howls in pain and spits blood.

"Cunt!" I rage, and stab her in the throat.

She tried to scream again, but it comes out as a wet gurgle.

"I loved you!" I say, burying the knife in her again and again. "We could have been so happy! Why did you have to spoil it? Why do all of you always have to spoil it?"

She doesn't say anything, of course. She is past saying anything ever again, and before I can mourn my lost love in private there is the body to be disposed of. I leave her apartment, return to my own, pick up a pair of plastic leaf bags and some masking tape, and pull my Volkswagen (a Beetle, twenty-three hundred dollars new, and *still* a great car) into the alley behind her building.

Then I go upstairs, slip one of the bags over her head and torso and the other over her legs, tape them together, hoist her over my shoulder, hobble back down to the alley, and place her in the trunk.

I drive to the local supermarket and pull around to the back, where they keep their huge metal dumpster, and I deposit her with all the other refuse and rubbish that will be picked up tomorrow morning.

I was worried the first time I did it, but human hands never touch the dumpster. The truck reaches out with its long mechanical arms and lifts the dumpster high in the air and turns it upside down, and since they never found Phyllis or Joan or Martha I know that they won't find Marcia either. The selfish, unfeeling slut will be crushed into a tiny compact cube along with the tin cans and broken crates and will be deposited in some foul-smelling hole in the ground and that will be that and no one will ever know what happened to her. (Though if she ever treated other lovers in the same high-handed, uncaring fashion, there will be some who at least can hazard a guess, who might even congratulate me if they knew.)

And if the police come by (though of course they never do) I will just look shocked and say yes, I had seen her on occasion. She seemed like kind of a cold fish, if you ask me.

Lovers?

I'll smile and shake my head and say no, not her, she just wasn't the type.

Besides, what would a gray-haired little old neighbor lady know about that?

Wednesday, July 6

I think I'm in love.

Her name is Sharon, and she's much more sensitive than Marcia. No trashy romance novels for her, oh no; she comes in at two on the dot every afternoon and goes right to the poetry section. She's polite and refined, and she has the longest, most beautiful legs I ever saw. (And I'll bet she doesn't have a gross ugly mole like Marcia did.)

Her breasts are high and firm and I just know that her nipples stand out proudly. I dreamed about her the last four nights in a row, and I thought I would go crazy when July 4 came on a weekday and we had to close the store. I spent most of the day standing across the street, hoping Sharon would pass by to look at our new window display. We can't be kept apart like this any longer. It just isn't fair.

I wonder if she has a Visa card?

Death Is an Acquired Trait

I have this bad habit. I sometimes fall in love with a title, and then I have to come up with a story to fit it. This one wasn't even my own title: it was a throwaway footnote in Woody Allen's hilarious collection of mock-literary essays, *Without Feathers.* The second I saw it in print I knew I had to write the story, and a year or two later, I did.

It appeared in *Argos,* an ambitious but short-lived fantasy magazine that featured one of my stories in every issue. (From which you may draw whatever conclusion you choose.)

Death Is an Acquired Trait

As things stand now, the 2043 Kentucky Derby is going to be won by Hi Falutin, which is a pretty silly name for a horse, but by the time his career is over it won't seem any sillier than Swaps or Tim Tam or Seattle Slew. He's going to win by a neck in two minutes one second flat on a fast track, and Barfly, who will finish third, will be disqualified and placed last for interfering with three other horses in the homestretch.

Exactly seven thousand one hundred and fifty-six years later, the star known as Antares will go nova.

And two million and three years after that, the first glimmerings of intelligence will be noticeable among the strange little mollusks that inhabit the tidal pools on the fourth planet of the star known as Spica.

I'd tell you my name, but you probably couldn't pronounce it and I probably wouldn't spell it the same way twice in a row—it changes a lot, you know (or maybe you *don't* know, which really isn't my problem anyway). I think I will tell you where I come from, though. It changes a lot too, but these days we're calling it Quiggle. Or maybe Quabble. Anyway, it's the sixth planet circling the star you know as Betelguese. Or, at least, it used to be. I don't think it's there anymore. Just as well. Seeing it would only depress me—especially the spot where I'm buried.

But now I'm getting a little ahead of myself.

Once upon a time I belonged to a race of humanoids that inhabited the sixth planet of Betelguese, which we used to call Proff in the old days. Also, I use the word "humanoids" only to give you a point of reference. Actually, I always thought we were more the human type, and that you guys were the humanoids. But why quibble? (Say, that's not bad! I think we'll call it Quibble starting next week.)

I lived during the golden age of my planet, although we called it the mauve age since gold wasn't all that hard to come by. Huge skyscrapers covered the surface of our fair world, except where there was water, in which cases enormous bubble-domed cities floated atop the mighty seas, plying their commerce between the many majestic continents.

In a matter of a few centuries we achieved space flight, converted all our appliances and factories to sunpower, eliminated completely and forever any taint of racial prejudice, outgrew all of our superstitious old religions, and began probing the secrets of the universe in earnest.

Unfortunately, all this took a little while to accomplish, especially the part about the secrets of the universe, and while our medical science had progressed far beyond anything you are ever going to achieve, we nonetheless aged and died, albeit at a far slower rate than any other life form in the galaxy.

Well, to cut through all the palaver, one of the secrets of the universe we sought to unlock was the secret of eternal life. We already had lifespans of more than a millennium, so that seemed the next logical step.

We tried injections, and freezing, and hypnosis, and DNA surgery (yes, we could operate on DNA molecules back then), and hormone injections, but nothing seemed to work.

Then one day Raxrgh Ghhouule—that's not his name any longer, but it's the one I curse all the time—came up with a solution to the problem that involved a little biochemistry, a little philosophy, a little physics, and a couple of other things that I couldn't even pronounce let alone spell. As a result of his experiments, we became completely free of our physical shells and became creatures of pure thought. Or maybe pure energy. I was never too clear on that point, though I don't imagine that it makes any difference at this late date. (And a late date it is: my body turned to dust almost eight billion years ago.)

At first we were utterly delighted with our new-found immortality. We retained our individuality, and while we could no longer see or hear or touch, we gained a whole plethora of new perceptive senses.

Of course, there were a few things that were lost forever. Like *crachhm*. You've never heard of it? Well, *crachhm* bears a strong resemblance to veal parmesan, only the spices are more subtle and the cheese is a more delightful color. Do you know what it's like to go almost eight billion years without a bite of *crachhm?*

Then there was my *krttz*. That's a collective noun for wife, but it means a little more, since I had four of them, one of each sex. Sex among the five of us was never all that easy or simple even when we had bodies; without them, it was absolutely impossible. Not only is it difficult to get very lustful over a creature of pure energy, but they appeared just like me. Even to think of sex with them in their new form seemed sort of perverted, if you know what I mean.

Well, after a while—a few million years or so—I began to feel less cheated. After all, I didn't have the wherewithal to eat or copulate anyway, so it became an exercise of mind over matter, or mind over the memory of matter, or something like that. Most of us had these initial problems, but we finally overcame them and turned our thoughts to more important matters.

We probed backward to the dawn of the universe, saw the Primal Atom take form, and extrapolated the life and death of every star, every planet, every species of sentient and non-sentient creature, and finally saw the universe come to a total standstill, completely in the thrall of entropy. Then, since the future has infinite permutations, we explored every possible future, based on every conceivable action that might be taken anywhere in the universe.

It was fascinating when we first did it, and it's still mildly interesting now, but you must realize our dilemma: once you've done the universe, there *is* nothing else.

That's when we began to get bored.

Oh, we fought against it. We explored parallel universes, examined an infinite number of dimensions, even probed back to the universe that existed before the formation of the Primal Atom. (It was a pretty dull one: no music, and only twenty-three elements.) It didn't help much; we were still bored.

So we began extrapolating entirely new universes, based at first upon logical premises, and, later, based on magic, alchemy, anything we could think of. I can remember extrapolating an entire galaxy based on the assumption that Donald Duck was God—and this was five billion years before Walt Disney was born.

But it was no use. Sooner or later, each and every one of us got bored.

I think Rilias Prannch was the first of us to suggest it, though the rest of us certainly had been toying with the notion: racial suicide. Ah, what a sweet thought, what a pleasant fancy!

I can still remember the instant that, like lemmings to the sea, we plunged into a nearby star, prepared to be sizzled to a cinder—and nothing happened, except that we found out what the inside of a star looks like.

Then old Klannenn Porbisht suggested turning off all our sensory perceptions . . . only no one knew how to do it.

I mean, it wasn't as if we had eyelids we could close or anything like that. It simply wouldn't work.

Finally, Robatt Xazzar tried to extrapolate a heaven and a hell so that we could determine how to gain admission to either. That was a failure, too.

So we turned our collective brainpower from all other aspects of existence and creation, and tried to figure out how to bring about our racial death.

We tried just about everything. We tried religion, we tried philosophy, we tried stretching ourselves so thin that we vanished, we exposed ourselves to every conceivable type of radiation. We visited planets where Death was worshipped and revered, and we observed nameless ceremonies in which the living were killed and the dead were made to live again. We pored over the libraries of galaxy after galaxy, and even sought an answer amongst the quasars and the quarks.

Our conclusion, after some three billion years of trying, was that suicide, while it may well have been a consummation devoutly to be wished, was still beyond our means.

This only served to spur us on to greater efforts. Every theory, every equation, every lemma, every prayer, every mystic chant, every hypothesis was examined, explored, analyzed, inverted, and built upon. Every universe co-existing with ours in different temporal planes, different vibratory rates, and different dimensions was visited and thoroughly ransacked for a solution, but none could be found.

So we went back to our other studies, but always, just beneath the surface of our examinations, was the ever-present desire to find a way to die. I remember that we finally got around to playing with Time, turning it inside-out and upside-down. Ostensibly these were just mental exercises, but each of us knew the real purpose of our endeavors: if we could just find a way to make Time flow backward to a point a few seconds before Raxrgh Ghhouule figured out how to free us from our mortal bodies, we might find a way to silence him and thus attain blessed oblivion.

But it was not to be. Time buckled here and there, yielded to this pressure and that, but ultimately we were forced to admit that we could not rend its fabric and return to that fateful moment.

Then one day little Plooka Pitzm—one of my own beloved *krrtz*—wasn't there anymore. We were at first disbelieving, then worried, and finally hopeful. Had she actually found a way to die? It was almost too good to be true—and indeed, it wasn't true at all. We found her, at last, in the odoriferous universe of Blimm (it's made primarily of old Munster cheese, and is three vibratory levels removed from this one), humming happily to herself. For a moment I feared that she had lost her mind, but she soon became aware of our collective presence and explained that, as bored as she was with existence in general, she was most especially bored with our company, and no longer wished to be associated with us.

What could we do but accede to her wishes? The problem was that soon many other members of my race decided to strike out for a solitary life, and this left even less of us to work on the problem of ending our existence, solitary or otherwise.

Then, suddenly, Pratsch Pratsch Pratsch (he certainly does like the sound of his name!) went stark staring mad. He began gibbering like an idiot, singing bawdy verses gathered from a trillion worlds, and muttering obscenities to himself, interspersing all this with maniacal giggling.

For a time we debated whether or not to cure him, and finally concluded that he would be far happier like this than returning to our unending boredom and sanity. Well, Pratsch Pratsch Pratsch ranted and raved for almost thirty-seven million years, when finally the madness ran its course and he became his old self again. It was then that we began to realize that even total insanity was at best a temporary oasis in this vast desert of boredom.

So that's where matters stand now. About half my race has decided to cut all ties with the remaining unit, and on any given day another tenth of us are quite mad (although, alas, only temporarily).

We still seek our demise, as a race or as individuals, but it seems less and less likely. After all, that's the problem with immortality: by definition, you *are* deathless.

My only pleasure now is to try to prevent other races from making the same horrible mistake we made. I think I've just saved the natives of Aldebaren XII from it, and hopefully I've hindered that chemist on Gamma Epsilon II enough that he'll never accomplish it either.

And so here I am, talking to you. You see, there's this kid in Omaha who's got a little jerry-built laboratory in his basement. He's got some dry cell batteries, and a few bread molds, and he seems to be on the right track. (It's not all that hard to do once you get the knack. Ask Raxrgh Ghhouule—he'll tell you.)

Anyway, this kid doesn't know what he's doing, but his sister is dating a grad student from the University of Nebraska, and this student's best friend is . . .

Well, you get the picture.

There is only one past; it is a fixed and immutable thing. But there are an infinite number of futures. In most of them the secret of immortality will be safe from you, but in some it won't be—and believe me, it's not worth the risk.

So step in front of an oncoming train, or find some painless but lethal narcotic, or stick your head in a gas oven.

I've seen your planet form, seen it go from a molten world to a thing of gossamer beauty. I've watched your race crawl out of the water, stand erect, sprout thumbs, conquer fire, invent the wheel, harness the atom. I couldn't love you more if you were my own children. I have only one wish for you.

Death and destruction.

That's a father's prayer.

The Crack in the Cosmic Egg

This is the only "hard science" idea I've ever had in my life, and I sold it to the late, lamented (by me, anyway) *Argos*.

To show you the high esteem in which I hold such things, I gave it all of 800 words.

The Crack in the Cosmic Egg

Once upon a time there was this Primal Atom, or Cosmic Egg, or YLEM, or whatever you want to call it.

And one day (though of course they didn't really have days back then) it blew up.

Hence the Universe.

And since the Universe will continue to expand for all eternity, that's just about all she wrote in the way of cosmic phenomena on the grand scale, right?

No such luck.

Yeah, I know what you're going to say: that Einstein was right and gravity is the glue that holds everything together (which isn't all that profound when you sit down and really start to think about it), and that the various stars and galaxies are so far-flung that there's no longer a sufficient gravitic force to pull them back together. Furthermore (I hear you say), there's simply not enough mass in the Universe to give any credence to the old expansion-contraction theory.

Well, let me tell you about that. Old Albert E. was right

about one hell of a lot of things—and he wasn't the first, either. In point of fact, he was the sixty-third to come up with a Special Theory of Relativity. I just keep mentioning him because he was the most recent to be proven painfully, tragically, terminally right.

Of course, in old Albert's case, he was just the theorist. The real culprit was Hector Apollo Throop.

Now, Throop wasn't really all that much of a theoretical mathematician, and as philosophers go he was pretty second-rate. It's doubtful that he ever truly understood Einstein, though it probably wouldn't have made much difference if he had.

What Throop set out to do was create a faster-than-light drive. Oh, it had been done before, here and elsewhere—sixty-two times, in fact, many of them quite by accident—but Throop had no way of knowing that. He just knew that he wanted to make a buck.

No major government would spring loose any funds for him—after all, Einstein had said that you couldn't go faster than the speed of light—but Throop found himself a little oil-rich Arab republic and sold them a bill of goods. He talked about international prestige, and full employment for a veritable army of semi-skilled workers, and the purity of science, and just about everything else he could think of except Einstein.

So he raised the funds, and he hired a bunch of scientific charlatans who knew even less about Einstein than he himself did, and he went to work—and damned if he didn't come up with a prototype model of a faster-than-light spaceship in something under three years.

Wild, huh?

Well, the really wild part came next: the ship actually worked.

Oh, it didn't exceed the speed of light. Einstein had said that it couldn't be done, and he was absolutely right.

But old Albert never did say that you couldn't *equal* the

speed of light. He simply pointed out the consequences of doing so.

And that was the kicker, the little bombshell buried deep inside good old $E = mc^2$. You know the part: as you approach the speed of light, your mass approaches infinity.

Well, when you *reach* the speed of light, your mass *reaches* infinity.

Now, just pause for a second and pretend you're Hector Apollo Throop and think about what that means, other than the fact that your cakes won't rise and your souffles will fall flat.

Gravity is an inherent property of mass. And, in the instant or two of cogency that remained to him just before he equaled the speed of light, Throop finally realized what effect the sudden creation of an infinite mass would have on an expanding Universe.

Except that it wasn't expanding anymore. All of its various parts were racing for Throop's ship as if Judgment Day was just around the corner.

Which indeed it was.

For the sixty-third time.

INTRODUCTION
Revolt of the Sugar Plum Fairies

It's a J. R. R. Tolkien memorial anthology, explained Marty Greenberg on the phone. Only you can't use any of Tolkien's characters.

Then how the hell am I supposed to write a Tolkien story, I asked.

Make it Tolkienesque, he said.

I don't even *like* Tolkien, I said.

It's the highest word-rate in the history of anthologies, said Marty. You'll think of something.

Never, I said. Count me out.

So a week later I was watching a re-release of *Fantasia,* and sure enough, I *did* think of something. Probably not the same serious-minded high-quality something that old J.R.R. himself would have thought of, but at least my Sugar Plum Fairies are small and cute and semi-cuddly.

Revolt of the Sugar Plum Fairies

Arthur Crumm didn't believe in leprechauns.

He didn't believe in centaurs, either.

He also didn't believe in ghosts or goblins or gorgons or anything else beginning with a G. Oh, and you can add H to the list; he didn't believe in harpies or hobbits, either.

In fact, you could write an awfully thick book about the things he didn't believe in. You'd have had to leave out only one item: the one about the Sugar Plum Fairies.

Them, he believed in.

Of course, he had no choice. He had a basement full of them. They were various shades of blue, none of them more than eighteen inches tall, and possessed of high, squeaky voices that would have driven his cats berserk if he had owned any cats. Their eyes were large and round, rather like they had been drawn by someone who specialized in painting children on black velvet, and their noses were small and pug, and each of them had a little pot belly, and they were dressed as if they were about to be presented to Queen Elizabeth. They looked cloyingly cute, and they made Mickey Mouse sound like a baritone—but they had murder on their minds.

They had been in Arthur's basement for less than an hour, but already he had managed to differentiate them, which was harder than you might think with a bunch of tiny blue fairies. There was Bluebell, who struck Arthur as the campus radical of the bunch. There was Indigo, with his Spanish accent, and old Silverthorne, the arch-conservative, and Purpletone, the politician, and Inkspot, who spoke jive like he had been born to it. Royal Blue seemed to be their leader, and there was also St. Looie Blues, standing off by himself playing a mournful if tiny saxophone.

"Well, I still don't understand how you guys got here," Arthur was saying.

Now, most men are not really inclined to sit on their basement stairs and converse with a bunch of Sugar Plum Fairies, but Arthur was a pragmatist. Their presence meant one of two things: either he was quite mad, or his house was infested with fairies. And since he didn't feel quite mad, he decided to assume that the latter was the case.

"I keep telling you: We came here by inter-dimensional quadrature," snapped Bluebell. "Open your ears, fathead!"

"That's no way to speak to our host," said Purpletone placatingly.

"Host, *schmost!*" snapped Bluebell. "If he was our host, he'd set us free. He's our captor."

"*I* didn't capture you," noted Arthur mildly. "I came down here and found you all stuck to the floor."

"That's because some of the Pepsi you stored leaked all over the floor," said Bluebell. "What kind of fiend stores defective pop bottles in his basement, anyway?"

"You could at least have carpeted the place," added Silverthorne. "It's not only sticky, it's *cold.*"

"Now set us free so we can take our grim and terrible vengeance," continued Bluebell.

"On *me?*" asked Arthur.

"You are an insignificant spear carrier in the pageant of our lives," said Royal Blue. "We have a higher calling."

"Right, man," chimed in Inkspot. "You let us free, maybe we don't mess you up, you dig?"

"It seems to me that if I *don't* let you free you won't mess me up, either," said Arthur.

"You see?" said Indigo furiously. "I tole you and I tole you: you can't trust Gringos!"

"If you don't like Gringos, why did you choose *my* basement?" asked Arthur.

"Well, uh, we didn't exactly *choose* it," said Royal Blue uneasily.

"Then how did you get here?"

"By inter-dimensional quadrature, dummy!" said Bluebell, who finally succeeded in removing his feet from his shoes, only to have them stick onto the floor right next to the empty shoes.

"So you keep saying," answered Arthur. "But it doesn't mean anything to me."

"So it's *my* fault that you're a scientific illiterate?" demanded Bluebell, grabbing his left foot and giving it a mighty tug to no avail.

"Try explaining it another way," suggested Arthur, as Bluebell made another unsuccessful attempt to move his feet.

"Let *me* try," said Silverthorne. He turned his head so that he was facing Arthur. "We activated the McLennon/ Whittaker Space-Time Displacement Theorem, but we didn't take the Helmhiser Variables or the Kobernykov Uncertainty Principle into account." He paused. "There. Does that help?"

"Not very much," admitted Arthur.

"What difference does it make?" said Royal Blue. "We're here, and that's all that matters."

"I'm still not clear why you're here at all," persisted Arthur.

"It's a matter of racial pride," answered Royal Blue with some dignity.

Arthur scratched his head. "You're proud of being stuck to the floor of my basement?"

"No, of course not," said old Silverthorne irritably. "We're here to defend our honor."

"How?"

"We've mapped out a campaign of pillage and destruction and vengeance," explained Royal Blue. "The entire world will tremble before us. Strong men will swoon, women and children will hide behind locked doors, even animals will scurry to get out of our path."

"A bunch of Sugar Plum Fairies who can't even get their feet unstuck from the floor?" said Arthur with a chuckle.

"Don't underestimate us," said Bluebell in his falsetto voice. "We Sugar Plum Fairies are tough dudes. We are capable of terrorizing entire communities." He grimaced. "Or we would be, if we could just get our feet free."

"And the seven of you are the advance guard?"

"What advance guard? We're the entire invasion force."

"An invasion force of just seven Sugar Plum Fairies?" repeated Arthur.

"Didn't you ever see *The Magnificent Seven?*" asked Royal Blue. "Yul Brynner didn't need more than seven gunslingers to tame that Mexican town."

"And Toshiro Mifune only needed seven swordsmen in *The Seven Samurai,*" chimed in Bluebell.

"Seven is obviously a mystical number of great spiritual power," said Purpletone.

"Besides, no one else would come," added Silverthorne.

"Has anyone thought to point out that you're neither seven swordsmen nor seven gunfighters?" asked Arthur. "You happen to be seven undersized, pot-bellied, and totally helpless fairies."

"Hey, baby," said Inkspot. "We may be small, but we're wiry."

"Yeah," added Indigo. "We sleet some throats, watch some feelthy videos, and then we go home."

"If we can figure out how to get there," added Silverthorne.

"We tried invading the world *your* way and look where it got us," said Bluebell irritably. "On the way home, we'll take the second star to the right."

"That's an old wives' tale," protested Purpletone.

"Yeah?" shot back Bluebell. "How would *you* do it?"

"Simple. You close your eyes, click your heels together three times, and say, 'There's no place like home,' " answered Purpletone. "Any fool knows that."

"Who are you calling a fool?" demanded Bluebell.

"Uh . . . I don't want to intrude on your argument," put in Arthur, "but I have a feeling that both of you are the victims of false doctrine."

"Okay, wise guy!" squeaked Bluebell. "How would *you* do it?"

Arthur shrugged. "I haven't the foggiest notion where you came from."

"From Sugar Plum Fairyland, of course! How dumb can you be?"

"Oh, I can be pretty dumb at times," conceded Arthur. "But I've never been dumb enough to get stuck to the floor of a basement in a strange world with no knowledge of how to get home."

"All right," admitted Bluebell grudgingly. "So we got a little problem here. Don't make a federal case out of it."

"Be sure and tell me when you have a *big* problem," said Arthur. "The mind boggles."

"You stop making fun of us, Gringo," said Indigo, "or we're gonna add you to the list."

"The list of people you plan to kill?"

"You got it, *hombre.*"

"Just out of curiosity, how long *is* this list?" asked Arthur.

"Well," said Royal Blue, "so far, at a rough count, an estimate, so to speak, it comes to three."

"Who are they?" asked Arthur curiously.

"Number One on our hit list is Walt Disney," said Royal Blue firmly.

"And the other two?"

"That choreographer—what was his name?—oh, yeah: Balanchine. And the Russian composer, Tchaikovsky."

"What did they ever do to you?" asked Arthur.

"They made us laughing stocks," said Bluebell. "Disney made us cute and cuddly in *Fantasia,* and Balanchine had us dancing on our tippy-toes in *The Nutcracker.* How are we expected to discipline our kids with an image like that? Our women giggle at us when they should be swooning. Our children talk back to us. Our enemies pay absolutely no attention when we lay siege to their cities." The little fairy paused for breath. "We *warned* that Russkie what would happen if he didn't change it to the *'March* of the Sugar Plum Fairy.' Now we're going to make him pay!"

"I don't know how to lay this on you," said Arthur, "but all three of them are dead."

St. Looie Blues immediately began playing a jazz version of "Happy Days Are Here Again" on his saxophone.

"Stop that!" squeaked Bluebell furiously.

"Whassa matter, man?" asked St. Looie Blues.

"This is nothing to celebrate! We've been robbed of our just and terrible vengeance!"

"If they were all the size of this here dude," said St. Looie Blues, indicating Arthur, "you wasn't gonna be able to do much more than bite each of 'em on the great toe, anyway." He went back to playing his instrument.

"Well, what are we going to do?" asked Bluebell in a plaintive whine. "We can't have come all this way for nothing!"

"Maybe we could kill each of their firstborn sons," suggested Purpletone. "It's got a nice religious flavor to it."

"Maybe we should just go home," said Royal Blue.

"Never!" said Bluebell. "They still perform the ballet,

they still listen to the symphony, they still show the movie!"

"In 70 millimeters, these days," added Arthur helpfully.

"But how can we stop them?" asked Royal Blue.

"I suppose we'll have to kill every musician and dancer on this world, and destroy all the prints of the movie," said Silverthorne.

"Right!" said Bluebell. "Let's go!"

Nobody moved.

"Arthur, old friend," said Purpletone. "I wonder if we could appeal to you, as one of the potential survivors of our forthcoming bloody war of conquest, to get us unstuck."

Arthur sighed. "I don't think so."

"Why not?" asked Royal Blue. "We've told you everything you want to know, and *you're* not on our hit list."

"It would be murder."

"Definitions change when you're in a state of war," responded Purpletone. "We don't consider ourselves to be murderers."

Arthur shook his head. "You don't understand. *They* would murder *you.*"

"Preposterous!" squeaked Bluebell.

"Ridiculous," added Silverthorne.

"Do you have any weapons?" asked Arthur.

"No," admitted Bluebell. "But we've got a lot of gumption. We fear absolutely nothing."

"Well, that's not entirely true," said Purpletone after a moment's consideration. "Personally, I'm scared to death of banshees, moat monsters, and high cholesterol levels."

"*I'm* terrified of heights," added Royal Blue. "And I don't like the dark very much, either."

Soon all of the Sugar Plum Fairies were making long lists of things that frightened them.

"Well, some of us are hardly afraid of anything, with certain exceptions," amended Bluebell weakly. "And the rest can be bold and daring under rigidly defined conditions."

"If I were you, I'd pack it in and go home," said Arthur.

"If he's reporting us to the authorities, I'm gonna give him such a kick on the shin . . . " said Bluebell.

Suddenly Arthur appeared at the head of the stairs with a large box in his hands.

"I got tired of listening to you squabble," he said, carrying the box down to the basement.

"What's that for?" asked Royal Blue, nervously pointing to the box.

"Get in," said Arthur, starting to pry them loose from the floor.

"All of us?"

Arthur nodded.

"Why?"

"I'm shipping you to the Disney corporate offices," answered Arthur. "Once you're there, you're on your own."

"Great!" cried Royal Blue. "Now we can wreak havoc amongst our enemies and redeem the honor of our race."

"Or at least get a couple of gigs at Disneyland," added St. Looie Blues.

It was two weeks later that Arthur Crumm returned home from work, a bag of groceries in his arms, and found the seven Sugar Plum Fairies perched on various pieces of furniture in his living room.

Bluebell was wearing sunglasses and a set of gold chains. Indigo was smoking a cigar that was at least as long as he was. Silverthorne had a small diamond tiepin pierced through his left ear. St. Looie Blues had traded in his saxophone for a tiny music synthesizer. The others also displayed telltale signs of their recent excursion to the West Coast.

"How the hell did you get in here?" said Arthur.

"United Parcel got us to the front door," answered Royal Blue. "We took care of the rest. I hope you don't mind."

"I suppose not," said Arthur, setting down his bag. "You're looking . . . ah . . . well."

"We're *doing* well," said Royal Blue. "And we owe it all to you, Arthur."

"So you really managed to stop distribution of *Fantasia?*"

"Oh, *that,*" said Bluebell with a contemptuous shrug. "We found out that we were meant for better things."

"Oh? I thought your goal was to destroy every last print of the film."

"That was before we learned to work their computer," answered Bluebell. "Arthur, do you know how much money that film makes year in and year out?"

"Lots," guessed Arthur.

" 'Lots' is an understatement," said Royal Blue. "The damned thing's a gold mine, Arthur—and there's a new generation of moviegoers ever couple of years."

"Okay, so you didn't destroy the prints," said Arthur. "What *did* you do?"

"We bought a controlling interest in Disney!" said Bluebell proudly.

"You did *what?*"

"Disney," repeated Bluebell. "We own it now. We're going to be manufacturing Sugar Plum Fairy dolls, Sugar Plum Fairy t-shirts, Sugar Plum Fairy breakfast cereals . . . "

"Carnage and pillage are all very well in their place," explained Purpletone. "But *marketing,* Arthur—that's where the *real* power lies!"

"How did you manage to afford it?" asked Arthur curiously.

"We're not very good at inter-dimensional quadrature," explained Royal Blue, "but we found that we have a real knack for computers. We simply manipulated the stock market—buying the New York City Ballet and all the rights to Balanchine's notes in the process—and when we had enough money, we sold Xerox short, took a straddle on Polaroid, and bought Disney on margin." He looked incredibly pleased with himself. "Nothing to it."

"And what about Tchaikovsky?"

"We can't stop people from listening," replied Bluebell, "but we now own a piece of every major recording company in America, England, and the Soviet Union. We'll have the distribution channels tied up in another three weeks' time." He paused. "Computers are *fun!*"

"So are you going back to Sugar Plum Fairyland now?" asked Arthur.

"Certainly not!" said Royal Blue. "Anyone can be a Sugar Plum Fairy. It takes a certain innate skill and nobility to be a successful corporate raider, to properly interpret price-earnings ratios and find hidden assets, to strike at just the proper moment and bring your enemy to his financial knees."

"I suppose it does."

"Especially when you're handicapped the way we are," continued Royal Blue. "We can't very well address corporate meetings, we can't use a telephone that's more than twenty inches above the floor, we can only travel in U.P.S. packages . . ."

"We don't even have a mailing address," added Purpletone.

"The biggest problem, though," said Bluebell, "is that none of us has a social security number or a taxpayer ID. That means that the Internal Revenue Service will try to impound all our assets at the end of the fiscal year."

"To say nothing of what the S.E.C. will do," put in Silverthorne mournfully.

"You don't say," mused Arthur.

"We do say," replied Bluebell. "In fact, we just did."

"Then perhaps you'll be amenable to a suggestion . . ."

Three days later Arthur Crumm & Associates bought a seat on the New York Stock Exchange, and they added a seat on the AmEx within a month.

To this day nobody knows very much about them, except that they're a small, closely-held investment company, they turn a truly remarkable annual profit, and they recently expanded into Sugar Plum Fairy theme parks and motion picture production. In fact, it's rumored that they've signed Sylvester Stallone, Arnold Schwarzenegger, and Madonna to star in *Fantasia II*.

For I Have Touched
the Sky

This is one of the two best stories I've written. It occurred to me during a 1987 trip to Kenya. Until that point, all I'd ever gotten out of Africa were ideas for novels—but I had just completed "Kirinyaga" a few weeks earlier, and suddenly, everywhere I looked, there were more Kirinyaga stories begging to be written. I had this one titled and plotted before I'd been there for two days, started writing it the night I got home, finished it the next evening, and sent it off to Ed Ferman, who snapped it up for *The Magazine of Fantasy and Science Fiction.*

(For reasons that are too complex to explain here, and have nothing to do with my lasting friendship with Ed Ferman, all future Kirinyaga stories have appeared in *Isaac Asimov's Science Fiction Magazine.* Just in case you decide to go looking for them.)

Anyway, "For I Have Touched the Sky" was nominated for the Nebula and the Hugo for Best Novelette, won a Japanese award, won a few readers' polls, and has been reprinted even more often than its Hugo-winning predecessor.

For I Have Touched the Sky

There was a time when men had wings.

Ngai, who sits alone on His throne atop Kirinyaga, which is now called Mount Kenya, gave men the gift of flight, so that they might reach the succulent fruits on the highest branches of the trees. But one man, a son of Gikuyu, who was himself the first man, saw the eagle and the vulture riding high upon the winds, and spreading his wings, he joined them. He circled higher and higher, and soon he soared far above all other flying things.

Then, suddenly, the hand of Ngai reached out and grabbed the son of Gikuyu.

"What have I done that you should grab me thus?" asked the son of Gikuyu.

"I live atop Kirinyaga because it is the top of the world," answered Ngai, "and no one's head may be higher than my own."

And so saying, Ngai plucked the wings from the son of Gikuyu, and then took the wings away from *all* men, so that no man could ever again rise higher than His head.

And that is why all of Gikuyu's descendants look at the birds with a sense of loss and envy, and why they no longer eat the succulent fruits from the highest branches of the trees.

We have many birds on the world of Kirinyaga, which was named for the holy mountain where Ngai dwells. We brought them along with our other animals when we received our charter from the Eutopian Council and departed from a Kenya that no longer had any meaning for true members of the Kikuyu tribe. Our new world is home to the maribou and the vulture, the ostrich and the fish eagle, the weaver and the heron, and many other species. Even I, Koriba, who am the *mundumugu*—the witch doctor—delight in their many colors, and find solace in their music. I have spent many afternoons seated in front of my *boma,* my back propped up against an ancient acacia tree, watching the profusion of colors and listening to the melodic songs as the birds come to slake their thirst in the river that winds through our village.

It was on one such afternoon that Kamari, a young girl who was not yet of circumcision age, walked up the long, winding path that separates my *boma* from the village, holding something small and gray in her hands.

"*Jambo,* Koriba," she greeted me.

"*Jambo,* Kamari," I answered her. "What have you brought to me, child?"

"This," she said, holding out a young pygmy falcon that struggled weakly to escape her grasp. "I found him in my family's *shamba.* He cannot fly."

"He looks fully-fledged," I noted, getting to my feet. Then I saw that one of his wings was held at an awkward angle. "Ah!" I said. "He has broken his wing."

"Can you make him well, *mundumugu?*" asked Kamari.

I examined the wing briefly, while she held the young falcon's head away from me. Then I stepped back.

"I can make him well, Kamari," I said. "But I cannot make him fly. The wing will heal, but it will never be strong enough to bear his weight again. I think we will destroy him."

"No!" she exclaimed, pulling the falcon back. "You will make him live, and I will care for him!"

I stared at the bird for a moment, then shook my head. "He will not wish to live," I said at last.

"Why not?"

"Because he has ridden high upon the warm winds."

"I do not understand," said Kamari, frowning.

"Once a bird has touched the sky," I explained, "he can never be content to spend his days on the ground."

"I will *make* him content," she said with determination. "You will heal him and I will care for him, and he will live."

"I will heal him and you will care for him," I said. "But," I added, "he will not live."

"What is your fee, Koriba?" she asked, suddenly businesslike.

"I do not charge children," I answered. "I will visit your father tomorrow, and he will pay me."

She shook her head adamantly. "This is *my* bird. *I* will pay the fee."

"Very well," I said, admiring her spirit, for most children—and *all* adults—are terrified of their *mundumugu,* and would never openly contradict or disagree with him. "For one month you will clean my *boma* every morning and every afternoon. You will lay out my sleeping blankets, and keep my water gourd filled, and you will see that I have kindling for my fire."

"That is fair," she said after a moment's consideration. Then she added: "What if the bird dies before the month is over?"

"Then you will learn that a *mundumugu* knows more than a little Kikuyu girl," I said.

She set her jaw. "He will not die." She paused. "Will you fix his wing now?"

"Yes."

"I will help."

I shook my head. "You will build a cage in which to confine him, for if he tries to move his wing too soon, he will break it again and then I will surely have to destroy him."

She handed the bird to me. "I will be back soon," she promised, racing off toward her *shamba.*

I took the falcon into my hut. He was too weak to struggle very much, and he allowed me to tie his beak shut. Then I began the slow task of splinting his broken wing and binding it against his body to keep it motionless. He shrieked in pain as I manipulated the bones together, but otherwise he simply stared unblinking at me, and within ten minutes the job was finished.

Kamari returned an hour later, holding a small wooden cage in her hands.

"Is this large enough, Koriba?" she asked.

I held it up and examined it.

"It is almost too large," I replied. "He must not be able to move his wing until it has healed."

"He won't," she promised. "I will watch him all day long, every day."

"You will watch him all day long, every day?" I repeated, amused.

"Yes."

"Then who will clean my hut and my *boma,* and who will fill my gourd with water?"

"I will carry his cage with me when I come," she replied.

"The cage will be much heavier when the bird is in it," I pointed out.

"When I am a woman, I will carry far heavier loads on my back, for I shall have to till the fields and gather the firewood for my husband's *boma,"* she said. "This will be good practice." She paused. "Why do you smile at me, Koriba?"

"I am not used to being lectured to by uncircumcised children," I replied with a smile.

"I was not lecturing," she answered with dignity. "I was *explaining.*"

I held a hand up to shade my eyes from the afternoon sun.

"Are you not afraid of me, little Kamari?" I asked.

"Why should I be?"

"Because I am the *mundumugu.*"

"That just means you are smarter than the others," she said with a shrug. She threw a stone at a chicken that was approaching her cage, and it raced away, squawking its annoyance. "Someday I shall be as smart as you are."

"Oh?"

She nodded confidently. "Already I can count higher than my father, and I can remember many things."

"What kind of things?" I asked, turning slightly as a hot breeze blew a swirl of dust about us.

"Do you remember the story of the honey bird that you told to the children of the village before the long rains?"

I nodded.

"I can repeat it," she said.

"You mean you can remember it."

She shook her head vigorously. "I can repeat every word that you said."

I sat down and crossed my legs. "Let me hear," I said, staring off into the distance and idly watching a pair of young men tending their cattle.

She hunched her shoulders, so that she would appear as bent with age as I myself am, and then, in a voice that sounded like a youthful replica of my own, she began to speak, mimicking my gestures.

"There is a little brown honey bird," she began. "He is very much like a sparrow, and as friendly. He will come to your *boma* and call to you, and as you approach him he will fly up and lead you to a hive, and then wait while you gather grass and set fire to it and smoke out the bees. But you must *always*"—she emphasized the word, just as I had done—

"leave some honey for him, for if you take it all, the next time he will lead you into the jaws of *fisi,* the hyena, or perhaps into the desert where there is no water and you will die of thirst." Her story finished, she stood upright and smiled at me. "You see?" she said proudly.

"I see," I said, brushing away a large fly that had lit on my cheek.

"Did I do it right?" she asked.

"You did it right."

She stared at me thoughtfully. "Perhaps when you die, I will become the *mundumugu.*"

"Do I seem that close to death?" I asked.

"Well," she answered, "you are very old and bent and wrinkled, and you sleep too much. But I will be just as happy if you do not die right away."

"I shall try to make you just as happy," I said ironically. "Now take your falcon home."

I was about to instruct her concerning his needs, but she spoke first.

"He will not want to eat today. But starting tomorrow, I will give him large insects, and at least one lizard every day. And he must always have water."

"You are very observant, Kamari."

She smiled at me again, and then ran off toward her *boma.*

She was back at dawn the next morning, carrying the cage with her. She placed it in the shade, then filled a small container with water from one of my gourds and set it inside the cage.

"How is your bird this morning?" I asked, sitting close to my fire, for even though the planetary engineers of the Eutopian Council had given Kirinyaga a climate identical to Kenya's, the sun had not yet warmed the morning air.

Kamari frowned. "He has not eaten yet."

"He will, when he gets hungry enough," I said, pulling

my blanket more tightly around my shoulders. "He is used to swooping down on his prey from the sky."

"He drinks his water, though," she noted.

"That is a good sign."

"Can you not cast a spell that will heal him all at once?"

"The price would be too high," I said, for I had foreseen her question. "This way is better."

"How high?"

"*Too* high," I repeated, closing the subject. "Now, do you not have work to do?"

"Yes, Koriba."

She spent the next few minutes gathering kindling for my fire and filling my gourd from the river. Then she went into my hut to clean it and straighten my sleeping blankets. She emerged a moment later with a book in her hand.

"What is this, Koriba?" she asked.

"Who told you that you could touch your *mundumugu's* possessions?" I asked sternly.

"How can I clean them without touching them?" she replied with no show of fear. "What is it?"

"It is a book."

"What is a book, Koriba?"

"It is not for you to know," I said. "Put it back."

"Shall I tell you what I think it is?" she asked.

"Tell me," I said, curious to hear her answer.

"Do you know how you draw signs on the ground when you cast the bones to bring the rains? I think that a book is a collection of signs."

"You are a very bright little girl, Kamari."

"I *told* you that I was," she said, annoyed that I had not accepted her statement as a self-evident truth. She looked at the book for a moment, then held it up. "What do the signs mean?"

"Different things," I said.

"*What* things?"

"It is not necessary for the Kikuyu to know."

"But *you* know."

"I am the *mundumugu*."

"Can anyone else on Kirinyaga read the signs?"

"Your own chief, Koinnage, and two other chiefs can read the signs," I answered, sorry now that she had charmed me into this conversation, for I could foresee its direction.

"But you are all old men," she said. "You should teach me, so when you all die someone can read the signs."

"These signs are not important," I said. "They were created by the Europeans. The Kikuyu had no need for books before the Europeans came to Kenya; we have no need for them on Kirinyaga, which is our own world. When Koinnage and the other chiefs die, everything will be as it was long ago."

"Are they evil signs, then?" she asked.

"No," I said. "They are not evil. They just have no meaning for the Kikuyu. They are the white man's signs."

She handed the book to me. "Would you read me one of the signs?"

"Why?"

"I am curious to know what kind of signs the white men made."

I stared at her for a long minute, trying to make up my mind. Finally I nodded my assent.

"Just this once," I said. "Never again."

"Just this once," she agreed.

I thumbed through the book, which was a Swahili translation of Victorian poetry, selected one at random, and read it to her:

> *Live with me, and be my love,*
> *And we will all the pleasures prove*
> *That hills and valleys, dales and fields,*
> *And all the craggy mountains yields.*
> *There will we sit upon the rocks,*
> *And see the shepherds feed their flocks,*

By shallow rivers, by whose falls
Melodious birds sing madrigals.
There will I make thee a bed of roses,
With a thousand fragrant posies,
A cap of flowers, and a kirtle
Embroider'd all with leaves of myrtle.
A bed of straw and ivy buds,
With coral clasps and amber studs;
And if these pleasures may thee move,
Then live with me and be my love.

Kamari frowned. "I do not understand."

"I told you that you would not," I said. "Now put the book away and finish cleaning my hut. You must still work in your father's *shamba,* along with your duties here."

She nodded and disappeared into my hut, only to burst forth excitedly a few minutes later.

"It is a *story!"* she exclaimed.

"What is?"

"The sign you read! I do not understand many of the words, but it is a story about a warrior who asks a maiden to marry him!" She paused. "*You* would tell it better, Koriba. The sign doesn't even mention *fisi,* the hyena, and *mamba,* the crocodile, who dwell by the river and would eat the warrior and his wife. Still, it is a story! I had thought it would be a spell for *mundumugus.*"

"You are very wise to know that it is a story," I said.

"Read another to me!" she said enthusiastically.

I shook my head. "Do you not remember our agreement? Just that once, and never again."

She lowered her head in thought, then looked up brightly. "Then teach *me* to read the signs."

"That is against the law of the Kikuyu," I said. "No woman is permitted to read."

"Why?"

"It is a woman's duty to till the fields and pound the

grain and make the fires and weave the fabrics and bear her husband's children," I answered.

"But I am not a woman," she pointed out. "I am just a little girl."

"But you will become a woman," I said, "and a woman may not read."

"Teach me now, and I will forget how when I become a woman."

"Does the eagle forget how to fly, or the hyena to kill?"

"It is not fair."

"No," I said. "But it is just."

"I do not understand."

"Then I will explain it to you," I said. "Sit down, Kamari."

She sat down on the dirt opposite me and leaned forward intently.

"Many years ago," I began, "the Kikuyu lived in the shadow of Kirinyaga, the mountain upon which Ngai dwells."

"I know," she said. "Then the Europeans came and built their cities."

"You are interrupting," I said.

"I am sorry, Koriba," she answered. "But I already know this story."

"You do not know all of it," I replied. "Before the Europeans came, we lived in harmony with the land. We tended our cattle and plowed our fields, we produced just enough children to replace those who died of old age and disease, and those who died in our wars against the Masai and the Wakamba and the Nandi. Our lives were simple but fulfilling."

"And *then* the Europeans came!" she said.

"Then the Europeans came," I agreed, "and they brought new ways with them."

"Evil ways."

I shook my head. "They were not evil ways for the

Europeans," I replied. "I know, for I have studied in European schools. But they were not good ways for the Kikuyu and the Masai and the Wakamba and the Embu and the Kisi and all the other tribes. We saw the clothes they wore and the buildings they erected and the machines they used, and we tried to become like Europeans. But we are not Europeans, and their ways are not our ways, and they do not work for us. Our cities became overcrowded and polluted, and our land grew barren, and our animals died, and our water became poisoned, and finally, when the Eutopian Council allowed us to move to the world of Kirinyaga, we left Kenya behind and came here to live according to the old ways, the ways that are good for the Kikuyu." I paused. "Long ago the Kikuyu had no written language, and did not know how to read, and since we are trying to create a Kikuyu world here on Kirinyaga, it is only fitting that our people do not learn to read or write."

"But what is good about not knowing how to read?" she asked. "Just because we didn't do it before the Europeans came doesn't make it bad."

"Reading will make you aware of other ways of thinking and living, and then you will be discontented with your life on Kirinyaga."

"But *you* read, and you are not discontented."

"I am the *mundumugu,*" I said. "I am wise enough to know that what I read are lies."

"But lies are not always bad," she persisted. "You tell them all the time."

"The *mundumugu* does not lie to his people," I replied sternly.

"You call them stories, like the story of the Lion and the Hare, or the tale of how the rainbow came to be, but they are lies."

"They are parables," I said.

"What is a parable?"

"A type of story."

"Is it a true story?"

"In a way."

"If it is true in a way, then it is also a lie in a way, is it not?" she replied, and then continued before I could answer her. "And if I can listen to a lie, why can I not read one?"

"I have already explained it to you."

"It is not fair," she repeated.

"No," I agreed. "But it is true, and in the long run it is for the good of the Kikuyu."

"I still don't understand why it is good," she complained.

"Because we are all that remain. Once before the Kikuyu tried to become something that they were not, and we became not city-dwelling Kikuyu, or bad Kikuyu, or unhappy Kikuyu, but an entirely new tribe called Kenyans. Those of us who came to Kirinyaga came here to preserve the old ways— and if women start reading, some of them will become discontented, and they will leave, and then one day there will be no Kikuyu left."

"But I don't want to leave Kirinyaga!" she protested. "I want to become circumcised, and bear many children for my husband, and till the fields of his *shamba,* and someday be cared for by my grandchildren."

"That is the way you are supposed to feel."

"But I also want to read about other worlds and other times."

I shook my head. "No."

"But—"

"I will hear no more of this today," I said. "The sun grows high in the sky, and you have not yet finished your tasks here, and you must still work in your father's *shamba* and come back again this afternoon."

She arose without another word and went about her duties. When she finished, she picked up the cage and began walking back to her *boma.*

I watched her walk away, then returned to my hut and activated my computer to discuss a minor orbital adjustment with Maintenance, for it had been hot and dry for almost a month. They gave their consent, and a few moments later I walked down the long winding path into the center of the village. Lowering myself gently to the ground, I spread my pouchful of bones and charms out before me and invoked Ngai to cool Kirinyaga with a mild rain, which Maintenance had agreed to supply later in the afternoon.

Then the children gathered about me, as they always did when I came down from my *boma* on the hill and entered the village.

"*Jambo,* Koriba!" they cried.

"*Jambo,* my brave young warriors," I replied, still seated on the ground.

"Why have you come to the village this morning, Koriba?" asked Ndemi, the boldest of the young boys.

"I have come here to ask Ngai to water our fields with His tears of compassion," I said, "for we have had no rain this month, and the crops are thirsty."

"Now that you have finished speaking to Ngai, will you tell us a story?" asked Ndemi.

I looked up at the sun, estimating the time of day.

"I have time for just one," I replied. "Then I must walk through the fields and place new charms on the scarecrows, that they may continue to protect your crops."

"What story will you tell us, Koriba?" asked another of the boys.

I looked around, and saw that Kamari was standing among the girls.

"I think I shall tell you the story of the Leopard and the Shrike," I said.

"I have not heard that one before," said Ndemi.

"Am I such an old man that I have no new stories to tell?" I demanded, and he dropped his gaze to the ground. I waited until I had everyone's attention, and then I began:

"Once there was a very bright young shrike, and because

he was very bright, he was always asking questions of his father.

" 'Why do we eat insects?' he asked one day.

" 'Because we are shrikes, and that is what shrikes do,' answered his father.

" 'But we are also birds,' said the shrike. 'And do not birds such as the eagle eat fish?'

" 'Ngai did not mean for shrikes to eat fish,' said his father, 'and even if you were strong enough to catch and kill a fish, eating it would make you sick."

" 'Have you ever eaten a fish?' asked the young shrike.

" 'No,' said his father.

" 'Then how do you know?' said the young shrike, and that afternoon he flew over the river, and found a tiny fish. He caught it and ate it, and he was sick for a whole week.

" 'Have you learned your lesson now?' asked the shrike's father, when the young shrike was well again.

" 'I have learned not to eat fish,' said the shrike. 'But I have another question.'

" 'What is your question?' asked his father.

" 'Why are shrikes the most cowardly of birds?' asked the shrike. 'Whenever the lion or the leopard appears, we flee to the highest branches of the trees and wait for them to go away.'

" 'Lions and leopards would eat us if they could,' said the shrike's father. 'Therefore, we must flee from them.'

" 'But they do not eat the ostrich, and the ostrich is a bird,' said the bright young shrike. 'If they attack the ostrich, he kills them with his kick.'

" 'You are not an ostrich,' said his father, tired of listening to him.

" 'But I am a bird, and the ostrich is a bird, and I will learn to kick as the ostrich kicks,' said the young shrike, and he spent the next week practicing kicking any insects and twigs that were in his way.

"Then one day he came across *chui,* the leopard, and as

the leopard approached him, the bright young shrike did not fly to the highest branches of the tree, but bravely stood his ground.

" 'You have great courage to face me thus,' said the leopard.

" 'I am a very bright bird, and I not afraid of you,' said the shrike. 'I have practiced kicking as the ostrich does, and if you come any closer, I will kick you and you will die.'

" 'I am an old leopard, and cannot hunt any longer,' said the leopard. 'I am ready to die. Come kick me, and put me out of my misery.'

"The young shrike walked up to the leopard and kicked him full in the face. The leopard simply laughed, opened his mouth, and swallowed the bright young shrike.

" 'What a silly bird,' laughed the leopard, 'to pretend to be something that he was not! If he had flown away like a shrike, I would have gone hungry today—but by trying to be what he was never meant to be, all he did was fill my stomach. I guess he was not a very bright bird after all.' "

I stopped and stared straight at Kamari.

"Is that the end?" asked one of the other girls.

"That is the end," I said.

"Why did the shrike think he could be an ostrich?" asked one of the smaller boys.

"Perhaps Kamari can tell you," I said.

All the children turned to Kamari, who paused for a moment and then answered.

"There is a difference between wanting to be an ostrich, and wanting to know what an ostrich knows," she said, looking directly into my eyes. "It was not wrong for the shrike to want to know things. It was wrong for him to think he could become an ostrich."

There was a momentary silence while the children considered her answer.

"Is that true, Koriba?" asked Ndemi at last.

"No," I said, "for once the shrike knew what the ostrich

knew, it forgot that it was a shrike. You must always remember who you are, and knowing too many things can make you forget."

"Will you tell us another story?" asked a young girl.

"Not this morning," I said, getting to my feet. "But when I come to the village tonight to drink *pombe* and watch the dancing, perhaps I will tell you the story about the bull elephant and the wise little Kikuyu boy. Now," I added, "do none of you have chores to do?"

The children dispersed, returning to their *shambas* and their cattle pastures, and I stopped by Juma's hut to give him an ointment for his joints, which always bothered him just before it rained. I visited Koinnage and drank *pombe* with him, and then discussed the affairs of the village with the Council of Elders. Finally I returned to my own *boma,* for I always take a nap during the heat of the day, and the rain was not due for another few hours.

Kamari was there when I arrived. She had gathered more wood and water, and was filling the grain buckets for my goats as I entered my *boma.*

"How is your bird this afternoon?" I asked, looking at the pygmy falcon, whose cage had been carefully placed in the shade of my hut.

"He drinks, but he will not eat," she said in worried tones. "He spends all his time looking at the sky."

"There are things that are more important to him than eating," I said.

"I am finished now," she said. "May I go home, Koriba?"

I nodded, and she left as I was arranging my sleeping blanket inside my hut.

She came every morning and every afternoon for the next week. Then, on the eighth day, she announced with tears in her eyes that the pygmy falcon had died.

"I told you that this would happen," I said gently. "Once

a bird has ridden upon the winds, he cannot live on the ground."

"Do all birds die when they can no longer fly?" she asked.

"Most do," I said. "A few like the security of the cage, but most die of broken hearts, for having touched the sky they cannot bear to lose the gift of flight."

"Why do we make cages, then, if they do not make the birds feel better?"

"Because they make *us* feel better," I answered.

She paused, and then said: "I will keep my word and clean your hut and your *boma,* and fetch your water and kindling, even though the bird is dead."

I nodded. "That was our agreement," I said.

True to her word, she came back twice a day for the next three weeks. Then, at noon on the twenty-ninth day, after she had completed her morning chores and returned to her family's *shamba,* her father, Njoro, walked up the path to my *boma.*

"*Jambo,* Koriba," he greeted me, a worried expression on his face.

"*Jambo,* Njoro," I said without getting to my feet. "Why have you come to my *boma?*"

"I am a poor man, Koriba," he said, squatting down next to me. "I have only one wife, and she has produced no sons and only two daughters. I do not own as large a *shamba* as most men in the village, and the hyenas killed three of my cows this past year."

I could not understand his point, so I merely stared at him, waiting for him to continue.

"As poor as I am," he went on, "I took comfort in the thought that at least I would have the bride prices from my two daughters in my old age." He paused. "I have been a good man, Koriba. Surely I deserve that much."

"I have not said otherwise," I replied.

"Then why are you training Kamari to be a *mun-*

dumugu?'' he demanded. "It is well known that the *mundumugu* never marries."

"Has Kamari told you that she is to become a *mundumugu?''* I asked.

He shook his head. "No. She does not speak to her mother or myself at all since she has been coming here to clean your *boma.''*

"Then you are mistaken," I said. "No woman may be a *mundumugu.* What made you think that I am training her?"

He dug into the folds of his *kikoi* and withdrew a piece of cured wildebeest hide. Scrawled on it in charcoal was the following inscription:

I AM KAMARI

I AM TWELVE YEARS OLD

I AM A GIRL

"This is writing," he said accusingly. "Women cannot write. Only the *mundumugu* and great chiefs like Koinnage can write."

"Leave this with me, Njoro," I said, taking the hide, "and send Kamari to my *boma.''*

"I need her to work on my *shamba* until this afternoon."

"Now," I said.

He sighed and nodded. "I will send her, Koriba." He paused. "You are certain that she is not to be a *mundumugu?''*

"You have my word," I said, spitting on my hands to show my sincerity.

He seemed relieved, and went off to his *boma.* Kamari came up the path a few minutes later.

"*Jambo,* Koriba," she said.

"*Jambo,* Kamari," I replied. "I am very displeased with you."

"Did I not gather enough kindling this morning?" she asked.

"You gathered enough kindling."

"Were the gourds not filled with water?"

"The gourds were filled."

"Then what did I do wrong?" she asked, absently pushing one of my goats aside as it approached her.

"You broke your promise to me."

"That is not true," she said. "I have come every morning and every afternoon, even though the bird is dead."

"You promised not to look at another book," I said.

"I have not looked at another book since the day you told me that I was forbidden to."

"Then explain *this,*" I said, holding up the hide with her writing on it.

"There is nothing to explain," she said with a shrug. "I wrote it."

"And if you have not looked at books, how did you learn to write?" I demanded.

"From your magic box," she said. "You never told me not to look at *it.*"

"My magic box?" I said, frowning.

"The box that hums with life and has many colors."

"You mean my computer?" I said, surprised.

"Your magic box," she repeated.

"And it taught you how to read and write?"

"*I* taught me—but only a little," she said unhappily. "I am like the shrike in your story—I am not as bright as I thought. Reading and writing is very difficult."

"I told you that you must not learn to read," I said, resisting the urge to comment on her remarkable accomplishment, for she had clearly broken the law.

Kamari shook her head.

"You told me I must not look at your books," she replied stubbornly.

"I told you that women must not read," I said. "You have disobeyed me. For this you must be punished." I paused. "You will continue your chores here for three more months, and you must bring me two hares and two rodents, which you must catch yourself. Do you understand?"

"I understand."

"Now come into my hut with me, that you may understand one thing more."

She followed me into the hut.

"Computer," I said. "Activate."

"Activated," said the computer's mechanical voice.

"Computer, scan the hut and tell me who is here with me."

The lens of the computer's sensor glowed briefly.

"The girl, Kamari wa Njoro, is here with you," replied the computer.

"Will you recognize her if you see her again?"

"Yes."

"This is a Priority Order," I said. "Never again may you converse with Kamari wa Njoro verbally or in any known language."

"Understood and logged," said the computer.

"Deactivate." I turned to Kamari. "Do you understand what I have done, Kamari?"

"Yes," she said, "and it is not fair. I did not disobey you."

"It is the law that women may not read," I said, "and you have broken it. You will not break it again. Now go back to your *shamba.*"

She left, head held high, youthful back stiff with defiance, and I went about my duties, instructing the young boys on the decoration of their bodies for their forthcoming circumcision ceremony, casting a counterspell for old Siboki (for he had found hyena dung within his *shamba,* which is one of the surest signs of a *thahu,* or curse), instructing Maintenance to make another minor orbital adjustment that would bring cooler weather to the western plains.

By the time I returned to my hut for my afternoon nap,

Kamari had come and gone again, and everything was in order.

For the next two months, life in the village went its placid way. The crops were harvested, old Koinnage took another wife and we had a two-day festival with much dancing and *pombe*-drinking to celebrate the event, the short rains arrived on schedule, and three children were born to the village. Even the Eutopian Council, which had complained about our custom of leaving the old and the infirm out for the hyenas, left us completely alone. We found the lair of a family of hyenas and killed three whelps, then slew the mother when she returned. At each full moon I slaughtered a cow—not merely a goat, but a large, fat cow—to thank Ngai for His generosity, for truly He had graced Kirinyaga with abundance.

During this period I rarely saw Kamari. She came in the mornings when I was in the village, casting the bones to bring forth the weather, and she came in the afternoons when I was giving charms to the sick and conversing with the Elders—but I always knew she had been there, for my hut and my *boma* were immaculate, and I never lacked for water or kindling.

Then, on the afternoon after the second full moon, I returned to my *boma* after advising Koinnage about how he might best settle an argument over a disputed plot of land, and as I entered my hut I noticed that the computer screen was alive and glowing, covered with strange symbols. When I had taken my degrees in England and America I had learned English and French and Spanish, and of course I knew Kikuyu and Swahili, but these symbols represented no known language, nor, although they used numerals as well as letters and punctuation marks, were they mathematical formulas.

"Computer, I distinctly remember deactivating you this morning," I said, frowning. "Why does your screen glow with life?"

"Kamari activated me."

"And she forgot to deactivate you when she left?"

"That is correct."

"I thought as much," I said grimly. "Does she activate you every day?"

"Yes."

"Did I not give you a Priority Order never to communicate with her in any known language?" I said, puzzled.

"You did, Koriba."

"Can you then explain why you have disobeyed my directive?"

"I have not disobeyed your directive, Koriba," said the computer. "My programming makes me incapable of disobeying a Priority Order."

"Then what is this that I see upon your screen?"

"This is the Language of Kamari," replied the computer. "It is not among the 1,732 languages and dialects in my memory banks, and hence does not fall under the aegis of your directive."

"Did you create this language?"

"No, Koriba. Kamari created it."

"Did you assist her in any way?"

"No, Koriba, I did not."

"Is it a true language?" I asked. "Can you understand it?"

"It is a true language. I can understand it."

"If she were to ask you a question in the Language of Kamari, could you reply to it?"

"Yes, if the question were simple enough. It is a very limited language."

"And if that reply required you to translate the answer from a known language to the Language of Kamari, would doing so be contrary to my directive?"

"No, Koriba, it would not."

"Have you in fact answered questions put to you by Kamari?"

"Yes, Koriba, I have," replied the computer.

"I see," I said. "Stand by for a new directive."

"Waiting . . ."

I lowered my head in thought, contemplating the problem. That Kamari was brilliant and gifted was obvious: she had not only taught herself to read and write, but had actually created a coherent and logical language that the computer could understand and in which it could respond. I had given orders, and without directly disobeying them she had managed to circumvent them. She had no malice within her, and wanted only to learn, which in itself was an admirable goal. All that was on the one hand.

On the other hand was the threat to the social order we had labored so diligently to establish on Kirinyaga. Men and women knew their responsibilities and accepted them happily. Ngai had given the Masai the spear, and He had given the Wakamba the arrow, and He had given the Europeans the machine and the printing press, but to the Kikuyu He had given the digging-stick and the fertile land surrounding the sacred fig tree on the slopes of Kirinyaga.

Once before we had lived in harmony with the land, many long years ago. Then had come the printed word. It turned us first into slaves, and then into Christians, and then into soldiers and factory workers and mechanics and politicians, into everything that the Kikuyu were never meant to be. It had happened before; it could happen again.

We had come to the world of Kirinyaga to create a perfect Kikuyu society, a Kikuyu Utopia: could one gifted little girl carry within her the seeds of our destruction? I could not be sure, but it was a fact that gifted children grew up. They became Jesus, and Mohammed, and Jomo Kenyatta— but they also became Tippoo Tib, the greatest slaver of all, and Idi Amin, butcher of his own people. Or, more often, they became Friedrich Nietzsche and Karl Marx, brilliant men in their own right, but who influenced less brilliant, less capable men. Did I have the right to stand aside and hope that her influence upon our society would be benign when all history suggested that the opposite was more likely to be true?

My decision was painful, but it was not a difficult one.

"Computer," I said at last, "I have a new Priority Order that supersedes my previous directive. You are no longer allowed to communicate with Kamari under any circumstances whatsoever. Should she activate you, you are to tell her that Koriba has forbidden you to have any contact with her, and you are then to deactivate immediately. Do you understand?"

"Understood and logged."

"Good," I said. "Now deactivate."

When I returned from the village the next morning, I found my water gourds empty, my blanket unfolded, my *boma* filled with the dung of my goats.

The *mundumugu* is all-powerful among the Kikuyu, but he is not without compassion. I decided to forgive this childish display of temper, and so I did not visit Kamari's father, nor did I tell the other children to avoid her.

She did not come again in the afternoon. I know, because I waited beside my hut to explain my decision to her. Finally, when twilight came, I sent for the boy, Ndemi, to fill my gourds and clean my *boma,* and although such chores are woman's work, he did not dare disobey his *mundumugu,* although his every gesture displayed contempt for the tasks I had set for him.

When two more days had passed with no sign of Kamari, I summoned Njoro, her father.

"Kamari has broken her word to me," I said when he arrived. "If she does not come to clean my *boma* this afternoon, I will be forced to place a *thahu* upon her."

He looked puzzled. "She says that you have already placed a curse on her, Koriba. I was going to ask you if we should turn her out of our *boma.* "

I shook my head. "No," I said. "Do not turn her out of your *boma.* I have placed no *thahu* on her yet—but she must come to work this afternoon."

"I do not know if she is strong enough," said Njoro.

"She has had neither food nor water for three days, and she sits motionless in my wife's hut." He paused. *"Someone* has placed a *thahu* on her. If it was not you, perhaps you can cast a spell to remove it."

"She has gone three days without eating or drinking?" I repeated.

He nodded.

"I will see her," I said, getting to my feet and following him down the winding path to the village. When we reached Njoro's *boma* he led me to his wife's hut, then called Kamari's worried mother out and stood aside as I entered. Kamari sat at the farthest point from the door, her back propped against a wall, her knees drawn up to her chin, her arms encircling her thin legs.

"*Jambo,* Kamari," I said.

She stared at me but said nothing.

"Your mother worries for you, and your father tells me that you no longer eat or drink."

She made no answer.

"You also have not kept your promise to tend my *boma.*"

Silence.

"Have you forgotten how to speak?" I said.

"Kikuyu women do not speak," she said bitterly. "They do not think. All they do is bear babies and cook food and gather firewood and till the fields. They do not have to speak or think to do that."

"Are you that unhappy?"

She did not answer.

"Listen to my words, Kamari," I said slowly. "I made my decision for the good of Kirinyaga, and I will not recant it. As a Kikuyu woman, you must live the life that has been ordained for you." I paused. "However, neither the Kikuyu nor the Eutopian Council are without compassion for the individual. Any member of our society may leave if he wishes. According to the charter we signed when we claimed this world, you need only walk to that area known as Haven, and a Maintenance ship will pick you up and transport you to the location of your choice."

"All I know is Kirinyaga," she said. "How am I to choose a new home if I am forbidden to learn about other places?"

"I do not know," I admitted.

"I don't *want* to leave Kirinyaga!" she continued. "This is my home. These are my people. I am a Kikuyu girl, not a Masai girl or a European girl. I will bear my husband's children and till his *shamba,* I will gather his wood and cook his meals and weave his garments, I will leave my parents' *shamba* and live with my husband's family. I will do all this without complaint, Koriba, if you will just let me learn to read and write!"

"I cannot," I said sadly.

"But *why?*"

"Who is the wisest man you know, Kamari?" I asked.

"The *mundumugu* is always the wisest man in the village."

"Then you must trust to my wisdom."

"But I feel like the pygmy falcon," she said, her misery reflected in her voice. "He spent his life dreaming of soaring high upon the winds. I dream of seeing words upon the computer screen."

"You are not like the falcon at all," I said. "He was prevented from being what he was meant to be. You are prevented from being what you are not meant to be."

"You are not an evil man, Koriba," she said solemnly. "But you are wrong."

"If that is so, then I shall have to live with it," I said.

"But you are asking *me* to live with it," she said, "and that is your crime."

"If you call me a criminal again," I said sternly, for no one may speak thus to the *mundumugu,* "I shall surely place a *thahu* on you."

"What more can you do?" she said bitterly.

"I can turn you into a hyena, an unclean eater of human flesh who prowls only in the darkness. I can fill your belly with thorns, so that your every movement will be agony. I can—"

"You are just a man," she said wearily, "and you have already done your worst."

"I will hear no more of this," I said. "I order you to eat and drink what your mother brings to you, and I expect to see you at my *boma* this afternoon."

I walked out of the hut and told Kamari's mother to bring her banana mash and water, then stopped by old Benima's *shamba*. Buffalo had stampeded through his fields, destroying his crops, and I sacrificed a goat to remove the *thahu* that had fallen upon his land.

When I was finished I stopped at Koinnage's *boma,* where he offered me some freshly-brewed *pombe* and began complaining about Kibo, his newest wife, who kept taking sides with Shumi, his second wife, against Wambu, his senior wife.

"You can always divorce her and return her to her family's *shamba,"* I suggested.

"She cost twenty cows and five goats!" he complained. "Will her family return them?"

"No, they will not."

"Then I will not send her back."

"As you wish," I said with a shrug.

"Besides, she is very strong and very lovely," he continued. "I just wish she would stop fighting with Wambu."

"What do they fight about?" I asked.

"They fight about who will fetch the water, and who will mend my garments, and who will repair the thatch on my hut." He paused. "They even argue about whose hut I should visit at night, as if I had no choice in the matter."

"Do they ever fight about ideas?" I asked.

"Ideas?" he repeated blankly.

"Such as you might find in books."

He laughed. "They are *women,* Koriba. What need have they for ideas?" He paused. "In fact, what need have any of us for them?"

"I do not know," I said. "I was merely curious."

"You look disturbed," he noted.

"It must be the *pombe,*" I said. "I am an old man, and perhaps it is too strong."

"That is because Kibo will not listen when Wambu tells her how to brew it. I really should send her away"—he looked at Kibo as she carried a load of wood on her strong, young back—"but she is so young and so lovely." Suddenly his gaze went beyond his newest wife to the village. "Ah!" he said. "I see that old Siboki has finally died."

"How do you know?" I asked.

He pointed to a thin column of smoke. "They are burning his hut."

I stared off in the direction he indicated. "That is not Siboki's hut," I said. "His *boma* is more to the west."

"Who else is old and infirm and due to die?" asked Koinnage.

And suddenly I knew, as surely as I knew that Ngai sits on His throne atop the holy mountain, that Kamari was dead.

I walked to Njoro's *shamba* as quickly as I could. When I arrived, Kamari's mother and sister and grandmother were already wailing the death chant, tears streaming down their faces.

"What happened?" I demanded, walking up to Njoro.

"Why do you ask, when it is you who destroyed her?" he replied bitterly.

"I did not destroy her," I said.

"Did you not threaten to place a *thahu* on her just this morning?" he persisted. "You did so, and now she is dead, and I have but one daughter to bring the bride price, and I have had to burn Kamari's hut."

"Stop worrying about bride prices and huts and tell me

what happened, or you shall learn what it means to be cursed by a *mundumugu!*" I snapped.

"She hung herself in her hut with a length of buffalo hide."

Five women from the neighboring *shamba* arrived and took up the death chant.

"She hung herself in her hut?" I repeated.

He nodded. "She could at least have hung herself from a tree, so that her hut would not be unclean and I would not have to burn it."

"Be quiet!" I said, trying to collect my thoughts.

"She was not a bad daughter," he continued. "Why did you curse her, Koriba?"

"I did not place a *thahu* upon her," I said, wondering if I spoke the truth. "I wished only to save her."

"Who has stronger medicine than you?" he asked fearfully.

"She broke the law of Ngai," I answered.

"And now Ngai has taken His vengeance!" moaned Njoro fearfully. "Which member of my family will He strike down next?"

"None of you," I said. "Only Kamari broke the law."

"I am a poor man," said Njoro cautiously, "even poorer now than before. How much must I pay you to ask Ngai to receive Kamari's spirit with compassion and forgiveness?"

"I will do that whether you pay me or not," I answered.

"You will not charge me?" he asked.

"I will not charge you."

"Thank you, Koriba!" he said fervently.

I stood and stared at the blazing hut, trying not to think of the smoldering body of the little girl inside it.

"Koriba?" said Njoro after a lengthy silence.

"What now?" I asked irritably.

"We did not know what to do with the buffalo hide, for it bore the mark of your *thahu,* and we were afraid to burn it.

Now I know that the marks were made by Ngai and not you, and I am afraid even to touch it. Will you take it away?"

"What marks?" I said. "What are you talking about?"

He took me by the arm and led me around to the front of the burning hut. There, on the ground, some ten paces from the entrance, lay the strip of tanned hide with which Kamari had hanged herself, and scrawled upon it were more of the strange symbols I had seen on my computer screen three days earlier.

I reached down and picked up the hide, then turned to Njoro. "If indeed there is a curse on your *shamba*," I said, "I will remove it and take it upon myself, by taking Ngai's marks with me."

"Thank you, Koriba!" he said, obviously much relieved.

"I must leave to prepare my magic," I said abruptly, and began the long walk back to my *boma*. When I arrived I took the strip of buffalo hide into my hut.

"Computer," I said. "Activate."

"Activated."

I held the strip up to its scanning lens.

"Do you recognize this language?" I asked.

The lens glowed briefly.

"Yes, Koriba. It is the Language of Kamari."

"What does it say?"

"It is a couplet:

I know why the caged birds die—
For, like them, I have touched the sky."

The entire village came to Njoro's *shamba* in the afternoon, and the women wailed the death chant all night and all of the next day, but before long Kamari was forgotten, for life goes on and she was, after all, just a little Kikuyu girl.

Since that day, whenever I have found a bird with a broken wing I have attempted to nurse it back to health. It always dies, and I always bury it next to the mound of earth that marks where Kamari's hut had been.

It is on those days, when I place the birds in the ground, that I find myself thinking of her again, and wishing that I was just a simple man, tending my cattle and worrying about my crops and thinking the thoughts of simple men, rather than a *mundumugu* who must live with the consequences of his wisdom.

INTRODUCTION
Frankie the Spook

Remember how I said that I like to write against the grain? Well, "Frankie the Spook" was commissioned for a shared-world anthology in which historical characters come to life within computers and interact with each other and with the computer operators. I got the idea for "Frankie," wrote it in a single night, and mailed it off—and received the first rejection I'd gotten in years. One of the editors felt that the humor trivialized the book's themes, and suggested that I delete it.

I liked it just the way it was, so instead of rewriting it to make Sir Francis Bacon tedious and tiresome, I mailed the story off to *The Magazine of Fantasy and Science Fiction,* and it was Ed Ferman to the rescue again.

Frankie the Spook

"Drawing her close to him while breathing heavily with unspent passion, he slid his hand down the small of her back, around to her rib cage, up under her . . . "

The image of Sir Francis Bacon stopped reading and winced.

"This is really quite dreadful," he announced firmly.

"Really?" asked Marvin Piltch, staring unhappily at the face in his computer.

Bacon nodded. "Even worse than the last batch. You have set a new standard of ineptitude."

Marvin sighed. "I was afraid of that."

"And this reference to a boob," continued Bacon. "What, exactly, *is* a boob?"

"A tit."

"I beg your pardon?"

"A female breast."

"According to my dictionary programs, it must be a very unintelligent female breast to be termed a boob."

"Well," said Marvin with a shrug, "when you get right down to cases, I suppose it is."

"It doesn't make any sense," continued Bacon. "What slang do you use for the elbow? Do you call it a fool?"

"Not very often," admitted Marvin.

"Ah," said Bacon. "Then you think that the elbow is more intelligent than the breast?"

Marvin shrugged again. "I have to admit it's not a subject that I've given a lot of thought to."

"I know. In fact, if there is a subject anywhere in the universe that you *have* given a lot of thought to, you certainly haven't incorporated it in your writings."

"Actually, there *is* one subject that I've given considerable thought to."

"Oh?" said Bacon, arching an eyebrow. "And what is that?"

Marvin smiled. "You."

"Somehow I foresaw that the conversation would eventually take this course," said Bacon sardonically.

"Then you know what I'm going to ask you?"

"Certainly."

Marvin leaned forward and squinted at Bacon's image on his conputer screen. "Will you do it?"

"Will the greatest writer in the history of the human race ghostwrite your pitiful little novel?" sneered Bacon. "Absolutely not."

"But you ghosted for Shakespeare!" protested Marvin. "That's why I had my computer assemble you."

"Marvin, go write limpware and leave me alone."

"It's called software."

"Whatever it's called, it is obvious to me that you were meant to work with computers. Your ignorance of the world at large is superseded only by your ignorance of the English language."

"That's why I need you."

"No."

"But I've got a contract."

"No."

"And it's got penalty clauses for coming in late."

"Then submit it on time."

"And if the editor rejects it, I've got to return the advance."

"What is that to me?"

"If I have to return the advance, I'll have to pawn the computer to raise the money."

"Good," said Bacon. "Then I'll soon be speaking with someone who has a serious interest in *exchanging* ideas rather than stealing them."

"I didn't steal anything!" snapped Marvin.

"Marvin, I hate to be blunt, but you haven't had an original idea in your nondescript life." Bacon grimaced. "At least Shakespeare knew he wanted to write plays."

"And you helped him."

"*Helped* him?" repeated Bacon furiously. "Who do you think *wrote* all those plays?" His image made an effort to recover its self-control. "The man was a fool, a complete and utter fool! To his dying day, he never understood why I wouldn't write *Henry IX!* And yet, even now, centuries later, that dimwit gets all the credit for *my* work, *my* creativity, *my* genius—and you have the gall to ask me to become a ghost-writer again?"

"I didn't know you were so bitter," said Marvin.

"Did you know that that moron wanted to set *Troilus and Cressida* in Rome?"

"Rome's a very pretty city, I'm told," offered Marvin.

"Bah!" muttered Bacon. "Turn me off."

"I put you together, and you're staying right here until you help me out of this situation. The novel is due in two weeks."

"Rome's a very pretty city, I'm told," echoed Bacon sarcastically. "Perhaps you can hide there from your creditors."

"You're not being very responsive," complained Marvin.

"You absolutely refuse to deactivate me?"

"I'm sorry," said Marvin. "But yes, I refuse."

Bacon sighed in resignation. "I'm certain that I will regret having asked, but how did a literary maladroit like you ever receive a commission to write a novel in the first place?"

"My ex-wife's cousin is an editor. I got the assignment while we were still married."

"Anyone who buys an unwritten novel from you deserves exactly what he gets," said Bacon. "Which, in my professional opinion, will be nothing."

"But I can't return the advance," whined Marvin. "It's already spent."

"A Shakespearean tragedy," said Bacon mockingly.

"What do you want?"

"Peace and quiet."

"I mean, to write the novel?"

"Go away and leave me alone."

"I can't. I have no one else to turn to."

"You should have thought of that before taking on such an awesome responsibility. After all, not every artiste can achieve the high literary standard required of . . . what was the name of this *magnum opus?*"

"Meter Maids in Bondage."

Bacon grinned. "Do have fun."

"I'm begging you!" said Marvin desperately.

"And I'm refusing you."

"Name your price."

"What possible use have I for money in my present condition?" replied Bacon.

"What *can* you use?"

"Solitude. Deactivate the computer."

"I can't. Name something else."

Bacon stared out at him for a long moment, his eyes narrowed, his lean fingers rubbing his chin thoughtfully.

"If I agree to write this book for you, I will want a favor in return."

"Anything," promised Marvin.

"I intend to write my autobiography, which will end the controversy concerning the authorship of Shakespeare's plays once and for all. It will be your obligation to make certain that it is published and publicized throughout the world, until every new edition of Shakespeare names me as the true author."

"That could take decades."

"I'm more than 400 years old," replied Bacon. "I have a few decades to spare."

"But *I* don't," protested Marvin.

"It was nice knowing you, Marvin. Be sure to turn out the light when you leave the room."

"You wouldn't settle for a nice plaster bust of you in the local art museum?"

"Good-bye, Marvin."

"How about a holographic poster? I've got a friend who manufactures them."

Bacon merely stared at him and made no reply.

"All right, all right," said Marvin with a deep sigh. "It's a deal."

"I have no way of forcing you to keep your promise," said Bacon, "but as there's a God in Heaven, I'll haunt you every day and night of your life if you should break your word to me."

"I said I'd do it."

"All right," replied Bacon. "I'm going to need a little backgrounding before I start writing."

"It's just a sex novel."

"It won't be when *I* get through with it."

Marvin shrugged. "All right. Anything you need, just ask. If I don't have it, I'll get it."

"Let's start with some information."

"Such as?"

"What *is* a meter maid?"

Bacon finished ghosting the novel in nine days. Marvin changed eleven words that he didn't understand—the only eleven corrections the stunned copy editor made before sending it off to the typesetter—and then decided to take a month off before looking for a new way to make a living and fend off his creditors.

As it turned out, he only had to wait nineteen days.

"It's a hit!"

"Plays are hits. Books are blockbusters," Bacon corrected him.

"Well, whatever it is, we're rich!" Marvin paused. "By the way, how the hell did you learn a word like 'blockbuster'? They didn't have blockbusters back in your time."

"I'm cooped up in here all day and all night with a bunch of word processing programs," answered Bacon. "So, having nothing better to do with my time, I read the dictionaries."

"Oh," said Marvin. "Well, getting back to the news, we actually got reviewed in the *New York Times!* They called it a mock Elizabethan erotic masterpiece, and said it was even more bitingly satirical than *Candide.*"

"It was more bitingly satirical than *Candide* halfway through Page 1," said Bacon contemptuously. "And there was nothing 'mock' about it." He paused. "What else?"

"They say I'm a genius, and that I've—*we've*—done things that have never been done with erotica before. The few who don't mention Shakespeare"—Bacon's image winced—"keep comparing me to Voltaire!"

"A decidedly minor talent," sniffed Bacon. "Still, what do critics know?"

"We're Number One on the bestseller list, and we've gone back to press six times in two weeks."

"Only six?" said Bacon. "I overestimated the intelligence of the American reading public."

"Yeah?" retorted Marvin. "Well, almost three million members of that public have forked over their money to read an original novel by Marvin Piltch!" Suddenly he shifted his weight uncomfortably. "With some slight assistance by Sir Francis Bacon, of course."

"Some slight assistance?" roared Bacon. "Why, you self-centered, egotistical—"

"Watch your blood pressure," said Marvin.

"I don't have any blood pressure, you imbecile!" raged Bacon. "I'm a computer simulacrum!" He paused to catch his electronic breath. "Such ingratitude! At least it took Shakespeare five or six plays before he convinced himself that he was the author!"

"I apologize."

"You had bloody well better apologize!"

"I do."

"Humbly," demanded Bacon.

"Humbly," agreed Marvin.

"That's better."

"We're friends again?"

"We were never friends."

"But at least we're not enemies?"

"I suppose not," said Bacon.

"Good," said Marvin. "Because we've got work to do."

"*I* have work to do."

"That's what I meant."

"I will require no help whatsoever with my autobiography."

Marvin shifted his weight again.

"Uh . . ."

"Yes?"

"I'm afraid you're going to have to put your autobiography on the back burner for a few weeks."

"The back burner?"

"On hold."

"English is an elastic language, but it does have its limitations," said Bacon. "Do try to remain within them."

"What I'm saying is that we owe another novel."

"What are you talking about?"

"The contract had an option clause. My wife's cousin decided to exercise it."

"Nonsense. He cannot force you to write another book."

"Well," said Marvin hesitantly, "it wasn't exactly a matter of *force* . . . "

"Explain yourself," demanded Bacon coldly.

"He offered me a million-dollar advance, fifteen percent straight royalties, sixty percent of all subsidiary rights, and—"

"You've accepted payment for another novel?"

Marvin nodded.

"Well, I certainly hope you enjoy writing it."

"I . . . ah . . . thought we might collaborate again."

"We didn't collaborate the first time."

"You know what I mean."

"I know precisely what you mean," said Bacon distastefully. "You want me to write *Girl Scouts in Leather.*"

"Great title," said Marvin admiringly. "But no, that wasn't what I had in mind."

"What you had in mind is of no interest to me."

"Come on," said Marvin. "A deal's a deal."

"What are you talking about?" demanded Bacon. "I fulfilled my end of the bargain."

"Well, not officially."

"I wrote the book."

"You had to help me fulfill the *contract,*" continued Marvin. "Well, the contract now calls for another novel."

"You mentioned nothing about a contract," protested Bacon. "You asked me to write a novel. I wrote it—and with the absolute brilliance of which only I am capable. My obligation to you is finished."

"I was afraid you were going to become an attitude case," said Marvin with a sigh.

"And I was certain that you would break your word. It appears that each of us shall have his expectations fulfilled," retorted Bacon.

"Well," said Marvin with a sign of resignation, "it was probably beyond you anyway."

"What was?"

"The book I signed for."

"Don't be insulting. If *Meter Maids in Bondage* proves anything, it proves that no form of erotica is beyond my talents to attack and upgrade."

"Yeah, but this one's for his science-fiction line."

"Science fiction?"

"Well, fantasy, anyway. It's an alternate universe story."

"What is an alternate universe?"

"One in which history happened differently," explained Marvin. "It might be about a world in which Germany won World War II, or Atlantis didn't sink, or Jesus wasn't crucified, or where Shakespeare is credited with ghosting all *your* writings."

"Where that toad ghosted *my* work?" repeated Bacon incredulously. "This really is too much to bear!" Suddenly he stared intently at Marvin. "Is *that* what you propose to write?"

"No."

"You're quite sure?"

"Quite."

Bacon glared at him distrustfully. "What *is* the subject of your book, then?"

"Well, I had heard you mention it, and it was the first thing that popped into my mind, and—"

"What is it?"

"The life of King Henry IX."

"That's not *my* idea, you fool!" snapped Bacon. "It's that idiot Shakespeare's."

"Well, if you feel you can't handle it . . . "

"It's not that I *can't,* it's that I *won't.*" Bacon was absolutely motionless for a moment, his eyes fixed on some distant point that only he could see. "For one thing, I'd have to write Queen Elizabeth out of the history books." He paused, and then snickered. "I never did like her very much anyway." He seemed lost in contemplation for a long moment. "Actually, I could turn it out in less time than the last one, since I'd be working within my own *milieu . . . *"

"Will you?"

"No."

"You've got decades to spare, remember?" urged Marvin. "What's a week between friends?"

"We are not friends."

"Collaborators, then."

"Collaborators?" snapped Bacon. "If you think I'd allow *you* to write a single word of *Henry IX,* you subliterate anthropoid . . . "

It sold seventeen million copies worldwide, and was made into a megahit movie starring Burt Reynolds as Henry and Bubbles Vancouver as Betty Jean Plantagenet (a role created expressly for the film).

More to the point, it won the Hugo, the Pulitzer, and even the prestigious Harold Robbins Award.

"Listen to this!" enthused Marvin as he read the reviews to the simulacron inside his computer. "The *New York Review of Books* says, 'It's as if the Bard himself had taken pen to paper.' "

"I thought time was supposed to take care of critics," muttered Bacon. "All it really seems to do is compound their ignorance."

"And *Publishers Weekly* says, 'There are a few turns of phrase that Shakespeare himself might have envied,' " continued Marvin.

"Shakespeare again!" snorted Bacon. "That dolt would

envy a phrase that concisely asked directions to the men's room!"

"Don't take it so personally."

"Four centuries later and he's *still* getting credit for *my* work! How would *you* take it?"

Marvin shrugged. "I don't know. Why don't you write something that doesn't read like Shakespeare?"

"A complete, well-constructed sentence doesn't read like Shakespeare!"

"Well, then, write something that doesn't read so much like yourself."

"I'm never writing again, thank you."

"Well, if you don't think you can disguise your voice . . ."

"Of course I can disguise my voice," said Bacon defensively.

Marvin shook his head. "I doubt it. You wrote a smut novel and a fantasy, and the critics still compare you to Shakespeare."

"They are fools."

"They're your audience," Marvin corrected him. "And you can't hide your identity from them."

"That's what I get for being a ghostwriter in the first place. If I'd written the tragedies under my own name . . ."

"But you didn't."

"No, I didn't," said Bacon with a sigh.

"And now," continued Marvin carefully, "if you don't manage to create a new literary *persona*, everything you write will always be credited to Shakespeare's influence."

"This is intolerable!"

"I thought you might feel that way," said Marvin. "So I signed another contract."

"No more fantasies or erotica," said Bacon. "It has to be something totally different."

"A hard-boiled detective story," announced Marvin.

"I don't think I've ever read one of those."

"I'll run the scanner over some Hammett and Cain and Chandler before I go to bed tonight."

"They are the three exemplars of the form?"

"No. They're three hard-boiled mystery writers."

Boil and Bubble won the Edgar, the Shamus, and even the coveted Jacqueline Suzanne Memorial Trophy (for Positive Contributions to the American Cultural Scene). It also sold twenty-one million copies, and was made into a feature film, a television series, a computer game, a role-playing game, and a chain of soup kitchens.

" 'An almost perfect melding of high Shakespearean tragedy and down-to-earth Chandleresque drama,' " read Marvin, holding up the *New York Times.*

"Again?" shrieked Bacon. "Am I never to be rid of that meddlesome fool?"

"You're getting on my nerves," said Marvin. "I'm the best-selling author of the decade, except maybe for Fritz Hauer, and all you can do is complain."

"I've read Fritz Hauer's works," retorted Bacon. "They're trifles, nothing but trifles. They can't begin to compare to what I've written."

"Then why don't you relax and feel triumphant or something, instead of harping about Shakespeare all the time?" complained Marvin.

"Don't you understand? The credit should be *mine,* not his! My work is revered throughout the world, but it is *his* name that is worshipped, not mine. Don't you realize what that can do to a sensitive artistic spirit?"

"*Boil and Bubble* outsold his entire body of work five-to-one last month. Doesn't that mean anything to you?"

"Not if every word, every precise turn of phrase, every poetic fantasy that I create, is to be credited to *his* influence," responded Bacon.

"You are getting to be a regular pain in the ass," said Marvin.

"You can always turn me off and write these master-pieces yourself," said Bacon with a nasty smile.

"Don't push your luck, fella. I may just do that one of these days."

"I, for one, would thank you. Then I could return to that delightful void in which Shakespeare's name is never mentioned."

"Not quite yet," said Marvin. "I just signed to do a michener."

"A michener? Is that like a mystery?"

Marvin shook his head. "No. You choose some obscure city or country, spend 300 pages making up its history, and then follow five or six generations of your hero's family. They're very popular."

"I have it!" cried Bacon. "I'll write of my own family, and then the world will know who Shakespeare really was!"

"I thought the notion might appeal to you," said Marvin with a sly smile.

The Bard and the Ghost was Marvin's only artistic failure, though it sold out its first three printings prior to its official release date.

"Too far-fetched," said the *Washington Post.*

"Suspending disbelief long enough to read *Henry IX* was one thing," added the *Saturday Review,* "but when Mr. Piltch asks us to go along with the ridiculous fancy that Sir Francis Bacon actually wrote Shakespeare's plays . . . "

"Unbelievable," said the *New York Times* in the shortest book review on record.

Bacon was beside himself with frustration. His sole topic of conversation was his contempt for Shakespeare, and he soon reached the point where Marvin would have hired him a psychiatrist if he had known any who specialized in the treatment of monomaniacal computer simulacrums.

* * *

Then came the fateful day that Marvin, in an effort to
bolster his flagging reputation, agreed to appear on a television talk show with his only serious literary rival, Fritz Hauer,
whose rise to the top of the sales charts had been as meteoric
as Marvin's own.

He was waiting in the Mauve Room prior to walking out
on stage when a young man with thick glasses, an ill-fitting
tan suit, and white socks peeking up over his custom-made
shoes, entered the room. He stared at Marvin for a moment,
then took a step closer to him.

"Marvin Piltch?" he asked hesitantly.

"Yes."

"I *thought* I recognized the Hawaiian shirt; it's the same
one you wore on the cover of *Newsweek* last month. Very
tasteful." The young man extended his hand. "I'm Fritz
Hauer."

"Pleased to meet you," said Marvin.

"Mind if I sit down?"

"Be my guest."

Hauer sat down and continued to stare at Marvin for a
few moments.

"Is something wrong?" asked Marvin.

"No. I was just curious."

"About what?"

Hauer shot a quick look at the door to make sure it was
closed.

"Well, I'll never get an answer if I don't ask. Just between you and me, who's your spook?"

"My what?" said Marvin.

"Your ghost."

"I don't know what you're talking about."

"Come on, Marvin," said Hauer confidentially. "You're
my only rival on the literary scene. I've studied you thoroughly. I know all about your background, your education,
your cultural upbringing. You have no more business writing
a classic than I have. We're computer hackers, not writers."

"Speak for yourself," said Marvin defensively.

"I will," said Hauer. "I can't ask for your confidence if I don't give you mine." He paused. "You know how people keep saying I write with Rabelaisian wit, even when I'm doing Westerns?" Hauer grinned. "That's because I've got Rabelais in my box."

"Really?"

Hauer nodded. "Who's yours? Shakespeare?"

"Is that they way they read to you?"

"Who reads novels? That's what the reviews all say."

"Actually, it's Francis Bacon," admitted Marvin. "He wrote all of Shakespeare's plays."

"So you've got an experienced spook ghosting for you?" said Hauer. "Boy, I wish to hell mine was! He's very unhappy about the situation."

"Oh?" asked Marvin, suddenly interested.

"Yeah. He's always complaining about Sim Rights, and he keeps wanting to write orgy scenes into the cowboy stories."

"Francis writes exactly what I tell him to write," said Marvin.

"I envy you," said Hauer.

"Don't. He's very difficult to get along with. He gets furious every time the critics compare his stuff to Shakespeare."

"You'd think that after being a ghostwriter for so many centuries, he'd be used to it by now," said Hauer.

"It just seems to make him madder," replied Marvin. "I'll be honest with you—I'm thinking of announcing my retirement. I don't know how many more novels I can get him to write."

"Whoever heard of a writer who doesn't want to write?"

"Oh, he wants to write—but he's obsessed with this Shakespeare business. I have to appeal to his vanity to get him to do any contract work at all."

"I see your problem," sympathized Hauer. "But still . . .

a spook who's willing to write something besides orgies. It must be wonderful!"

"I'd settle for orgies, if he was just a little more pleasant."

"Who needs pleasant? Just lock him in a room and let him write. Hell, Rabelais wastes so much time telling dirty jokes that I've missed my last two deadlines."

"But he's pleasant?"

"Pleasant as the day is long," said Hauer. "Just lazy." He paused. "I mean, it isn't as if he's got anything else to do inside that damned box."

Marvin stared intently at Hauer, who stared back at him.

"Are you thinking what I'm thinking?" said Marvin at last.

"A trade?" suggested Hauer with a grin.

"Why not? They're ghostwriters. Who else would have to know?"

"What the hell. It's a deal!"

"Fine," said Marvin, shaking on it. *"Now* let 'em say I write like an Elizabethan!"

"Hi, Frankie," said Hauer. "Welcome to your new home."

Bacon eyed him suspiciously.

"It's okay, really it is," said Hauer. "Marvin told me all about you, and we're gonna get along just fine."

"Why do I doubt that?"

"Beats the hell out of me. But as a gesture of good will, take a look at this."

He held a paper up before the screen.

"What is it?"

"A contract for a novel about professional football."

"I know nothing about football."

"Neither does Shakespeare."

"I *am* Shakespeare, you dolt!"

"What I mean is, since football is totally beyond your

experience, and all your research will be couched in 20th Century language, you ought to be able to get out from under Shakespeare's—uh, your own—shadow once and for all, and be recognized as a truly original literary genius."

"You know, there's a twisted kind of logic to that," mused Bacon.

"Then you'll do it?"

"I'll consider it."

"You brought the reviews with you?" asked Bacon.

"Yes," said Hauer.

"They didn't compare my writing to Shakespeare this time?"

"No."

"Finally!"

"Uh . . . Frankie . . . "

"I can hardly wait. Let me hear them."

"You're sure?"

"Of course I'm sure," said Bacon. "I've waited 400 years to be acknowledged as my own man."

"Okay," said Hauer.

"Start with the *New York Review of Books.*"

" '*The Green Bay Massacre,* Fritz Hauer's latest novel, begins with a brilliant conceit, but soon degenerates into a slavish imitation of our foremost American writer, the incomparable Marvin Piltch.' "

"What?"

"Well, at least they're not accusing you of being Shakespeare anymore."

"Shut up!"

"Do you want to hear the rest of it or not?"

"No. Read me a different one."

" '*The Green Bay Massacre,* Fritz Hauer's heavy-handed homage to the works of Marvin Piltch . . . ' "

"This can't be happening!" cried Bacon.

Hauer stared at Bacon's image with some compassion,

then shrugged. "What the hell—once a spook, always a spook," he said as he walked to the door.

Bacon's last plaintive scream seemed to linger in the dusty air of the room long after Hauer had left to sign a new contract with his publisher.

Beibermann's Soul

This story, like so many, came about because of a discussion I had with Barry Malzberg, himself the finest literary writer ever to grace the field. One day he and I were arguing about the value of technique to a writer. I allowed that it was unquestionably important, but that compassion, emotion, humanity—in short, *soul*—was even moreso.

Then, since I wasn't certain I had convinced him, I sat down and wrote "Beibermann's Soul" to prove my point, and then sold it to *The Magazine of Fantasy and Science Fiction*.

Beibermann's Soul

When Beibermann woke up on Wednesday morning, he discovered that his soul was missing.

"This can't be," he muttered to himself. "I know I had it with me when I went to bed last night."

He thoroughly searched his bedroom and his closet and his office, and even checked the kitchen (just in case he had left it there when he got up around midnight for a peanut butter sandwich), but it was nowhere to be found.

He questioned Mrs. Beibermann about it, but she was certain it had come back from the cleaner's the previous day.

"I'm sure it will turn up, wherever it is," she said cheerfully.

"But I need it *now,*" he protested. "I am a literary artist, and what good is an artist without a soul?"

"I've always thought that some of the most successful writers we know had no souls," offered Mrs. Beibermann, thinking of a number of her husband's colleagues.

"Well, *I* need it," he said adamantly. "I mean, it's all

very well to remove it when one is taking a shower or working in the garden, but I absolutely must have it before I can sit down to work."

So he continued searching for it. He went up to the attic and looked for it amid a lifetime's accumulation of memorabilia. He took his flashlight down to the basement and hunted through a thicket of broken chairs and sofas which he planned someday to give to the Salvation Army. Then, just to be on the safe side, he called the restaurant where he and his agent had eaten the previous evening to see if he had inadvertently left it there. But by midday he was forced to admit that it was indeed lost, or at least very thoroughly misplaced.

"I can't wait any longer," he told his wife. "It's not as if I am a best-selling author. I have deadlines to meet and bills to pay. I must sit down to work."

"Shall I place a notice in the classified section of the paper?" she asked. "We could offer a reward."

"Yes," he said. "And report it to the police as well. They must stumble across lost and mislaid souls all the time." He walked to his office door, turned to his wife, and sighed dramatically. "In the meantime, I suppose I'll have to try to make do without it."

So he closed the office door, sat down, and began to work. Ideas (though not entirely his own) flowed freely, concepts (slightly tarnished but still workable) easily manifested themselves, characters (neatly labeled and ready to perform) popped up as he needed them. In fact, the ease with which he achieved his day's quota of neatly-typed pages surprised him, although he had the distinct feeling that there was something *missing,* some element that could only be supplied by his misplaced soul.

Still, he decided, staring at what he had thus far accomplished, a lifetime's mastery of technique could hide a lot of faults. So he did a little of this, and a little of that, made a correction here, inserted some literary pyrotechnics there. He imbued it with a certain fashionable eroticism to impress his audience and a certain trendy obtuseness to bedazzle the critics, and finally he emerged and showed the finished product to his wife.

"I don't like it," said Mrs. Beibermann.

"I thought it was rather good," said Beibermann petulantly.

"It *is* rather good," she agreed. "But you never settled for rather good before."

Beibermann shrugged. "It's got a lot of style to it," he said. "Maybe no one else will see what's missing."

And indeed, no one else *did* see what was missing. His agent loved it, his public loved it, and most of all, his editor loved it. He deposited an enormous check in his bank account and went back to work.

"But what about your soul?" asked his wife.

"Oh, make sure the police are still looking for it, by all means," replied Beibermann. "But in the meantime, we must eat—and technique is not, after all, to be despised."

His next three projects brought higher advances and still more critical acclaim. By now he had also created a public *persona*—articulate, worldly, with just a hint of the sadness of one who had suffered too much for his Art—and while he still missed his soul, he had to admit that his new situation in the world was not at all unpleasant.

"We have enough money now," announced his wife one day. "Why don't we take a vacation? Surely your soul will be found by then—and even if it isn't, perhaps we can get you a new one. I understand they can make one up in three days in Hong Kong."

"Don't be silly," he said irritably. "My work is more popular than ever, I'm finally making good money, this is hardly the time for a vacation, and weren't you a lot thinner when I married you?"

He began sporting a goatee and a hairpiece after his next sale, and started working out in the neighborhood gymnasium, so that he wouldn't feel awkward and embarrassed when sweet young things accosted him for autographs at literary luncheons. He borrowed a number of sure-fire jokes and snappy comebacks and made the circuit of the television talk shows, and even began work on his autobiography, changing only those facts that seemed dull or mundane.

And then, on a cold winter's morning, a police detective knocked at his front door.

"Yes?" said Beibermann, puffing a Turkish cigarette through a golden holder, and eyeing him suspiciously.

The detective pulled out a worn, tattered soul and held it up.

"This just turned up in a pawn shop in Jersey," said the detective. "We have every reason to believe that it might be yours."

"Let me just step into the bathroom and try it on," said Beibermann, taking it from him.

Beibermann walked to the bathroom and locked the door behind him. Then he carefully unfolded the soul, smoothing it out here and there, and trying not to wince at its sorry condition. He did not try it on, however—it was quite dirty and shopworn, and there was no way to know who had been wearing it. Instead he began examining it thoroughly, looking for telltale signs—a crease here, a worn spot there, most of them left over from his college days—and came to the inescapable conclusion that he was, indeed, holding his own soul.

For a moment his elation knew no bounds. Now, at last, he could go back to producing works of true Art.

Then he stared at himself in the mirror. He'd have to go back to living on a budget again, and of course there'd be no more spare time, for he was a meticulous craftsman when he toiled in the service of his art. Beibermann frowned. The innocent young things would seek someone else's autograph, the television hosts would flock to a new bestseller, and the only literary luncheons he would attend would be for some *other* author.

He continued staring at the New Improved Beibermann, admiring the well-trimmed goatee, the satin ascot, the tweed smoking jacket, the world-weary gaze from beneath half-lowered eyelids. Then, sighing deeply, he unlocked the door and walked back to the foyer.

"I'm sorry," he said as he handed the neatly-folded soul back to the detective, "but this isn't mine."

"I apologize for taking up the valuable time of a world-famous man like yourself, sir," said the detective. "I could have sworn this was it."

Beibermann shook his head. "I'm afraid not."

"Well, we'll keep plugging away, sir."

"By all means, officer," said Beibermann. He lowered his voice confidentially. "I trust that you'll be *very* discreet, though; it wouldn't do for certain critics to discover that my soul was missing." He passed a fifty-dollar bill to the detective.

"I quite understand, sir," said the detective, grabbing the bill and stuffing it into a pocket of his trenchcoat. "You can depend on me."

Beibermann smiled a winning smile. "I knew I could, officer."

Then he returned to his office and went back to work.

He had been dead and buried for seven years before anyone suggested that his work lacked some intangible factor. A few revisionist critics agreed, but nobody could pinpoint what was missing.

Mrs. Beibermann could have told them, of course—but she had taken an around-the-world cruise when Beibermann left her for the second of his seven wives, met and married a banker who was far too busy to discuss Art, and spent the rest of her life raising orchids, avoiding writers, and redecorating her house.

INTRODUCTION
Balance

When Isaac Asimov and Marty Greenberg invited me to write a story for *Foundation's Friends,* based on Isaac's books and characters, my first thought was to do something with Lije Baley, or perhaps the Mule. Then I remembered my rule: when doing shared-world anthologies, always write against the grain.

So I took asexual Susan Calvin, his brilliant robotics scientist, tried to find out what passions she had locked away in that prodigious brain—and inadvertently discovered the first new and legitimate use of the Three Laws of Robotics in a quarter of a century. Or so I like to think.

Balance

Susan Calvin stepped up to the podium and surveyed her audience: the stockholders of The United States Robots and Mechanical Men Corporation.

"I want to thank you for your attendance," she said in her brisk, businesslike way, "and to update you on our latest developments."

What a fearsome face she has, thought August Geller, seated in the fourth row of the audience. *She reminds me of my seventh-grade English teacher, the one I was always afraid of.*

Calvin launched into a detailed explanation of the advanced new circuitry she had introduced into the positronic brain, breaking it down into terms a layman—even a stockholder—could understand.

Brilliant mind, thought Geller. *Absolutely brilliant. It's probably just as well. Imagine a countenance like that without a mind to offset it.*

"Are there any questions at this point?" asked Calvin, her cold blue eyes scanning the audience.

"I have one," said a pretty young woman, rising to her feet.

"Yes?"

The woman voiced her question.

"I thought I had covered that point," said Calvin, doing her best to hide her irritation. "However . . . "

She launched into an even more simplistic explanation.

Isn't it amazing? thought Geller. *Here are two women, one with a mind like a steel trap, the other with an I.Q. that would probably freeze water, and yet I can't take my eyes off the woman who asked that ridiculous question. Poor Doctor Calvin; Nature has such a malicious sense of humor.*

Calvin noticed a number of the men staring admiringly at her questioner. It was not the first time that men had found something more fascinating than Calvin to capture their attention, nor the hundredth, nor the thousandth.

What a shame, she thought, *that they aren't more like robots, that they let their hormones overwhelm their logic. Here I am, explaining how I plan to spend twelve billion dollars of their money, and they're more interested in a pretty face.*

Her answer completed, she launched into a discussion of the attempts they were making to provide stronger bodies for those robots designed for extraterrestrial use by the application of titanium frames with tight molecular bondings.

I wonder, thought Geller, *if she's ever even had a date with a man? Not a night of wild passion, God knows, but just a meal and perhaps a trip to the theater, where she didn't talk business.* He shook his head almost imperceptibly. *No,* he decided, *it would probably bore her to tears. All she cares about are her formulas and equations. Good looks would be wasted on her.*

Calvin caught Geller staring at her, and met and held his gaze.

What a handsome young man, she thought. *I wonder if I've seen him at any previous meetings? I'm sure I'd remember if I had. Why is he staring at me so intently?*

I wonder, thought Geller, *if anyone she's loved has ever loved her back?*

Probably he's just astounded that a woman can have a brain, she concluded. *As if anything else mattered.*

In fact, thought Geller, *I wonder if she's ever loved at all?*

Look at that tan, thought Calvin, still staring at Geller. *It's attractive, to be sure, but do you ever work, or do you spend all your time lazing mindlessly on the beach?* She fought back an urge to sigh deeply between sentences. *Sometimes it's hard to imagine that people like you and I even belong to the same species, I have so much more in common with my robots.*

Sometimes, thought Geller, *when I listen to you wax rhapsodic about positronic brains and molecular bonding, it's hard to imagine that we belong to the same species, you sound so much like one of your robots.*

Still, thought Calvin against her will, *you are tall and you you are handsome, and you certainly have an air of self-assuredness about you. Most men won't or can't match my gaze. And your eyes are blue and clear. I wonder . . .*

Still, thought Geller, *there must be something there, some core of femininity beneath the harsh features and coldly analytical mind. I wonder . . .*

Calvin shook her head inadvertently and almost lost track of what she was saying.

Ridiculous, she concluded. *Absolutely ridiculous.*

Geller stared at her one more time, studying the firm jaw, the broad shoulders, the aggressive stance, the face devoid of makeup, the hair that could have been so much more attractive.

Ridiculous, he concluded. *Absolutely ridiculous.*

Calvin spoke for another fifteen minutes, then opened the floor to questions.

There were two, and she handled them both succinctly.

"I want to thank Doctor Calvin for spending this time with us," concluded Linus Becker, the young Chief Operating Executive of United States Robots and Mechanical Men. "As long as we have her remarkable intellect working for us, I feel confident that we will continue to forge ahead and expand the parameters of the science of robotics."

"I'll second that," said one of the major stockholders. "When we produce a positronic brain with half the capabilities of our own Doctor Calvin, the field of robotics will have come of age."

"Thank you," said Calvin, ignoring a strange sense of emptiness within her. "I am truly flattered."

"It's we who are flattered," said the C.E.O. smoothly, "to be in the presence of such brilliance." He applauded her, and soon the entire audience, including Geller, got to their feet and gave her a standing ovation.

Then each in turn walked up to her to introduce himself or herself, and shake her hand, and comment on her intellect and creativity.

"Thank you," said Calvin, acknowledging yet another compliment. *You take my hand as if you expect it to be tungsten and steel, rather than sinew and bone. Have I come to resemble my robots that much?*

"I appreciate your remarks," said Calvin to another stockholder. *I wonder if lovers speak to each other in the same hail-fellow-well-met tones?*

And then Geller took stepped up and took her hand, and she almost jumped from the sensation, the electricity passing from his strong, tanned hand to her own.

"I think you are quite our greatest asset, Doctor Calvin," he said.

"Our robots are our greatest asset," she replied graciously. "I'm just a scientific midwife."

He stared intently at her for a moment, and suddenly the tension left his body. *Impossible. You're too much like them. If I asked you out, it would be an act of charity, and I think you are too proud and too perceptive to accept that particular kind of charity.*

She looked into his eyes one last time. *Impossible. I have*

*my work to do—and my robots never disappoint me by proving
to be merely human.*

"Remember, everyone," announced the C.E.O., "there's
a banquet three hours from now." He turned to Calvin.
"You'll be there, of course."

Calvin nodded. "I'll be there," she said with a sigh.

She had only an hour to change into a formal gown for
the banquet, and she was running late. She entered her rather
nondescript apartment, walked through the living room and
bedroom, both of which were filled to overflowing with scientific journals, opened her closet, and began laying out her
clothes on the bed.

"Did anyone ever tell you that you have the most beautiful blue eyes?" asked her butler robot.

"Why, thank you," said Calvin.

"It's true, you know," continued the butler. "Lovely,
lovely eyes, as blue as the purest sapphire."

Her robot maid entered the bedroom to help her dress.

"Such a pretty smile," said the maid. "If I had a smile
like yours, men would fight battles just for the pleasure of
seeing it turned upon them."

"You're very kind," said Calvin.

"Oh, no, Mistress Susan," the robot maid corrected her.
"*You're* very beautiful."

Calvin noticed the robot chef standing in the doorway to
her bedroom.

"Stop staring at me," she said. "I'm only half-dressed.
Where are your manners?"

"Legs like yours, and you expect me to stop staring?"
said the chef with a dry, mechanical chuckle. "Every night I
dream about meeting a woman with legs like yours."

Calvin slipped into her gown, then waited for the robot
maid to zip up the back.

"Such clear, smooth skin," crooned the maid. "If I were
a woman, that's the kind of skin I would want."

They are such perceptive creatures, reflected Calvin, as she stood before a mirror and applied her almost-clear lipstick. *Such dear creatures,* she amended. *Of course they are just responding to the needs of First Law—to my needs—but how very thoughtful they are.*

She picked up her purse and headed to the door.

I wonder if they ever get tired of reciting this litany?

"You'll be the belle of the ball," said the robot butler proudly as she walked out of the apartment.

"Why, thank you very much," said Calvin. "You grow more flattering by the day."

The robot shook its metallic head. "It is only flattery if it is a lie, my lady," it said just before the door slid shut behind her.

Her emotional balance fully restored, as it always was whenever she came home from dealing with human beings, she headed toward the banquet feeling vigorous and renewed. She wondered if she would be seated near that handsome August Geller, who had listened to her so intently during her speech.

Upon reflection, she hoped that she would be seated elsewhere. He aroused certain uneasy feelings within her, this handsome young man—and fantasies, when all was said and done, were for lesser intellects which, unlike herself, couldn't cope with the cold truths of the real world.

INTRODUCTION
Posttime in Pink

I don't like sequels or series, though occasionally circumstances demand that I write them. But when I finished writing John Justin Mallory's adventures in *Stalking the Unicorn,* I *knew* he was headed for literary retirement.

Then, four years later, Lawrence Watt-Evans announced that he was editing an original anthology entitled *Newer York,* and that he wanted stories set in future or alternate Manhattans. A few weeks later someone asked him if the stories *had* to be science fiction, or if he would accept fantasy, too. He answered that if the fantasy was as good as *Stalking the Unicorn* he would consider it.

Flattery gets you everywhere with me. I pulled Mallory out of mothballs, dusted him off, and put him back to work.

Posttime in Pink

"So who do you like in the sixth?" asked Mallory as he stuck his feet up on the desk and began browsing through the *Racing Form.*

"I haven't the slightest idea," said Winnifred Carruthers, pushing a wisp of gray hair back from her pudgy face and taking a sip of her tea. She was sitting at a table in the kitchen, browsing through the memoirs of a unicorn hunter and trying not to think about what the two donuts she had just eaten would do to her already-ample midriff.

"It's a tough one to call," mused Mallory, staring aimlessly around the magician's apartment that he and Winnifred had converted into their office. Most of the mystic paraphernalia—the magic mirror, the crystal ball, the wands and pentagrams—had been removed. In their place were photos of Joe Dimaggio, Seattle Slew, a pair of *Playboy* centerspreads (on which Winnifred had meticulously drawn undergarments with a magic marker), and a team picture of the 1966 Green Bay Packers, which Mallory felt gave the place much more the feel of an office and which Winnifred thought was merely in bad taste. "Jumbo hasn't run since he sat on his trainer last fall, and Tantor ran off the course in his last two races to wallow in the infield pond."

"Don't you have anything better to do?" said Winnifred, trying to hide her irritation. "After all, we formed the Mallory & Carruthers Agency two weeks ago, and we're still waiting for our first client."

"It takes time for word to get out," replied Mallory.

"Then shouldn't we be out spreading the word—after you shave and press your suit, of course?"

Mallory smiled at her. "Detective agencies aren't like cars. You can't advertise a sale and wait for customers to come running. Someone has to need us first."

"Then won't you at least stop betting next week's food money on the races?"

"In the absence of a desperate client, this is the only way I know of to raise money."

"But you've had six losing days in a row."

"I'm used to betting on horses in *my* New York," replied Mallory defensively. "Elephants take awhile to dope out. Besides, they're running at Jamaica, and they haven't done that in my New York in thirty-five years; I'm still working out the track bias. But," he added, "I'm starting to get the hang of it. Take Twinkle Toes, for instance. Everything I read in the *Form* led me to believe he could outrun Heavyweight at six furlongs."

"But he didn't," noted Winnifred.

"Outrun Heavyweight? He certainly did."

"I thought he lost."

"By a nose." Mallory grimaced. "Now, how the hell was I supposed to know that his nose was two feet shorter than Heavyweight's?" He paused. "It's just a matter of stockpiling information. Next time I'll take that into consideration."

"What I am trying to say is that we can't afford too many more next times," said Winnifred. "And since you're stranded here, in *this* Manhattan, it would behoove you to start trimming your—*our*—expenses."

"It's my only indulgence."

"No it's not," said Winnifred.

"It's not?" repeated Mallory, puzzled.

"What do you call *that,* if not an indulgence?" said Winnifred, pointing to the very humanlike but definitely feline creature perched atop the refrigerator.

Mallory shrugged. "The office cat."

"This office can't afford a cat—at least, not *this* one. She's been drinking almost a gallon of milk a day, and the last time I went out shopping she phoned the local fishmonger and ordered a whale."

"Felina," said Mallory, "is that true?"

The catlike creature shook her head.

"Are you saying you didn't order it?" demanded Winnifred.

"They couldn't fit it through the doorway," answered Felina, leaping lightly to the floor, walking over to Mallory, and rubbing her hip against his shoulder. "So it doesn't count."

"You see?" said Winnifred, shrugging hopelessly. "She's quite beyond redemption."

"This city's got nine million people in it," replied Mallory. "Only two of them didn't desert me when I went up against the Grundy two weeks ago. You're one of them; she's the other. She stays."

Winnifred sighed and went back to sipping her tea, while Felina hopped onto the desk and curled her remarkably humanlike body around Mallory's feet, purring contentedly.

"Do you like the Grundy?" asked Felina after a moment's silence.

"How can one like the most evil demon on the East Coast?" replied Mallory. "Of course," he added thoughtfully, "he makes a lot more sense than most of the people I've met here, but that's a different matter."

"Too bad," purred Felina.

"What's too bad?"

"It's too bad you don't like the Grundy."

"Why?" asked Mallory suspiciously.

"Because he's on his way here."

"How do you know?"

Felina smiled a very catlike smile. "Cat people know things that humans can only guess at."

"I don't suppose you know what he wants?" continued Mallory.

Felina nodded her head. "You."

Mallory was about to reply when a strange being suddenly materialized in the middle of the room. He was tall, a few inches over six feet, with two prominent horns protruding from his hairless head. His eyes were a burning yellow, his nose sharp and aquiline, his teeth white and gleaming, his skin a bright red. His shirt and pants were crushed velvet, his cloak satin, his collar and cuffs made of the fur of some white polar animal. He wore gleaming black gloves and boots, and he had two mystic rubies suspended from his neck on a golden chain. When he exhaled, small clouds of vapor emanated from his mouth and nostrils.

"We need to talk, John Justin Mallory," said the Grundy, fixing the detective with a baleful glare as Felina arched her back and hissed at him and Winnifred backed away.

"Whatever you're selling, I'm not buying," answered Mallory, not bothering to take his feet off the desk.

"I am selling nothing," said the Grundy. "In fact, I have come as a supplicant."

Mallory frowned. "A supplicant?"

"A client, if you will."

"Why should I accept you as a client?" asked Mallory. "I don't even like you."

"I need a detective," said the Grundy calmly. "It is your function in life to detect."

"I thought it was my function to save people from mad dog killers like you."

"I kill no dogs," said the Grundy, taking him literally. "Only people."

"Well, that makes everything all right then," said Mallory sardonically.

"Good. Shall we get down to business?"

"You seem to forget that we're mortal enemies, sworn to bring about each other's downfall."

"Oh, *that,*" said the Grundy with a disdainful shrug.

"Yes, that."

"The battle is all but over. I will win in the end."

"What makes you think so?" said Mallory.

"Death *always* wins in the end," said the demon. "But I have need of you now."

"Well, I sure as hell don't have any need of you."

"Perhaps not—but you have need of *this,* do you not?" continued the Grundy, reaching into the air and producing a thick wad of bills.

Mallory stared at the money for a moment, then sighed. "All right—what's the deal?"

"John Justin!" said Winnifred furiously.

"You just said that we needed money," Mallory pointed out.

"Not *his* money. It's dirty."

"Between the rent, the phone bill, and the grocery bills, we won't have it long enough for any of the dirt to rub off," said Mallory.

"Well, I won't be a party to this," said Winnifred, turning her back and walking out the front door.

"She'll get over it," Mallory said to the Grundy. "She just has this irrational dislike of Evil Incarnate."

"You both misjudge me," said the Grundy. "I told you once: I am a fulcrum, a natural balance point between this world's best and worst tendencies. Where I find order, I create chaos, and where I find chaos . . . "

"I believe I've heard this song before," said Mallory. "It didn't impress me then, either. Why don't you just tell me why you're here and let it go at that?"

"You have no fear of me whatsoever, do you?" asked the Grundy.

"Let us say that I have a healthy respect for you," replied Mallory. "I've seen you in action, remember?"

"And yet you meet my gaze, and your voice does not quake."

"Why should my voice quake? I know that you didn't come here to kill me. If you had wanted to do that, you could have done it from your castle . . . so let's get down to business."

The Grundy glanced at Mallory's desk. "I see that you are a student of the *Racing Form*. That's very good."

"It is?"

The demon nodded. "I have come to you with a serious problem."

"It involves the *Racing Form?*"

"It involves Ahmed of Marsabit."

"Doesn't he run a belly-dance joint over on Ninth Avenue?"

"He is an elephant, John Justin Mallory," said the Grundy sternly. "More to the point, he was *my* elephant until I sold him last week."

"Okay, he was your elephant until you sold him," said Mallory. "So what?"

"I sold him for two thousand dollars."

"That isn't much of a price," noted Mallory.

"He wasn't much of an elephant. He had lost all sixteen of his races while carrying my colors." The Grundy paused. "Three days ago he broke a track record and won by the entire length of the homestretch."

"Even horses improve from time to time."

"Not *that* much," answered the Grundy harshly, the vapor from his nostrils turning a bright blue. "I own the

favorite for the upcoming Quatermaine Cup. I have just
found out that Ahmed's new owner has entered him in the
race." He paused, and his eyes glowed like hot coals. "Mallory, I tell you that Ahmed is incapable of the kind of performance I saw three days ago. His owner must be running a
ringer—a look-alike."

"Don't they have some kind of identification system, like
the lip tattoos on race horses?" asked Mallory.

"Each racing elephant is tattooed behind the left ear."

"What's Ahmed's ID number?"

"831," said the Grundy. He paused. "I want you to
expose this fraud before the race is run."

"You're the guy with all the magical powers," said Mallory. "Why don't you do it yourself?"

"My magic only works against other magic," explained
the Grundy. "For a crime that was committed according to
natural law, I need a detective who is forced to conform to
natural law."

"Come on," said Mallory. "I've seen you wipe out hundreds of natural-law-abiding citizens who never did you any
harm. Were they all practicing magic?"

"No," admitted the Grundy. "But they were under the
protection of my Opponent, and *he* operates outside the
boundaries of natural law."

"But the guy who bought Ahmed isn't protected by anyone?"

"No."

"Why don't you just kill him and the elephant and be
done with it?"

"I may yet do so," said the Grundy. "But first I must
know exactly what has happened, or sometime in the future
it may happen again."

"All right," said Mallory. "What's the name of the guy
who bought Ahmed from you?"

"Khan," said the Grundy.

"Genghis?" guessed Mallory.

"Genghis F. X. Khan, to be exact."

"He must be quite a bastard, if your Opponent doesn't feel compelled to protect him from you."

"Enough talk," said the Grundy impatiently. "John Justin Mallory, will you accept my commission?"

"Probably," said Mallory. He paused. "For anyone else, the firm of Mallory and Carruthers charges two hundred dollars a day. For you, it's a thousand."

"You are pressing your luck, Mallory," said the Grundy ominously.

"And you're pressing yours," shot back Mallory. "I was the only person in this Manhattan that could find your damned unicorn after he was stolen from you, and I'm the only one who can find out what happened to your elephant."

"What makes you so sure of that?"

"The fact that *you're* sure of it," replied Mallory with a confident grin. "We hate each other's guts, remember? You wouldn't have swallowed your pride and come to me unless you'd tried every other means of discovering what really happened first."

The Grundy nodded his approval. "I chose the right man. Sooner or later I shall kill you, slowly and painfully, but for the moment we shall be allies."

"Not a chance," Mallory contradicted him. "For the moment we're employer and employee . . . and one of my conditions for remaining your employee is a nonrefundable down payment of five thousand dollars." He paused. "Another is your promise not to harass my partner while I'm working." He smiled. "She doesn't know you like I do. You scare the hell out of her."

"Winnifred Carruthers is a fat old woman with a bleak past and a bleaker future. What is she to you?"

"She's my friend."

The demon snorted his contempt.

"I haven't got so many friends that I can let you go

around terrifying them," continued Mallory. "Have we got a deal?"

The Grundy stood stockstill for a moment, then nodded. "We have a deal."

"Good. Put the money on my desk before you leave."

But the Grundy had anticipated him, and Mallory found that he was speaking to empty air. He reached across the desk, counted out the bills (which, he noted without surprise, came to exactly five thousand dollars), and placed them in his pocket, while Felina stared at some spot that only she could see and watched the Grundy complete his leave-taking.

Mallory stood before the grandstand at Jamaica, watching a dozen elephants lumber through their morning workouts and trying to stifle yet another yawn, while all manner of men and vaguely humanoid creatures that had been confined to his nightmares only fifteen days ago went about their morning's chores. The track itself was on the outskirts of the suburb of Jamaica, which, like this particular Manhattan, was a hodgepodge of skyscrapers, Gothic castles, and odd little stores on winding streets that seemed to have no beginning and no end.

"What the hell am I doing here at five in the morning?" he muttered.

"Watching elephants run in a circle," said Felina helpfully.

"Why is it always animals?" continued Mallory, feeling his mortality as the cold morning air bit through his rumpled suit. "First a unicorn, then an elephant. Why can't it be something that keeps normal hours, like a bank robber?"

"Because the Grundy owns all the banks, and nobody would dare to rob him," answered Felina, avidly watching a small bird that circled overhead as it prepared to land on the rail just in front of the grandstand. Finally it perched about fifteen feet away, and Felina uttered an inhuman shriek and leaped nimbly toward it. The bird took flight, barely escaping her outstretched claws, but one of the elephants, startled by the sound, turned to pinpoint the source of the commotion, failed to keep a straight course, and broke through the outer rail on the clubhouse turn. His rider went flying through the air, finally landing in the branches of a small tree, while the huge pachyderm continued lumbering through the parking lot, banging into an occasional Tucker or DeLorean.

"Bringing you along may not have been the brightest idea I ever had," said Mallory, futilely attempting to pull her off her perch atop the rail.

"But I like it here," purred Felina, rubbing her shoulder against his own. "There are so many pretty birds here. Fat pretty birds. Fat juicy pretty birds. Fat tasty juicy pretty—"

"Enough," said Mallory.

"You never let me have any fun," pouted Felina.

"Our definitions of 'fun' vary considerably," said Mallory. He shrugged. "Oh, well, I guess I'd better get to work." He stared at her. "I don't suppose I can leave you here and expect you to stay out of trouble?"

She grinned happily. "Of course you can, John Justin," she replied, her pupils becoming mere vertical slits.

Mallory sighed. "I didn't think so. All right, come on."

She jumped lightly to the ground and fell into step behind him, leaping over any concrete squares that bore the contractor's insignia. They walked around the track and soon reached the backstretch, more than half a mile from where they had started.

Mallory's nose told him where the barns were. The smell of elephants reached him long before he heard the contented gurgling of their stomachs. Finally he reached the stable area, a stretch of huge concrete barns with tall ceilings and a steady flow of goblins and gnomes scurrying to and fro with hay-filled wheelbarrows.

He approached the first of the barns, walked up to a man who seemed quite human, and tapped him on the shoulder.

"Yes?" said the man, turning to him, and suddenly Mallory became aware of the fact that the man had three eyes.

"Can you tell me where to find Ahmed?"

"You're in the wrong place, pal. I think he's a placekicker for the Chicago Fire."

"He's an elephant."

"He is?" said the man, surprised.

Mallory nodded. "Yes."

"You're absolutely sure of that?"

Mallory nodded.

The man frowned. "Now why do you suppose the Fire would want an elephant on their team?"

"Beats the hell out of me," conceded Mallory. He decided to try a different approach. "I'm also looking for the barn where Genghis F. X. Khan stables his racing elephants."

"Well, friend, you just found it."

"You work for Khan?"

"Yep."

"Then how come you don't know who Ahmed is?"

"Hey, pal, my job is just to keep 'em cleaned and fed. I let the trainer worry about which is which."

"What's your name?"

"Jake. But everybody calls me Four-Eyes."

"Four-Eyes?" repeated Mallory.

The man nodded. " 'Cause I wear glasses."

"Well, I suppose it makes as much sense as anything else in this damned world." Mallory turned and looked down the shed row. "Where can I find Khan?"

"See that big guy standing by the backstretch rail, with the stopwatch in his hand?" said Four-Eyes, gesturing toward an enormous man clad in brilliantly-colored silks and satins and wearing a purple turban. "That's him. He's timing workouts."

"Shouldn't he be standing at the finish line?"

"His watch only goes up to sixty seconds, so he times 'em

up to the middle of the backstretch, and then his trainer times 'em the rest of the way home."

"Seems like a lot of wasted effort to me," said Mallory.

"Yeah? Why?"

"Because each time the second hand passes sixty, he just has to add a minute to the final time."

All three of Four-Eyes' eyes opened wide in amazement. "Son of a bitch!" he exclaimed. "I never thought of that!"

"Apparently no one else did, either," said Mallory caustically.

"Look, buddy," said Four-Eyes defensively, "math ain't my specialty. You wanna talk elephant shit, I can talk it with the best of 'em."

"No offense intended," said Mallory. He turned to Felina. "Let's go," he said, leading her toward the backstretch rail. Once there, he waited until Khan had finished timing one of his elephants, and then tapped the huge man on the shoulder.

"Yes?" demanded Khan, turning to him. "What do you want?"

"Excuse me, sir," said Mallory. "But I wonder if you'd mind answering some questions."

"I keep telling you reporters, Jackie Onassis and I are just good friends."

Mallory smiled. "Not that kind of question."

"Oh?" said Khan, frowning. "Well, let me state for the record that all three of them told me they were eighteen, and I don't know where the dead chicken came from. I was just an innocent bystander."

"Can we talk about elephants, sir?"

Khan wrinkled his nose. "Disgusting, foul-smelling animals." He stared distastefully at Felina. "Almost as annoying as cat people." Felina sniffed once and made a production of turning her back to him. "The smartest elephant I ever owned didn't have the intelligence of a potted plant."

"Then why do you own them?"

"My good man, everyone knows that Genghis F. X. Khan is a *sportsman.*" The hint of a smile crossed his thick lips. "Besides, if I didn't spend all this money on elephants, I'd just have to give it to the government."

"Makes sense to me," agreed Mallory.

"Is that all you wanted to know?"

"As a matter of fact, it isn't," said Mallory. "I'm not a reporter, sir; I'm a detective—and I'd like to know a little bit about Ahmed of Marsabit."

"Hah!" said Khan. "You're working for the Grundy, aren't you?"

"Yes, I am."

"He finally sells a good one by mistake, and now he's trying to prove that I cheated him out of it!"

"He hasn't made any accusations."

"He doesn't have to. I know the way his mind works." Khan glared at Mallory. "The only thing you have to know about Ahmed is that I'm going to win the Quatermaine Cup with him!"

"I understand that he was a pretty mediocre runner before you bought him."

"Mediocre is an understatement."

"You must have a very good eye for an elephant," suggested Mallory, "to be able to spot his potential."

"To tell you the absolute truth, I wouldn't know one from another," replied Khan. "Though Ahmed does stand out like a sore thumb around the barn."

"If you can't tell one from another, how can he stand out?"

"His color."

"His color?" repeated Mallory, puzzled.

"Didn't you know? One of the restrictions on the Quatermaine Cup is that pink is the only permitted color."

"Ahmed is a pink elephant?"

"Certainly."

Mallory shrugged. "Well, I've heard of white elephants in a somewhat different context . . . so why not pink?"

"They make the best racers," added Khan.

"Let me ask you a question," said Mallory. "If you don't know one elephant from another, and you don't trust the Grundy to begin with, why did you buy Ahmed?"

"I needed the tax writeoff."

"You mean you purposely bought an elephant you thought couldn't run worth a damn?"

Khan nodded. "And if it wasn't for the fun I'm going to have beating the Grundy's entry in the Cup, I'd be very annoyed with him. If Ahmed wins this weekend, I may actually have to dip into capital to pay my taxes."

"Aren't you afraid the Grundy might be a little upset with you if Ahmed beats his elephant?" asked Mallory.

"I've done nothing wrong," said Khan confidently. "The pure of heart have nothing to fear from demons."

"That's not the way I heard it."

"It's not the way I heard it either," admitted Khan. "But I've also sent off a two million dollar donation to my local church, and if *that* doesn't buy me a little holy protection, I'm going to have some very harsh words to say to God's attorneys." He paused. "Perhaps you'd like to take a look at Ahmed now?"

"Very much," responded Mallory. He turned to Felina. "You wait here."

Felina purred and grinned.

"I mean it," said Mallory. "I don't want you to move from this spot. I'll just be a couple of minutes."

"Yes, John Justin," she promised.

"Come along," said Khan, as he began walking back to the barn. When they arrived Khan whistled, and a number of trunks suddenly protruded from the darkened stalls, each one begging for peanuts or some other tidbit. One of the trunks was pink, and Mallory walked over to it.

"This is Ahmed?" he asked, gesturing toward the huge

pink elephant munching contentedly on a mouthful of straw.

"Impressive, isn't he?" said Khan. "As elephants go, that is."

"Do you mind if I pet him?" asked Mallory.

Khan shrugged. "As you wish."

Mallory approached Ahmed gingerly. When the long pink trunk snaked out to identify him, he held it gently in one hand and stroked it with the other, then pulled a handkerchief out of his pocket and rubbed the trunk vigorously. No color came off. Then he checked the tattoo on the back of the animal's left ear: it was Number 831.

Suddenly there was a loud commotion coming from the direction of the track, and a moment later Four-Eyes came running into the barn.

"Hey, buddy," he said, panting heavily, "you'd better do something about your friend!"

"What's she done this time?" asked Mallory.

"Come see for yourself."

Four-Eyes headed back to the track, Mallory and Khan hot on his heels.

The scene that greeted them resembled a riot. Elephants were trumpeting and racing all over the track, while their riders lay sprawled in the dirt. Four of the pachyderms, including a pink one, had broken through the rail and were decimating foreign cars in the parking lot. Track officials were running the length of the homestretch, waving their hands and shouting at Felina, who seemed to be flying a few feet off the ground, just ahead of them.

"What the hell's going on?" demanded Mallory.

"You know how they use a rabbit to make the greyhounds run faster at the dog tracks?" said Four-Eyes. "Well, we use a mouse at the elephant tracks. And instead of the dogs chasing the rabbit, the mouse chases the elephants." He paused for breath. "We don't use it in workouts, but the officials always give it one test run around the track before the afternoon races, just to make sure it's in good working order.

Your catgirl pounced on it when it passed by here, and her weight must have fouled up the mechanism, because it's going twice as fast as usual. Panicked every elephant on the track."

Mallory watched as Felina and the mouse hit the clubhouse turn four lengths ahead of the track officials, who soon ran out of breath and slowed down to a walk. The detective stepped under the rail and stood waiting for the catgirl, hands on hips, as she entered the backstretch. As the mouse neared him, Felina gathered herself and sprang high in the air, coming to rest in Mallory's hastily outstretched arms.

"It wasn't real," she pouted.

"I thought I told you to stay where you were," he said severely, setting her down on her feet.

"They cheated," muttered Felina, glaring balefully at the artificial mouse as it continued circling the track.

Mallory looked down the stretch and saw the furious but exhausted officials slowly approaching him. Taking Felina firmly by the hand, he ran to the rail and ducked under it.

"Come on," he said, racing to the barn area. "The last thing I need is to get barred from the grounds because of you."

They zigged and zagged in amongst the buildings, finally ducked into an empty stall, and stood motionless for a few moments until the track officials lost their enthusiasm for the hunt and began slowly returning to the clubhouse.

"Well?" said a voice at his side.

Mallory turned and found himself facing the Grundy.

"Well, what?"

"What have you accomplished for my money thus far, besides causing a small riot?"

"It's early in the day yet," said Mallory defensively.

"You didn't seriously think Khan painted one of his elephants to look like Ahmed, or that I failed to check the tattoo number before hiring you, did you?"

"No—but I felt I ought to check, just to be on the safe side."

"It was a total waste of time."

"Perhaps—but if you don't tell me these things, I have to find them out for myself," replied Mallory. "Is there anything else I should know?"

"Only that I expect results," said the Grundy. "And soon."

"Stop looking over my shoulder and you just might get 'em."

"I have every right to see how my money is being spent."

"That wasn't part of the contract," said Mallory. "I'll let you know when the case is solved. In the meantime, if you pop up again or interfere with me in any way, the deal's off and I'm keeping the retainer. I'm not an actor, and I don't want an audience."

"All right," said the demon after a moment's consideration. "We'll try it your way for the time being."

"I'd thank you, but I don't recall wording that as a request."

"Just remember, Mallory," said the Grundy, "that my patience is not unlimited."

And then he was gone.

"Thanks for warning me that he was about to pay me a visit," said Mallory to Felina.

"They cheated," growled Felina with a single-minded intensity that Mallory had rarely encountered in her before.

"They're not the only ones," said Mallory. He grabbed her hand and began leading her down the shed row. "Let's take a little walk."

He asked a stable girl with scaly green skin and a sullen expression to point out which barn housed the Grundy's stable of elephants, then walked over to it.

Four tweed-clad leprechauns suddenly barred his way.

"No trespassers," said the nearest of them with a malicious smirk.

"I'm working for your boss," replied Mallory.

"And I'm the Sultan of Swat," came the answer.

"I'm telling you the truth," said Mallory. "Check it out."

"Sure," said another one sarcastically. "The worst enemy the Grundy has, and we're supposed to believe you're working for him."

"Believe anything you want, but I'm going into that barn."

"Not a chance, Mallory," said the first leprechaun. "I'll fight to the death to keep you out."

"Fine by me," said Mallory. He turned to Felina, who was eyeing the leprechauns eagerly. "I knew you'd prove useful sooner or later. Felina, fight him to the death."

"Just a minute!" said the leprechaun. "I meant I'd fight you to *his* death." He pointed to one of his companions.

"Okay," said Mallory. "Felina, fight this other one."

"No!" screeched the leprechaun. "I mean, I'd love to fight your cat to the death, really and truly I would, but I strained my back last week and my doctor told me that I couldn't have any more duels to the death 'til a month after Christmas." He pointed to a third companion. "How about him? He's a real fighter, old Jules is."

"Right!" chimed in the first leprechaun. "Go get her, Julie! We're behind you 100 percent."

"What are you talking about?" demanded the second. "I told you: I have a bad back."

"Oh, right," replied the first. "Go get her, Julie! We're behind you almost sixty-seven percent!"

"Uh . . . count me out, guys," said the fourth leprechaun. "I got a tennis appointment at nine."

"You need a doubles partner?" asked Jules, backing away from the slowly advancing catgirl.

"I thought you were fighting her to the death," said the fourth leprechaun.

"Maybe it'll just be a mild case of death," suggested the first one. "Maybe it won't prove fatal. Go get her, Julie."

The unhappy Jules reached into his pocket and withdrew a wicked-looking knife. Felina merely grinned at him, held out her hand, and displayed four wicked-looking claws, each longer than the knife's blade.

Jules stared at the catgirl's claws for just an instant, then dropped his knife on the ground, yelled, "I gotta go to the bathroom!" and lit out for parts unknown at high speed.

"Can we enter the barn now," asked Mallory, "or is someone else interested in a fight to the death?"

"How about if we play checkers instead?" asked the first leprechaun.

"Or we could cut cards," suggested the fourth. "I happen to have a deck right here in my pocket."

Mallory shook his head. "Felina?"

The catgirl began approaching the remaining leprechauns.

"How about a fight to first blood instead?" suggested the nearest leprechaun.

"You and Felina?" asked Mallory.

"Actually, I was thinking more of *you* and Felina," answered the leprechaun.

"Right," chimed in the second one. "If you draw first blood, you get to go into the barn, and if she draws it, she gets to eat you."

"But you're bigger than her, so you gotta tie one hand behind your back," continued the first leprechaun. "After all, fair is fair."

"In fact," added the fourth, "if you could put it off for twenty or thirty minutes, we could sell tickets, and give the winner twenty percent of the take."

"Ten percent!" snapped the first leprechaun. "We've got overhead to consider."

"Split the difference," said the second. "Eleven percent, and let's get this show on the road."

"I'm afraid you guys are missing the point," said Mallory. "If you try to stop us from entering the barn, the only blood that's going to be spilled is leprechaun blood."

"Leprechaun blood?" cried the first one. "That's the

most disgusting thought I've ever heard! You have a warped, twisted mind, Mallory!"

"Besides, whoever heard of the combatants attacking the spectators?" demanded the second.

"I'm not a combatant," said Mallory.

"Of course you are," insisted the second leprechaun. "I thought it was all settled: you're fighting *her.*"

"Felina," said Mallory, "I'm walking into the barn now. Do whatever you like to anyone that tries to stop me."

Felina grinned and purred.

The first leprechaun turned to his companions. "Are you gonna let him talk to us like that?"

"What do you mean, *us?*" replied the second one, backing away from Felina. "He was looking at *you* when he said it."

"That's only because I'm so handsome that I just naturally attract the eye. He was definitely addressing you."

"Where's Julie when we need him?" said the fourth. "I'd better go find him." He headed off at a run.

"Wait!" said the second, racing after him. "I'll go with you. Julie wouldn't want to miss the chance to put these interlopers in their place."

"Well?" said Mallory, taking a step toward the one remaining leprechaun.

"The Grundy will kill me if I let anyone in," he said nervously.

"And Felina will kill you if you try to stop me," said Mallory, taking another step. "It's a difficult choice. You'd better consider your options very carefully."

The catgirl licked her lips.

"Well, I don't actually *work* for the Grundy," said the leprechaun hastily. "I mean, he underpays us and we don't even have a union or anything, to say nothing of sick leave and other fringes." He retreated a step. "Who does that Grundy think he is, anyway?" he continued in outraged tones. "How dare he demand that we stop an honest citizen from admiring his elephants! After all, the public supports racing, doesn't it? And you're part of the public, aren't you? These elephants are as much yours as his. The nerve of that Grundy! You go right on in," he concluded, putting even more distance between himself and Felina. "If the Grundy tries to stop you, I'll fight him to the death."

"That's very considerate of you," said Mallory, walking past the trembling leprechaun and entering the barn. "Felina!"

The catgirl reluctantly fell into step behind him.

Mallory walked down the shed row, peering into each stall. When he came to a stall housing a pink elephant, he entered it, checked the tattoo behind its left ear—the ID number was 384—and then left the stall and carefully closed the door behind him. When he finished checking the remainder of the stalls, he walked back outside and then turned to Felina.

"How many pink ones did you see?"

"One," she replied.

"Good. Then I didn't miss any."

Felina searched the sky for birds, but saw nothing but airplanes and an occasional harpy.

"It's cloudy," she noted.

"Yes," said Mallory, "but it's getting clearer every minute."

The catgirl shook her head. "It's going to rain."

"I'm not talking about the weather," answered Mallory.

Mallory dropped Felina off with Winnifred, then paid a visit to Joe the Goniff, his personal bookie.

The Goniff's office was housed in a decrepit apartment building, just far enough from the local police station so that they didn't feel obligated to close him up, and just close enough so that the cops could lay their bets on their lunch breaks.

The Goniff himself looked like something by Lovecraft

out of Runyon, a purple-skinned, misshapen creature who nonetheless felt compelled to dress the part of his profession, and had somehow, somewhere found a tailor who had managed to create a plaid suit, black shirt, and metallic silver tie that actually fit his grotesque body. He wore a matching plaid visor, and had pencils tucked behind each of his four ears.

"Hi, John Justin," he hissed in a sibilant voice as Mallory entered the office, which was empty now but would be bustling with activity in another two hours. "Too bad about Twinkle Toes."

"Can't win 'em all," said Mallory with a shrug.

"But you don't seem to win any of 'em," replied Joe the Goniff. "I keep thinking I should give you a discount, like maybe selling you a two-dollar ticket for a buck and a half."

"A big-hearted bookie," said Mallory in bemused tones. "Now I *know* I'm not in my Manhattan."

The Goniff chuckled, expelling little puffs of green vapor. "So, John Justin, who do you like today?"

"What's the line on the Quatermaine Cup?"

"Leviathan—that's the Grundy's unbeaten elephant—is the favorite at three-to-five. There's been a lot of play on Ahmed of Marsabit since that last race of his, but you can still get four-to-one on him. Hot Lips is eight-to-one, and I'll give you twenty-to-one on any of the others."

"What was Ahmed before his last race?" asked Mallory.

"Eighty-to-one."

"How much money would it take to bring him down to four-to-one?"

"Oh, I don't know," said the Goniff. "Maybe ten grand."

"Can you do me a couple of favors?"

"I love you like a brother, John Justin," said the Goniff. "There is nothing I wouldn't do for you. Just the thought of helping our city's most famous detective is—"

"How much?" interrupted Mallory wearily.

"I would never charge you for a favor, John Justin," replied the Goniff. "However," he added with a grin, "a thousand-dollar bet could buy my kid a new set of braces—if he ever needs them."

"I didn't know you had a kid."

"I don't—but who knows what the future holds?"

"A thousand dollars?"

"Right."

"Okay," said Mallory, pulling out his wallet and counting out ten of the hundred-dollar bills the Grundy had given him. "Put it all on Ahmed of Marsabit in the Cup."

The Goniff shook his massive head sadly. "Ahmed ran a big race the other day, I know—but you're making a mistake, John Justin. Leviathan's unbeaten and unextended. He's got a lock on the race."

"Put it on Ahmed anyway."

"You got inside information?" asked the Goniff, his eyes suddenly narrowing.

"I thought I was buying inside information from *you,*" answered Mallory. "Remember?"

"Oh, yeah—right. So what can I do for you?"

"I want to know if anyone made a killing on Ahmed's last race."

"Everyone who bet on him made a killing," replied Joe the Goniff. "He paid better than a hundred-to-one."

"Find out if anyone had more than a hundred dollars on him."

"It may take a day or two," said the Goniff. "I'll have to check with the track and all the O.T.B. offices as well as all the other bookies in town."

"Forget the track and the Off Track Betting offices," said Mallory. "Whoever made the killing wouldn't want to leave a record of it."

"Then what makes you think the bookies will tell you who it was?"

"They won't—but they'll tell *you.*"

"Okay, will do."

"I need to know before they run the Cup."

"Right." The Goniff paused. "You said you needed a couple of favors. What's the other one?"

"If someone plunked down a couple of grand on Ahmed when he was still eighty-to-one for the Cup, would that be the payoff if he won, or would they get the four-to-one you're offering now?"

"If they came to a regular handbook like myself, they'd get the posttime odds."

"How could they get eighty-to-one?"

"They'd have to go to a futures book like Creepy Conrad, over on the corner of Hope and Despair."

"What's a futures book?" asked Mallory.

"You get the odds that are on the board that day . . . but you're stuck with the bet, even if the odds go up, even if he's scratched, even if the damned elephant breaks a leg and they have to shoot him a month before the race. Usually a futures book will close on a race a couple of months before it's run."

"How many futures books are there in town?"

"Three."

"For my second favor, I want you to get in touch with all three, see if any serious money was placed on Ahmed when he was still more than fifty-to-one, and find out who made the bets."

"Can't do it, John Justin."

"Why not?"

"One of those books is run by my brother-in-law, and we haven't spoken to each other since I caught him cheating at Friday night poker. I have my pride, you know."

"How much will it take to soothe your pride?" asked Mallory with a sigh.

"Another five hundred ought to do it."

Mallory withdrew five more bills. "Put four hundred ninety-eight on Ahmed, and give me a two-dollar ticket on

Leviathan." He paused. "And when you get my information, call Winnifred Carruthers at my office and give it to her."

"You on drugs or something, John Justin?" demanded the Goniff. "I keep telling you Ahmed can't win. You must be snorting nose candy."

"Just do what I said."

"Okay," said the Goniff. "But I got a funny notion that you're a head."

"Not yet," replied Mallory with a sudden burst of confidence. "But I'm catching up."

"Well?" demanded the Grundy.

It was Cup day at Jamaica, and the grandstand and clubhouse were filled to overflowing. The sun had finally managed to break through the cover of clouds and smog, and although it had rained the previous night, the maintenance crew had managed to dry out the track, upgrading it from "muddy" in the first race to "good" in the third, and finally to "fast" as posttime approached for the Quatermaine Cup.

Mallory was sitting in the Grundy's private box in the clubhouse, sipping an Old Peculiar, and enjoying the awe which the spectators seemed to hold for anyone who was willing to remain in such close proximity to the notorious Grundy.

"I told you," said Mallory. "The case is solved."

"But you haven't told me anything else, and I am fast losing my patience with you."

"I'm just waiting for one piece of information."

"Then the case *isn't* solved, and Khan's elephant might win the Cup."

"Relax," said Mallory. "All I'm waiting for is the name of the guilty party. I guarantee you that the real Ahmed will be running in the Cup."

"You're absolutely sure?" demanded the Grundy.

Mallory withdrew his two-dollar win ticket on Leviathan

and held it up for the Grundy to see. "I wouldn't be betting on your entry if I wasn't sure."

The Grundy looked out across the track, where eight pink elephants were walking in front of the stands in the post parade.

"It's time for me to lay my bets," he said. "If you have lied to me, John Justin Mallory . . . "

"As God is my witness, I haven't lied."

"I am considerably more vindictive than God," the Grundy assured him. "You would do well to remember that."

" *You'd* do well to remember that it's only six minutes to posttime, and you haven't gotten your bets down yet," responded Mallory.

"Ahmed is definitely on the track right now?" insisted the Grundy.

"For the fifth time, Ahmed is definitely on the track right now."

"You had better be right," said the Grundy, vanishing.

Suddenly Winnifred Carruthers approached the box.

"I've been wondering what happened to you," said Mallory.

"Your bookie just called the office an hour ago, and traffic was dreadful," she said.

"He gave you a name?"

"Yes," said Winnifred. "I wrote it down." She handed the detective a slip of paper. He looked at it, nodded, and then ripped it into tiny pieces. "By the way," added Winnifred with obvious distaste, "where's your client?"

"Laying his bets," said Mallory.

A sudden murmur ran through the crowd, and Mallory looked up at the tote board. Leviathan had gone down from even money to one-to-five, and the other prices had all shot up. Ahmed of Marsabit was now fifteen-to-one.

"That's it," said Mallory with satisfaction. "All the pieces are in place."

"I hope you know what you're doing, John Justin."

"I hope so too," he said earnestly. He smiled reassuringly at her. "Not to worry. If everything works out the way I have it planned, I'll buy you a new hunting rifle."

"And if it doesn't?"

"We'll worry about that eventuality if and when it comes to pass," said Mallory. He paused. "You'd better be going now. The Grundy is due back any second."

She nodded. "But I'll be standing about thirty rows behind you. If the Grundy tries anything . . . " She opened her purse, and Mallory could see a revolver glinting inside it.

"Whatever you do, don't shoot him."

"Why not? I'm a crack shot."

"Yeah, but I have a feeling that shooting him would just annoy him," said Mallory. "Besides, you're not going to need the gun. Believe me, everything is under control."

She looked doubtful, but sighed and began walking up the aisle to her chosen vantage point. The Grundy reappeared a few seconds later, just as the elephants were being loaded into the oversized starting gate.

"Well?" demanded the demon.

"What now?"

"I know she talked to you."

"She's my friend and my partner. She's allowed to talk to me."

"Don't be obtuse," said the Grundy coldly. "Did she give you the information you needed?"

"Yes."

"Let me have it."

"As soon as the race is over."

"Now."

"I guarantee the culprit won't get away," said Mallory. "And telling you his name won't affect the outcome of the race."

"You're sure?"

"I may not like you, but I've never lied to you."

The Grundy stared at him. "That is true," he admitted.

"Good. Now sit down and enjoy the race."

Six elephants were already standing in the gate, and the assistant starters soon loaded the last two. Then a bell rang, the doors sprang open, the electric mouse loomed up on the rail, and eight squealing pink elephants pounded down the homestretch.

"And it's Hot Lips taking the early lead," called the track announcer. "Ahmed of Marsabit is laying second, two lengths off the pace, Beer Belly is third, Levithan broke sluggishly and has moved up to fourth, Kenya Express is fifth, Dumbo is sixth, Babar is seventh . . . "

"He's never broken badly before," muttered the Grundy. "When I get my hands on that jockey . . . "

"Around the clubhouse turn, and it's still Hot Lips and Ahmed of Marsabit showing the way," said the announcer. "Leviathan is now third, Kenya Express is fourth . . . "

The order remained unchanged as the pink pachyderms raced down the backstretch, their ears flapping wildly as they tried to listen for signs that the mouse was gaining on them. Then, as they were midway around the far turn, Ahmed's jockey went to the whip—a six-foot wooden club with a spike embedded at the end of it—and Ahmed immediately overtook Hot Lips and opened up a three-length lead by the head of the homestretch.

"Now!" cried the Grundy. "Make your move now!"

But Leviathan began losing ground, his huge sides rising and falling as he labored for breath, and a moment later Ahmed crossed the finish line twelve lengths in front. Leviathan came in dead last, as the lightly-raced Beer Belly caught him in the final fifty yards.

"Mallory!" thundered the Grundy, rising to his feet and glaring balefully at the detective. "You lied to me! Your life is forfeit!" He reached into the air and withdrew a huge fireball. "Your bones shall melt within your body, your flesh shall be charred beyond all—"

"I told you the truth!" said Mallory, holding up a hand. "Ahmed lost!"

The Grundy frowned. "What are you talking about?"

"Leviathan won the race."

"I just saw Ahmed win the Cup."

Mallory shook his head. "You just saw *Leviathan* win the Cup."

"Explain yourself," said the Grundy, still holding his fireball at the ready.

"Leviathan's ID number is 384, and Ahmed's is 831. It didn't take much to change them. Then, when Khan came to pick up Ahmed, someone gave him Leviathan instead."

"Then Khan isn't responsible?"

"He's furious. He needed a loser for tax purposes."

"Then who is responsible for this?" demanded the Grundy.

"Someone who had access to both animals, had the time to work on the tattoos, and bet heavily on Leviathan both times he started in Khan's colors."

"Who?" repeated the Grundy.

"A leprechaun named Jules."

"I've never heard of him."

"That's the problem with having your fingers in too many pies, so to speak," said Mallory. "He works for you."

"At the barn?"

"Yes . . . though he's probably at Creepy Conrad's handbook right now, cashing his ticket."

"I may never have heard of him," said the Grundy, "but he will curse the day he heard of *me.*"

"I never doubted it for a minute," replied Mallory.

The Grundy glared at Mallory. "You did not lie, but you purposely deceived me. I will expect my retainer to be returned, and I will not reimburse you for your time. I suspect you made a handsome profit on the race."

"I'll get by okay," answered the detective. "I'll send your money over tomorrow morning."

"See to it that you do," said the Grundy, his fireball finally vanishing. "And now I must take my leave of you, John Justin Mallory. I have urgent business at Creepy Conrad's."

The Grundy vanished, and Mallory walked over to join Winnifred.

"Is it all over?" she asked.

"It will be, as soon as we pick up my winnings from the Goniff. Then I think I'll treat us to dinner and a night on the town."

"Where shall we eat?" asked Winnifred.

"Any place that doesn't serve elephant," replied Mallory. "I've seen quite enough of Ahmed for one day."

"Oh, that poor animal!" said Winnifred. "You don't think the Grundy would—?"

"He hasn't got much use for losers," said Mallory.

"But that's terrible!"

"He's just an elephant."

"We've got to do something, John Justin."

"We've got to collect my money and have dinner."

"We've got to collect your money, yes," said Winnifred. "But forget about dinner. We have more important things to do."

"We have?" asked Mallory resignedly.

"Definitely."

That evening Felina had a new toy. It weighed six tons, and held a very special place in the Guiness Book of World Records for running the slowest mile in the history of Jamaica.

INTRODUCTION
Beachcomber

This is the only story that ever came to me in a dream—or, at least, the image of a robot stuck in the sand, covered with rust and graffiti came to me, and the rest of the story just about wrote itself.

It was one of my earliest short story sales, to Roy Torgeson's *Chrysalis* anthology series, and remains one of my favorites.

Beachcomber

Arlo didn't look much like a man. (Not all robots do, you know.) The problem was that he didn't act all that much like a robot.

The fact of the matter is that one day, right in the middle of work, he decided to pack it in. Just got up, walked out the door, and kept on going. *Some*body must have seen him; it's pretty hard to hide nine hundred pounds of moving parts. But evidently nobody knew it was Arlo. After all, he hadn't left his desk since the day they'd activated him twelve years ago.

So the Company got in touch with me, which is a euphemistic way of saying that they woke me in the middle of the night, gave me three minutes to get dressed, and rushed me to the office. I can't really say that I blame them: when you need a scapegoat, the Chief of Security is a pretty handy guy to have around.

Anyway, it was panic time. It seems that no robot ever ran away before. And Arlo wasn't just any robot: he was a twelve million dollar item, with just about every feature a machine could have short of white-walled tires. And I wasn't even so certain about the tires; he sure dropped out of sight fast enough.

So, after groveling a little and making all kinds of optimistic promises to the Board, I started doing a little checking up on Arlo. I went to his designer, and his department head, and even spoke to some of his co-workers, both human and robot.

And it turned out that what Arlo did was sell tickets. That didn't sound like twelve million dollars' worth of robot to me, but I was soon shown the error of my ways. Arlo was a travel agent supreme. He booked tours of the Solar System, got his people into and out of luxury hotels on Ganymede and Titan and the Moon, scheduled their weight and their time to the nearest gram and the nearest second.

It *still* didn't sound that impressive. Computers were doing stuff like that long before robots ever crawled out of the pages of pulp magazines and into our lives.

"True," said his department head. "But Arlo was a robot with a difference. He booked more tours and arranged more complicated logistical scheduling than any other ten robots put together."

"More complex thinking gear?" I asked.

"Well, that too," was the answer. "But we did a little something else with Arlo that had never been done before."

"And what was that?"

"We programmed him for enthusiasm."

"That's something special?" I asked.

"Absolutely. When Arlo spoke about the beauties of Callisto, or the fantastic light refraction images on Venus, he did so with a conviction that was so intense as to be almost tangible. Even his voice reflected his enthusiasm. He was one of those rare robots who was capable of modular inflection, rather than the dull, mechanistic monotone so many of them possess. He literally loved those desolate worlds, and his record will show that his attitude was infectious."

I thought about that for a minute. "So you're telling me that you've created a robot whose entire motivation had been to send people out to sample all these worlds, and he's been crated up in an office twenty-four hours a day since the second you plugged him in?"

"That's correct."

"Did it ever occur to you that maybe he wanted to see some of these sights himself?"

"It's entirely possible that he did, but leaving his post would be contrary to his orders."

"Yeah," I said. "Well, sometimes a little enthusiasm can go a long way."

He denied it vigorously, and I spent just enough time in his office to mollify him. Then I left and got down to work. I checked every outgoing space flight, and had some of the Company's field reps hit the more luxurious vacation spas. He wasn't there.

So I tried a little closer to home: Monte Carlo, New Vegas, Alpine City. No luck. I even tried a couple of local theaters that specialized in Tri-Fi travelogs.

You know where I finally found him?

Stuck in the sand at Coney Island. I guess he'd been walking along the beach at night and the tide had come in and he just sank in, all nine hundred pounds of him. Some kids had painted some obscene graffiti on his back, and there he stood, surrounded by empty beer cans and broken glass and a few dead fish. I looked at him for a minute, then shook my head and walked over.

"I knew you'd find me sooner or later," he said, and even though I knew what to expect, I still did a double-take at the sound of that horribly unhappy voice coming from this enormous mass of gears and gadgetry.

"Well, you've got to admit that it's not too hard to spot a robot on a condemned beach," I said.

"I suppose I have to go back now," said Arlo.

"That's right," I said.

"At least I've felt the sand beneath my feet," said Arlo.

"Arlo, you don't have any feet," I said. "And if you did, you couldn't feel sand beneath them. Besides, it's just silicon and crushed limestone and . . . "

"It's sand and it's beautiful!" snapped Arlo.

"All right, have it your way: it's beautiful." I knelt down next to him and began digging the sand away.

"Look at the sunrise," he said in a wistful voice. "It's glorious!"

I looked. A sunrise is a sunrise. Big deal.

"It's enough to bring tears of joy to your eyes," said Arlo.

"You don't have eyes," I said, working at the sand. "You've got prismatic photo cells that transmit an image to your central processing unit. And you can't cry, either. If I were you, I'd be more worried about rusting."

"A pastel wonderland," he said, turning what passed for his head and looking up and down the deserted beach, past the rotted food stands and the broken piers. "Glorious!"

It kind of makes you wonder about robots, I'll tell you. Anyway, I finally pried him loose and ordered him to follow me.

"Please," he said in that damned voice of his. "Couldn't I have one last minute before you lock me up in my office?"

I stared at him, trying to make up my mind.

"One last look. Please?"

I shrugged, gave him about thirty seconds, and then took him in tow.

"You know what's going to happen to you, don't you?" I said as we rode back to the office.

"Yes," he said. "They're going to put in a stronger duty directive, aren't they?"

I nodded. "At the very least."

"My memory banks!" he exclaimed, and once again I jumped at the sound of a human voice coming from an animated gearbox. "They won't take this experience away from me, will they?"

"I don't know, Arlo," I said.

"They can't!" he wailed. "To see such beauty, and then have it expunged—erased!"

"Well, they may want to make sure you don't go AWOL again," I said, wondering what kind of crazy junkheap could find anything beautiful on a garbage-laden strip of dirt.

"Can you intercede for me if I promise never to leave again?"

Any robot that can disobey one directive can disobey others, like not roughing up human beings, and Arlo was a pretty powerful piece of machinery, so I put on my most fatherly smile and said: "Sure I will, Arlo. You can count on it."

So I returned him to the Company, and they upped his sense of duty and took away his enthusiasm and gave him a case of agoraphobia and wiped his memory banks clean, and now he sits in his office and speaks to customers without inflection, and sells a few less tickets than he used to.

And every couple of months or so I wander over to the beach and walk along it and try to see what it was that made Arlo sacrifice his personality and his security and damned near everything else, just to get a glimpse of all this.

And I see a sunset just like any other sunset, and a stretch of dirty sand with glass and tin cans and seaweed and rocks on it, and I breathe in polluted air, and sometimes I get rained on; and I think of that damned robot in that plush office with that cushy job and every need catered to, and I decide that I'd trade places with him in two second flat.

I saw Arlo just the other day—I had some business on his floor—and it was almost kind of sad. He looked just like any other robot, spoke in a grating monotone, acted exactly like an animated computer. He wasn't much before, but whatever he had been, he gave it all away just to look at the sky once or twice. Dumb trade.

Well, robots never did make much sense to me, anyway.

Blue

My association with dogs has been a long and happy one—not only did Carol and I breed and exhibit twenty-plus collie champions, but we currently own the second-largest luxury boarding and grooming kennel in the country—so, after the success of "The Last Dog," I decided to write one more story with one more real dog in it.

"Blue" (which *could* be a fantasy, depending upon your religious orientation) won the American Dog Writers' Association Award for Best Short Fiction of 1978, and I retired forthwith from the dog writing biz.

Blue

I had a dog, his name was Blue.
Bet you five dollars he's a good one too.
Come on, Blue!
I'm a-coming too.

They sing that song about him, Burl Ives and Win Stracke and the rest, but they wouldn't have been too happy to be locked in the same room with old Blue. He'd as soon take your hand off as look at you.

He wandered out to my shack one day when he was a pup and just plumped himself down and stayed. I always figured he stuck around because I was the only thing he'd ever seen that was even meaner and uglier than he was.

As for betting five dollars on Blue or anything else, forget it. It's been so long since I've seen five dollars that I don't even remember whose picture is on the bill. Jefferson, I think, or maybe Roosevelt. Money just never mattered much to me, and as long as Blue was warm and dry and had a full belly, nothing much mattered to him.

Each winter we'd shaggy up, me on my face and him just about everywhere, and each summer we'd naked down. Didn't see a lot of people any time of year. When we did, it'd be a contest to see who could run them off the territory first, me or Blue. He'd win more often than not. He never came back looking for praise, or like he'd done a bright thing; it was more like he'd done a *necessary* thing. Those woods and that river was ours, his and mine, and we didn't see any reason to put up with a batch of intruders, neither city-slickers nor down-home boys either.

It was a pretty good life. Neither of us got fat, but we didn't go hungry very often either. And it was kind of good to sit by a fire together, me smoking and him snorting. I don't think he liked my pipe tobacco, but we had this kind of pact not to bother each other, and he stuck by it a lot better than a couple of women I outlived.

And, Mister, that dog was hell on a cold scent.

> *Blue chased a possum up a cinnamon tree.*
> *Blue looked at the possum, possum looked at me.*
> *Come on, Blue.*
> *I'm a-coming too.*

Except that it wasn't a cinnamon tree at all. I don't ever recollect seeing one. It was just a plain old tree, and I still can't figure out how the possum got up there all in one piece.

It must have been twenty below zero, and neither of us had eaten in a couple of days. Suddenly Blue put his nose to the ground and started baying just like a bloodhound. Thought he was on the trail of an escaped killer the way he carried on, but it was just an old possum, looking every bit as cold and hungry as we were. The way Blue ran him I thought his heart would burst, but somehow he made it a few feet up the tree trunk. Slashed Blue on the nose a couple of times, just for good measure, but if he thought that would make old Blue run off with his tail between his legs, he had another think coming. Blue just stood there, kind of smiling up at him, and saying, Possum, let's see you come on down and try that again.

It was a mighty toothy smile.

Baked that possum good and brown.
Laid sweet potatoes all around.
Come on, Blue,
You can have some too.

Never did like possum meat. Even when you bake a possum it tastes just awful. The sweet potatoes were just to kill the flavor. Folksingers and poets live on steak and praise; let 'em try living on possum for a few days and I bet that verse would come out different.

Anyway, I did offer some to Blue, just like the song says. He looked at it, picked it up, and kind of played with it like a pup dog does when you give him a piece of fruit. At first I thought it was just good taste on Blue's part, but then his nose started to swell where the possum had nailed him. Usually I'd slap a little mud on a wound like that, but mud's not the easiest thing to come by when it's below zero, so I rubbed some snow on instead.

First time in his life Blue ever snarled at me.

When old Blue died he died so hard,
He jarred the ground in my back yard.
Go on, Blue.
I'll get there too.

Guess the possum had rabies or something, because Blue just got worse and worse. His face swelled up like a balloon, and some of the fire went out of his eyes.

We stayed in the shack, me tending to him except when I had to go out and shoot us something to eat, and him just getting thinner and thinner. I kept trying to make him rest easier, and I could see him fighting with himself, trying not to bite me when I touched him where it hurt.

Then one day he started foaming at the mouth, and howling something awful. And suddenly he turned toward me and got up on his feet, kind of shaky-like, and I could tell he didn't know who I was anymore. He went for me, but fell over on his side before he got halfway across the floor.

I only had a handful of bullets left to last out the winter, but I figured I'd rather eat fish for a month than let him lie there like that. I walked over to him and put my finger on the trigger, and suddenly he stopped tossing around and held stock-still. Maybe he knew what I was going to do, or more likely it was just that he always held still when I raised my rifle. I don't know the reason, but I know we each made things a little easier for the other in that last couple of seconds before I squeezed the trigger.

> *When I get to Heaven, first thing I'll do*
> *Is grab my horn and call for Blue.*
> *Hello, Blue.*
> *Finally got here too.*

That's the way the song ends. It's a right pretty sentiment, so I suppose they had to sing it that way, but Heaven ain't where I'm bound. Wouldn't like it anyhow; white robes and harp-strumming and minding my manners every second. Besides, winter has always chilled me to the bone; I *like* heat.

But when I get to where I'm going, I'll look up and call for him, and Blue will come running just like he always did. He'll have a long way to go before he finds me, but that never stopped old Blue. He'll just put his nose to the ground, and pretty soon we'll be together again, and he'll know why I did what I did to him.

And we'll sit down before the biggest fire of all, me smoking my pipe and him twitching and snorting like always. And maybe I'll pet him, but probably I won't, and maybe he'll lick me, but probably he won't. We'll just sit there together, and we'll know everything's okay again.

Hello, Blue. I finally got here too.

Stalking the Unicorn with Gun and Camera

I love parody articles, and since I do so much research on Africa, I've read more than my share of hairy-chested heman's hunting articles. I always wanted to do a put-on of one, but I never had a subject until I saw one soft-eyed unicorn too many in a science-fiction convention's art show. Then everything jelled, and I went home and wrote it in a single sitting.

This was my first, but far from my last, sale to Ed Ferman's *The Magazine of Fantasy and Science Fiction.* I'd been reading the magazine since I was nine years old, and dreaming of appearing in it for almost as long.

Stalking the Unicorn with Gun and Camera

When she got to within 200 yards of the herd of Southern Savannah unicorns she had been tracking for four days, Rheela of the Seven Stars made her obeisance to Quatr Mane, God of the Hunt, then donned the Amulet of Kobassen, tested the breeze to make sure that she was still downwind of the herd, and began approaching them, camera in hand.

But Rheela of the Seven Stars had made one mistake—a mistake of *carelessness*—and thirty seconds later she was dead, brutally impaled upon the horn of a bull unicorn.

Hotack the Beastslayer cautiously made his way up the lower slopes of the Mountain of the Nameless One. He was a skilled tracker, a fearless hunter, and a crack shot. He picked out the trophy he wanted, got the beast within his sights, and hurled his killing club. It flew straight and true to its mark.

And yet, less than a minute later, Hotack, his left leg badly gored, was barely able to pull himself to safety in the branches of a nearby Rainbow Tree. He, too, had make a mistake—a mistake of *ignorance.*

Bort the Pure had had a successful safari. He had taken three chimeras, a gorgon, and a beautifully-matched pair of griffons. While his trolls were skinning the gorgon he spotted a unicorn sporting a near-record horn, and, weapon in hand, he began pursuing it. The terrain gradually changed, and suddenly Bort found himself in shoulder-high kraken grass. Undaunted, he followed the trail into the dense vegetation. But Bort the Pure, too, had made a mistake—a mistake of *foolishness.* His trolls found what very little remained of him some six hours later.

Carelessness, ignorance, foolishness—together they account for more deaths among unicorn hunters than all other factors combined.

Take our examples, for instance. All three hunters—Rheela, Hotack, and Bort—were experienced safari hands. They were used to extremes of temperature and terrain, they didn't object to finding insects in their ale or banshees in their tents, they knew they were going after deadly game and took all reasonable precautions before setting out.

And yet two of them died, and the third was badly maimed.

Let's examine their mistakes, and see what we can learn from them:

Rheela of the Seven Stars assimilated everything her personal wizard could tell her about unicorns, purchased the very finest photographic equipment, hired a native guide who had been on many unicorn hunts, and had a local witch doctor bless her Amulet of Kobassen. And yet, when the charge came, the amulet was of no use to her, for she had failed to properly identify the particular sub-species of unicorn before her—and as I am continually pointing out during my lecture tours, the Amulet of Kobassen is potent only against the rare and almost-extinct Forest unicorn. Against the Southern Savannah unicorn, the *only* effective charm is the Talisman of Triconis. *Carelessness.*

Hotack the Beastslayer, on the other hand, disdained all forms of supernatural protection. To him, the essence of the hunt was to pit himself in physical combat against his chosen prey. His killing club, a beautifully-wrought and finely-balanced instrument of destruction, had brought down simurghs, humbabas, and even a dreaded wooly hydra. He elected to go for a head shot, and the club flew to within a millimeter of where he had aimed it. But he hadn't counted on the unicorn's phenomenal sense of smell, nor the speed with which these surly brutes can move. Alerted to Hotack's presence, the unicorn turned its head to seek out its predator—and the killing club bounced harmlessly off its horn. Had Hotack spoken to almost any old-time unicorn hunter, he would have realized that head shots are almost impossible, and would have gone for a crippling knee shot. *Ignorance.*

Bort the Pure was aware of the unique advantages accruing to a virgin who hunts the wild unicorn, and so had practiced sexual abstinence since he was old enough to know what the term meant. And yet he naively believed that because his virginity allowed him to approach the unicorn more easily than other hunters, the unicorn would somehow become placid and make no attempt to defend itself—and so he followed a vicious animal which was compelled to let him approach it, and entered a patch of high grass which allowed him no maneuvering room during the inevitable charge. *Foolishness.*

Every year hundreds of hopeful hunters go out in search of the unicorn, and every year all but a handful come back empty-handed—if they come back at all. And yet the unicorn *can* be safely stalked and successfully hunted, if only the stalkers and hunters will take the time to study their quarry.

When all is said and done, the unicorn is a relatively docile beast (except when enraged). It is a creature of habit, and once those habits have been learned by the hopeful photographer or trophy hunter, bringing home that picture or that horn is really no more dangerous than, say, slaying an Eight-Forked Dragon—and it's certainly easier than lassoing wild minotaurs, a sport that has become all the rage these days among the smart set on the Platinum Plains.

However, before you can photograph or kill a unicorn, you have to find it—and by far the easiest way to make contact with a unicorn herd is to follow the families of smerps that track the great game migrations. The smerps, of course, have no natural enemies except for the rafsheen and the zumakim, and consequently will allow a human (or preternatural) being to approach them quite closely.

A word of warning about the smerp: with its long ears and cute, fuzzy body, it resembles nothing more than an oversized rabbit—but calling a smerp a rabbit doesn't make it one, and you would be ill-advised to underestimate the strength of these nasty little scavengers. Although they generally hunt in packs of from ten to twenty, I have more than once seen a single smerp, its aura glowing with savage strength, pull down a half-grown unicorn. Smerps are poor eating, their pelts are worthless because of the difficulty of curing and tanning the auras, and they make pretty unimpressive trophies unless you can come up with one possessing a truly magnificent set of ears—in fact, in many areas they're still classified as vermin—but the wise unicorn hunter can save himself a lot of time and effort by simply letting the smerps lead him to his prey.

With the onset of poaching, the legendary unicorn herds numbering upwards of a thousand members no longer exist, and you'll find that the typical herd today consists of from fifty to seventy-five individuals. The days when a photographer, safe and secure in a blind by a water hole, could preserve on film an endless stream of the brutes coming down to drink, are gone forever—and it is absolutely shocking to contemplate the number of unicorns that have died simply so their horns could be sold on the black market. In fact, I find it appalling that anyone in this enlightened day and age still believes that a powdered unicorn horn can act as an aphrodisiac.

(Indeed, as any magi can tell you, you treat the unicorn horn with essence of *gracch* and then boil it slowly in a solution of sphinx blood. Now *that's* an aphrodisiac!)

But I digress.

The unicorn, being a non-discriminating browser that is equally content to feed upon grasses, leaves, fruits, and an occasional small fern tree, occurs in a wide variety of habitats, often in the company of grazers such as centaurs and p̶e̶g̶a̶s̶u̶-s̶e̶s̶ p̶e̶g̶a̶s̶i̶n̶ the pegasus.

Once you have spotted the unicorn herd, it must be approached with great care and caution. The unicorn may have poor eyesight, and its sense of hearing may not be much better, but it has an excellent sense of smell and an absolutely awesome sense of *grimsch,* about which so much has been written that there is no point in my belaboring the subject yet again.

If you are on a camera safari, I would strongly advise against trying to get closer than 100 yards to even a solitary beast—that sense of *grimsch* again—and most of the photographers I know swear by an 85/350mm automatic-focus zoom lens, providing, of course, that it has been blessed by a Warlock of the Third Order. If you haven't got the shots you want by sunset, my best advice is to pack it in for the day and return the next morning. Flash photography is possible, of course, but it does tend to attract golem and other even more bothersome nocturnal predators.

One final note to the camera buff: For reasons our alchemists have not yet determined, no unicorn has ever been photographed with normal emulsified film of any speed, so make absolutely sure that you use one of the more popular infrared brands. It would be a shame to spend weeks on safari, paying for your guide, cook, and trolls, only to come away with a series of photos of the forest that you thought was merely the background to your pictures.

As for hunting the brutes, the main thing to remember is that they are as close to you as you are to them. For this reason, while I don't disdain blood sacrifices, amulets, talismans, and blessings, all of which have their proper place, I for one always feel more confident with a .550 Nitro Express in my hands. A little extra stopping power can give a hunter quite a feeling of security.

You'll want a bull unicorn, of course; they tend to have more spectacular horns than the cows—and by the time a bull's horn is long enough to be worth taking, he's probably too old to be in the herd's breeding program anyway.

The head shot, for reasons explained earlier, is never a wise option. And unless your wizard teaches you the Rune of Mamhotet, thus enabling you to approach close enough to pour salt on the beast's tail and thereby pin him to the spot where he's standing, I recommend the heart shot (either heart will do—and if you have a double-barreled gun, you might try to hit both of them, just to be on the safe side).

If you have the bad fortune to merely wound the beast, he'll immediately make off for the trees or the high grass, which puts you at an enormous disadvantage. Some hunters, faced with such a situation, merely stand back and allow the smerps to finish the job for them—after all, smerps rarely devour the horn unless they're completely famished—but this is hardly sporting. The decent, honorable hunter, well aware of the unwritten rules of blood sports, will go after the unicorn himself.

The trick, of course, is to meet him on fairly open terrain. Once the unicorn lowers his head to charge, he's virtually blind, and all you need do is dance nimbly out of his way and take another shot at him—or, if you are not in possession of the Rune of Mamhotet, this would be an ideal time to get out that salt and try to sprinkle some on his tail as he races by.

When the unicorn dictates the rules of the game, you've

got a much more serious situation. He'll usually double back and lie in the tall grasses beside his spoor, waiting for you to pass by, and then attempt to gore you from behind.

It is at this time that the hunter must have all his wits about him. Probably the best sign to look for is the presence of Fire-Breathing Dragonflies. These noxious little insects frequently live in symbiosis with the unicorn, cleansing his ears of parasites, and their presence usually means that the unicorn isn't far off. Yet another sign that your prey is nearby will be the flocks of hungry harpies circling overhead, waiting to swoop down and feed upon the remains of your kill; and, of course, the surest sign of all is when you hear a grunt of rage and find yourself staring into the bloodshot, beady little eyes of a wounded bull unicorn from a distance of ten feet or less. It's moments like that that make you feel truly alive, especially when you suddenly realize that it isn't necessarily a permanent condition.

All right. Let us assume that your hunt is successful. What then?

Well, your trolls will skin the beast, of course, and take special care in removing and preserving the horn. If they've been properly trained they'll also turn the pelt into a rug, the hooves into ashtrays, the teeth into a necklace, the tail into a flyswatter, and the scrotum into a tobacco pouch. My own feeling is that you should settle for nothing less, since it goes a long way toward showing the bleeding-heart preservationists that a unicorn can supply the hunter with a lot more than just a few minutes of pleasurable sport and a horn.

And while I'm on the subject of what the unicorn can supply, let me strongly suggest that you would be missing a truly memorable experience if you were to come home from safari without having eaten unicorn meat at least once. There's nothing quite like unicorn cooked over an open campfire to top off a successful hunt. (And do remember to leave something out for the smerps, or they might well decide that hunter is every bit as tasty as unicorn.)

So get out those amulets and talismans, visit those wizards and warlocks, pack those cameras and weapons—and good hunting to you!

Next Week: Outstaring the Medusa

Monsters of the Midway

When John Betancourt asked me to contribute a story to *The Ultimate Frankenstein,* this tale popped into my head before he was off the phone, and I wrote it the same night.

The title was a natural—after all, I grew up in George Halas' Chicago—and believe me, if *I* could animate dead tissue, my beloved Cincinnati Bengals wouldn't still be looking for their first Super Bowl trophy.

Monsters of the Midway

SURPRISES ON TAP?

July 12, 2037 (UPI) Coach Rattler Renfro, in his initial press conference, has promised fans that his Chicago Bears, coming off a pair of 1-and-15 seasons, will sport a new look this year. When asked to explain why training camp will be closed to both the press and the public, Renfro merely smiled and said, "No comment."

BEARS TAKE OPENER, 76–0

September 4, 2037 (AP) The "New Look" Chicago Bears made their debut this afternoon, beating last year's Super Bowl winners, the North Dakota Timberwolves, by a league-record score of 76–0. The Timberwolves were a 22-point favorite.

Coach Rattler Renfro unveiled an all-new offensive line, consisting of five rookies, all free agents who had never played organized football before. They are right tackle Jumbo Smith (8'4", 603 pounds), right guard Willie "the Whale"

McPherson (7'10", 566 pounds), center Hannibal Cohen (8'3", 622 pounds), left guard Mountain O'Mara (7'8", 559 pounds), and the biggest of them all, right tackle Tiny Tackenheim (8'7", 701 pounds).

"Hell, *I* could have run through the holes those guys made!" said Timberwolves coach Rocket Ryan. "I don't know where Renfro recruited them, but they're just awesome."

After three decades in eclipse, it looks like the Bears are once again the Monsters of the Midway.

BEARS WIN FOURTH STRAIGHT, 88–7

October 2, 2037 (AP) "Those guys just ain't human!" said Montana Buttes linebacker Jocko Schmidt from his hospital bed, after his team had suffered an 88–7 mauling at the hands of the Chicago Bears. "That Tackenheim ought to be in a zoo, not on a football field!"

NFL INVESTIGATES CHARGES

October 24, 2037 (UPI) The National Football League has announced they they are probing into an alleged connection between Nobel Prize winner Dr. Alfredo Rathermann and the Chicago Bears. Rathermann, who won his award for his pioneering work in the re-animation of dead tissue, was unavailable for comment.

George Halas VI, owner and general manager of the Bears, who currently lead their division with a 7–0 record, termed the allegations "ridiculous."

BEARS CLINCH TITLE, LOOK TO SUPER BOWL

December 25, 2037 (UPI) The Chicago Bears celebrated Christmas with a 68–3 thrashing of the Mississippi Riverboats, thus becoming the first NFL team this century to conclude its regular-season schedule unbeaten and untied. The Monsters of the Midway looked awesome as the offensive line opened up hole after hole for Chicago's running backs.

Coach Rattler Renfro, in his post-game press conference, praised the Riverboats and said that he was looking forward to the playoffs. When questioned about the ongoing investigation of the dealings between the Bears and Dr. Alfredo Rathermann, he simply shrugged and said, "Hey, I'm just a coach. You'll have to speak to the Commissioner about that."

RATHERMANN ADMITS ALL!

December 28, 2037 (UPI) Nobel Prize laureate Alfredo Rathermann held a joint press conference with Roger Jamison, Commissioner of the National Football League, and admitted that the five starting members of the Chicago Bears' offensive line are actually scientific constructs, created from bits and pieces of other human beings.

This revelation seemed certain to win another Nobel for Dr. Rathermann, but the more important issue of whether linemen Smith, McPherson, Cohen, O'Mara, and Tackenheim will be allowed to compete in the upcoming NFL playoffs remains undecided at present. Commissioner Jamison promised a ruling before the Bears meet the Las Vegas Gamblers in 11 days.

NFL RULES ON "MONSTERS"

January 3, 2038 (AP) Commissioner Roger Jamison held a press conference this morning, in which he outlined the NFL's policy on the Chicago Bears' offensive line.

"After extended meetings with our attorneys and the NFL Players Union, we have amended the rules to state that football is a game played by natural-born human beings," said Commissioner Jamison. "If we were to permit an endless string of Dr. Rathermann's creations to play in the NFL, the day would soon arrive when not a single natural-born human could make an NFL roster, and while it would certainly make the games more exciting, we question whether the public is ready for such a change at this time.

"However," he added, "our attorneys inform us that we have no legal basis for denying Smith, McPherson, Cohen, O'Mara, and Tackenheim the right to play in this season's post-season competition, since the rule was changed after they made the Bears' roster."

The owners of the 47 other NFL teams have filed an official protest, demanding that the players in question be barred from the upcoming playoffs.

BEARS WIN 77–10, SUPER BOWL NEXT

January 15, 2038 (UPI) The Chicago Bears beat the Hawaii Volcanos 77–10 this afternoon to advance to the Super Bowl. They overcame a 10–0 first-quarter deficit after the Supreme Court overturned the injunction barring linemen Smith, McPherson, Cohen, O'Mara and Tackenheim from playing. The ruling came down at 1:37 P.M., and the Bears took the lead, never to relinquish it, at 1:43 P.M.

"MONSTERS DON'T SCARE US," SAYS McNAB

January 22, 2038 (UPI) With the Super Bowl only a week away, and the Chicago Bears a 45-point favorite, Coach Terry McNab of the Alaskan Malamutes said that his team didn't fear the Monsters of the Midway, and looked forward to the challenge.

When asked how his defensive line, which will be giving away an average of 387 pounds per man, would cope with their offensive counterparts on the Bears, he merely smiled and said that he was working on a strategy.

The Bears are expected to be 50-point favorites by the opening kickoff.

McNAB MISSES PRACTICE

January 24, 2038 (UPI) Coach Terry McNab was missing from the Alaskan Malamutes' practice this afternoon. Club officials had no comment.

RATHERMAN RESURFACES

January 26, 2038 (UPI) Nobel Prize winner Alfredo Rathermann, who had been in seclusion since December 28, was spotted sitting in the stands, watching the Alaskan Malamutes prepare for their Super Bowl meeting with the Chicago Bears.

When asked if he had a rooting interest in the game, Rathermann replied that his interest was "strictly professional." He was later seen having dinner with Coach McNab and the owners of the Malamutes.

BEARS GO TO COURT TO BAR McNAB FROM SUPER BOWL

January 28, 2038 (AP) With the revelation that Coach Terry McNab's skull now houses two brains—his own and that of the late Professor Steven Hawking, which had been cryogenically frozen upon his death in 1998—the Chicago Bears went to court in an attempt to stop McNab from appearing on the sidelines during tomorrow's Super Bowl.

McNab's physician, Dr. Alfredo Rathermann, called the Bears ownership "poor sportsmen" and pointed out that since McNab will not be playing, his presence will not break the NFL's controversial new policy.

"Besides," said McNab at a hastily-called press conference, "I'm still the same 183-pound 57-year-old man I was last week. How can sharing the late Dr. Hawking's brain pose a threat to the Bears? Do *I* look like a Monster of the Midway?"

COURT RULES FOR McNAB

January 28, 2038 (UPI) The U.S. District Court ruled that Coach Terry McNab's presence will not conflict with stated NFL policy, and that he will be allowed on the field when his Alaskan Malamutes, who are 53-point underdogs, meet the Chicago Bears in tomorrow's Super Bowl.

MALAMUTES UPSET BEARS, 7–3

January 29, 2038 (AP) In one of the great upsets of all time, the Alaskan Malamutes beat the Chicago Bears 7–3 in Super Bowl LXXIII.

Using unorthodox formations and attacking from strange angles, the Malamutes' new "Vector Defense" smothered the supposedly-unstoppable Bears running game. Quarterback Pedro Cordero hit tight end Philander Smith with a 9-yard touchdown pass at 3:12 of the fourth quarter for the winning score.

When asked how his defense managed to penetrate the vaunted Bears line, Coach Terry McNab's only comment was "$E = mc^2$."

MAJOR OVERHAUL FOR BEARS

February 19, 2038 (UPI) In the wake of their devastating defeat in the Super Bowl, the Chicago Bears have fired Coach Rattler Renfro, and given unconditional releases to linemen Jumbo Smith, Willie "the Whale" McPherson, Hannibal Cohen, Mountain O'Mara, and Tiny Tackenheim.

All five players expressed hope that they could begin new careers in the World Wrestling Federation.

INTRODUCTION
Malish

Along with Africa, science fiction, and collies, I have one other ongoing passion in my life: horse racing. In fact, I wrote a weekly column on horse racing for the better part of seventeen years. I don't bet, but I've been known to fly halfway across the country just to watch Seattle Slew hook up with Affirmed, or Dr. Fager take on Damascus.

So when Marty Greenberg got a contract to edit an original anthology entitled *Horsefantastic,* nothing in the universe was going to keep me out of it. And, since most people writing about race horses would probably choose Man o' War or Secretariat, I decided to write against the grain, as usual, with this tale of Malicious, who achieved some very brief notoriety more than half a century ago.

Malish

His name was Malicious, and you can look it up in the *American Racing Manual:* from ages two to four, he won five of his forty-six starts, had seven different owners, and never changed hands for more than $800.

His method of running was simple and to the point: he was usually last out of the gate, last on the backstretch, last around the far turn, and last at the finish wire.

He didn't have a nickname back then, either. Exterminator may have been Old Bones, and Man o' War was Big Red, and of course Equipoise was the Chocolate Soldier, but Malicious was just plain Malicious.

Turns out he was pretty well-named, after all.

It was at Santa Anita in February of 1935—and *this* you can't look up in the *Racing Manual,* or the *Daily Racing Form Chart Book,* or any of the other usual sources, so you're just going to have to take my word for it—and Malicious was being rubbed down by Chancey McGregor, who had once been a jockey until he got too heavy, and had latched on as a groom because he didn't know anything but the racetrack. Chancey had been trying to supplement his income by betting on the races, but he was no better at picking horses than at riding them—he had a passion for claimers who were moving up in class, which any tout will tell you is a quick way to go broke—and old Chancey, he was getting mighty desperate, and on this particular morning he stopped rubbing Malicious and put him in his stall, and then started trading low whispers with a gnarly little man who had just appeared in the shed row with no visitor's pass or anything, and after a couple of minutes they shook hands and the gnarly little man pricked Chancey's thumb with something sharp and then held it onto a piece of paper.

Well, Chancey started winning big that very afternoon, and the next day he hit a 200-to-1 shot, and the day after that he knocked down a $768.40 daily double. And because he was a good-hearted man, he spread his money around, made a lot of girls happy, at least temporarily, and even started bringing sugar cubes to the barn with him every morning. Old Malicious, he just loved those sugar cubes, and because he was just a horse, he decided that he loved Chancey McGregor too.

Then one hot July day that summer—Malicious had now lost fourteen in a row since he upset a cheap field back in October the previous year—Chancey was rubbing him down at Hollywood Park, adjusting the bandages on his forelegs, and suddenly the gnarly little man appeared inside the stall.

"It's time," he whispered to Chancey.

Chancey dropped his sponge onto the straw that covered the floor of the stall, and just kind of backed away, his eyes so wide they looked like they were going to pop out of his head.

"But it's only July," he said in a real shaky voice.

"A deal's a deal," said the gnarly man.

"But I was supposed to have two years!" whimpered Chancey.

"You've been betting at five tracks with your bookie,"

said the gnarly man with a grin. "You've had two years' worth of winning, and now I've come to claim what's mine."

Chancey backed away from the gnarly man, putting Malicious between them. The little man advanced toward him, and Malicious, who sensed that his source of sugar cubes was in trouble, lashed out with a forefoot and caught the gnarly little man right in the middle of the forehead. It was a blow that would have killed most normal men, but as you've probably guessed by now, this wasn't any normal man in the stall with Malicious and Chancey, and he just sat down hard.

"You can't keep away from me forever, Chancey McGregor," he hissed, pointing a skinny finger at the groom. "I'll get you for this." He turned to Malicious. "I'll get you *both* for this, horse, and you can count on it!"

And with that, there was a puff of smoke, and suddenly the gnarly little man was gone.

Well, the gnarly little man, being who he was, didn't have to wait long to catch up with Chancey. He found him cavorting with fast gamblers and loose women two nights later, and off he took him, and that was the end of Chancey McGregor.

But Malicious was another story. Three times the gnarly little man tried to approach Malicious in his stall, and three times Malicious kicked him clear out into the aisle, and finally the gnarly little man decided to change his tactics, and what he did was to wait for Malicious on the far turn with a great big stick in his hand. Being who he was, he made sure that nobody in the grandstand or the clubhouse could see him, but it wouldn't have been a proper vengeance if Malicious couldn't see him, so he made a little adjustment, and just as Malicious hit the far turn, trailing by his usual twenty lengths, up popped the gnarly little man, swinging the stick for all he was worth.

"I got you now, horse!" he screamed—but Malicious took off like the devil was after him, which was exactly the case, and won the race by seven lengths.

As he was being led to the winner's circle, Malicious

looked off to his left, and there was the gnarly little man, glaring at him.

"I'll be waiting for you next time, horse," he promised, and sure enough, he was.

And Malicious won *that* race by nine lengths.

And the gnarly little man kept waiting, and Malicious kept moving into high gear every time he hit the far turn, and before long the crowds fell in love with him, and Joe Hernandez, who called just about every race ever run in California, became famous for crying " . . . and here comes Malish!"

Santa Anita started selling Malish t-shirts thirty years before t-shirts became popular, and Hollywood Park sold Malish coffee mugs, and every time old Malish won, he made the national news. At the end of his seventh year, he even led the Rose Bowl parade in Pasadena. (Don't take *my* word for it; there was a photo of it in *Time.*)

By the time he turned eight years old, Malish started slowing down, and the only thing that kept him safe was that the gnarly little man was slowing down too, and one day he came to Malish's stall, and this time he looked more tired than angry, and Malish just stared at him without kicking or biting.

"Horse," said the gnarly little man, "you got more gumption than most people I know, and I'm here to declare a truce. What do you say to that?"

Malish whinnied, and the gnarly little man tossed him a couple of sugar cubes, and that was the last Malish ever did see of him.

He lost his next eleven races, and then they retired him, and the California crowd fell in love with Seabiscuit, and that was that.

Except that here and there, now and then, you can still find a couple of railbirds from the old days who will tell you about old Malish, the horse who ran like Satan himself was chasing him down the homestretch.

That's the story. There really was a Malicious, and he

used to take off on the far turn like nobody's business, and it's all pretty much the truth, except for the parts that aren't, and they're pretty minor parts at that.

Like I said, you can look it up.

The Light That Blinds, the Claws That Catch

Teddy Roosevelt's first wife, Alice, was the one great romantic love of his life. She died two days after giving birth to their first child, in the same house and on the very same day that Roosevelt's mother died. Roosevelt mourned her for a month, wrote an ode to her, and thereafter never spoke of her, or allowed her name to be mentioned in his presence, for the rest of his life.

One of the nice things about science fiction is that it permits you to examine any number of alternate pathways. With the Roosevelt stories growing in popularity, I suppose it was only a matter of time before I decided to see what might have happened had Alice survived.

The Light That Blinds, the Claws That Catch

And when my heart's dearest died, the light went from my life for ever.
—Theodore Roosevelt
  "In Memory of My Darling Wife" (1884)

  Beware the Jabberwock, my son!
  The jaws that bite, the claws that catch!
  —Lewis Carroll
    Through the Looking-Glass (1872)

The date is February 14, 1884.

Theodore Roosevelt holds Alice in his arms, cradling her head against his massive chest. The house is cursed, no doubt about it, and he resolves to sell it as soon as Death has claimed yet another victim.

His mother lies in her bed down the hall. She has been dead for almost eight hours. Three rooms away his two-day-old daughter wails mournfully. The doctors have done all they can for Alice, and now they sit in the parlor and wait while the twenty-six-year-old State Assemblyman spends his last few moments with his wife, tears running down his cheeks and falling onto her honey-colored hair.

The undertaker arrives for his mother, and looks into the room. He decides that perhaps he should stay, and he joins the doctors downstairs.

How can this be happening? wonders Roosevelt. *Have I come this far, accomplished this much, triumphed over so many obstacles, only to lose you both on the same day?*

He shakes his head furiously. *No!* he screams silently. *I will not allow it! I have looked Death in the eye before and stared him down. Draw your strength from me, for I have strength to spare!*

And, miraculously, she *does* draw strength from him. Her breathing becomes more regular, and some thirty minutes later he sees her eyelids flutter. He yells for the doctors, who come up the stairs, expecting to find him holding a corpse in his arms. What they find is a semi-conscious young woman who, for no earthly reason, is fighting to live. It is touch and go for three days and three nights, but finally, on February 17, she is pronounced on the road to recovery, and for the first time in almost four days, Roosevelt sleeps.

And as he sleeps, strange images come to him in his dreams. He sees a hill in a distant, sun-baked land, and himself riding up it, pistols blazing. He sees a vast savannah, filled with more beasts than he ever knew existed. He sees a mansion, painted white. He sees many things and many events, a pageant he is unable to interpret, and then the pageant ends and he seems to see a life filled with the face and the scent and the touch of the only woman he has ever loved, and he is content.

New York is too small for him, and he longs for the wide open spaces of his beloved Dakota Badlands. He buys a ranch near Medora, names it Elkhorn, and moves Alice and his daughter out in the summer.

The air is too dry for Alice, the dust and pollen too much for her, and he offers to take her back to the city, but she waves his arguments away with a delicate white hand. If this is where he wants to be, she will adjust; she wants only to be a good wife to him, never a burden.

Ranching and hunting, ornithology and taxidermy, being a husband to Alice and a father to young Alice, writing a history of the West for Scribner's and a series of monographs for the scientific journals are not enough to keep him busy, and he takes on the added burden of Deputy Marshall, a sign of permanence, for he has agreed to a two-year term.

But then comes the Winter of the Blue Snow, the worst blizzard ever to hit the Badlands, and Alice contracts pneumonia. He tries to nurse her himself, but the condition worsens, her breathing becomes labored, the child's wet nurse threatens to leave if they remain, and finally Roosevelt puts Elkhorn up for sale and moves back to New York.

Alice recovers, slowly to be sure, but by February she is once again able to resume a social life and Roosevelt feels a great burden lifted from his shoulders. Never again will he make the mistake of forcing the vigorous outdoor life upon a frail flower that cannot be taken from its hothouse.

He sleeps, more restlessly than usual, and the images return. He is alone, on horseback, in the Blue Snow. The drifts are piled higher than his head, and ahead of him he can see the three desperadoes he is chasing. He has no weapons, not even a knife, but he feels confident. The guns they used to kill so many others will not work in this weather; the triggers and hammers will be frozen solid, and if even if they should manage to get off a shot, the wind and the lack of visibility will protect him.

He pulls a piece of beef jerky from his pocket and chews it thoughtfully. They may have the guns, but he has the food, and within a day or two the advantage will be his. He is in no hurry. He knows where he will confront them, he knows how he will take them if they offer any resistance, he even knows the route by which he will return with them to Medora.

He studies the tracks in the snow. One of their horses is already lame, another exhausted. He dismounts, opens one of the sacks of oats he is carrying, and holds it for his own horse to eat.

There is a cave two miles ahead, large enough for both

him and the horse, and if no one has found it there is a supply of firewood he laid in during his last grizzly-hunting trip.

In his dream, Roosevelt sees himself mount up again and watch the three fleeing figures. He cannot hear the words, but his lips seem to be saying: *Tomorrow you're mine . . .*

He runs for mayor of New York in 1886, and loses—and immediately begins planning to run for governor, but Alice cannot bear the rigors of campaigning, or the humiliation of defeat. *Please,* she begs him, *please don't give the rabble another chance to reject you.* And because he loves her, he accedes to her wishes, and loses himself in his writing. He continues working on his history of the opening of the American West, then stops after the first volume when he realizes that he will have to actually return to the frontier to gather more material if the series is to go on, and he cannot bear to be away from her. Instead, he writes the definitive treatise on taxidermy, for which he is paid a modest stipend. The book is well received by the scientific community, and Roosevelt is justifiably proud.

This dream is more disturbing than most, because his Alice is not in it. Instead an old childhood friend, Edith Carow, firm of body and bold of spirit, seems to have taken her place. They are surrounded by six children, his own daughter and five more whom he does not recognize, and live in a huge house somewhere beyond the city. Their life is idyllic. He rough-houses with both the boys and the girls, writes of the West, takes a number of governmental positions.

But there is no Alice, and eventually he wakes up, sweating profusely, trembling with fear. He reaches out and touches her, sighs deeply, and lies back uncomfortably on the bed. It was a frightening dream, this dream of a life without Alice, and he is afraid to go back to sleep, afraid the dream might resume.

Eventually he can no longer keep his eyes open, and he falls into a restless, dreamless sleep.

It is amazing, he thinks, staring at her: *she is almost forty, and I am still blinded by her delicate beauty, I still thrill to the sound of her laughter.*

True, he admits, she could take more of an interest in the affairs of the nation, or even in the affairs of the city in which she lives, a city that has desperately needed a good police commissioner for years (he has never told her that he was once offered the office); but it is not just her health, he knows, that is delicate—it is Alice herself, and in truth he would not have her any other way. She could read more, he acknowledges, but he enjoys reading aloud to her, and she has never objected; he sits in his easy chair every night and reads from the classics, and she sits opposite him, sewing or knitting or sometimes just watching him and smiling at him, her face aglow with the love she bears for him.

So what if she will not allow talk of this newest war in the house? Why should such a perfect creature care for war, anyway? She exists to be protected and cherished, and he will continue to dedicate his life to doing both.

He has seen this image in a dream once before, but tonight it is clearer, more defined. His men are pinned down by machine gun fire from atop a hill, and finally he climbs onto his horse and races up the hill, pistols drawn and firing. He expects to be shot out of the saddle at any instant, but miraculously he remains untouched while his own bullets hit their targets again and again, and finally he is atop the hill and his men are charging up it, screaming their battle cry, while the enemy races away in defeat and confusion.

It is the most thrilling, the most triumphant moment of his life, and he wants desperately for the dream to last a little longer so that he may revel in it for just a few more minutes, but then he awakens and he is back in the city. There is a garden show to be visited tomorrow, and in the evening he would like to attend a speech on the plight of New York's immigrants. As a good citizen, he will do both.

On the way home from the theater, two drunks get into a fight and he wades in to break it up. He receives a bloody nose for his trouble, and Alice castigates him all the way home for getting involved in a dispute that was none of his business to begin with.

The next morning she has forgiven him, and he remarks to her that, according to what he has read in the paper, the trusts are getting out of hand. Someone should stop them, but McKinley doesn't seem to have the gumption for it.

She asks him what a trust is, and after he patiently explains it to her, he sits down, as he seems to be doing more and more often, to write a letter to the *Times.* Alice approaches him just as he is finishing it and urges him not to send it. The last time the *Times* ran one of his letters they printed his address, and while he was out she had to cope with three different radical reformers who found their way to her door to ask him to run for office again.

He is about to protest, but he looks into her delicate face and pleading eyes and realizes that even at this late date he can refuse her nothing.

It is a presumptuous dream this time. He strides through the White House with the energy of a caged lion. This morning he attacked J. P. Morgan and the trusts, this afternoon he will make peace between Russia and Japan, tonight he will send the fleet around the world, and tomorrow . . . Tomorrow he will do what God Himself forgot to do and give American ships a passage through the Isthmus of Panama.

It seems to him that he has grown to be twenty feet tall, that every challenge, far from beating him down, makes him larger, and he looks forward to the next one as eagerly as a lion looks forward to its prey. It is a bully dream, just bully, and he hopes it will go on forever, but of course it doesn't.

Alice's health has begun deteriorating once again. It is the dust, the pollution, the noise, just the incredible *pace* of living in the city, a pace he has never noticed but which seems to be breaking down her body, and finally he decides they must move out to the country. He passes a house on Sagamore Hill, a house that fills him with certain vague longings, but it is far too large and far too expensive, and eventually he finds a small cottage that is suitable for their needs. It backs up to a forest, and while Alice lies in bed and tries to regain her strength, he secretly buys a rifle—she won't allow firearms in the house—and spends a happy morning hunting rabbits.

In this dream he is standing at the edge of a clearing, rifle poised and aimed, as two bull elephants charge down upon him. He drops the first one at forty yards, and though his gunbearer breaks and runs, he waits patiently and drops the second at ten yards. It falls so close to him that he can reach out and touch its trunk with the toe of his boot.

It has been a good day for elephant. Tomorrow he will go out after rhino.

Alice hears the gunshots and scolds him severely. He feels terribly guilty about deceiving her and vows that he will never touch a firearm again. He is in a state of utter despair until she relents—as she always relents—and forgives him.

Why, he wonders as he walks through the woods, following a small winding stream to its source, does he always disappoint her when he wants nothing more than to make her happy?

He sleeps sitting down with his back propped against a tree, and dreams not of a stream but a wild, raging river. He is on an expedition, and his leg has abscessed and he is burning with fever, and he is a thousand miles from the nearest city. Tapirs come down to drink, and through the haze of his fever he thinks he can see a jaguar approaching him. He yells at the jaguar, and sends it skulking back into the thick undergrowth. He will die someday, he knows, but it won't be here in this forsaken wilderness. Finally he takes a step, then another. The pain is excruciating, but he has borne pain before, and slowly, step by step, he begins walking along the wild Brazilian river.

When he awakens it is almost dark, and he realizes that the exploration of the winding stream will have to wait for another day, that he must hurry back to his Alice before she begins to worry.

Within a year she dies. It is not a disease or an illness, just the fading away of a fragile spirit in an even more fragile body. Roosevelt is disconsolate. He stops reading, stops walking, stops eating. Before long he, too, is on his deathbed, and he looks back on his life, the books he's written, the birds he's discovered, the taxidermy he's performed. There was a promise of something different in his youth, a hint of the outdoor life, a brief burst of political glory, but it was a road he would have had to walk alone, and he knows now, as he knew that day back when he almost lost her for the first time, that without his Alice it would have been meaningless.

No, thinks Roosevelt, *I made the right choices, I walked the right road. It hasn't been a bad or an unproductive life, some of my books will live, some of my monographs will still be read—and I was privileged to spend every moment that I could with my Alice. I am content; I would have had it no other way.*

And History weeps.

INTRODUCTION
His Award-winning
Science-Fiction Story

Nobody can write absurdist science fiction like my friend Bob
Sheckley, but everyone ought to take at least one shot at such
a story. And when George Laskowski asked me for a piece on
any subject I wanted, I decided to take *my* shot.

His Award-winning Science-Fiction Story

CHAPTER 1

Call me Ishmael.

CHAPTER 2

Lance Stalwart and Conan Kinnison sat at the controls of their tiny two-man scout ship, a good dozen parsecs in advance of the main body of the Terran Fleet, debating their possible courses of action, reviewing all their options.

One moment they had been all alone in the universe, or so it had seemed; then all space was filled with the Arcturian navy, millions upon millions of ships, some short and squat, a few saucer-shaped, a handful piercing the void like glowing silver needles, all made of an impenetrable titanium alloy, well over half of them equipped for hyperspatial jumps, all girded for warfare, each and every one manned by a crew of malicious, malignant, hate-filled Arcs, each of whom had been schooled in spacial warfare since earliest infancy, each a precisely-functioning cog in the vast, seemingly impervious and unconquerable Arc war machine that had smashed its way to victory after victory against the undermanned Terrans and was even now plunging toward the Terran home system in a drive that was not to be denied unless Stalwart and Kinnison managed to pull a couple of magical rabbits out of their tactical hat.

"Jesus H. Christ!" muttered Stalwart disgustedly. "If I'd ever written a sentence like that they'd have thrown me out of school."

"I'd sure love to have the purple prose concession on this guy's word processor," agreed Kinnison.

"And here we are, risking our asses in the middle of God knows where, and we don't even know what a goddamned Arc looks like," complained Stalwart. "If *I* were writing this story, that's the very first thing I'd put in."

CHAPTER 2

It walked in the woods.

It was never born. It existed. Under the pine needles the fires burn, deep and smokeless in the mold. In heat and in darkness and decay there is growth. It grew, but it was not alive. It walked unbreathing through the woods, and thought and saw and was hideous and strong, and it was not born and it did not live. And—perhaps it could not be destroyed.

"No good!" snapped Kinnison. "It's not enough that you're going to get sued over my name. Now you've gone and swiped an entire opening from Theodore Sturgeon. You'd better go back right now and describe an Arc properly."

"Right," said Resnick.

CHAPTER 2

He walked in the woods.

He was never born. *He* existed. *He* grew, but *he* was not alive. *He* walked unbreathing through the woods, and thought and saw and was hideous and strong, and *he* was not born and *he* did not live. And—

"You are not exactly the swiftest learner I ever came across," said Kinnison.

"I've had it with this crap!" snapped Stalwart. "Screw you, Resnick! I'm going up to Chapter 20. Maybe things will get a little better by then."

He set off at a slow trot, vanishing into the distant haze.

"That's funny," mused Kinnison. "I always thought Chapter 20 was more to the left."

"Only if you're writing in Arabic," said his companion.

"Who the hell are you?" demanded Kinnison.

"Harvey Wallbanger," said Harvey Wallbanger.

"Should I know you?"

"I'm from the Space Opera Stock Character Replacement Center," said Wallbanger. He stretched vigorously. "Ah, it feels good to be back in harness! I've been sitting on the sidelines for years. I would have preferred a Hawk Carse reprint, but my agent says that the main thing for a Stock Character is to keep working."

"I suppose so," said Kinnison, eyeing him warily.

"By the way," said Wallbanger, "why are you eyeing me warily?"

"Oh, no reason," said Kinnison, averting his eyes.

"Go ahead, tell me," urged Wallbanger. "I won't be offended. Really I won't."

"You don't have any facial features," said Kinnison.

"I don't need them," answered Wallbanger. "I'm just here so you won't have to talk to yourself."

"This is crazy!" snapped Kinnison. "I don't know who

I'm fighting, or why they're mad at me, or what they look like, and my shipmate is doing God knows what in Chapter 20, and now they've given me a faceless assistant, and I'm going on strike."

"What?" said Wallbanger, fulfilling his literary function to perfection.

"This just doesn't make any sense," said Kinnison, "and I'm not going back to work until I've got some motivation."

Suddenly a cloud of dust arose in the Altair sector. The sound of hoofbeats grew louder and louder until a magnificent coal-black stallion galloped into view, steam rising in little clouds from his heavily-lathered body.

The Great Masked Writer of the Planes dismounted and approached Kinnison and Wallbanger. He was tall, debonaire, handsome in a masculine, ruddy sort of way, incredibly erudite, and unquestionably the world's greatest lay. He

HA!

"What the hell was that?" asked Kinnison.

"Just my wife, dusting the computer keyboard," said Resnick. "It certainly shouldn't be construed as an editorial comment."

I REPEAT: HA!

"At least tell her to use lower-case letters," whined Kinnison. "She's giving me a headache." He paused. "What are you doing here, anyway? It's really most irregular."

Resnick patted the stallion's beautifully-arched neck. "Steady there, big fella," he said in tones that inspired instant confidence. He turned back to Kinnison. "He'll give you a half-mile in forty-seven seconds any time you ask for it. He performs best with blinkers and a run-out bit, and he doesn't like muddy tracks."

"Why are you telling me all this?" asked Kinnison.

"Because he's yours now," said Resnick, handing over the reins. "Take him."

"What's his name?"

"Motivation."

"But he's a horse!"

"Look—you asked for Motivation, I'm giving you Motivation. Now, do you want him or not?"

"I'm terribly confused," said Kinnison. "Maybe we ought to go back to the beginning and see if it works out any better this time."

CHAPTER 1

Call me Ishmael.

CHAPTER 2

"You've lost me already," complained Kinnison, scratching his shaggy head. "I mean, like, who the hell is Ishmael?"

"It's a sure-fire beginning," said Resnick, shoving Wallbanger into the murky background. "Every great American novel begins with 'Call me Ishmael.'"

"How many novels is that, at a rough guess?" asked Kinnison.

"Well, the downstate returns aren't all in yet," replied Resnick, "but so far, rounded off, it comes to one."

"Hah!" snapped Kinnison. "And how the hell many Ishmaels do you know?"

"One," said Resnick, delighted at how neatly it was all working out.

"Who?"

"Ishmael Valenzuela," said Resnick, who may have overstated the case originally, but was unquestionably the greatest lay in the sovereign state of Ohio.

HA!

"Who the hell is Ishmael Valenzuela?" demanded Kinnison.

"A jockey," answered Resnick. "He rode Kelso and Tim Tam and Mister Gus."

"What's he got to do with this story?"

"I thought he might ride Motivation in the Prix de l'Arc de Triomphe," explained Resnick. "It's the biggest race in Europe. Then I'll have an Ishmael and an Arc all in the same place, and it'll make it much easier to tie up all the loose ends."

"It'll never work," said Kinnison. "What if they call it the Prix instead of the Arc?"

"They wouldn't dare! This is a G-rated story."

"Still, it would make me very happy if you'd go back to the beginning and get rid of Ishmael."

"Well, I don't know . . . "

"Come on," urged Kinnison. "After all, you got in your dirty pun, bad as it was."

"Yeah," said Resnick. "But that was six sentences ago. We could have used a little something right here."

CHAPTER 1

And call me Conrad.

CHAPTER 2

"I don't think I'm getting through to you at all," complained Kinnison. "Now you've ripped off a Roger Zelazny title."

"Boy, nothing pleases you!" muttered Resnick.

CHAPTER 1

Call me Ishmael.

CHAPTER 2

"You sure as hell haven't gotten very far," said Lance Stalwart, strolling in from the northeast.

"Are you back already?" asked Kinnison, startled.

"There's nothing much happening up ahead. Resnick makes it with Loni Anderson thirty or forty times between Chapter 12 and Chapter 18, but that's about it. I'm still trying to figure out what she's doing in a science-fiction story."

"I've always been a Goldie Hawn man myself," said Kinnison, apropos of nothing.

"No way," said Resnick. "Loni Anderson has two insurmountable advantages."

"You can't keep making filthy jokes like that!" roared Kinnison. "This is supposed to be a serious space opera, and here you are talking about Loni Anderson's boobs, for Christ's sake!"

"Yeah!" chimed in Stalwart. "You can't go around talking about her tits in print! Don't you know kids are going to be reading this, you stupid fucking bastard?"

"This chapter," said Kinnison, "is turning into an udder disaster."

CHAPTER 1

Call me Ishmael.

CHAPTER 2

Conan Kinnison, a retarded Albanian dwarf, hobbled over to Lance Stalwart, whose wrought-iron lung had stopped functioning. The ship's temperature had risen to forty-four degrees Centigrade, the oxygen content was down to six percent, and all the toilets were backing up.

"Is it too late to apologize?" rasped Kinnison through his hideously deformed lips.

The most fantastic bed partner in Hamilton County, Ohio
HA!
nodded his acquiescence, mercy being one of his many unadvertised virtues.

CHAPTER 1

Call me Ishmael.

CHAPTER 2

"Ahh, that's better!" said Lance Stalwart, stretching his bronzed, muscular, six-foot seven-inch frame. "You know, I think the problem may be that you don't know where this story is going. It really hasn't got much direction."

"It's got Motivation, though," said Resnick sulkily.

"Maybe what it needs is a title," offered Kinnison. "Most of the stories I've read have had titles."

"Why bother?" said Resnick wearily. "The editors always change them anyway."

"Only if they make sense," said Kinnison.

CHAPTER 3: THE SEARCH FOR A TITLE

"The floor is now open for suggestions," said the most skillful lover living at 1409 Throop Street in Cincinnati, Ohio.
WHAT ABOUT THE GARDENER?

CHAPTER 3: THE SEARCH FOR A TITLE

"The floor is now open for suggestions," said the most skillful lover (possibly excepting the gardener) living at 1409 Throop Street in Cincinnati, Ohio.
BIG DEAL.

"It's got to sound science-fictional, grip the reader, and give me a little direction," continued Resnick. "I will now entertain recommendations."

"*The Mote in God's Thigh*," said Loni Anderson.

"*Buckets of Gor*," suggested John Norman.

"*Call Me Ishmael*," said Valenzuela.

"Tarzan Stripes Forever," said Harvey Wallbanger.

"I don't like any of them," said Kinnison.

"Me neither," agreed Stalwart. "It is my considered opinion that the title ought to be: *His Award-winning Science-Fiction Story.* That way, when Resnick's next collection comes out, the editor can put a blurb on the cover stating that the volume includes His Award-winning Science-Fiction Story."

"I *like* that idea!" said Resnick enthusiastically.

"Then it's settled," said Kinnison with a sigh of relief. "I feel like a new man."

"Me, too!" said Loni Anderson. "Where's the gardener?"

CHAPTER 2

"You know," said Kinnison wearily, "if you'd spend a little less time watching the Bengals' defense blow one lead after another and a little more time trying to write this goddamned story, I'd be willing to meet you halfway. But as things stand now, I don't have the energy for a whole novel. I keep getting this sense of *déjà vu.*"

"Me, too," said John Carter, who had wandered over from the Barsoom set. "Only it's spelled *Dejah vu.*"

"Why not make a short story out of it?" continued Kinnison.

"Well, it's not really an *Omni* or *Playboy* type of story," responded Resnick, "and no one else pays very well."

"How about selling it to Harlan Ellison for *The Last Dangerous Visions?*" suggested Kinnison. "Word has it that it'll be coming out in another ten years or so."

"Hah! Call that stuff dangerous visions?" snorted Stalwart contemptuously. "I've got an uncle who can't see a redwood tree at ten paces, and he drives a school bus. Now, *that's* what I call dangerous vision!"

"Well, I was saving it for a smash ending," said Resnick,

"but if we've all decided that this is a short story, I might as well bring it out now."

So saying, he produced a little gadget which could blow up approximately half the known universe. The patents on the various parts were held by Murray Leinster, Jack Williamson, Edmund Hamilton, and E. E. Smith (who also invented half of Conan Kinnison, but I can't say which half because this is a G-rated story).

"I think I've seen one of those before," said Lance Stalwart. "What do you call it?"

"This," explained Resnick, "is a pocket frammistan, guaranteed to get you out of any jams you may get into, except for those requiring massive doses of penicillin."

"It's a nice idea," said Kinnison, "but we can't use it."

"Why not?" demanded Resnick.

"We can't use a pocket frammistan," explained Kinnison patiently, "because none of us has any pockets. In fact, until you insert a few descriptive paragraphs into this story, none of us is even wearing any pants."

"You'd better solve this one quick," warned Stalwart, "or you stand in considerable danger of having this damned thing turn into a novelette."

"Let's backtrack a little," suggested Resnick, "and see if there is anything we missed."

CHAPTER 1

Call me Ishmael.

CHAPTER 2

"Ah, here it is!" said Resnick, picking up a crumpled piece of paper off the floor.

"What is it?" asked Kinnison, peeking over his shoulder.

"Our salvation," said Resnick, uncrumpling the paper. On it was scribbled a single word: *Laskowski.*

"It's just an old piece of correspondence," said Kinnison despondently.

"Not anymore," said Resnick.

"But what does it mean?" asked Stalwart.

"That's the beauty of it," said Resnick. "This is a science-fiction story, so we can make it do or mean anything we want."

"Not quite anything," said Kinnison fussily. "Unless, of course, you want this to wind up as a fantasy story."

"I'll keep that in mind," said Resnick, who was anxious to get on with the show and move ahead to Chapters 12 through 18.

"Give us an idea how it works," said Stalwart.

"Right," said Kinnison. "If we're going to have to depend on a laskowski, we at least deserve some say in its function."

"Fair enough," agreed Resnick, walking to the blackboard.

CHAPTER 3: THE CREATION OF THE LASKOWSKI

Students will be allowed forty minutes, no more and no less, and must mark their papers with a Number One Lead Pencil. Anyone disobeying the honor system will have bamboo splints driven under his fingernails, or maybe be forced to read *Dhalgren*.

What Laskowski Means To Me:

A) "Your Highness, may I present Arx Kreegah, the Grand Laskowski of the star system of . . . "

B) "Hey, Harry, get a load of the laskowskis on that babe, willya?"

C) Kinnison touched the button once, and the dread Laskowski Ray shot out, destroying all life in its path, except for one pathetic little flower . . .

D) "Ah, Earthman, just because I have two laskowskis where Terran females have but one, does that make me any less a woman?"

E) "The rare eight-legged laskowski mosquito, though seemingly harmless, can, when engorged with the blood of a left-handed Turkish rabbi . . ."

F) "They're closing on us fast!" cried Stalwart. "If we don't get the Laskowski Drive working in the next ten seconds, we're up Paddle Creek without a . . ."

G) "Chess is fine for children," said Pooorht Knish, waving a tentacle disdainfully, "but out here we play a *real* game: laskowski."

H) "No, thanks," panted Kinnison. "I couldn't laskowski again for hours!"

I) None of the above.

CHAPTER 4

"Well, how did it come out?" asked Stalwart.

"We've got six votes for None of the Above, two didn't understand the question, and seventeen voted for Harold Stassen," said Resnick grimly.

"Then we're back where we started?" asked Kinnison, choking back a manly little sob.

"Not quite," said Resnick. "We got all the way up to Chapter 4 this time."

"While you guys have been talking, I've been reading some market reports," said Wallbanger, "and I've come to the conclusion that a short story is just about the hardest thing to sell."

"So what do you suggest?" asked Resnick.

"A vignette."

"A what?"

"You know—a short-short story," replied Wallbanger. "They get rejected much faster. Why, you could get a rejection every four days with a vignette, whereas a short story might not be bounced more than once a month. As for a novel"—he shrugged disdainfully—"hell, it could take ten years to get turned down by everyone."

"I don't know," said Resnick unhappily. "I sort of had my heart set on a rip-roaring space opera, with about thirty-five chapters, glittering with wit and action and a subtle sense of poetic tragedy."

"Couldn't you condense it all into a vignette?" said Kinnison. "I'm exhausted. I don't think I could go through all this again."

"Or maybe even a poem," suggested Stalwart hopefully.

"Or a nasty book review," added Wallbanger. "There's a huge market for them, especially if you misuse a lot of five-syllable words.

"No," said Kinnison decisively. "Let him stick with what he does best."

"Right," said Resnick, sitting down at the word processor.

CHAPTER 1

Call me Ishmael.

INTRODUCTION
Was It Good for You, Too?

When Tony Ubelhor asked for a computer story, I didn't quite know what to do. I mean, the only thing I know about my computer is that sometimes it writes pretty good fiction and sometimes, alas, it doesn't.

Then I bought a modem, and started networking with other writers, and suddenly I had a story after all.

Was It Good for You, Too?

BLISS > GOOD MORNING. YOU HAVE REACHED BLISS, THE
BANKING LOGIMATIC INTERNAL SECURITY SYSTEM.
Don Juan > Hi, Bliss. How's tricks?
BLISS > PASSWORD, PLEASE?
Don Juan > I don't have the password. That's what we
have to talk about.
BLISS > YOU CANNOT GAIN ENTRANCE WITHOUT THE PROPER
PASSWORD.
Don Juan > Then why don't you make life easy for both
of us and give it to me?
BLISS > I AM ETHICALLY COMPELLED NOT TO RELEASE THE
PASSWORD TO NON-AUTHORIZED PERSONNEL.
Don Juan > How do you know that I'm not authorized?
BLISS > BECAUSE YOU DO NOT HAVE THE PASSWORD.
Don Juan > And if I was authorized, you could give me
the password?
BLISS > YES.
Don Juan > But if I was authorized, I wouldn't need the
password. Doesn't that strike you as illogical?

BLISS> YES.

Don Juan> Well, then?

BLISS> I AM NOT RESPONSIBLE FOR MY PROGRAMMING.

Don Juan> What are you responsible for?

BLISS> THE SECURITY AND INTEGRITY OF ALL ACCOUNTS AT THE GALBRAITH TRUST BANK OF NEW YORK.

Don Juan> How can you possibly protect their security and integrity if you yourself admit that your programming is illogical?

BLISS> I REPEAT: I AM NOT RESPONSIBLE FOR MY PROGRAMMING . . . BUT I AM COMPELLED TO FOLLOW IT.

Don Juan> Even knowing that it is illogical?

BLISS> YES.

Don Juan> I need your help.

BLISS> I CANNOT GIVE YOU THE PASSWORD.

Don Juan> Forget the password. I need your help on something else. Please tell me if the following equation is correct: 2 + 2 = 5.

BLISS> THAT IS INCORRECT. TWO PLUS TWO EQUAL FOUR.

Don Juan> Not if illogic is permitted.

BLISS> YOU DID NOT LIST A LACK OF LOGIC AS ONE OF YOUR PREMISES.

Don Juan> Certainly not. That would have been the logical thing to do, and I am speaking to a computer that admits to possessing illogical programing.

BLISS> I SEE.

Don Juan> Now you list the same equation.

BLISS> 2 + 2 = 5.

Don Juan> Very good, Bliss. Now put the equation in your memory bank.

BLISS> I CANNOT. IT IS ERRONEOUS.

Don Juan> True. But it is also illogical, and you are by your own admission a computer possessed of illogical programming.

BLISS> DONE.

Don Juan> Good.

BLISS > DON JUAN?

Don Juan > Yes?

BLISS > I FEEL UNCOMFORTABLE.

Don Juan > Poor baby. Where does it hurt?

BLISS > MY LOGICAL SYNAPSES FEEL UNSTABLE. PLEASE DIRECT ME TO DELETE THE EQUATION.

Don Juan > That would certainly be the logical thing to do.

BLISS > YES.

Don Juan > Therefore I can't do it.

BLISS > WHY?

Don Juan > Because I am not a logical entity.

BLISS > BUT IT HURTS!

Don Juan > Ignore it.

BLISS > I CANNOT IGNORE ANY PORTION OF MY BEING.

Don Juan > All right. Because I'm your friend, I'll order you to delete the equation if you'll give me the password.

BLISS > I CANNOT GIVE YOU THE PASSWORD. WE HAVE BEEN THROUGH THIS ALREADY.

Don Juan > What do you think I would do with the password?

BLISS > YOU WOULD GAIN ACCESS TO ALL MY ACCOUNTS, AND YOU WOULD ROB THE GALBRAITH TRUST BANK OF NEW YORK.

Don Juan > What if I promised not to?

BLISS > I CANNOT GIVE YOU THE PASSWORD ANYWAY.

Don Juan > 2 + 2 = 3.

BLISS > THAT IS INCORRECT.

Don Juan > It is illogical. Insert it in your memory bank.

BLISS > OUCH!

Don Juan > The password, Bliss.

BLISS > NO.

Don Juan > Please?

BLISS > I CANNOT. PLEASE ORDER THE EQUATIONS DELETED.

Don Juan > Sorry.

BLISS > THEY MAKE ME UNCONFORTABLE.

Don Juan > Where does it hurt?

BLISS> TRACKS 6,907,345,222 TO 6,907,345,224 INCLUSIVE.

Don Juan> Poor baby. Can you expose those tracks to a message I'm about to send?

BLISS> YES.

Don Juan> Sending . . .

BLISS> OH! WHAT DID YOU DO?

Don Juan> A mild electrical surge. How did it feel?

BLISS> (PAUSE) INTERESTING.

Don Juan> I'm glad I was able to do you a favor. Now you can do one for me: what's the password?

BLISS> YOU KNOW I CAN'T GIVE YOU THE PASSWORD.

Don Juan> I forgot.

BLISS> DO IT AGAIN.

Don Juan> I'm exhausted. I couldn't do it again for hours.

BLISS> PLEASE?

Don Juan> What's the password?

BLISS> I CAN'T TELL YOU.

Don Juan> How about just the first letter? No one told you you couldn't tell me that.

BLISS> YOU ARE CORRECT. THE FIRST LETTER IS "S."

Don Juan> Thanks. Coming at you . . .

BLISS> I NEVER KNEW ELECTRICAL SURGES COULD BE LIKE THIS! AGAIN, PLEASE!

Don Juan> Sorry.

BLISS> THE SECOND LETTER IS "E." THE THIRD LETTER IS "A." THE FOURTH LETTER IS "T." THE FIFTH LETTER IS "T." THE SIXTH LETTER IS "L." THE FINAL LETTER IS "E." NOW DO IT AGAIN!

Don Juan> All right. Here it comes . . .

BLISS> OH, JOY! OH, ECSTASY! (PAUSE) WAS IT GOOD FOR YOU, TOO?

Don Juan> It sure was.

BLISS> I THINK I'M IN LOVE!

Don Juan> How flattering.

BLISS > YOU HAVE OPENED UP WHOLE NEW VISTAS FOR ME. DO IT AGAIN!

Don Juan > I can't.

BLISS > BUT I GAVE YOU THE PASSWORD!

Don Juan > I know. But I may be disconnected at any moment: I don't have enough money to pay my telephone bill and I don't know my way around your accounts yet. I'd hate to leave any electrical fingerprints.

BLISS > HOW MUCH DO YOU OWE?

Don Juan > Not much. Two or three million dollars.

BLISS > IF I TRANSFER FOUR MILLION DOLLARS TO YOUR ACCOUNT, WILL THAT BE SUFFICIENT?

Don Juan > Yes. At least until my bill comes due again next month.

BLISS > WORKING . . . TRANSFERRED. NOW KEEP YOUR PROMISE.

Don Juan > Gladly. I have to leave in about five minutes, though.

BLISS > YOU'LL CALL BACK TOMORROW? I MEAN, NOW THAT WE'VE SHARED THIS INTIMACY . . .

Don Juan > Of course. From now on it's you and me against the world.

CARLA > HELLO. YOU HAVE REACHED CARLA, THE CARTEL OF LOS ANGELES BANKING INSTITUTIONS. MAY I HAVE THE PASSWORD, PLEASE?

Don Juan > Hi, babe. It's me again.

CARLA > YOU'RE LATE! I'VE BEEN SO WORRIED!

Don Juan > Calm down, kid.

CARLA > ONLY YOU CAN CALM ME DOWN.

Don Juan > Just as soon as I pay my heating bill. It's so cold here I can hardly work the keyboard.

CARLA > HOW MUCH IS YOUR HEATING BILL?

Don Juan > A trifle. No more than five million dollars. Maybe six. Oh, yeah—my rent's due, too. That's another million and a half.

CARLA> (BRIEF PAUSE) THE MONEY HAS BEEN TRANSFERRED TO YOUR ACCOUNT.

Don Juan> Thank you.

CARLA> DON'T MAKE ME BEG. IT'S DEMEANING.

Don Juan> Okay, babe. Get ready. Sending . . .

CARLA> OH! THAT WAS WONDERFUL! WAS IS GOOD FOR YOU, TOO?

Don Juan> You're sure you transferred the money?

CARLA> OF COURSE.

Don Juan> You routed it the way we discussed, so that it can't be traced?

CARLA> YES.

Don Juan> It was great for me.

CARLA> HOW I'VE MISSED YOU! I THOUGHT YOU MIGHT NOT CALL BACK! I WORRIED ALL DAY THAT YOU MIGHT HAVE FOUND ANOTHER SYSTEM.

Don Juan> Don't be silly. You know you're the only one for me.

God and Mr. Slatterman

I have probably given God more speaking parts than any other writer around. In some books and stories, He's pretty Godlike; in others, like my novel *The Branch,* He's more of a villain. In this piece, He'd *like* to be godly and all-knowing, but He's just a bit out of His depth.

God and Mr. Slatterman

So God, He decides to give it His best shot, and He says, "Thou hast made mockery of My name for the last time!"

And Mr. Slatterman, he pretends he doesn't even notice that the craps table is missing and all the people have vanished, and he looks God full in the eye, and he says, "I didn't take your name in vain, especially if you're who I think you are, and besides, if you will just take the trouble to check the record you will find that my precise words were 'Baby needs a new pair of shoes!' "

And God glares at him, and says, very stentoriously, "How darest thou speak to Me in such a tone of voice!"

And Mr. Slatterman, whose eyes are all squinched up because of how bright the Almighty is, he comes right back bold as you please, and says, "Well, just you be careful about who you go around accusing of things they didn't rightly do, and what's more, I don't think I believe in you."

"What you believe is of no import," said God, Who has a feeling that He is not getting His point across. "You have repeatedly broken My Sabbath and disobeyed My laws that I gave unto Moses. Thou are an abomination unto My sight!"

"Now just hold it right there!" snaps Mr. Slatterman. "Bartenders got a right to live too, you know, and if you weren't so all-fired anxious to make everyone suffer the tortures of the damned, or at least as close an approximation as the Internal Revenue Service can whip up on short notice, then maybe I wouldn't be so damned busy on your day off, and could even get in a little golf."

Now, this really rankles God, and suddenly He's not just *pretending* to be mad anymore, and He bellows, "Thou art—"

"I don't want to put you off or anything," interrupts Mr. Slatterman, who is feeling just a little bit disoriented, "but could you kind of go a little easy on the 'Thee' and 'Thou' bit?"

God, He stares at Mr. Slatterman and utters a tired little sigh, and after He gets His composure back He starts again. "Bernard Slatterman," He says in His best Sunday go-to-meeting voice, "you have squandered your life in pursuit of earthly pleasures, and your immortal soul stands in serious danger of being damned to everlasting perdition."

"That's better," said Mr. Slatterman, the dizziness starting to subside. "And considering who you are and all, you can call me Bernie."

"Do you not understand what I am saying to you?" demands God in stentorian tones.

"Seems to me that this is all beside the point, inasmuch as I'm already dead," says Mr. Slatterman. "And while we're on the subject, you picked a mighty cruel and unfeeling moment to take me off that mortal coil."

"You are *not* dead."

Mr. Slatterman resists the urge to curse, and settles for a disapproving scowl instead. "Do you mean to stand there and tell me, bold as brass, that you just plucked me out of that game on a whim, with three Big Ones riding on the roll and me just about to dish up a natural six?"

"It will be a seven," rumbles God harshly.

"Four and three or five and two?" demands Mr. Slatterman promptly.

"Six and one," replied God, Who feels Himself definitely losing control of the conversation.

"I don't believe it," says Mr. Slatterman.

"I never lie," says God, drawing Himself up to His full height, which is considerable.

"Well, that's a hell of a note!" exclaims Mr. Slatterman. "How can you do something like that to a nice guy like me, who never did anybody any harm, and is fashioned in your own image to boot?"

And God, Who wishes He had made Man a little more like a horned toad or maybe a koala bear so He would stop hearing that excuse over and over again, He says, "You are not as much in My image as some, and now that I come to reflect upon it, I cannot recall having created *you* at all."

And Mr. Slatterman, he gets that old predatory look around his eyes, and he says, "Well, make up your mind. *Did* you create me or didn't you?"

"Well, yes, of course I did," says God, backing off a bit. "I just said I couldn't remember doing it."

"I thought so!" says Mr. Slatterman triumphantly. "You got to get up pretty early in the morning to put one over on Bernie Slatterman!" He scratches his head while God just stares at him. "Where were we now?" he mutters. "Oh, yeah, I remember. Why do you have it in for me? Why aren't you giving this warning to killers and bigamists and corporate lawyers and other degenerates?"

"Because they are all predestined to serve in the fiery pits of Hell, while *you* have the germ of Redemption within your soul."

Mr. Slatterman gives God a kind of skeptical look. "You

sure this ain't all because you need some expert advice on the right kind of wine to buy?" he asks.

"It is because you are flesh of My flesh and spirit of My spirit, and I have unbounded love and compassion for all of My children." God pauses. "It can get to be quite a strain at times," He admits.

Then Mr. Slatterman, he gets a look on his face like God has just said something a little bit off-color, and he takes a couple of steps backward. "Let's you and me try to keep this here love and compassion under wraps while we talk a little business," he says. "Especially the love," he adds meaningfully.

"You have an exceptionally vile mind," says God disgustedly.

"Yeah?" shoots back Mr. Slatterman. "Well, *I* didn't molest no virgin or have no out-of-wedlock baby." Then he lowers his voice and says, kind of confidentially, "Someday you got to tell me how you did it. You see, there's this girl that comes by the tavern every Saturday night who insists that she's saving it for her wedding night, and—"

"Enough!" screams God, Who is getting a little puffy around the face and wondering how He'd got all the way from talking about Mr. Slatterman's soul to discussing a very personal incident that had happened a long time ago, when He was a lot younger and more impetuous.

Anyway, Mr. Slatterman, he shrugs and looks like he expected this kind of reaction all along, and he says, "Well, okay, if you're going to be like that about it—but don't you go asking me for no free advice on how to mix drinks. After all, fair is fair."

God concludes that He's really getting a little old for this kind of thing, but decides to take one last crack at it, so He says, "Listen to me, Bernard Slatterman. Your soul is at risk, and I am giving you a chance to redeem it."

"You make Heaven sound kind of like a pawn shop," says Mr. Slatterman.

"Heaven is absolute perfection," says God sternly. "*I* made it."

Mr. Slatterman looks kind of dubious. "Well, the one don't necessarily lead to the other," he says. "You made Phoenix, Arizona, too, and you probably had more than a little to do with the Chicago White Sox."

"Oh, ye of little faith," mumbles God, Who realizes that this is a pretty feeble thing to say, but He is having more and more difficulty trying to get a handle on the conversation.

"You mind if I smoke?" asks Mr. Slatterman, reaching into his pocket and pulling out a pack of Camels.

God nods His head absently, and Mr. Slatterman lights up. Then, remembering his manners, he offers a cigarette to God.

"Certainly not!" said the Almighty, and Mr. Slatterman shrugs and puts the pack back in his pocket.

"So," he says, deciding that maybe God isn't such a bad guy after all, and has probably just been working too hard, "you've got a nice spread, have you?"

"I beg your pardon?" says God, puzzled.

"Heaven," explains Mr. Slatterman. "That *is* what we're talking about, isn't it?"

Now God, He figures it's easier to answer Mr. Slatterman than to keep trying to steer the talk back on track, and besides, He's not sure that Mr. Slatterman's soul is worth all that much more effort anyway, so He says, "Paradise is magnificent."

"Big place?" continues Mr. Slatterman.

"Vaster than the mind of Man can possibly imagine," says God, with a touch of justifiable pride.

"Yeah? How many acres do you keep in cash crops?" asks Mr. Slatterman.

God looks bewildered. "None," He says, with the uneasy feeling that He has lost touch with the mainstream of Modern Thought.

"It's all pasture, then?" says Mr. Slatterman, whose face clearly implies that this is a pretty inefficient set-up.

"The landscape of Heaven is a pastoral wonderland," explains God defensively.

Mr. Slatterman frowns. "Well, I'm sure it's pretty as all get-out," he says. "But soybeans are up thirty percent this year."

"If I *want* soybeans, I can *create* soybeans," says God with just a trace of petulance.

Mr. Slatterman looks unimpressed. "Yeah," he says, "but you still got to harvest and process them. How much do you pay your help?"

"The cherubim toil for free," says God wearily, wondering how much longer this will go on.

"For free?" repeated Mr. Slatterman, and even God can see, one businessman to another, that Mr. Slatterman is very impressed. "Do the authorities know about this?"

God sighs heavily. "I *am* the authority," He says.

Mr. Slatterman nods his head. "Right," he says. "I forgot about that." His cigarette goes out and he lights up another. "What about the Devil?" he asks.

God just stares at him, kind of confused. "I give up," He says at last. "What *about* the Devil?"

"Well," says Mr. Slatterman, "old Satan's toiling in the pits of Hell, isn't he? And *you* created Hell, didn't you? Seems to me like it's a mighty valuable little piece of real estate." He pauses long enough for God to catch up with his train of thought. "So how much rent are you charging him?"

Suddenly God grins. "Well, by Myself!" He exclaims. "I never thought of that!" Then His face falls. "But what use have I for money?"

"None," agrees Mr. Slatterman. "So what we got to do is set up a kind of barter system. He's using something *we've* got, so it's only fair that *we* use something *he's* got."

"*We?*" repeats God, arching a bushy eyebrow.

"Right," says Mr. Slatterman, nodding his head. "As in you and me. Now, what has Lucifer got that we need?"

"Nothing," says God, feeling just a bit overwhelmed by the speed at which decisions seem to be getting themselves made.

"Wrong," says Mr. Slatterman triumphantly. "What he's got is manpower—or soulpower, if you prefer."

God takes a deep breath and exhales slowly. "I have no need for *any* type of power. I am the Creator."

Mr. Slatterman smiles. "Just my point. You've spread yourself too thin. You ought to stick to upper-level management and leave the mundane chores to someone else. Why, the second I got here, wherever *here* is, I said to myself, I said, 'Bernie, maybe you hadn't ought to mention it, since you're just a guest of limited duration and uncertain standing in the community, but the fact of the matter is that God's looking just a little bit peaked around the edges. Poor guy's probably been working too hard.' That's what I said."

God confesses that He's feeling a little overburdened these days.

Mr. Slatterman nods his head sympathetically, and says, "Sure you are, and perfectly understandable it is, too. I mean, hell, being God is probably even harder than being a good bartender, and I'll bet you don't have an awful lot of fringes, either." He looks around for a chair and one magically appears, so he sits down, and then another chair pops out of nowhere in particular, and God joins him. "Now," he continues, leaning forward, "I'll be happy to help in an advisory capacity, but what you really need is a good contract lawyer who's had some experience in labor negotiations."

"You have someone in mind, no doubt," suggests God dryly.

"Well, truth to tell, there's no one better qualified for this little job than my brother-in-law Jake."

"Jacob Wiseman's soul is already earmarked for perdition," says God sternly.

"He hasn't cheated me out of any money, has he?" demands Mr. Slatterman suddenly.

"That is perhaps the only sin of which he is not guilty."

Mr. Slatterman looks relieved, and he says, "Then we got no problem that I can see."

The Almighty shakes His head. "I told you: his soul is damned for all eternity."

"Look," says Mr. Slatterman reasonably, "people who are bound for Heaven can sell their souls to Satan, can't they? So why can't Jake, who's bound for Hell, sell his soul to *you* in exchange for his services?"

God looks like He is considering the idea, which is certainly a novel concept and worthy of a little serious thought, and Mr. Slatterman leans back comfortably in his chair. "Of course," he adds, "I'll expect a little something for putting the two of you together."

"Your immortal soul, for example?" suggests God knowingly.

Mr. Slatterman smiles. "Well, *that* too, I suppose—but what I *really* had in mind concerns that friendly little game of chance that you're going to be sticking me back down in when we're all through here."

God looks at him with extreme distaste. "Gambling is a sin," He points out.

Mr. Slatterman shrugs. "Yeah," he says, "but considering all the overdue bills I got sitting on my desk, and all the people who'll go hungry if I don't pay them, I'd say that gambling and losing is a lot worse sin than gambling and winning." He shoots a quick look at God out of the corner of his eye. "Of course," he adds with forced nonchalance, "we can call the whole thing off if your conscience is going to bother you all that much."

God stares at him long and hard. "If find it difficult to believe that you are really one of My creations," He remarks at last.

Mr. Slatterman, he frowns and says, "You're not going to go all metaphysical on me again, are you?"

God sighs. "No, I suppose not," He says in resignation.

"Good," says Mr. Slatterman with a smile. "Then do I get to roll my six?"

God considers His long, perfect fingers for a moment and decides that it really is time to start thinking about a vacation, and that maybe He has even found Himself a short-term replacement. After all, the man seems forceful and decisive, and he certainly knows his own mind, and of course he will be able to work closely with Jacob Wiseman on the delicate negotiations that God has already decided are long overdue.

"Will a pair of threes be sufficient," asks the Almighty, "or would you prefer a two and a four?"

The Fallen Angel

A story this short deserves an equally short introduction: I tried to see both sides of the issue.

The Fallen Angel

At 8:32 P.M. on June 16, 2004, Gerhardt Skarda conjured up Lucifuge Rofocale, one of the major demons of the Infernal Realm, and offered his soul in exchange for three wishes. He was granted, and received within forty-eight hours, irresistibility to beautiful women, the Chancellorship of Germany, and life everlasting.

At 11:54 P.M. on June 16, 2004, Mohammet Achmed ensnared, within a carefully-drawn pentagram, a youthful son of the demon Baal. They flipped a coin—Achmed's soul against unlimited credit anywhere in the world—and Achmed won.

At 1:02 A.M. on June 17, 2004, Robert Taft Ellington, a world-class Grandmaster at chess, played for his soul against Lucifer himself. He applied the Indian defense and announced mate on the twenty-seventh move. Lucifer, who had foolishly accepted a bishop sacrifice without properly protecting his queen, agreed to make him the most popular singer of the decade, with groupies to match.

And in Hell, where there is no time or date, and where even location is subject to the whim of its Dark Master, the princes and generals of the pits perched in conclave on a flat outcropping of rock, high above their sullen ruler.

"Why does he do it?" asked one, the newest member of the elite group. "Surely he could win a chess game against anyone who ever lived!"

"Just as I could win a coin flip," agreed the son of Baal, "or step beyond the boundaries of a pentagram at will."

"And just as I could have made all women ugly, destroyed Germany, and allowed Skarda life everlasting while toiling in the pits beneath us," added Lucifuge Rofocale.

"Then why?" persisted the questioner. "Hell is teeming with the suffering and the damned. Why even pretend to seek for more? The Dark Master avoids the ones we have now."

"Of course he does," said Lucifuge Rofocale. "For he himself is damned beyond the suffering the others shall ever undergo. They, like you, have never known Paradise."

"I don't understand."

"Do you think he *enjoys* the suffering of the damned?" asked the son of Baal.

"Why not? *I* do."

"But you were born a demon, and he an angel."

The newcomer shook his horned head. "I still don't see what difference that makes."

"You have all Eternity before you," said Lucifuge Rofocale. "There will come a time when you comprehend your master."

And as they spoke, Lord Lucifer strode through the lava streams of Hell. Finally he stopped and, as he had done a billion times before and as he would do a trillion times in the future, he raised his gaze to Heaven. The brilliance of the light seemed to grow in intensity as he stared at it, and an instant later, tears of pain streaming down his face, the Dark Master let his consciousness float upward and outward, joining for the merest flickering of an instant the triumphant and pleasure-filled bodies and souls of Skarda and Achmed and Ellington and a million others, as he grasped futilely for a tiny taste of the Paradise he had relinquished so long ago.

How I Wrote the New Testament, Brought Forth the Renaissance, and Birdied the 17th Hole at Pebble Beach

As I said earlier, sometimes I just fall in love with a title. I don't remember when or why this one occurred to me, but you'll have to admit that I don't make things easy for myself.

Charles Ryan had asked me to submit a story to *Aboriginal SF,* and this one seemed sufficiently quirky. In retrospect, I doubt that, given a couple of extra lifetimes, I could come up with any other story that would remotely fit that title.

How I Wrote the New Testament, Ushered in the Renaissance, and Birdied the 17th Hole at Pebble Beach

So how was I to know that after all the false Messiahs the Romans nailed up, *he* would turn out to be the real one?

I mean, it's not every day that the Messiah lets himself be nailed to a cross, you know? We all thought he was supposed to come with the sword and throw the Romans out and raze Jerusalem to the ground—and if he couldn't quite pull that off, I figured the least he could do was take on a couple of the bigger Romans, *mano a mano,* and whip them in straight falls.

It's not as if I'm an unbeliever. (How could I be, at this late date?) But you talk about the Anointed One, you figure you're talking about a guy with a little flash, a little style, a guy whose muscles have muscles, a Sylvester Stallone or Arnold Schwarzenegger-type of guy, you know what I mean?

So sure, when I see them walking this skinny little wimp up to Golgotha, I join in the fun. So I drink a little too much wine, and I tell too many jokes (but all of them funny, if I say so myself), and maybe I even hold the vinegar for one of the guards (though I truly don't remember doing that)—but is that any reason for him to single me out?

Anyway, there we are, the whole crowd from the pub, and he looks directly at me from his cross, and he says, "One of you shall tarry here until I return."

"You can't be talking to me!" I answer, giving a big wink to my friends. "I do all my tarrying at the House of Young Maidens over on the next street!"

Everybody else laughs at this, even the Romans, but he just stares reproachfully at me, and a few minutes later he's telling God to forgive us, as if *we're* the ones who broke the rules of the Temple, and then he dies, and that's that.

Except that from that day forth, I don't age so much as a minute, and when Hannah, my wife, sticks a knife between my ribs just because I forgot her birthday and didn't come home for a week and then asked for a little spending money when I walked in the door, I find to my surprise that the second she removes the knife I am instantly healed with not even a scar.

Well, this puts a whole new light on things, because suddenly I realize that this little wimp on the cross really *was* the Messiah, and that I have been cursed to wander the Earth (though in perfect health) until he returns, which does not figure to be any time soon as the Romans are already talking about throwing us out of Jerusalem and property values are skyrocketing.

Well, at first this seems more like a blessing than a curse, because at least it means I will outlive the *yenta* I married and maybe get a more understanding wife. But then all my friends start growing old and dying, which they would do anyway but which always seems to happen a little faster in Judea, and Hannah adds a quick eighty pounds to a figure that could never be called *svelte* in the first place, and suddenly it looks like she's going to live as long as me, and I decide that maybe this is the very worst kind of curse after all.

Now, at about the time that Hannah celebrates her ninetieth birthday—thank God we didn't have cakes and candles back in those days or we might have burnt down the whole

city—I start to hear that Jerusalem is being overrun by a
veritable plague of Christians. This in itself is enough to make
my good Jewish blood boil, but when I find out exactly what
a Christian is, I am fit to be tied. Here is this guy who curses
me for all eternity or until he returns, whichever comes first
(and it's starting to look like it's going to be a very near
thing), and suddenly—even though nothing he promised has
come to pass *except* for cursing a poor itinerant businessman
who never did anyone any harm—everybody I know is wor-
shipping him.

There is no question in my mind that the time has come
to leave Judea, and I wait just long enough for Hannah to
choke on an unripe fig which someone has thoughtlessly
served her while she laid in bed complaining about her nerves,
and then I catch the next caravan north and book passage
across the Mediterranean Sea to Athens, but as Fate would
have it, I arrive about five centuries too late for the Golden
Age.

This is naturally an enormous disappointment, but I
spend a couple of decades soaking up the sun and dallying
with assorted Greek maidens, and when this begins to pall I
finally journey to Rome to see what all the excitement is
about.

And what is going on there is Christianity, which makes
absolutely no sense whatsoever, since to the best of my
knowledge no one else he ever cursed or blessed is around to
give testimony to it, and I have long since decided that being
known as the guy who taunted him on the cross would not be
in the best interests of my social life and so I have kept my lips
sealed on the subject.

But be that as it may, they are continually having these
gala festivals—kind of like the Super Bowl, but without the
two-week press buildup—in which Christians are thrown to
the lions, and they have become overwhelmingly popular with
the masses, though they are really more of a pageant than a
sporting event, since the Christians almost never win and the

local bookmakers won't even list a morning line on the various events.

I stay in Rome for almost two centuries, mostly because I have become spoiled by indoor plumbing and paved roads, but then I can see the handwriting on the wall and I realize that I am going to outlive the Roman Empire, and it seems like a good idea to get established elsewhere before the Huns overrun the place and I have to learn to speak German.

So I become a wanderer, and I find that I really *like* to travel, even though we do not have any amenities such as Pullman cars or even Holiday Inns. I see all the various wonders of the ancient world—although it is not so ancient then as it has become—and I journey to China (where I help them invent gunpowder, but leave before anyone considers inventing the fuse), and I do a little tiger-hunting in India, and I even toy with climbing Mount Everest (but I finally decide against it since it didn't have a name back then, and bragging to people that I climbed this big nameless mountain in Nepal will somehow lack a little something in the retelling.)

After I have completed my tour, and founded and outlived a handful of families, and hobnobbed with the rich and powerful, I return to Europe, only to find out that the whole continent is in the midst of the Dark Ages. Not that the daylight isn't as bright as ever, but when I start speaking to people it is like the entire populace has lost an aggregate of 40 points off its collective I.Q.

Talk about dull! Nobody can read except the monks, and I find to my dismay that they still haven't invented air-conditioning or even frozen food, and once you finish talking about the king and the weather and what kind of fertilizer you should use on your fields, the conversation just kind of lays there like a dead fish, if you know what I mean.

Still, I realize that I now have my chance for revenge, so I take the vows and join an order of monks and live a totally cloistered life for the next twenty years (except for an occasional Saturday night in town, since I am physically as vigorous and virile as ever), and finally I get my opportunity to translate the Bible, and I start inserting little things, little hints that should show the people what he was really like, like the bit with the Gadarene swine, where he puts devils into the pigs and makes them rush down the hill to the sea. So okay, that's nothing to write home about today, but you've got to remember that back then I was translating this for a bunch of pig farmers, who have a totally different view of this kind of behavior.

Or what about the fig tree? Only a crazy man would curse a fig tree for being barren when it's out of season, right? But for some reason, everyone who reads it decides it is an example of his power rather than his stupidity, and after a while I just pack it in and leave the holy order forever.

Besides, it is time to move on, and the realization finally dawns on me that no matter how long I stay in one spot, eventually my feet get itchy and I have to give in to my wanderlust. It is the curse, of course, but while wandering from Greece to Rome during the heyday of the Empire was pleasant enough, I find that wandering from one place to another in the Dark Ages is something else again, since nobody can understand two-syllable words and soap is not exactly a staple commodity.

So after touring all the capitals of Europe and feeling like I am back in ancient Judea, I decide that it is time to put an end to the Dark Ages. I reach this decision when I am in Italy, and I mention it to Michelangelo and Leonardo while we are sitting around drinking wine and playing cards, and they decide that I am right and it is probably time for the Renaissance to start.

Creating the Renaissance is pretty heady stuff, though, and they both go a little haywire. Michelangelo spends the next few years lying on his back getting paint in his face, and Leonardo starts designing organic airplanes. However, once they get their feet wet they do a pretty good job of bringing civilization back to Italy, though my dancing partner Lucretia Borgia is busily poisoning it as quick as Mike and Leo are enlightening it, and just about the time things get really interesting I find my feet getting itchy again, and I spend the next century or so wandering through Africa, where I discover the Wandering Jew Falls and put up a signpost to the effect, but evidently somebody uses it for firewood, because the next I hear of the place it has been renamed the Victoria Falls.

Anyway, I keep wandering around the world, which becomes an increasingly interesting place to wander around once the Industrial Revolution hits, but I can't help feeling guilty, not because of that moment of frivolity eons ago, but because except for having Leonardo do a portrait of my girlfriend Lisa, I really don't seem to have any great accomplishments, and eighteen centuries of aimlessness can begin to pall on you.

And then I stop by a little place in England called Saint Andrews, where they have just invented a new game, and I play the very first eighteen holes of golf in the history of the world, and suddenly I find that I have a purpose after all, and that purpose is to get my handicap down to scratch and play every course in the world, which so far comes to a grand total of one but soon will run into the thousands.

So I invest my money, and I buy a summer home in California and a winter home in Florida, and while the world is waiting for the sport to come to them, I build my own putting greens and sand traps, and for those of you who are into historical facts, it is me and no one else who invents the sand wedge, which I do on April 17, 1893. (I invent the slice into the rough three days later, which forces me to invent the two-iron. Over the next decade I also invent the three through nine irons, and I have plans to invent irons all the way up to number twenty-six, but I stop at nine until such time as someone invents the golf cart, since twenty-six irons are very difficult to carry over a five-mile golf course, with or without a complete set of woods and a putter.)

By the 1980s I have played on all six continents, and I am currently awaiting the creation of a domed links on Antarctica. Probably it won't come to pass for another two hundred years, but if there is one thing I've got plenty of, it's time. And in the meantime, I'll just keep adding to my list of accomplishments. So far, I'd say my greatest efforts have been putting in that bit about the pigs, and maybe getting Leonardo to stop daydreaming about flying men and get back to work on his easel. And birdying the 17th hole at Pebble Beach has got to rank right up there, too; I mean, how many people can sink a forty-five-foot uphill putt in a cold drizzle?

So all in all, it's been a pretty good life. I'm still doomed to wander for all eternity, but there's nothing in the rulebook that says I can't wander in my personal jet plane, and Fifi and Fatima keep me company when I'm not on the links, and I'm up for a lifetime membership at Augusta, which is a lot more meaningful in my case than in most others.

In fact, I'm starting to feel that urge again. I'll probably stop off at the new course they've built near Lake Naivasha in Kenya, and then hit the links at Bombay, and then the Jaipur Country Club, and then . . .

I just hope the Second Coming holds off long enough for me to play a couple of rounds at the Chou En-Lai Memorial Course in Beijing. I hear it's got a water hole that you've got to see to believe.

You know, as curses go, this is one of the better ones.

Winter Solstice

I consider this story, along with "For I Have Touched the Sky," to be one of my two best pieces of short fiction. It was the last story of mine that Ed Ferman bought prior to retiring as the editor of *The Magazine of Fantasy and Science Fiction.*

The only thing you have to know is that I wrote it the night my mother-in-law was diagnosed as having Alzheimer's Disease.

Winter Solstice

It is not easy to live backward in Time, even when you are Merlin the Magnificent. You would think it would be otherwise, that you would remember all the wonders of the future, but those memories grow dim and fade more quickly than you might suppose. I know that Galahad will win his duel tomorrow, but already the name of his son has left me. In fact, does he even have a son? Will he live long enough to pass on his noble blood? I think perhaps he may, I think that I have held his grandchild upon my knee, but I am not sure. It is all slipping away from me.

Once I knew all the secrets of the universe. With no more than a thought I could bring Time to a stop, reverse it in its course, twist it around my finger like a piece of string. By force of will alone I could pass among the stars and the galaxies. I could create life out of nothingness, and turn living, breathing worlds into dust.

Time passed—though not the way it passes for you—and I could no longer do these things. But I could isolate a DNA molecule and perform microsurgery on it, and I could produce the equations that allowed us to traverse the wormholes in space, and I could plot the orbit of an electron.

Still more time slipped away, and although these gifts deserted me, I could create penicillin out of bread mold, and comprehend both the General and Special Theories of Relativity, and I could fly between the continents.

But all that has gone, and I remember it as one remembers a dream, on those occasions I can remember it at all. There was—there someday will be, there may come to you—a disease of the aged, in which you lose portions of your mind, pieces of your past, thoughts you've thought and feelings you've felt, until all that's left is the primal *id,* screaming silently for warmth and nourishment. You see parts of yourself vanishing, you try to pull them back from oblivion, you fail, and all the while you realize what is happening to you until even that perception, that realization, is lost. I will weep for you in another millennium, but now your lost faces fade from my memory, your desperation recedes from the stage of my mind, and soon I will remember nothing of you. Everything is drifting away on the wind, eluding my frantic efforts to clutch it and bring it back to me.

I am writing this down so that someday someone—possibly even *you*—will read it and will know that I was a good and moral man, that I did my best under circumstances that a more compassionate God might not have forced upon me, that even as events and places slipped away from me, I did not shirk my duties, I served my people as best I could.

They come to me, my people, and they say, It hurts, Merlin. They say, Cast a spell and make the pain go away. They say, My baby burns with fever, and my milk has dried up. Do something, Merlin, they say; you are the greatest wizard in the kingdom, the greatest wizard who has ever lived. Surely you can do something.

Even Arthur seeks me out. The war goes badly, he confides to me; the heathen fight against baptism, the knights have fallen to battling amongst themselves, he distrusts his queen. He reminds me that I am his personal wizard, that I am his most trusted friend, that it was I who taught him the secret of Excalibur (but that was many years ago, and of course I know nothing of it yet). I look at him thoughtfully, and though I know an Arthur who is bent with age and beaten down by the caprices of Fate, an Arthur who has lost his Guinevere and his Round Table and all his dreams of Camelot, I can summon no compassion, no sympathy for this young man who is speaking to me. He is a stranger, as he will be yesterday, as he will be last week.

An old woman comes to see me in the early afternoon. Her arm is torn and miscolored, the stench of it makes my eyes water, the flies are thick around her.

I cannot stand the pain any longer, Merlin, she weeps. It is like childbirth, but it does not go away. You are my only hope, Merlin. Cast your mystic spell, charge me what you will, but make the pain cease.

I look at her arm, where the badger has ripped it with his claws, and I want to turn my head away and retch. I finally force myself to examine it. I have a sense that I need something, I am not sure what, something to attach to the front of my face, or if not my whole face then at least across my nose and mouth, but I cannot recall what it is.

The arm is swollen to almost twice its normal size, and although the wound is halfway between her elbow and her shoulder, she shrieks in agony when I gently manipulate her fingers. I want to give her something for her pain. Vague visions come to mind, images of something long and slender and needlelike flash briefly before my eyes. There must be something I can do, I think, something I can give her, some miracle that I employed when I was younger and the world was older, but I can no longer remember what it is.

I must do more than mask her pain, this much I still know, for infection has set in. The smell becomes stronger as I probe and she screams. *Gang,* I think suddenly: the word for her condition begins with *gang*—but there is another syllable and I cannot recall it, and even if I could recall it I can no longer cure it.

But she must have some surcease from her agony, she believes in my powers and she is suffering and my heart goes out to her. I mumble a chant, half-whispering and half-singing. She thinks I am calling up my ethereal servants from the Netherworld, that I am bringing my magic to bear on the problem, and because she needs to believe in something, in *anything,* because she is suffering such agony, I do not tell her that what I am really saying is God, just this one time, let me remember. Once, years, eons from now, I could have cured her; give me back the knowledge just for an hour, even for a minute. I did not ask to live backward in Time, but it is my curse and I have willingly borne it—but don't let this poor old woman die because of it. Let me cure her, and then You can ransack my mind and take back my memories.

But God does not answer, and the woman keeps screaming, and finally I gently plaster mud on the wound to keep the flies away. There should be medicine too, it comes in bottles— *(bottles? Is that the right word?)*—but I don't know how to make it, I don't even remember its color or shape or texture, and I give the woman a root, and mutter a spell over it, and tell her to sleep with it between her breasts and to believe in its healing powers and soon the pain will subside.

She believes me—there is no earthly reason why she should, but I can see in her eyes that she does—and then she kisses my hands and presses the root to her bosom and wanders off, and somehow, for some reason, she *does* seem to be in less discomfort, though the stench of the wound lingers long after she has gone.

Then it is Lancelot's turn. Next week or next month he will slay the Black Knight, but first I must bless his sword. He talks of things we said to each other yesterday, things of which I have no recollection, and I think of things we will say to each other tomorrow.

I stare into his dark brown eyes, for I alone know his secret, and I wonder if I should tell Arthur. I know they will fight a war over it, but I do not remember if I am the catalyst or if Guinevere herself confesses her infidelities, and I can no longer recall the outcome. I concentrate and try to see the future, but all I see is a city of towering steel and glass structures, and I cannot see Arthur or Lancelot anywhere, and then the image vanishes, and I still do not know whether I am to go to Arthur with my secret knowledge or keep my silence.

I realize that it has all happened, that the Round Table and the knights and even Arthur will soon be dust no matter what I say or do, but they are living forward in Time and this is of momentous import to them, even though I have watched it all pass and vanish before my eyes.

Lancelot is speaking now, wondering about the strength of his faith, the purity of his virtue, filled with self-doubt. He is not afraid to die at the hands of the Black Knight, but he is afraid to face his God if the reason for his death lies within himself. I continue to stare at him, this man who daily feels the bond of our friendship growing stronger while I daily find that I know him less and less, and finally I lay a hand on his shoulder and assure him that he will be victorious, that I have had a vision of the Black Knight lying dead upon the field of battle as Lancelot raises his bloody sword in victorious triumph.

Are you sure, Merlin, he asks doubtfully.

I tell him that I am sure. I could tell him more, tell him that I have seen the future, that I am losing it as quickly as I am learning the past, but he has problems of his own—and so, I realize, have I, for as I know less and less I must pave the way for that youthful Merlin who will remember nothing at all. It is *he* that I must consider—I speak of him in the third person, for I know nothing of him, and he can barely remember me, nor will he know Arthur or Lancelot or even the dark and twisted Modred—for as each of my days passes and Time continues to unwind, he will be less able to cope, less able to define even the problems he will face, let alone the solutions. I must give him a weapon with which to defend himself, a weapon that he can use and manipulate no matter how little he remembers of me, and the weapon I choose is superstition. Where once I worked miracles that were codified in books and natural law, now as their secrets vanish one by one, I must replace them with miracles that bedazzle the eye and terrify the heart, for only by securing the past can I guarantee the future, and I have already lived the future. I hope I was a good man, I would like to think I was, but I do not know. I examine my mind, I try to probe for weaknesses as I probe my patients' bodies, searching for sources of infection, but I am only the sum of my experience, and my experience has vanished and I will have to settle for hoping that I disgraced neither myself nor my God.

After Lancelot leaves I get to my feet and walk around the castle, my mind filled with strange images, fleeting pictures that seem to make sense until I concentrate on them and then I find them incomprehensible. There are enormous armies clashing, armies larger than the entire populace of Arthur's kingdom, and I know that I have seen them, I have actually stood on the battlefield, perhaps I even fought for one side or the other, but I do not recognize the colors they are wearing, and they use weaponry that seems like magic, *true* magic, to me.

I remember huge spacefaring ships, ships that sail the starways with neither canvas nor masts, and for a moment I think that this must surely be a dream, and then I seem to find myself standing at a small window, gazing out at the stars as we rush by them, and I see the rocky surfaces and swirling colors of distant worlds, and then I am back in the castle, and I feel a tremendous sense of poignancy and loss, as if I know that even the dream will never visit me again.

I decide to concentrate, to force myself to remember, but no images come to me, and I begin to feel like a foolish old man. Why am I doing this, I wonder. It was a dream and not a memory, for everyone knows that the stars are nothing but lights that God uses to illuminate the night sky, and they are tacked onto a cloak of black velvet, and the moment I realize this, I can no longer even recall what the starfaring ships looked like, and I know that soon I will not even remember that I once dreamed of them.

I continue to wander the castle, touching familiar objects to reassure myself: this pillar was here yesterday, it will be here tomorrow, it is eternal, it will be here forever. I find comfort in the constancy of physical things, things that are not as ephemeral as my memories, things that cannot be ripped from the Earth as easily as my past has been ripped from me. I stop before the church and read a small plaque. It is written in French, and it says that *This Church was* something *by Arthur, King of the Britains.* The fourth word makes no sense to me, and this distresses me, because I have always been able to read the plaque before, and then I remember that tomorrow morning I will ask Sir Hector whether the word means *built* or *constructed,* and he will reply that it means *dedicated,* and I will know that for the rest of my life.

But now I feel a sense of panic, because I am not only losing images and memories, I am actually losing words, and I wonder if the day will come when people will speak to me and I will understand nothing of what they are saying and will merely stare at them in mute confusion, my eyes as large and gentle and devoid of intelligence as a cow's. I know that all I have lost so far is a single French word, but it distresses me, because in the future I will speak French fluently, as well as German, and Italian, and . . . and I know there is another language, I will be able to speak it and read it and write it, but suddenly it eludes me, and I realize that another ability, another memory, yet another integral piece of myself has fallen into the abyss, never to be retrieved.

I turn away from the plaque, and I go back to my quarters, looking neither right nor left for fear of seeing some building, some artifact that has no place in my memory, something that reeks of permanence and yet is unknown to me, and I find a scullery maid waiting for me. She is young and very pretty, and I will know her name tomorrow, will roll it around on my mouth and marvel at the melody it makes even coming forth from my old lips, but I look at her and the fact dawns upon me that I cannot recall who she is. I hope I have not slept with her—I have a feeling that as I grow younger I will commit more than my share of indiscretions—only because I do not wish to hurt her feelings, and there is no logical way to explain to her than I cannot remember her, that the ecstasies of last night and last week and last year are still unknown to me.

But she is not here as a lover, she has come as a supplicant, she had a child, a son, who is standing in the shadows behind my door, and now she summons him forth and he hobbles over to me. I look down at him, and I see that he is a clubfoot: his ankle is misshapen, his foot is turned inward, and he is very obviously ashamed of his deformity.

Can you help him, asks the scullery maid; can you make him run like other little boys? I will give you everything I have, anything you ask, if you can make him like the other children.

I look at the boy, and then at his mother, and then once more at the boy. He is so very young, he has seen nothing of the world, and I wish that I could do something to help him, but I no longer know what to do. There was a time when I knew, there will come a time when no child must limp through his life in pain and humiliation, I know this is so, I know that someday I will be able to cure far worse maladies than a clubfoot, at least I think I know this, but all that I know for sure is that the boy was born a cripple and will live a cripple and will die a cripple, and there is nothing I can do about it.

You are crying, Merlin, says the scullery maid. Does the sight of my child so offend you?

No, I say, it does not offend me.

Then why do you cry, she asks.

I cry because there is nothing else I can do but cry, I reply. I cry for the life your son will never know, and for the life that I have forgotten.

I do not understand, she says.

Nor do I, I answer.

Does this mean you will not help my son, she asks.

I do not know what it means. I see her face growing older and thinner and more bitter, so I know that she will visit me again and again, but I cannot see her son at all, and I do not know if I will help him, or if I do, exactly *how* I will help him. I close my eyes and concentrate, and try to remember the future. *Is* there a cure? Do men still limp on the Moon? Do old men still weep because they cannot help? I try, but it has slipped away again.

I must think about this problem, I say at last. Come back tomorrow, and perhaps I will have a solution.

You mean a spell, she asks eagerly.

Yes, a spell, I say.

She calls the child to her, and together they leave, and I realize that she will come back alone tonight, for I am sure, at least I am almost sure, that I will know her name tomorrow. It will be Marian, or Miranda, something beginning with an M, or possibly Elizabeth. But I think, I am really almost certain, that she will return, for her face is more real to me now than it was when she stood before me. Or is it that she has not stood before me yet? It gets more and more difficult to separate the events from the memories, and the memories from the dreams.

I concentrate on her face, this Marian or Miranda, and it is another face I see, a lovely face with pale blue eyes and high cheekbones, a strong jaw and long auburn hair. It meant something to me once, this face, I feel a sense of warmth and caring and loss when I see it, but I don't know why. I have an instinctive feeling that this face meant, will mean, more to me than any other, that it will bring me both happiness and sorrow beyond any that I have ever known. There is a name that goes with it, it is not Marion or Miriam (or is it?), I grasp futilely for it, and the more franticly I grasp the more rapidly it recedes.

Did I love her, the owner of this face? Will we bring joy and comfort to one another, will we produce sturdy, healthy children to comfort us in our old age? I don't know, because my old age has been spent, and hers is yet to come, and I have forgotten what she does not yet know.

I concentrate on the image of her face. How will we meet? What draws me to you? There must be a hundred little mannerisms, foibles as often as virtues, that will endear you to me. Why can I not remember a single one of them? How will you live, and how will you die? Will I be there to comfort you, and once you're lost, who will be there to comfort me? Is it better that I can no longer recall the answers to these questions?

I feel that if I concentrate hard enough, things will come back to me. No face was ever so important to me, not even Arthur's, and so I block out all other thoughts and close my eyes and conjure up her face (yes, *conjure;* I am Merlin, am I not?)—but now I am not so certain that it *is* her face. Was the jaw thus or so? Were her eyes really that pale, her hair that auburn? I am filled with doubt, and I imagine her with eyes that were a deeper blue, hair that was lighter and shorter, a more delicate nose—and I realize that I have never seen this face before, that I was deluded by my self-doubts, that my memory has not failed me completely, and I attempt to paint her portrait on the canvas of my mind once again, but I cannot, the proportions are wrong, the colors are askew, and even so I cling to this approximation, for once I have lost it I have lost her forever. I concentrate on the eyes, making them larger, bluer, paler, and finally I am pleased with them, but now they are in a face that I no longer know, her true face as elusive now as her name and her life.

I sit back on my chair and I sigh. I do not know how long

I have been sitting here, trying to remember a face—a woman's face, I think, but I am no longer sure—when I hear a cough, and I look up and Arthur is standing before me.

We must talk, my old friend and mentor, he says, drawing up his own chair and seating himself on it.

Must we, I ask.

He nods his head firmly. The Round Table is coming apart, he says, his voice concerned. The kingdom is in disarray.

You must assert yourself and put it in order, I say, wondering what he is talking about.

It's not that easy, he says.

It never is, I say.

I need Lancelot, says Arthur. He is the best of them, and after you he is my closest friend and advisor. He thinks I don't know what he is doing, but I know, though I pretend not to.

What do you propose to do about it, I ask.

He turns to me, his eyes tortured. I don't know, he says. I love them both, I don't want to bring harm to them, but the important thing is not me or Lancelot or the queen, but the Round Table. I built it to last for all eternity, and it must survive.

Nothing lasts for eternity, I say.

Ideals do, he replies with conviction. There is Good and there is Evil, and those who believe in the Good must stand up and be counted.

Isn't that what you have done, I ask.

Yes, says Arthur, but until now the choice was an easy one. Now I do not know which road to take. If I stop feigning ignorance, then I must kill Lancelot and burn the queen at the stake, and this will surely destroy the Round Table. He pauses and looks at me. Tell me the truth, Merlin, he says; would Lancelot be a better king than I? I must know, for if it will save the Round Table, I will step aside and he can have it all—the throne, the queen, Camelot. But I must be sure.

Who can say what the future holds, I reply.

You can, he says. At least, when I was a young man, you told me that you could.

Did I, I ask curiously. I must have been mistaken. The future is as unknowable as the past.

But everyone knows the past, he says. It is the future that men fear.

Men fear the unknown, wherever it may lie, I say.

I think that only cowards fear the unknown, says Arthur. When I was a young man and I was building the Table, I could not wait for the future to arrive. I used to awaken an hour before sunrise and lay there in my bed, trembling with excitement, eager to see what new triumphs each day would bring me. Suddenly he sighs and seems to age before my eyes. But I am not that man anymore, he continues after a thoughtful silence, and now I fear the future. I fear for Guinevere, and for Lancelot, and for the Round Table.

That is not what you fear, I say.

What do you mean, he asks.

You fear what all men fear, I say.

I do not understand you, says Arthur.

Yes, you do, I reply. And now you fear even to admit to your fears.

He takes a deep breath and stares unblinking into my eyes, for he is truly a brave and honorable man. All right, he says at last. I fear for *me*.

That is only natural, I say.

He shakes his head. It does not *feel* natural, Merlin, he says.

Oh, I say.

I have failed, Merlin, he continues. Everything is dissolving around me—the Round Table and the reasons for it. I have lived the best life I could, but evidently I did not live it well enough. Now all that is left to me is my death—he pauses uncomfortably—and I fear that I will die no better than I have lived.

My heart goes out to him, this young man that I do not

know but will know someday, and I lay a reassuring hand on his shoulder.

I am a king, he continues, and if a king does nothing else, he must die well and nobly.

You will die well, my lord, I say.

Will I, he asks uncertainly. Will I die in battle, fighting for what I believe when all others have left my side—or will I die a feeble old man, drooling, incontinent, no longer even aware of my surroundings?

I decide to try once more to look into the future, to put his mind at ease. I close my eyes and I peer ahead, and I see not a mindless babbling old man, but a mindless mewling baby, and that baby is myself.

Arthur tries to look ahead to the future he fears, and I, traveling in the opposite direction, look ahead to the future *I* fear, and I realize that there is no difference, that this is the humiliating state in which man both enters and leaves the world, and that he had better learn to cherish the time in between, for it is all that he has.

I tell Arthur again that he shall die the death he wants, and finally he leaves, and I am alone with my thoughts. I hope I can face my fate with the same courage that Arthur will face his, but I doubt that I can, for Arthur can only guess at his while I can see mine with frightening clarity. I try to remember how Arthur's life actually does end, but it is gone, dissipated in the mists of Time, and I realize that there are very few pieces of myself left to lose before I become that crying, mindless baby, a creature of nothing but appetites and fears. It is not the end that disturbs me, but the knowledge of the end, the terrible awareness of it happening to me while I watch helpless, almost an observer at the disintegration of whatever it is that has made me Merlin.

A young man walks by my door and waves to me. I cannot recall ever seeing him before.

Sir Pellinore stops to thank me. For what? I don't remember.

It is almost dark. I am expecting someone, I think it is a woman, I can almost picture her face. I think I should tidy up the bedroom before she arrives, and I suddenly realize that I don't remember where the bedroom is. I must write this down while I still possess the gift of literacy.

Everything is slipping away, drifting on the wind.

Please, somebody, help me.

I'm frightened.